The

Melissa Nathan is the author of the incredibly successful novel *The Nanny*, which hit the *Sunday Times* top ten in the spring of 2003. Born and raised in Hertfordshire, Melissa now lives in north London with her family. She was a journalist for twelve years before turning to writing novels full-time. She is a Jane Austen aficionado, a fact reflected in her two earliest novels, *Pride, Prejudice and Jasmin Field* and *Persuading Annie*. Both were witty new spins on two of the nation's favourite novels *Pride and Prejudice* and *Persuasion*.

Praise for Melissa Nathan's previous novels

'This is one to gobble up in a single sitting' *Company*

'Hugely enjoyable' *heat*

'A witty novel about love' *B*

'Tremendous fun' Jilly Cooper

'A wow of a love story' *Essentials*

'A modern day Lizzy and Darcy tale you won't be able
to put down' *Company*

'A witty spin on the nation's favourite novel . . .
with a loveable, contemporary heroine at its heart'
Good Housekeeping

'Hugely entertaining . . . a memorable read –
funny, warm and intelligent' *Woman's.Own*

Also by Melissa Nathan

The Waitress

MELISSA NATHAN

arrow books

Published by Arrow in 2004

1 3 5 7 9 10 8 6 4 2

First published in the United Kingdom in 2004 by Century

Arrow Books
Random House Group Limited
20 Vauxhall Bridge Road, London SW1V 2SA

Random House Australia (Pty) Limited
20 Alfred Street, Milsons Point, Sydney,
New South Wales 2061, Australia

Random House New Zealand Limited
18 Poland Road, Glenfield
Auckland 10, New Zealand

Random House (Pty) Limited
Endulini, 5a Jubilee Road, Parktown 2193, South Africa

Random House Group Limited Reg. No. 954009

www.randomhouse.co.uk

A CIP catalogue record for this book is available
from the British Library

Papers used by Random House
are natural, recyclable products made from wood grown in
sustainable forests. The manufacturing processes conform to
the environmental regulations of the country of origin

ISBN 0 09 942798 2

Typeset by SX Composing DTP, Rayleigh, Essex
Printed and bound in Great Britain by
Bookmarque Ltd, Croydon, Surrey

To Samuel Mark

Acknowledgements

It is a rare privilege to be able to genuinely thank someone for saving your life. Thank you, Alison Jones, for letting me see this year. Thank you all at 81, especially Marianne, Denise and Caroline, for making my visits as easy as poosible.

Thank you Rosy Daniel, for making Samuel more than just a dream.

Thank you everyone at the amazing Waiting Rooms café in Palmers Green: Phillip Chard, who created its special, unique atmosphere; thank you Destina Philippou, who taught me how to make cappuccino and didn't lose her temper when I burnt the toast, and also thanks to Angela Delusu and Nick Green. Please never forget that this is a work of fiction and the only thing that remotely resembles your café is the sense of fun and friendship at Crichton Brown's.

Thank you Corinne Rodriguez, Sarah Sutcliffe and Rob Salter for your insights and anecdotes.

And, as ever, thank you to my fantastic team-mates in this team effort: Kate Elton, my editor, who doesn't let her keen eye and business mind get in the way of her infectious excitement and warm heart. And thank you to all at Random house, especially Georgina Hawtrey-Woore, Rina Gill, Ron Beard, Susan Sandon, Rob Waddington and Faye Brewster.

Thank you Maggie for being more than my agent, and all at Ed Victor, for that perfect combination of professionalism and fun.

I am lucky enough to be surrounded by people who make my life a joy. Thank you, as ever, to Andrew, Mum, Dad, Jeremy and Deborah for helping me keep body and soul together. And thank you Sammy Mark, for helping me keep going.

1

It was one of those parties that would live on in the collective memory, ripening over the years with significance and irony; a party that would launch a hundred favourite anecdotes and change lives. But to actually experience it was hell. It was full of tomorrow's celebs and high-fliers, yesterday's love affairs and embarrassments. The laughter was loud and the talk thunderous, the noise almost drowning out the din from the music deck but not making a dent in the clash of egos.

Katie sipped at her paper cup of sweet punch again because she'd forgotten how disgusting it was. Ex-boyfriend number three, Hugh, was bellowing at her over the thumping bass. She hadn't seen him for four years, and was frowning so hard to hear him that she looked as if she was straining. Hugh did not have a naturally loud voice, but what he lacked in ability he made up for in motivation.

'. . . but the annual bonus,' he trumpeted, 'you see, is a golden handcuff.'

'A golden what?'

'Handcuff. Uncouth to go into details, but they really know what they're doing.'

'Excellent. So, how is –'

'I mean put it this way, we're talking more than –'

And then he did an impression of a person whose trousers had been set on fire. Katie was impressed. He'd rarely been so interesting. As he re-landed, the grinning face of their hostess, Sandy, appeared beside him. It was Sandy's engagement party and she was very, very drunk.

'Hello everybody!' she greeted them. 'Hello Hugh-Poo. If I wasn't a taken woman, you'd be in trouble.'

Hugh gave a tight smile. 'Anyway, if you'll excuse me.' His voice was slightly pained.

'Oh dear,' said Sandy. 'You're not leaving on my account, are you?'

'No, no,' said Hugh. 'I must just . . .' As he limped off, Sandy turned to Katie.

'It's so hard not to do it to him,' she whispered into Katie's left eye.

'I know.'

'It's his face.'

'I know.'

'How am I going to be mature enough to get married?'

'Show me the ring again!'

Sandy extended her hand in glee and Katie ooh-ed at the beautiful diamond in its platinum setting. As she did so, Geraldine, Sandy's flatmate appeared as if from nowhere.

'Oh my *God*,' she muttered. 'You're not still showing that thing off are you?'

They looked up at her.

'Hello Gerry,' greeted Katie. 'Sprinkling happy fairy-dust all around, as usual?'

2

Ignoring Katie, Geraldine looked down at her flatmate. 'People will think you're getting married for all the wrong reasons, you know.'

Sandy gave a regretful look at her ring. 'I just think it's beautiful.' She gave a little sigh.

'It is!' squealed Katie. 'Let me see it again.'

Sandy, never one to stay unhappy for long, extended her hand again, as Geraldine tutted. 'Have you been remembering to take pictures?' she asked.

Sandy gasped, 'Oh no!' She rushed off on heels that seemed to have turned her ankles to sponge.

'I knew it,' Geraldine said to Katie. 'All that money on the newest digital camera and she hasn't taken one shot. Money to burn.'

'You know, you should be careful,' warned Katie. 'People will think you're jealous.'

It was Geraldine's turn to gasp. 'Me? Jealous? Are you mad? I wouldn't marry that man unless he . . . I don't know . . .'

Katie raised her eyebrows. 'Proposed?'

Geraldine sighed. 'Piss off.' She took a gulp of punch and then grimaced. 'I told her she put too much sugar in this. It's like medicine,' she said before finishing it in one. 'I just assumed I'd get married before her.'

'Do you want to talk about it?' asked Katie.

Then Geraldine was off. 'All the way through college – three goddam years – I had to listen to her *pathetic* relationship problems – that girl has the emotional maturity of a boohbah. I could become a relationship counsellor just off the back of being her flatmate. The hours I wasted listening to her waffle. And all the time,' she took a deep breath, 'I thought I was on to a sure-fire thing with that *wanker*. A man whose idea of commitment is to buy a newspaper. Mr Emotional-Retard.'

'Well,' sighed Katie, 'you should have guessed from his name.'

'And can you believe,' squeaked Geraldine, 'two years together and he chucks me during a Pizza Express meal – *a Pizza Express meal* – and then comes to the party tonight?'

'Your ex?'

'Yes. You know what he is, don't you?'

'An emotional retard?'

'He's a *fucking* emotional retard.'

'So, where is he?' Katie looked round the expanse of oak-floored room.

'In the corner,' said Geraldine. '*Don't look*!' She yanked the back of Katie's halter-neck dress. 'Jesus, Katie, I don't want him to think we're talking about him. He's arrogant enough already.'

'Did you invite him?' choked Katie, rearranging herself.

'Of course I did. We're good friends. I'm completely over him.'

'As long as no one looks at him.'

All right then Miss Smarty-pants. I'll introduce you – and then you can tell me what an emotional retard you think he is.'

'Ooh, I can't wait. Lead on McMadwoman.'

Just as they turned round, Hugh blocked their path. He gave them both a big grin and Geraldine abandoned Katie to his monologue.

4

'Right,' he said. 'Goolies all straightened. Now, where was I?'

Despite herself, after talking to Hugh for a while Katie remembered why she'd been able to stay with him for so long. Ten months and three weeks to be precise. There was a comfy solidity about him, a warm reassurance that seemed to emanate from his M&S cardi. And then he started to dance. As the drum and bass shifted to a new rhythm, he did things with his hips that reminded her of her Great-Aunt Edna trying to walk on a damp day. His pupils were now so dilated they looked as if they were in the last stages of labour.

'So where's Maxine?' she asked.

'Away on business,' said Hugh, almost losing his balance and giving up on the hip movement. 'She does a lot of travelling with her work. She's doing very well. They're talking promotion within the year. How's your work?'

'Brilliant!'

'Really?'

'Yep,' nodded Katie firmly. 'Decided what I'm going to do.'

She looked briefly round the room, so as to avoid Hugh's reaction. When she heard him say 'Good for you,' enthusiastically, she felt as if she'd just told him that today she'd learnt how to count to ten and spell 'fish'.

'I'm going to be an educational psychologist,' she informed him.

There was a pause.

'Oh by the way, we're moving into your area,' said Hugh.

'Really?'

'Yeah. Time to move out of the flat and into a house. You can get so much more for your money out your way. How's your little flat?'

'Fine.'

'And the waiting?'

Katie frowned. 'Waiting?'

'I mean, being a waitress. The waiting at table.'

Katie shrugged. 'It pays the bills. Until I get trained up as an educational psych—'

'Oh yes, that's right,' interrupted Hugh. 'So what happened to your dreams of running your own restaurant?'

Katie pushed the memory of confiding this to Hugh in bed one Sunday afternoon to the back of her mind. 'Ah, those innocent dreams,' she smiled. 'After a few years of work you realise why it was so easy being idealistic as a student. Because you hadn't worked yet.'

'Tell me about it,' said Hugh. 'Mind you, I'm not doing too badly. Bonuses are amazing. Guess how much –'

'Oh my God!' whispered Katie, staring beyond Hugh's shoulder. 'Look!'

Hugh looked and turned back, unimpressed. Standing behind him was Dave Davies, champion oarsman, part-time model and lead role in all the best plays during their years at Oxford.

'He's come out, you know,' said Hugh. 'Completely and utterly gay. His boyfriend's called Kevin.'

Katie gasped. 'You're *kidding*!'

Hugh sighed. 'Yes. But a man can dream.'

Then, before she knew it, Katie was enjoying herself

with this man who had threatened to do something silly all those years ago when she'd told him It Was Over. Of course, she hadn't taken Hugh's threat seriously, but sure enough he did go and do something silly, almost immediately. He went and found solace in the form of Maxine White – and four years on, he was still with her. Maxine White, she of the pointless questions in lectures, she of the stick-thin legs, no bottom, and shoulder-blades like pistons, she of the shiny lipstick and no lips. She of the figure a pencil would be proud of.

Maxine White had been one of Katie and Hugh's favourite in-jokes for their entire ten months and three weeks together – Katie had been especially proud of the nickname she'd given her: Karen D'Ache – so it was only natural that, almost instantly after their abrupt break-up, when Hugh started taking Maxine seriously, Katie had taken such disloyalty personally.

However, after he had stayed with Pencil for the first year – longer than he'd been with Katie – Katie began to entertain the thought that he might not be doing it to make her jealous. It took until she spotted them introducing their parents to each other at graduation to finally acknowledge that their relationship was probably not a sub-plot in the oeuvre that was Katie's Life. It took her another six months to regain confidence in the powers of the petite, hourglass figure over the long tall stick look.

Ever since then, whenever she'd seen Hugh at college get-togethers he was with Maxine. In fact, now Katie thought about it, this was the first time she'd seen him on his own, without Maxine in gobbing distance, since that fateful night when he'd dreamily told her that their first

7

son would have to be named after his great grandfather who'd died in the First World War. Until then, as far as she could remember, they'd been happy enough, but his casual reference to the assumption that one day she would be the proud mother of one Obadiah Oswald caused such a strong reaction in Katie that she had yet to fully recover.

The thought of that night still gave her shivers. There they'd been, cosily entwined under his *Thunderbirds* duvet, when he'd started talking about The Future. She hadn't known blank terror quite like it since seeing the child-snatcher in *Chitty Chitty Bang Bang*. She'd completely panicked and, there and then, chucked her longest-surviving boyfriend faster than she would have chucked a pinless grenade that had plopped into her lap, and with about as much finesse.

And that was it. They were never alone again.

Since then they'd both discovered all they needed to know about each other through the grapevine. She'd discovered that he blamed her for being a heartless bitch and he'd discovered that she was too busy enjoying herself to blame him for anything. The next thing he was dating Maxine White.

In recent years, the grapevine had withered and died and she'd forgotten about him. She'd also forgotten that if you gave him time, he became a very sympathetic listener.

He concentrated as she listed the merits of becoming an educational psychologist. He nodded earnestly when she told him This Was It, the career she'd been looking for, the reason she'd been 'waiting' – yes, in both senses of the word – before choosing the right path. Only last month she'd thought she wanted to be a teacher, but an educational psychologist was the natural progression – and of course, she already had the right psychology degree. It seemed this was meant for her. Most importantly, he laughed at her jokes and even made some good ones of his own. It was nice. Not nice enough to lose all reason and agree to name your first son Obadiah Oswald, but nice none the less.

They both blinked as a flash went off in their faces.

'Gotcha!' cried Sandy, waving a digital camera the size of a compact in the air. 'I'll print it out later and e-mail it to you.'

'Don't you dare,' said Hugh. 'Maxine'll kill me.' He turned suddenly to Katie. 'Not that – she's just . . . you know.'

'Of course,' she said. 'Anyway, I really should find my friend, she doesn't know anyone else here.'

'Right. Fine.'

'She was a bit nervous.'

'Absolutely. Right. I have to . . . you know . . .'

'OK.'

They turned away from each other in one swift, concluding move only to land facing each other again. Hugh then did the decent thing – gave Katie a firm, nodding grin and turned back into the living room, oozing decisiveness.

Katie almost dived to the safe sanctuary of her best mate, Sukie and her flatmate, Jon. They always stayed in the kitchen at parties. If Jon had had the choice, he'd have climbed into the oven, but they were using it to heat pizzas. If Sukie had had the choice, she'd have climbed on the table and sung Waterloo, but they were using it to serve drinks.

Katie pushed her way through the crowd, stopped occasionally by the obligatory catch-up chat (Are you still a waitress? You're not going to believe it, but I'm engaged/married/divorced . . .) and joined them by the sink. Sukie was sitting on the sideboard, cocktail in hand and Jon was leaning against it mixing a new one. They greeted her with obvious delight.

'Katie!' greeted Sukie. 'Jon's just created the best cocktail in the world! We have to think of a name.'

'No, we have to go,' replied Katie. 'This is the worst party I've ever been to.'

'But everyone here's so successful,' said Jon. 'They're all *frightfully* clever.'

Katie and Sukie turned to him.

'So are you,' reminded Katie. 'Mr First.'

'Classics doesn't count,' he mumbled, swaying alarmingly.

'Oh no.' Katie turned to Sukie. 'You've let him get drunk, haven't you?'

'I'm a talentless git,' moaned Jon, his chin dropping to his chest.

Katie slumped. 'I have to go home with this, you know,' she grumbled to Sukie.

'He's only just turned,' said Sukie. 'I promise.'

'And nobody cares,' Jon told the floor.

'I care,' Katie told him, rather sternly. 'I'm the one who'll have to listen to you all bloody night.'

'Ah Katie,' smiled Jon tearfully, putting his arms round her neck. 'You're my best friend.'

The flash made them all blink.

'Ooh that was *lovely*!' cried Sandy, waving her digital

camera perilously close to their faces. 'I'll round robin it by snail. I mean –'

'I've got a machine back at the flat,' belched Jon. 'E-mail it to us.'

'Excellent!' said Sandy. 'Well done Jon!'

'It's all I'm good for,' Jon told her. 'An e-mail address.'

'I think it's time to go home,' Katie told Sandy. 'I'll just go and get my coat, it's in the other room.'

'Right,' said Sandy, 'Jon, what's your e-mail address?'

Katie squeezed out of the kitchen and into the wide living room. Geraldine and Sandy's flat – soon to be just Geraldine's – was vast for London living. Geraldine's parents had bought it in the mid-80s' property drop and then taken heavy rent from her friends. Sandy was the third to be leaving. The crowd was thinning slightly and Katie saw a very nice-looking sight approaching. Just before it reached her, Geraldine appeared suddenly.

'Katie!' she almost yelled. 'Have you met Dan? He's my ex.'

Katie smiled up at Geraldine's ex and stopped. He smiled back and stopped too.

'Hello,' she grinned, as her pelvic floor tightened.

She wasn't sure if the drink had suddenly hit home, or if she'd been swallowed whole by a Magic Eye book, but as far as Katie was concerned, everything else was suddenly a blur around the sharply focused vision smiling down at her. So this was Dan, she thought. This was Geraldine's famous ex. The mysterious ex-Oxford student, now rich city slicker, who had come to visit Geraldine every fourth weekend of the month for two years, whom they'd all thought was a figment of her imagination. No wonder she'd kept him to herself. He was a humdinger. A cappuccino-crème-brulée of a man. A warm-out-of-the-bag Peshwari Naan of a man. And she should know, she was a waitress.

Later, she couldn't remember how the conversation had started, or exactly when they'd sat down together on the beanbags in the corner of the room, or how they'd ended up discussing their various hopes and dreams. All she could remember was the feeling she had while she was with him and that semi-vague, semi-distinct sensation that he was feeling it too.

'So,' she said, after he'd sat back down with more drinks for them both. 'Who do you know here? Apart from Geraldine, of course.'

'Ah yes. Apart from Geraldine.'

'You're good friends now, I hear.'

'Is that what you hear?'

Katie grinned.

'Yes,' said Dan. 'For the record, it was fine going out with her when I saw her once a month. As soon as I was seeing her every week it all sort of . . . petered out. You know.'

Katie nodded, wondering which she should be more worried about: Geraldine's contradictory version or the fact that he used phrases like 'for the record'.

'What was the question again?' asked Dan.

'Who else do you know here?'

'My mate,' said Dan, indicating a friend with a nod of his head. 'He's the one over there in the lurid green shirt underneath that girl with the pigtails.'

12

Katie looked over and could just make out the form of two people playing human jigsaw on a sofa.

'He looks nice.'

'He is nice,' sighed Dan. 'Unfortunately, so's his girlfriend.'

'She looks nice too.'

'She's in Mauritius.'

'Oh dear.'

'I was under strict instructions to keep him occupied – he's been known to do this before – but I got a bit distracted.'

Katie grimaced. 'You can get back to him if you want.'

'Well, between you and me and probably everyone else in this room, I think it's a bit late now.'

'Yes.'

'I mean, there's only so much hiding from the truth you can do, isn't there? If it wasn't this party it would have been another. I love him like a brother, but just not a brother I'd let my sister date.'

'Do you have a sister?'

'No.'

'Phew.'

'And anyway, there's only so much you can listen to about quantum physics at a party.'

'Are you going to tell his girlfriend?'

'She'll find out soon enough,' said Dan flatly. 'He's snogging her best friend.'

They watched the couple for a moment.

'So,' said Dan suddenly. 'Who did you arrive with?'

'My flatmate Jon, who's in the kitchen getting depressed because that's what he does at parties and

Sukie, my best friend, who's in the kitchen getting loud because that's what she does at parties.'

'How long have you and Jon been flatmates?'

'Since college. He's actually my landlord; his parents helped him make an investment in London. We're like brother and sister.'

'Like the brother and sister from *Flowers in the Attic*?'

'No.'

'Good. I hated that book.'

'We're nothing like that. Jon's not blond.'

Dan nodded thoughtfully. 'Excellent.'

Just then Katie saw Sukie out of the corner of her eye, looking at her questioningly. When Katie gave a tiny frown and turned back to Dan, she sensed Sukie returning to the kitchen.

'So,' she said to Dan. 'What have you been up to since Uni?'

Dan smiled a wide smile that created a crease in his cheek Katie was tempted to ask to borrow. He inclined his head towards her.

'Well, I suppose I'm what you'd call "something in the city".'

'Ooh, what? A skyscraper?'

'But, you see . . .' Dan now shifted round so he was facing her and leant towards her intently. She met him halfway. She noticed that one of his eyes was deep blue, the other, deep blue with a dash of hazel. She didn't know which one to look at first. Happily, her inebriated state meant that in passing moments she could see both at the same time, just before his nose joined them and she had to blink. 'My dad always said that the best thing a man could

14

do for himself was set up his own business.'

'Wow,' said Katie, concentrating on which was fuller, his upper lip or his lower lip.

'That's what he did,' said Dan. 'A self-made man, my dad. Brought up on a council estate.'

'Wow.' Lower lip was fuller. Just.

'One day I'd like to do that.'

'Wow.'

'And settle down and have a family of course.'

Katie was deciding what to say instead of wow, when Dan gave her another creasy smile.

'Wow,' she said.

They laughed together. Nice teeth, one slightly crooked.

'Anyway, enough about me,' he said. 'What do you do?'

'Oh, I'm going to be an educational psychologist.'

His eyes widened.

'Wow!' he said.

By the time the camera flash went off in their faces, they'd had enough beers not to really notice or care. They turned slowly to face Sandy.

'Lovely!' she beamed. 'I'll e-mail it to you both.'

'Perfect,' said Dan.

'It may be a bit blurry,' said Sandy. 'Or is that me?' She had hysterics before turning her attention to the couple on the sofa taking full advantage of their mutual friend being in Mauritius.

'You do realise,' Katie heard Dan say quietly in her ear, 'that once I have your e-mail address I may pester you for a date.'

15

Katie looked up at him. Their noses were almost touching.

'I should think so too,' she murmured.

And then, hey presto, they were kissing.

If Katie were the type of girl to be into Lists, this Kiss would have had all the necessary components to make it a Top Kiss. Her limbs went limp, her closed eyes saw sparks and her organs spoke. They said 'Thank you.'

By the time she left the party, she had a date for next weekend, a spring in her step and a warm glow where it mattered.

2

By the next morning, the warm glow where it mattered had transformed into a thumping great pain where it hurt. By Monday morning it had developed into a dull ache all over.

Katie had a morning shift at the café, and as everyone in the café business knows, morning shifts are the pits. They're almost as bad as afternoon shifts, which are nearly as horrendous as evening shifts.

She woke up edgily, her first conscious thought being that she wanted to be asleep again. Then she remembered that she had a date with Dan and knew all was right with the world. Then she realised she had a dull ache all over her body and the date would probably be a disaster.

It was going to be a long day.

She ripped herself untimely out of bed and was so traumatised that her entire body went into hibernation mode, huddling against itself for warmth. Her teeth were chattering so loudly she could almost make out what they were saying.

Wrapping herself tightly in her ancient towelling robe, she tiptoed down the hall, past Jon's closed door and into the shower. Twenty minutes later, she came out clean, refreshed, as awake as she was going to get, and now late for work. After diving into her work clothes – the nearest things that were clean and comfortable – brushing her hands through her urchin hair and setting off for work, most of her optimism had faded.

The walk into work was usually a pleasant-enough interlude. Katie craved routine and she made a point of taking the same route every day. It grounded her and gave her a sense of context. Unless she was so dramatically late or exhausted that she needed to take the bus, she liked to pop into the grocer's to pick up something healthy to eat on her way to the newsagent's where she bought her usual chocolate bar.

Today, however, was a bus day. She kept her eyes down and her head supported. She didn't read, she didn't make eye contact, she didn't smile. She fitted right in.

Porter's Green was what up-and-coming people called 'up-and-coming', and what its oldest inhabitants called 'shot to pieces'. Its borders touched the borders of an already up-and-come part of north London, which boasted borders abutting an area so up-and-come it had blue plaques splattered on its houses like bird-droppings.

The process of an area 'coming up' included a rapid change in local shops, people and events, which spoke to its newest inhabitants of buzz and excitement. And word spread. Eager potential home-owners would first feel disappointment at not being able to afford even a bijou garage near a blue-plaqued property in central London, and then dismay at not being able to afford a good-sized flat on the borders. Finally, they'd find a spacious, family home in Porter's Green and discover that not only were the amenities superior, the shops more practical, the people less pretentious and the atmosphere more cosy, but, even better, within the next few years it was all going to change.

And so an entire set of New-Labour voters moved in next-door to Old-Labour voters and set about transforming their old Victorian houses into up-dated Victorian pads with more mod cons and fewer internal walls. At weekends, they'd drive into the neighbouring up-and-come village to take brunch in the cafés that had yet to arrive in their high street. Meanwhile the oldies, who had woken up one day to find themselves living in an unrecognisable, overpriced village where you couldn't get a decent cup of tea any more but could get 150 different types of coffee, made the bus journey in the opposite direction to find the bargains they could now no longer find in their own high street.

Katie's bus dropped her off about twenty yards from the café where she worked. She could see it from here, but usually tried not to. Her workplace, the thirty square yards where she spent up to sixty hours a week, was called, unsurprisingly enough, 'The Café'. One had to be inside to fully realise the leap of imagination that had created such a name.

She opened the door, her entrance heralded as usual by the tired jangle of what passed for a bell but sounded like a cat being slowly strangled. The same instant, a stifling warmth and sticky smell invaded her nostrils and pores.

Head down, she focused on her shoes as they stuck to the discoloured lino, unsure whether it was the fluorescent lighting making her feel sick or just the fact that it was Monday morning.

'Oh look! It's Herself!' came a reedy voice from the darkest corner.

She glanced up at the grimy clock-face above the coffee machine. Damn. Three minutes after seven.

'Morning Alec.'

'Only just.'

She looked over to where her boss was sitting and gave him a full beam, taking in his greasy hair and ever-present half-moustache. 'How was your weekend?' she asked.

Alec's right eyebrow twitched. 'Get your pinny on and help Sukie with the coffees.'

Katie walked past the coffee machine through the staff door into the kitchen. She stuffed her coat under the work-top, took out the pinny she'd washed on her Sunday off and wound the fraying belt several times round her waist. She barely noticed that Matt, the dishwasher, wasn't here yet and there was already a pile of dirty coffee cups waiting. She walked back into the main part of the café.

The sense that no one in The Café wanted to be here, but through no fault of their own had ended up here, seeped into one's consciousness via the plastic seats and Formica tables. Usually Monday mornings made Katie want to go straight to the meat knives and commit hara-kiri. Luckily they were blunt.

It was hard to believe that three years ago, she'd popped into The Café on a whim one sunny afternoon. She'd just moved into Jon's flat nearby, straight after her year of travelling had ended. When she got the job she'd thought she was on the first rung of a ladder she wanted to stay on forever, and they'd even celebrated that night with a bottle of wine. One day she'd get a manager's job in a respectable London restaurant and from there start her journey towards owning her own restaurant franchise. With the waitressing job to pay her rent, she'd have time to go for interviews, money to buy an interview suit and relevant experience to discuss.

At first it had felt heaven-sent. There she'd met Sukie, an out-of-work actress, and they had clicked immediately. Katie's flair for cooking blossomed and she often came up with inspired and delicious menu ideas that her boss was happy to let her make as well as serve. She liked her employer, a circular Greek woman who called her Sweetie and gave her delicious home-made leftovers that she and Jon would devour. But then her boss's husband became ill and she sold the café quickly to become his full-time carer. The farewell party was sad yet not without hope. That was because they hadn't met their new boss yet.

The first thing Alec did as owner was open up The Café two hours earlier each morning to catch the city commuters who set out every morning from the station directly below. Then he cut his staff by half, doubled the price of coffee, shrank the menu and only cooked fresh food twice a week. After that, the next step was easy – make customers spend their money and then leave.

Katie couldn't remember when she stopped looking in the papers for a new job. Was it after she got scared of going for interviews because she knew she'd be too tired to do herself justice? Or after she realised her interview suit was out of fashion, and she couldn't afford another one and refused to ask her parents for a handout? Or after she realised she'd have to give a convincing answer to why she'd worked at a crappy local café for so long?

Whichever it was, it didn't matter. All that mattered was that she had to get out of here.

Back in the café, she joined Sukie who was already attacking the coffee machine with gusto. The first commuter queue had started. The 7.14 into Euston was notoriously unreliable. It either came in late or smack bang on time but at the wrong platform, so that fifty knackered commuters had to race over the bridge to catch it. There was usually no tannoy announcement, so they had to be alert to spot whether it was their train or the 7.24 straight through to Brighton. Their morning coffees were not a luxury, they were a necessary tool in making it into the office instead of to the south coast.

If The Café staff resented making coffee for tired, ungrateful and often surly commuters, the commuters resented buying it, with knobs on. For a start, they would rather be in bed. Then there was the flickering fluorescent light that always pissed them off. And what did they have to look forward to? A crowded, over- or under-heated train where they probably wouldn't get a seat, followed by a job that didn't even pay them enough to be able to live near the borders of a place splattered with blue plaques – and that was if they were lucky and didn't catch the Brighton train.

'Double espresso, two sugars.'

Sukie took the change from one customer, nodded to let the next one know she'd heard him and whizzed back to the coffee machine. Katie joined her and spoke to commuter number three in the queue.

'Good morning! How can I help you this fine day.'

'Black coffee.'

'Black coffee coming up. It'll be my absolute pleas—'

'Excuse me,' cut in commuter number five, a man whose face seemed to have been pummelled in the night. Number four in the queue had overtaken him on the stairs up to the café and he wanted to knife him. 'Some of us have got trains to catch.'

'Right,' said Katie and she turned to the coffee machine.

'Will you spit in his coffee or shall I?' muttered Sukie without breaking from her task.

'Someone's already trodden on his face,' muttered Katie back. 'Give the guy a break.'

They both whizzed back round, coffees in hands, smiles on lips and continued with the queue until it had finished and the last train from Porter's Green to the city had left (the 8.54: only two minutes late, right platform, but minus two carriages), its commuters stuffed into each others' armpits, dreaming of Friday.

The sudden dip in custom on a Monday morning was usually Katie's lowest point of the week. This was when she had time to face the reality of her working day. Alec would approach them and, summoning up a spirit of excitement and eagerness for the week ahead, would command the same thing every single Monday morning.

'Right. First day of the week girls, first day of the week. Here we go. Salads out front, chip oil frying in back, make your boss a nice cup of coffee.'

And Sukie and Katie would reply the same thing every single Monday morning.

'Make it yourself, you lazy bastard,' from Sukie.

'You've got hands, haven't you?' from Katie.

And Alec would make himself a cup of coffee, while expressing his doubts over their parentage with imagination and spirit.

Today, though, Katie did not feel swamped by the usual onslaught of misery and failure. Today, the rudeness of the commuters, the miserable fug of the café and the dismal attempts at leadership from Alec had the opposite effect – all because of what had happened to her late on Friday afternoon.

For she had had an epiphany. She was going to become an educational psychologist.

It all happened during a double-shift that had gone so painfully slowly that she thought she must have actually died and gone to hell. She'd started chatting to a customer. It wasn't the done thing – it was hard to chat freely with Alec around – but he'd been oppressing someone in the kitchen at the time and the customer had been at table 18, right by the door, so it had felt a fairly safe risk.

The woman had had a quiet Friday at work and had popped in for a quick coffee before getting home to a house full of overtired children and an underpaid nanny. She'd started chatting to Katie about the weather and somehow Katie had found herself telling her that she was considering becoming a teacher. This thought had occurred to her only the week before, after she'd seen a reality TV show about an inner city school where a teacher had got locked in the girls' toilets and had escaped through a window. It seemed like an adventurous job. It

24

just so happened that the woman had been a teacher once, a while ago, before she'd started training to be an educational psychologist. Once you'd been a teacher for two years, all you needed was a masters degree and voilà! An educational psychologist. Much better for pulling at parties, the woman told Katie, and better still, you didn't have to wait for a bell to go to the toilet.

Katie was reborn. Not only did she already have the requisite psychology degree (from Oxford no less) but she'd always liked children. They liked her too – she had an affinity with them. By the time she had deposited the warmed croissant on a plate and taken it to the woman, Katie's new future was set; restaurant franchises were a dim and distant memory. This woman was *meant* to come into the café that day, and she, Katie Simmonds, had been *meant* to see that TV programme the week before. It was destiny.

So here she was, starting the first week of the rest of her life. Which was why today, The Café's usual Monday morning depression didn't seep into her bones and numb her; instead it reminded her – as if she'd already mentally escaped this place – of what she'd left behind.

'Table 8 wants serving.'

Katie turned to Alec, who was still sitting by the till, the steam from his coffee cup mingling with the smoke from his hand-rolled cigarette. He nodded briefly over at table 8. He always sat in the near corner by the till because he said it gave him a good view of everything in The Café as well as the window-front. By happy coincidence, it also gave a good view of any passing policemen who might want to check his kitchen for illegal substances and any passing traffic wardens who might disagree with him that laziness was a disability.

Katie walked over to where two men were having a morning meeting, both pretending that their self-made careers were going excellently and that they were content to be in a café rather than a pub.

'Two English breakfasts and two coffees,' said one man, returning the menu to Katie without looking at her.

'One decaffeinated,' added the other, briefly examining her chest.

Katie walked away, muttering, 'I'm going to be an educational psychologist, I'm going to be an educational psychologist.'

Keith the 'chef' had just arrived, a man not driven by demons as much as devoured by them. He had so many phobias it was a wonder he made it from his flat down the street into the café. He was telling Sukie about his weekend. Katie could tell this, because she kept hearing Sukie's regular murmurs of 'Oh dear.'

'Two fried breakfasts,' interrupted Katie.

Keith turned to her. 'Morning Katie,' he said. 'I was just telling Sukie my neighbours are trying to drive me out of my flat.'

'Oh dear,' murmured Katie.

Sukie and Katie made brief eye contact before Katie went to make the coffees and give them to the men at table 8.

'Are you sure that's decaffeinated?' asked one, examining her chest again.

'Yes.' Katie smiled at his bald patch.

He smelt it warily.

'I can smell coffee.'

'Well,' said Katie gravely, crossing her arms so he couldn't give it back to her. 'That's because it's so good.' She turned away and walked back to the kitchen, muttering, 'Believe me, if I wanted to put something in your drink, it wouldn't be coffee.' Then she repeated under her breath, 'I know the names of everyone in the Cabinet, I know the names of everyone in the Cabinet.'

As she walked to the kitchen, Matt appeared. He was seventeen and working as a part-time dishwasher while studying for his A-Levels.

'Matt!' greeted Katie.

Matt grunted.

'Nice to see you too,' she answered.

He grunted again and followed her in.

'I've got something that will cheer you up,' said Katie. She went to her bag and pulled out an A-4 sized piece of paper. Because of Sandy's software package, there were four pictures from Saturday's party, which she'd e-mailed the day before. It had only taken her five attempts and two hours. There was a photo of Jon, Sukie and Katie, all a little worse for drink, one of an unnamed couple in a clinch (the man in an almost luminous green shirt), one of Hugh and Katie chatting and one of Katie in deep conversation with an unknown man.

'Ta-da!' trumpeted Katie. 'My new date.'

Keith, Sukie and Matt all approached and Sukie took the piece of paper out of Katie's hand. They all studied Dan and made approving noises. Then Sukie performed the now cherished ritual of adding the latest photos to the dairy fridge. Both fridges were covered with beaming glossy faces of various members of staff in poses with friends, partners, lovers, exes, but the meat fridge door was entirely filled with photos of Katie with men. It was titled 'The Ones Who Got Away.'

Sukie coughed loudly.

'May I have everyone's attention please? I hereby call this relationship . . .' she stared at the photo, as if for inspiration, 'Doomed.' She Blu-Tacked it with all the other staff photos. It had become a bit of a standing joke just how fussy Katie was with her men. In fact, Sukie had hardly been surprised to discover that last weekend's party had been so full of Katie's exes. She'd been highly amused to see that Katie hadn't even recognised some of them because she'd extricated herself from the relationships so quickly.

'I have a feeling this one will last,' insisted Katie.

'Really?' said Sukie. 'And I have a feeling Matt will lose his virginity before next year.'

'Piss off,' said Matt.

'Don't talk to *me* about sex,' began Keith.

'OK,' chorused Katie and Sukie.

'Oh go on,' said Matt.

Alas, just then Alec came in and the chef's sexual anecdotes had to be left for another occasion.

3

Even though Katie now knew she wanted to be an educational psychologist, she was glad that today she had a job that didn't need any concentration. She'd have found it hard to concentrate, what with her mind replaying every nuance of her conversation with Dan and planning and re-planning what she should wear for her date with him.

Every time the café door had opened to the bizarrely welcoming sound of a strangled cat, she'd had a very silly daydream that did no one any good at all. Briefly, the daydream was that she would turn round to find, standing there in the doorway, surrounded by a halo of light and accompanied by a brass fanfare and choral blast, Dan. Their eyes would meet, their hearts would explode, etc etc etc. Well, it kept a girl going.

Every time she remembered certain key points about Dan, such as the way his cheek crinkled when he smiled, the way his legs stretched all the way up to his bottom and the undeniable look of keenness in his eyes, she felt invulnerable. He was on her mind so much that had he suddenly appeared – wham! out of nowhere – it

29

would have felt more like witchcraft than coincidence.

After their shift was over, Sukie and Katie went home to live their lives of wonder, fulfil their dreams and see what was on TV. They ambled up Asherman's Hill together.

'So when's the date then?' asked Sukie.

Katie closed her eyes in little girl glee.

'Sunday night.'

'Interesting,' considered Sukie, nodding slowly. 'A Sunday. OK. Not too obvious, but still keen.' Katie took in this new opinion like an expert taster swilling a new wine round her tongue. 'I once got asked out on a Wednesday morning,' continued Sukie. 'Not a good sign.'

'What happened?'

'I ended up helping on his dad's market stall.'

'How old were you?'

'Fourteen. It was the summer holidays.'

'I think that's sweet,' smiled Katie. 'A way of getting to know you.'

'Oh, *he* wasn't there,' said Sukie. 'It was just me and his dad. He was off skateboarding with his mates.'

Katie nodded. 'Actually,' she said eventually, 'Dan suggested Saturday, but I'm away at my folks this weekend so I'll come home early for the date. It was that or wait till the following weekend because I'm too knackered mid-week.'

'That's completely different,' said Sukie. 'He's desperate.'

'Excellent. What shall I wear?'

'It doesn't matter. He's after what's underneath.'

'But how do I make what's underneath as alluring as possible?'

'Turn up.'

They parted at the top of the road.

'What you up to this afternoon?' asked Sukie, putting on her old, brightly coloured, woolly gloves.

'Re-writing my CV,' replied Katie, blowing into her hands. 'I'm hoping I can get Jon to help me. Have you got any auditions today?'

'Nope. Going to see my agent.'

'Oh good, why?'

'Because I'm not depressed enough already.'

They said their farewells and parted company.

Twenty minutes later, Katie opened her flat door, picked up all the post, twitched her nose like Mole smelling his home, and knew from all the signs that either Jon's writing was going well today, or he was still sleeping off last night's bar shift. If it was the former, she was in with a chance of getting first-class help with her latest CV.

She knocked on his door and at the murmured greeting, opened it into a rank writing den. Jon was sitting at his laptop, tapping away, wearing a dressing gown that could have sat up and probably written its own novel by itself.

'Want a coffee?' she asked, breathing through her mouth.

Jon blinked his intense black eyes up at her through his glasses.

'Hello,' he said. 'Left work early?'

'No, Jon. It's three o'clock. Children are leaving school. The sun is nearly going down. Please wash that dressing gown.'

'I'd love a coffee thanks.'

He stretched up and gave a big yawn, and Katie backed her head out of the room.

'I won't make you one unless you shower first,' she said. 'I'll make you some white toast and chocolate spread too.'

'OK, you win,' grinned Jon. 'I was just about to finish for today anyway. It's going to be a brilliant book, even though I say so myself.'

'Excellent!' Katie felt a warm glow wash over her. All was well, Jon's book was brilliant, she was going to be an educational psychologist and Dan was in the world.

'Are you doing a shift at the bar tonight?' she asked.

Jon looked at his clock. 'Yeah, but much later. I've got till twelve.'

'Fancy helping me with my CV?'

Jon left a beat. 'What do you want to be this time?'

'Educational psychologist.'

She could see his mind beginning to whirr.

'Why not?' he grinned. 'I'm feeling creative.'

Meanwhile Sukie's bus journey was taking even longer than she'd expected. At each stop there was another old person who took up precious *Countdown* time heaving themselves and their wheelie shoppers on. The driver was one of those types who felt he'd made his contribution to world peace having waited for them. She wouldn't have minded if she was sure the little trip was going to be worthwhile, but deep down, she knew this agonisingly slow journey was a self-deceptive ploy to make her feel she was doing something positive in the tidal wave of negativity that was her career.

She was a living, breathing cliché: the out-of-work

actress who worked as a waitress. How did she get here? Most people at least went to LA for this humiliation, but she hadn't even managed that. She sighed and rubbed the condensation on the window with her gloved hand. She leant her forehead against the cold glass and watched busy shoppers bent in the cold until her eyes shut.

It had seemed, at one point, as if she was going to be one of the lucky ones. She had gone straight into a fringe production out of drama college. It wasn't West End, but it was paid work. She got her Equity card with that first job and her agent was always ringing her with auditions. Before long, she was a regular on the fringe circuit. Then things went quiet. To tide her over she got a waitressing job. The next year, she started getting things in mainstream theatres. She started becoming a regular. But now she felt she couldn't return to the fringe, so, when she had 'resting' periods, she worked as a waitress again – reliable money, good tips and she wasn't risking ruining her climb up the ladder by stepping down a rung or two. The third year though, things weren't quite as regular. It was a bad year for actresses: a couple of theatres closed down and, by coincidence, others took on plays that had few or even no parts for women.

She knew it was bad when she could no longer watch television without wanting to throw things at it when the acting was bad. That was when she and her agent decided they had to change tack. They would re-invent her. She would become a telly actress instead of a theatre actress. Then, once she had made her name, she could return to her first love as a safe-bet for strapped theatres. However, it didn't seem to be working and sometimes she couldn't risk watching *EastEnders* or she might smash her telly for good.

The bus journey finally approached its end. She jumped up and rang the bell.

She felt calmer and more positive almost as soon as she turned the corner of her agent's street. The big red door beckoned to her like a beacon of hope. She knew she could have phoned, but seeing Greta face-to-face was always so much better. She needed to know that for the short moment Greta was talking to her, she was actually thinking about her too.

After being buzzed in and asked to wait in Reception, she was eventually summoned into the biggest office in the place.

'Sukie!' greeted Greta, arms outstretched.

'Greta!' Sukie practically ran to her arms.

Greta came out from behind her desk, resplendent in a vermilion woollen two-piece with matching hair and lipstick, and clasped Sukie to her bosom like a long-lost child. Sukie fought the tears.

'How's my Vivienne Leigh?' soothed Greta.

'Fine,' gasped Sukie.

Greta released her, sat back down behind her desk and intercom'd her receptionist. 'Two coffees, my love, strong and sweet.' She winked at Sukie, stood up, opened a sash window behind her – 'Let's let the room breathe' – and sat back down behind her desk, shifting piles of *Spotlights*, CVs and scripts out of the way, so that she could still be seen.

Sukie sat upright on the edge of the deep leather couch framing the office.

34

'I was just passing and wondered if there was anything I should know about, or . . .'

Greta's phone went. She thrust her hand up in the air, ceasing all talk, and picked up.

'Greta.'

A pause.

'*Darling!*'

Sukie stared, transfixed. As snippets of Greta's conversation wafted over, ('I have just the boy . . .', 'don't be put off by his accent . . .', 'marvellous as Romeo at Guildford . . .'), she ruminated on what it would be like to be Greta's only client. Sometimes she felt like one of hundreds of infants in an orphanage where Greta had come searching for the perfect child. Which may have explained why she often had the unnerving compulsion to curl up on Greta's lap. While Greta made all the right noises into the phone, her receptionist brought coffee and biscuits. Sukie ignored the biscuits – she was a good-looking actress, and there weren't many parts for good-looking actresses turning to fat. She started the hot coffee without enthusiasm. After serving fresh ground coffee with different forms of heated milk all day, it always irked her to be given instant with cold milk.

Just as she finished it, Greta put down the phone.

'National's new assistant,' she explained. 'They're doing a new Eldridge.'

Sukie leant forward eagerly with the expression of a stray cat in the rain.

Greta gave her a smile so sympathetic it was almost another hug. 'Darling,' she murmured, 'it's not for you.'

'Why?'

'Because they're looking for a thirty-year-old black male. Trust me. I know what I'm doing.'

Sukie tried to smile.

'Now now, do I detect a soupçon of dejection in that lovely, Greta Garbo face?'

'It's been two months,' said Sukie in a small voice. 'Christmas is coming.'

'I know, sweetest heart, I know.'

'I was working more when I was doing fringe.'

'Darling,' said Greta, launching into one of her speeches. 'I've never *seen* a Beatrice like yours. Such *passion*, such *fire*. And your Titania at the Open Air Theatre when you got drenched in the hail – *exquisite* poignancy. And your Rosalind – such *spunk*, such *sensitivity*, such *humour*. I cannot wait for the call from the National to say they're doing Macbeth and need his lady. You're the next Judi Dench, my dear. You are standing *In. Her. Wings.*'

Sukie drank it all in.

'The trick is my love,' continued Greta, softening her tone slightly, 'you have to relive those moments *when it counts.*'

'What do you mean?'

Greta came and sat next to Sukie on the couch, took her hand in hers and placed it in her small lap.

'Television directors are different from theatre directors.'

'I know.'

'There are a lot of new, young TV directors out there who think Judi Dench *is actually* Queen Victoria. They think a British Classic is a re-run of *Dr Who*. And unlike in the theatre, they don't give you a chance to shine because, bless their *little* hearts, they don't know *how* to. They think if they can capture you on tape, they can capture your *soul*.'

'Greta, just tell me what to do.'

Greta took a deep breath and began.

'The audition is *not* a time to be yourself,' she said slowly. 'It's a time to be who they want you to be.' She closed her eyes. 'Lose yourself. Give yourself over to the Muse.' She opened her eyes again and they shone at Sukie. 'Start performing before you've opened the door.'

'I thought I was.'

'They have said "Action" before you have walked into that room.'

Greta sighed the sigh of a movie star and Sukie caught a glimpse of the young, lithe actress inside her agent. 'My dear,' began Greta. 'First impressions count more than anything, especially in this business. It's a fact.'

'You mean pretend to be who I'm not,' repeated Sukie dully.

Greta flinched dramatically. 'I mean act – perform –'

'Lie –'

Greta clasped her hand to her heart. 'Inhabit the role before you walk in.'

'Pretend I'm a hardened Northern pathologist before I walk in –'

'*Yes* –'

'Pretend I'm really a Victorian lesbian music-hall star?'

'Yes – well –'

'They're idiots.'

'*Yes*! Now we're getting somewhere.'

Sukie grimaced.

'Darling,' another squeeze of the hand, 'you re-think your definition of lying and I will have another look at some of the scripts on my desk with you in mind, with the beautiful, exciting knowledge that you will be as sublime in the auditions as you can be on stage.'

'OK,' said Sukie firmly.

'OK, dearest heart.'

'I can do it.'

'I have every faith.'

Sukie nodded.

'Meanwhile,' said Greta, returning to her desk, 'I've got a *lovely* voice-over audition, 5 p.m. today, for an Anusol advert on Essex Radio with *your name* on it.'

While Jon squinted at the screen at her previous CV, Katie stood by the printer watching her new one emerge, thinking of Dan.

'What was this old one for?' asked Jon. 'I've forgotten.'

'Teacher. How lame was that?'

'What was the one before that?

'Film director.' She laughed.

'And the one before that?'

She thought hard. 'Dentist I think. Weird.' She shivered.

'And the one before that?'

'Can't remember.' Katie made herself comfortable on his bed.

Jon gave her a long look.

'What?' she asked him impatiently.

He shrugged. 'It's just . . . are you sure we aren't wasting our time? We could be watching *Pop Idol*. I taped it.'

Katie pointed at his computer. 'You said you'd help me.'

'But you're only going to change your mind again.'

'I am not!'

'Do you realise my folder of Katie's CVs is almost as big as my book? Two great works of fiction.'

'Thanks!' She laughed. 'Just because we don't all have a vocation like you.'

'Hmm.'

'Mr Tortured Writer.'

'All right. Point made.'

They sat in silence for a moment before Jon spoke.

'If I don't get an agent I don't know what I'll do.'

'You will get an agent. It's only a matter of time.'

Jon shook his head.

'Yes you will,' insisted Katie. 'They keep asking to meet you after just reading three chapters.'

'Yeah and then I'm too terrified to meet them because I know I'll spill my coffee or laugh too loud or fart, or just . . . I don't know, spontaneously combust.'

'You just need some assertiveness training.'

'I just need a stunt double.'

'Maybe you need a makeover.'

Jon looked up at her. 'Oh cheers!'

'I just mean . . .' she came towards him, took off his glasses, swept his hair aside, undid the neck zip of his fleece and pushed him in front of the mirror.

'What do you think?' she asked him.

'Where's everything gone?' he squinted.

She put his glasses back on him. 'Image is everything Jon,' she told his reflection. 'Contact lenses, a new hairstyle and a trip to the shops – you'll have an agent.'

'And then spill my coffee, laugh too loud and fart.'

She pointed at him in the mirror. 'Ah yes, but it won't matter because you'll look so good. Now,' she said, giving his shoulders a squeeze. 'Let's get going on my CV, then I can go to the library and get some prospectuses.'

'Or watch *Pop Idol.*'

'Or watch *Pop Idol.*'

That evening, student and The Café's dishwasher Matt was sitting in his bedroom, staring at his A-Level French book. His school counsellor had told him that this stage of his life would probably be the hardest time ever, and it had only just occurred to him that the word 'probably' meant that it might never get better than this.

The truth was that Matt didn't know what to be depressed about first: the unpredictability of exam questions, the predictability of acne, the fear of turning into a commuter and, worst of all, the terror of his virginity becoming a fact of life rather than a phase he'd grow out of.

These were just some of his favourite musings. Global warming, the risk of being wrongfully imprisoned for murder, being buried alive and his unruly hair were some of the others. The fact that his body (once a haven he'd felt totally at home in, now an enemy that could attack when least expected) didn't seem satisfied with being six-foot and was intent on making him the tallest boy at college, the fact that all his mates seemed to have been 'doing it' since they were twelve, and the fact that his mother had a tendency to ask his friends questions like 'Boys, enlighten me, what's a golden shower?' were a few of the minor leaguers. On the way home from The Café this afternoon, he'd realised that if he got run over and killed today, he would actually *die* a virgin.

Darkness was now falling mid-afternoon and Matt stared out of his bedroom window at the silky red snake of sunset filling his aluminium-framed square of sky. For a few seconds, he had an out-of-body sensation of contentment. At moments like this he could believe he was just another normal bloke and his life was going to be fine. His body would stop growing, all the other boys' bodies would catch up, his mother would lose her voice and he'd get a shag. Then, all too soon, the sun had set and he was stuck in his harshly lit room staring at his French vocab. As he glanced back up at the blue-black sky, he heard his mother's voice calling him for dinner. He turned off his lamp, shut his book and went downstairs.

By Friday morning, Katie was in such a state of nervous excitement about her date with Dan on Sunday, she could barely eat. Tomorrow she was off to spend the weekend with her family in Glossop, Derbyshire, but she'd be coming home early for the date. She usually took the train, but, because there was work on the track now for the foreseeable future, she was taking the car. All she had to get through was seven hours of café hell before the fun commenced.

It had been a long week. Christmas shopping had begun in earnest in Porter's Green and the stress levels were seeping into The Café. Two women had almost had a punch-up when one realised the other had been the very person who'd bought Woolies' very last Snowboarding Barbie. Everyone had so many bags of shopping that The Café's cumbersome chairs and heavy tables had become a nuisance. On Wednesday, Katie mentioned to Alec that it might be a great idea to put a couple of comfy sofas in the window, but he looked at her like she'd just suggested he juggle nude. She would have persisted, but she had four tables to wait on.

By Tuesday, the weather had turned and it was now raining from dawn to dusk. Umbrellas littered the floor and radiators, which meant that wet umbrella steam was now added to the coffee machine steam. People were slipping on wet patches of floor and The Café reeked of damp coats. Unsurprisingly, more customers were smoking and the smell of cigarettes clung to the damp fabric. Overall, this was not somewhere anyone wanted to stay for too long, which meant its customers wanted to be served sharp. Which was a shame, because there was now double the usual amount of them with the same amount of staff. On Wednesday morning, Katie suggested taking on part-time staff for the Christmas rush. Alec listened to this suggestion thoughtfully and then said, 'Table 4 wants serving.'

On Thursday, Katie had not had a chance to go to the toilet until noon. The Cafe only had one Ladies and one Gents, so she stood outside in the corridor, jiggling quietly as she watched the people who had just ordered food from her get increasingly irate that it hadn't yet arrived. It was a tough decision, but she decided it would be preferable to make them wait rather than have an accident in front of them.

She put her ear to the door. Inside, she could hear the distinct voice of a woman on a phone.

'I must talk to you about Playstation,' she could hear. She started shifting from foot to foot again. Was someone using the toilet as a phone booth? She looked out into the café. Alec was on the prowl.

'I'll see you at school later anyway,' came the voice inside.

Eventually, Katie decided she'd have to take some action. She gave two quiet but firm knocks at the door.

Silence. Then, 'Who is it?' came the voice.

Katie was nonplussed.

'Katie.'

There was a pause.

'Katie who?'

Katie blinked. She looked to her right and left.

'Simmonds.'

There was another pause.

'Yes?' came the voice. 'I'm on the phone.'

'Yes,' Katie told the door. 'I wondered if I could use the toilet.'

'Well, I'm on that too,' came the voice impatiently. Then she heard it say, 'Look, I'll have to call you back.'

When the lady came out, Katie tried a smile. It didn't work. The lady gave her a look that would sour chocolate.

Katie locked the door behind her. She was so grateful to sit down in a quiet room that she closed her eyes and blocked out the noise of the café outside. Her body ached so much she wasn't sure if she'd ever be able to stand up again. She rolled her head from side to side.

Two loud bangs on the door made her jump.

'Hello?' she called out.

'Are you sure you're comfortable?' came Alec's voice. 'Only I don't want to disturb you. Would you like some cushions perhaps? Or a bed?'

She tensed. She was about to answer when she realised her eyes were watering. She took a deep breath to steady her voice.

'That is you, isn't it, Katie?' Alec's voice was suddenly less harsh.

'I'll just check,' she said drily, staring at her shoes.

There was a pause outside and she knew Alec would be frowning.

She closed her eyes for a full minute. 'Yes!' she called out. 'It's me.'

There was another pause. Had Alec heard her?

'I've just had a complaint, young lady!' he shouted.

'Would you like to come in?' She was now shouting back.

'Get your fanny out here immediately.' She knew he was reversing sharp back to the café.

'*It's busy*,' she yelled at the door.

She knew that if she stayed one second longer in the toilet she'd start crying and that wouldn't help anyone. Thankfully, she knew – as well as Alec did – that he lacked the courage to actually reprimand her when there wasn't the security of a locked door between them. Instead he made sarcastic comments whenever she came near about customers complaining while staff were in the toilet. By the end of the day, she just wanted to punch him.

On Friday morning, she was exhausted. It had been a monumental effort to get up today, even though she'd gone to bed at nine the night before. The backs of her knees were still aching from yesterday and today had barely begun.

She dragged herself out of the kitchen to join Sukie at the coffee machine and work her way through the queue of wet, shivering commuters, all of whom were so clenched they seemed to have lost their necks on the way in. She naturally assumed that Sukie's heavy shoulders, general air of dejection and unusual lethargy were due to the crapness of the day. It wasn't until they were on their last two customers of the 7.14 train to Euston that Sukie told Katie, 'You're looking at the person behind the voice behind the Anusol advert.'

'Wow!'

'On Essex Radio.'

'Wow!'

'I just found out I got the job.'

'Wow!'

'As soon as I've spent my earnings, I'm going to kill myself.'

'Oh.'

Sukie spun round to face the customers. 'Would you like sugar in that?' she asked.

'Yes,' said the woman.

She turned to get the sugar.

'*No!*' the woman cried suddenly.

Sukie turned back to her.

'Yes or no?'

The woman hesitated. 'I don't know.'

Sukie blinked.

'What do you think?' asked the woman.

Sukie blinked again.

'I think you deserve the sugar,' said Katie quickly, as Sukie's face registered exactly what she thought.

'Yes,' the woman turned to Katie. 'I have been good all week.'

'Well then,' Katie went to pick up the sugar.

'But I'm being weighed tomorrow,' said the woman quickly. 'It would be a shame to waste all the good work I've done this week.'

'It would,' said Katie.

'Half,' said the woman.

Katie didn't move. 'Final answer?'

The woman nodded firmly.

'Final answer. Half a sugar.'

Katie obliged. As the woman walked out of The Café with her black coffee and half a sugar, Katie said dully, 'I know all the names of the shadow Cabinet.'

Sukie nodded. 'I'm the voice behind the Anusol advert on Essex Radio.'

They stood there for a while watching the rain.

Early Saturday afternoon, Katie threw her last bag into her car. She hadn't intended to leave for her parents' this late – it was now starting to get dark – but the temptation of having three whole car seats to fill with luggage had proved too much and her packing time had extended way beyond the usual, even though she was only going for one night. She'd also started packing much later than she'd planned because she'd completely overslept and then had needed a hot bath to get her body working properly. Forty minutes after getting into it, she'd woken up, chilled and wrinkly. She had a coffee and phoned her mum to tell her she might be late. The journey would be easy. Just a few motorways and she'd be home. She'd packed her CDs and was raring to go, boosted by the fact that the next time she hit London, she'd be on her way to her date with Dan.

4

So far it had taken Katie four hours. Weekend traffic didn't help the fact that she took the wrong turning off the motorway twice which resulted in a loss of confidence so complete that she missed the next two exits and had to double-back twice. By the time she got home she would need a valium and a shower.

As would most of her family.

Katie had a condition that was prevalent in her family, which the men dubbed Locational Dyslexia, the women A Crap Sense Of Direction. It didn't much matter what it was called; the result was the same. She couldn't direct herself out of a paper bag with an exit sign.

And now she was having a nightmare roundabout experience. As she approached, she saw that none of the locations she had memorised were mentioned – even briefly – on this roundabout sign. She glanced in her mirror – cars were slowing down behind her and there was no time to stop. She didn't have a chance to look and see if any of the names on the signpost were even in the same direction as home. Needles of sweat pricked her armpits and her heart quickened. Getting nearer to the roundabout, she moved across into the middle lane. Perhaps the signs painted on the roads would help her – but what if she was in the wrong lane? She watched all the other drivers already on the roundabout, envious of their apathetic expressions. Couldn't she just plump for a car and follow it?

A wide space emerged, leaving her enough time to pull out comfortably. She glanced behind her again – a queue of cars – there was no alternative, she would have to get on to the roundabout. Hoping that somehow there would be more clues once on it, she edged forward and, staying in the middle lane, went round as slowly as possible, reading the signs intently.

Still nothing. Not one sign gave her any information she could do anything with.

She was now grimacing heavily, panic having levelled out into misery. She completed the roundabout once more. Still nothing. Of the three exits, one was a no-go. She could see that it took the drivers on a dual-carriageway from which there was no return. Just looking at it traumatised her. Of the other two exits, one extended as far as the eye could see, with no possibilities of a U-turn, the other, seemingly, went straight back to London.

She rounded the circle again, muttering uselessly to herself.

After her fourth round-trip, she phoned home on the hands-free.

'I'm on a roundabout,' she shouted.

'Well done!' cried her father cheerfully.

'I can't get off it.'

'I'll get your mother.'

It only took Deanna two roundabout trips to get to the phone, by which time Katie was starting to get giddy and a bit depressed.

'What are the exits?' Deanna asked calmly.

'I'm just coming up to them again . . .' said Katie, slowing down accordingly. She read them all off to her mother.

'Hmm,' Deanna said thoughtfully. 'That's odd.'

'Why?' Katie's voice trembled. 'Am I on the wrong roundabout?'

'Ah! Just as I thought. You want the third exit. How misleading.'

The never-ending road.

'Are you sure?' she asked. 'I'm not going to end up in Birmingham?'

'Sweetheart,' said her mother. 'Would I ever send you to Birmingham?'

'Right, I'm indicating now.'

'Good girl.'

'I'm going off the roundabout.'

'Good girl!'

Almost immediately she drove past another sign, and this one now mentioned, bottom of its list, the location she needed.

'It's right!' she cried. 'You were right! I'm going the right way!'

By the end of the journey, her entire family had been navigating her from home via one phone line and three extensions. It had not been a smooth process. Deanna had shouted at Katie's pregnant sister, her brother had said 'Bugger' while his parents were on the line and, horrifyingly, her father had said 'Bollocks' while all of them were on the line. The shock waves of silence that reverberated down the phone after that almost caused Katie to miss another turning.

'Darling,' she heard her mother's voice cut through the silence, 'are you still there?'

'Yes,' she said in a small voice.

'Bea?' Deanna asked Katie's older sister. 'Are you still there?'

'Yes,' said Bea, 'but I might have lost the baby.'

'That's *not* funny,' said Deanna. 'Cliffie? Are you still there?'

'God yes,' came the voice of their younger brother. 'I wouldn't miss this for the world.'

'Sydney?' said Deanna. 'Are you still there? Or would you like to go and calm down?'

'No I would bloody well not like to go and calm down,' came the voice of Katie's father.

When she finally heard the comforting sound of gravel crunching under her car's wheels and saw the warm lights of the family front room through the topiary, Katie almost wept with relief.

Deanna came to the door followed by her two golden retrievers. Katie stepped out of the car, her leg muscles doing a Bambi, and within minutes everyone was feeling much better. The journey hadn't caused any permanent damage to the Simmonds family – at least nothing a swift round of whisky and some group therapy couldn't sort out.

Later, her mother and sister joined her in the cosy cliché kitchen, complete with Aga, oak table and dresser, while she ate her re-heated dinner. Meanwhile her father, brother and brother-in-law caught the latest rugby scores on the news.

'They're going to the pub to watch the rugby in the morning, so we can have a nice catch-up then,' said Deanna.

'I hope they're back for Sunday lunch,' said Bea.

'Oh, Mum, I won't be staying long after lunch,' said Katie.

'Why?'

'I have a date.'

Bea and Deanna were all ears.

'He's called Dan.'

'And?'

'No, Dan.'

She finished off her apple and rhubarb crumble with hot custard. 'He's ex-Oxford, he's made enough money in the city to start his own business and he's got a crinkle in his cheek when he smiles.'

'What did he study at Oxford?' asked Deanna.

'What colour eyes?' asked Bea.

'What time are you going?' asked Deanna.

'How tall?'

Katie took a deep breath. 'The date's at eight, so considering how long it took me to get here, I'll probably have to leave in about half an hour. Blue eyes, about six-foot tall, don't know what he studied.'

The conversation was interrupted by The Men appearing. Deanna leapt up to attend their needs, whether it be making a pot of tea, washing up a glass or fetching a home-made cookie from the pantry.

As Katie watched her family with an affectionately critical eye, she couldn't help but wonder how her sister, the arbiter of taste, the queen of aesthetics, could ever have married Maurice. Maurice didn't really have a face, he had a chin with optional extras, and the older he got, the more colonial his chin became. It had already taken over his neck and looked set to march triumphantly onward to his ears. Katie wondered if her sister would wake up one day and discover that it had annexed his entire head.

To her mind, what must have made things rather painful for Bea was that Maurice's mother was a rare beauty, with a neatness in the chin area not found in any of her husband's ancestors' portraits, and Katie could only wonder how Bea, competitive in all things womanly, felt about having this much to live up to. The only hope was that her children – the first of which was already a neat little bulge under Bea's Jaeger cashmere – would, if it had to take after anyone from Maurice's family, take after his mother. They'd all find out in three months' time.

'How's it going sis?' asked Cliffie, taking one of Deanna's home-made spiced cookies and eating it in one. 'Recovered from the journey yet?'

Katie yawned her yes.

'Someone's a sleepyhead,' nodded Sydney, her father. 'I think it's time for bed.'

Katie dragged her feet up the wide, shallow staircase to her small, neat attic bedroom, unchanged since she left for college and beyond, all those years ago. Blue-and-white check wallpaper and matching curtains set off the single bed with its Princess-and-the-Pea-style headboard. She felt

53

instantly soothed by the room's delicate tranquillity, a quality she'd never been aware of as she grew up. After leaving her clothes on the blue-and-white-check corner armchair she slipped into the cool sheets and turned off her blue-and-white-check bedside lamp. She closed her eyes, and tried to squeeze in some snapshot moments of last week's party before sleep tiptoed in to snatch her away.

Downstairs, Bea and Maurice got themselves comfy in their bed in Bea's old bedroom. It had been four years after her eldest daughter's wedding before Deanna had finally replaced Bea's bed and Maurice stopped having to use the old put-you-up. Deanna had said she'd never got round to it, but the fact was that a mere wedding licence and year-long pre-nuptual preparations had not suddenly made her and Sydney able to deal with the fact that their daughter was officially no longer a virgin.

After Bea and Maurice had spent their third entire Christmas season with Maurice's family, Bea had finally admitted to her parents that Maurice just couldn't bear the thought of having to sleep in 'that bed' during 'what was meant to be a holiday'. Deanna had finally capitulated. She bought an Emperor-size bed; a bed big enough for them never to know they were in it together. How their daughter and son-in-law spent their nights under their roof was obviously their business, but Deanna and Sydney certainly spent *their* nights sleeping easier knowing that it was physically possible for Bea to be sleeping on the opposite side of the bedroom to her husband.

Cliffie's room had never had to change. At twenty-one, he had yet to leave home, and everyone knew he wouldn't. He had a very nice local job and was content to stay cosseted by the heat and comfort of the family fire.

Spartacus and Hector, the family's retrievers, settled down in the porch off the kitchen, whiffling against the Wellingtons, and the grandfather clock's chimes echoed softly in the dead of night. Outside, November's night brought a frost that traced gossamer patterns over the Simmonds' rambling back-garden, and silence fell, soft as a Walt Disney fairy, dense as the night-sky, all over Glossop.

At seven the next morning, Katie woke to the smell of sizzling bacon and frying eggs, the sound of hot water clunking its way through the house's old radiators and the sensation of being cushioned in a comfort zone so soft she thought she was floating. She lay still, savouring the moment, letting her eyes adjust to her room with the morning's light casting new angles and corners to it. When she heard the dogs' excited barking she knew The Men must be on their way out, which meant she hadn't missed too much of the day. She waited until the prospect of leaving her bed metamorphosed from an unbearable one of cold discomfort, to a pleasant one of hot breakfast, family gossip and a clean body. The process took fifteen minutes, by which time she could hear Bea's bath running. She knew that her mother would already be dressed, having breakfasted all the men and Bea, and would now be waiting for her.

She gingerly grasped the duvet, slowly moving it away from her, leaving her with nothing but fleece pyjamas protecting her against the elements. She waited for the cold but the temperature change was painless. She sat up, swung her legs out of bed, wriggled her toes in the old thick-pile carpet and stood up. She padded over to her wooden-framed, double-glazed attic window and opened her curtains. Hazy winter sunlight streamed into her room, showing up the dancing dust particles and making the frost outside look all the more magical.

Downstairs in the kitchen, her mother sat at the head of the long oak table, dogs at her feet, teapot, butter dish and milk jug in front of her on the table, *Telegraph* open beside them. She beamed up at her daughter.

'Aha!' she exclaimed, jumping to her feet. 'You're up!' She walked to the fridge. 'There's a fresh pot just made,' she said, bending down to take out bacon and eggs. Katie knew there was no point telling her mother not to make her breakfast. It would be like telling the dogs not to wag their tails. She poured herself a cup of tea, topped up her mother's, flicked through the paper and watched her mother prepare breakfast, complete with buttered mushrooms and grilled tomatoes. Deny it though she might, being looked after could be incredibly nice sometimes.

As she finished her breakfast, Katie realised she was waiting for two little words to jar the morning's ease. She knew Bea wouldn't be too much longer upstairs and this might be the only opportunity her mother had to quiz her all weekend. She finished her breakfast and waited patiently. Her mother had earned the right to voice the words; breakfast was perfect.

'So,' asked Deanna, taking the plate to the sink. Katie could almost see the two words forming at the back of her mother's throat. 'How's work?'

'Fine.'

'Yes?'

'Yes.'

With her back to her daughter, Deanna squashed the suds against the plate.

'Anything interesting happen recently?'

Katie considered this. 'We had a woman in with a beard the other day.'

Her mother's back curved towards the sink and Katie couldn't work out if this was because she was putting elbow grease into the washing up or crying. 'Hm.'

'Unless it was a man with breasts of course.'

No response.

'And a blind man hit Alec in the shin with his stick.'

Her mother turned round, Marigolds dripping on the tiled floor, fringe in her eyes.

They stared at each other across the kitchen.

'And that's interesting, is it, Katherine?'

Katie shook her head resignedly. 'No,' she said. 'Not really. But it was funny.'

Deanna took off her gloves, left them on the draining board and came and sat at the table.

'Darling,' she said, patting her hair out of her eyes, 'I am seriously worried.'

'Mm.'

'This is not something you can keep putting off.'

'I'm not putting it off.'

'It's bad enough you can't commit to a man, but at least try and commit to a job. You need direction.'

Katie counted to ten. 'Well, we all know I've got a lousy sense of direction,' she said.

'Don't change the subject,' said Deanna tartly.

There was a pause.

'You need a career,' she clarified.

'*You* didn't.'

'I certainly did, young lady,' scoffed Deanna. 'I brought up a family of three. Like Bea probably will. But you're different. Can you imagine marrying someone like Maurice?'

'God, no.'

'Katherine.'

'Sorry.'

'All you have to do is decide. Great-Aunt Edna is just waiting for the word.'

'How is she?'

'She's fine. But the point is she's determined to give you her money only when you decide what you truly want to do. Not a moment before. She's so rigidly principled that she complete refuses to take our advice and give it to you sooner rather than later.'

'Good. Well perhaps you could take a leaf out of her book.'

'Oh for goodness sake, Katie,' shouted Deanna, leaning forward over the table. 'Don't you see?'

'See what?'

'She's an old woman.'

'What's that got to do with it?'

'She may die before she changes her will.'

'Why does she need to change her will?'

'Because,' sighed Deanna, 'at the moment she's leaving small amounts to loads of people she doesn't really care about. But as soon as she hears from you, she'll change her will and give you everything.'

'What, and take money out of other people's hands?' asked Katie. 'Why would I want her to do that?'

'Because these are people who will hardly remember her,' said Deanna fiercely, 'and the amounts are not enough, to remotely transform their lives. Whereas if she changes her will, your life will be dramatically improved. But,' she pointed out, 'she cannot change her will if she's dead.'

'Well,' retorted Katie. 'That'll give her something to live for.'

Deanna sat back in her chair. 'You're just like her,' she muttered. 'Mad.'

'Thank you.'

Deanna shut her eyes. 'It's your future, Katie.'

'So why can't she just put it in a trust fund for me?'

'I will pretend I didn't hear that.'

'That's good of you,' said Katie, contrite.

'Your Great-Aunt Edna has always been . . . eccentric, shall we say, and it matters to her that she's not just giving you money to squander. She thinks if you have a trust fund you won't become self-sufficient, you'll become spoilt. She wants you to find a career. Although she probably had no idea it would take you quite this long to find one.'

'Mum, I can't decide my future because a weird old lady might die.'

'Katie!'

'Sorry.'

'That money is not to be sniffed at. You're incredibly lucky that she's picked you.'

'Am I?'

'Of course you are,' exclaimed Deanna.

Katie sighed. 'I don't know. If I didn't have this Damocles sword hanging over me –'

'*Damocles sword*!' Deanna exploded. 'Seventy thousand pounds and you call it –'

'Yes but it comes with such strings attached. At least Bea and Cliffie know they'll get her antiques and will be able to do what they want with them.'

Deanna snorted. 'I doubt it. Those antiques of hers are incredibly precious and I bet there'll be some disclaimer in the will about what they do with them. Anyway, she's making it tough for your own sake.'

'If you choose to give, you give for the sake of giving . . .'

Deanna shook her head firmly. 'No,' she said. 'She's just ahead of her time and knows what's best. Her mother was marching for votes for the likes of you.'

'I know, I know.' Katie had heard it all before.

'I hope you'll be visiting her before lunch.'

'I suppose.'

'Good.'

They heard Bea thump down the stairs, moaning with the temporary added weight and internal discomfort.

'Fresh cup?' asked Deanna.

'Ooh lovely,' said Katie.

Bea walked into the kitchen.

'Cup of tea?' asked Deanna brightly.

Bea wasn't fooled. 'You're not discussing it again, are you?'

'Of course we are,' sighed Deanna.

'It's what I come home for,' sang Katie. 'I long for these discussions.'

'If only you could decide –' said Deanna.

'Actually, I have decided,' Katie interrupted.

Her mother perked up considerably. 'You could have said something.'

'I'm going to be an educational psychologist,' announced Katie, 'I think.' There was silence. 'And guess what?' she continued. 'It only takes four more years' training. I've even got the right degree.' There was more silence. 'Any more tea in the pot?'

The three women stared at each other.

'Don't you want to do something *nice*?' Deanna asked eventually. 'How about a nice job in publishing? You could get yourself a lovely little flat in Fulham –'

'I don't want a lovely little flat in Fulham –'

'– or Chelsea. How about working for Sothebys?'

'*Mu-um.*'

'Breda Witherspoon's daughter Vanessa started off as a receptionist at that big publishing house' – Deanna ignored Katie's head dropping on to the table – 'the one that started eating up all the little ones, and now she's Children's Books editor for one of the companies they bought. She's so happy. And she earns a lovely little salary. Breda's so pleased; it means she's self-sufficient but can't afford luxuries so still needs a man.'

Katie started humming quietly into the wood of the table.

'Barbara Maythorpe's daughter Sandra,' continued Deanna, louder, 'has a *lovely* little job at Sotheby's, where she has to look after a place when Sotheby's go in and stock-take after someone wealthy's snuffed it. She says it's absolutely fascinating. Absolutely adores it.'

Katie lifted her head. 'No thanks.'

'And she meets all these wonderful men through it. Men who share her interest in antiques.'

Deanna cupped the teapot with one hand and stretched across to flick the kettle on with the other.

'You can't tell me,' she said, a hint of firmness in her voice, 'you just *can't* – that you'd rather train for four more years, or wait tables in a crummy little café than get a nice job in publishing.'

Katie scrunched her eyes shut.

'I simply refuse to believe it,' continued Deanna. 'Waitressing is what you were doing at sixteen.'

'You were proud of me then.' Katie sat up.

'Of course. It showed initiative *then*. You were going to become the next Conran restaurateur.'

'Yes well,' said Katie. 'We all have silly dreams.'

'Exactly,' said Deanna.

'How are they all at Ye Olde Tea Shoppe?' asked Katie.

'Fine. They always ask after you. Mrs Blatchett sends her love.'

'Is she still alive?'

Her mother closed her eyes in answer.

'It's a perfectly sensible question,' Katie told Bea, who nodded agreement.

'Yes,' sighed Deanna, slowly opening her eyes. 'She's still alive.'

'Although it's hard to tell from the service,' muttered Bea.

'The service isn't quite as fast as it used to be,' conceded Deanna, 'but she's still got all her marbles.'

'Just make sure you never go their hungry,' said Bea.

'Mum,' started Katie. 'I don't wait tables *instead* of working in publishing. I wait tables until I know what I want to do.'

'But when will you find out? You're twenty-four –'

'I know how old I am.'

'I don't want to see you throw all that potential away,' said Deanna.

'Please stop sending me job applications in the post, Mum. I recognise your hand-writing,' continued Katie. 'Not sending me a note inside does not make them anonymous.'

'Oh, what are we going to do with you?' sighed Deanna.

'You're not going to do anything with me. I'm big enough and ugly enough to do what I want.'

'You are not ugly. Or big.'

'That's me,' said Bea happily, putting another slice of toast in her mouth.

'I will decide what I want to do in my own time,' explained Katie, 'and when I decide, I will follow a career path of my own choosing.'

Her mother chewed her lip. 'You're not serious about becoming an educational psychologist are you?' she asked eventually.

Katie sighed before shaking her head, suddenly certain. 'No.' Since her epiphany she'd watched all the children in the café with new interest. 'Children are revolting,' she said. Bea gasped. 'Not yours of course,' she rushed. 'Yours will be beautiful.'

'Well, it'll be a baby first,' said Bea, a little quietly. 'Maybe that will help.'

'I'm sure it will,' assured Katie, 'but I still couldn't be an educational psychologist.'

'Thank God for small mercies,' sighed Deanna.

One hour later, Katie rang the bell of Great-Aunt Edna's cottage and could hear sounds of movement from within. It wasn't that she didn't like her mother's aunt, she just didn't know her very well. Apparently, as a baby she'd bonded with her and would go only to her at family functions. This had worked its charm on the old bird and now Katie was to get the money – if she decided what she wanted to be before Great-Aunt Edna died – and Bea and Cliffie the contents of her minuscule rented cottage which was stuffed with antiques.

'Just a minute!' came a thin voice. Katie wrapped her scarf tighter round her neck. Great-Aunt Edna had a thing about saving money, so rarely had the heating on.

The door opened and a wisp of a woman stood before her. A thinning cloud of white hair was swept off her face, highlighting the sharpness of her blue eyes. Katie was always struck by her aunt's frailty, until the woman spoke. Her body and features might be slowly shrivelling, but her mind was as sturdy as ever.

'Let me have a look at you,' she said, clasping her favourite great-niece's chin.

Their eyes met. Great-Aunt Edna grinned. 'Not bad,' she beamed proudly. 'You'll do, you'll do.'

They kissed hello and then made their way slowly down the cold dark hall into the kitchen. 'What will you have to drink?' asked Edna, patting Katie's arm, which made her feel like a giant in Mrs Tiggywinkle's house. Once in the kitchen, a hot blast of air hit her – this was clearly where Great-Aunt Edna spent her day. The old woman settled herself at the table and instructed Katie where to get the things out for tea. Everything in the cottage, from the priceless ornaments to be exquisitely decorated cups and saucers, was old, collectible and in pristine condition. As soon as Great-Aunt Edna had become unable to manage it herself, she had taken on a girl from the village to help clean her home. She was not a spendthrift, but she was proud and determined that nobody could say she kept a dirty home.

Katie made the tea and sat with her back against the wall, the kitchen clock chiming every precious quarter of an hour.

'So,' said Great-Aunt Edna, pouring milk from the jug into the china cups. 'What have you got to tell me?' Desperate not to talk about work and not to leave too long a gap before answering, Katie found herself saying, 'I've met a man.'

Great-Aunt Edna's eyebrows, fine arches of smoke, rose as she took the tea cosy off the teapot.

'Is he handsome?'

Katie smiled. 'Yes, he is.'

Great-Aunt Edna nodded as she placed the tea strainer on to the cup.

'Is he wealthy?'

Katie considered this. 'I suppose he must be,' she answered.

Great-Aunt Edna placed one hand on the teapot lid and slowly poured out two perfect cups of tea. She placed the pot down heavily, just missing the doily, then she neatly replaced the tea cosy.

They drank their tea.

'So he could be a provider then,' considered Great-Aunt Edna.

'I hadn't thought of it like that.'

'You probably didn't realise you did,' said Great-Aunt Edna, 'but you've been conditioned to think of exactly that.'

Katie frowned. 'I just like him.'

Great-Aunt Edna placed her teacup in its saucer and treated herself to a custard cream straight out of the biscuit tin. ('We don't need to stand on ceremony here.')

'Would you like him as much if he were as poor as a church-mouse?' she asked, dunking the custard cream into her tea and sucking thoughtfully on it.

'Yes,' said Katie. 'In fact, I'd probably have preferred him.'

Great-Aunt Edna bit into the rest of her biscuit. 'Ah dear,' she said. 'If only it was irrelevant.'

Katie nodded. 'Yes,' she said. 'But I suppose you could say the same about him.'

Great-Aunt Edna smiled at her great-niece, her eyes suddenly pretty in their red-rimmed sockets.

'Yes dear,' she said warmly. 'If you weren't quite the lovely girl you are, he probably wouldn't be interested.'

'Thank you,' said Katie.

'Oh it wasn't a compliment, my dear,' the old woman said, dunking the last of her custard cream. 'It's pure economics.'

The kitchen clock had chimed the quarters four times

before Katie finally made her way back through the chilly hall. She had asked Great-Aunt Edna to join them for lunch, as she always did whenever she did her duty visit. And Great-Aunt Edna had smiled and said thank you but no, as she always did whenever asked.

By the time Katie got back home, her body slushing with tea, Bea was helping Deanna with lunch and there were distinct noises of The Men's arrival. There were also distinct noises of more than the usual amount of men. Katie glanced out of the hall window and could see at least six making their way to the house for lunch. Her father had brought home eligible guests. At least their presence would stop her mother from pestering her. She bounded down the stairs and made her way into the kitchen.

'Ah, Katie!' greeted her father enthusiastically. From the swift response from his entourage – she hadn't seen men swivel round so fast since her brother played bobbing apples at a Halloween party ten years before and walloped Mrs Higginbottom – it became apparent that she'd probably been promised as dessert. Her father approached and gave her a bear-hug.

'Here's my youngest daughter,' he told the men, like he was presenting a prize calf. 'Katie, meet your old dad's young drinking buddies.' Katie felt herself being scrutinised by three pairs of well-practised eyes. She knew well enough that to men like this she was somewhat lacking in the most vital criteria. She didn't have Bea's Boadicea bearing, her hips were far from child-bearing and her petite frame did not signal a good homely cook. To London men she always felt fine, but to country men she felt like the runt of the family. She murmured something about helping the women, who were so busy adjusting their lunch-time menu to stretch to eight that their movements were almost a blur.

'First,' said her father, taking Katie by the arm, 'you must meet everyone. This is Basher, this is Toby and this is Foxy.' The three guests acknowledged her with politely interested nods and varying widths of smile. 'And of course,' he continued jovially, nodding to Cliffie and Maurice, 'you know those two rascals.' Cliffie grabbed her in a brotherly arm-lock and then darted out of the way before she elbowed him in the ribs.

'Right,' said Sydney, clapping his big red hands together, 'time for a pre-lunch drink, I think.' And suddenly, as if by magic, the men disappeared.

'What's wrong with Basher's head?' whispered Bea.

'I think that's his face,' replied Katie.

'Quiet, girls' said Deanna, 'and help me with the vegetables.'

It was at the table that Katie had the opportunity to examine thoroughly why she didn't want to marry any of these men. Basher ate like a horse, Toby's idea of Women's Lib meant letting women out to do flower-arranging 'if they showed an aptitude' and Foxy was so-called because if you looked really carefully you could see his nasal hairs came out at such an angle that they looked like whiskers. But most importantly, none of them were Dan.

After lunch, Sydney appeared in the kitchen.

'Well?' he asked Katie, clearly proud of his potential date selection. Before she had to answer, Deanna swept in front of her.

'Come on with you,' she told her husband, tight-lipped, almost brushing him out of the room with her hand like she would unsightly dust. 'Out from under our feet. We've work to do. We've just served a four-course lunch for eight and you're in here with your "Well?"'

Sydney moved out of the way to give the women more room to clear the kitchen, his contribution to Sunday lunch. 'Toby's great-uncle's an Earl,' he whispered excitedly over Deanna's head at Katie, as he reached the door.

'And his mother's a horse, by the looks of things,' Deanna retorted, flushed with heat and exertion. 'Get along with you. She's got a date tonight with a nice boy from Oxford, stop interfering.'

'Oh really?' said Sydney, body half out of the room, 'and what does his father do?'

'Minds his own business, probably,' scolded his wife. 'Get out of my kitchen or there'll be no tea.'

Sydney winked at Katie and tapped his nose before the door was shut firmly behind him.

Katie put down the cutlery she was drying. 'Thanks Mum,' she said. 'I was starting to have nasty visions of an arranged marriage there.'

'Arranged marriage my *foot*,' said Deanna. 'I'm not having my daughter married off like some pig at auction.'

'Thanks, Mum.'

'Not until you've got a career to fall back on.'

'Oooh!' said Bea suddenly. 'It's kicking!' She turned to face her mother and sister and sure enough, her bulge was dancing its own little rumba.

'Ooh!' echoed Katie. 'It's going to be a dancer!'

'No it's *not*!' retorted Bea fiercely. 'Rugby, centre back.'

'Won't she get teased about that at ballet?' asked Katie.

They looked again at the amazing dancing tummy, before Bea replied, fondly stroking her bump, 'It's a boy, I just know it.'

They all beamed the same Simmonds smile and silently made the same vow with God that they didn't mind if it was a boy or girl, as long as it was healthy and didn't have its father's chin.

At three o'clock that afternoon, about the time that Katie set off back from Glossop, the London sky gave up all pretence of providing any light. And Sukie could hold out no longer. She knew it was frowned upon, but if Greta had not wanted to be phoned at home, she wouldn't have given out her home number.

It only rang once.

'Greta Michaels?'

'Greta, it's me, Sukie.'

'Sukie, darling. Everything all right?'

'Yes I'm fine. Sorry to phone you at home –'

'What's up?'

'I just –'

'Did you get the voice-over?'

'Yes, I just –'

'Well done! I knew you could do it.'

'I just wanted to ask you a bit more about how I can improve things at audition.'

'Darling, it's not about improving things, you're a – oh hold on, I just have to let the cats out – you're a natural. It's about redefining what auditions *are*.'

'Right. Re-defining.'

'Yes.'

'I just wondered if there was anything else I can do,' repeated Sukie. 'I mean, seeing as I haven't got any auditions next week and the voice-over's only one afternoon.'

She could hear Greta fiddling with papers in the background.

'I tell you what, my dear,' said Greta after a pause. 'I'm just reading your CV. Now that we're re-inventing you as a telly actress, it could do with changing.'

'Oh. How?'

'Well, TV directors don't really need to know that you can jazz dance and fence. You don't see many jazz-dancing fencers in your average sitcom.'

'What do they want?'

'They want to know things like whether you'll do nudity and what your measurements are.'

'You don't get many naked scenes in your average sitcom either.'

'I know darling, but you know what I mean. Take a look at your CV.' More rustling. 'Ooh, and your letter, darling. It needs to be *completely* rewritten.'

'Right. Completely rewritten.'

'When you've got those to me, we'll get you back on the audition road.'

'You mean, you won't put me forward for auditions until I've done my CV and letter?'

'Well, darling, once you've re-read them, you won't want me to. I'm *so* glad you phoned. Now we can really get the ball rolling.'

By the time Sukie put down the phone, she had already

promised herself never to phone Greta at home again. That would teach her to be so undisciplined. She pinned a note to her fridge saying 'Only phone Greta when happy.' Then she phoned her mother for some utterly biased support.

'I think you should change your agent,' said her mother helpfully.

'No, Greta's wonderful,' replied Sukie wearily. How was it possible to be so supportive that it made things worse?

'But she's not helping you at all,' argued her mother, 'and she's making you depressed. I think she's harmful.'

'No she's not. She's trying to advance my career.'

'Yes, but are you *happy*?'

When she got off the phone, Sukie added to her fridge note, 'And Mum.' Then she phoned Katie's mobile and left a message saying she needed to talk. Then she texted Katie's mobile saying '*Agent and Mum mad. Am going to yours via offie.*' Then she went round to Katie's flat in the hope that Jon was in so that she could wait for Katie to get home.

5

Katie always found it so much easier getting back to London, so just three hours later, she was trying to find a parking space within a five-mile radius of her flat. She only had one hour before her date with Dan to get the feeling back in her bottom.

She very rarely used her car, for two very sensible London reasons. One, it was cheaper to walk or get public transport, and two, it meant she didn't have to faff around trying to find a parking space once she got to her destination. Some bastard must have seen her set off on Saturday and nipped into her spot. He probably wouldn't move for a month. She carefully balanced her weight from one numbed buttock to another.

Suddenly, she heard a front door bang shut. Then she saw someone leave a flat further up the road and walk to their car. She was there in an instant, her indicator clicking territorially as he drove away. Within seconds she was in his space, never to leave again. Hah. That would teach him to go out on a Sunday evening.

She turned off her engine and sat in the dark car. Oh dear. She knew the signs. She was almost unbearably nervous about this date. It hadn't been many days since Dan asked her out, but it had been enough for it to turn into a Terrifying Prospect. Day One it had just been a nice tingly feeling of something to look forward to. Day Two the tingly feeling had grown into a tingly feeling with tense undertones as the reality of a date with Dan crept nearer. Day Three onwards, no tingly feeling left, just tension.

As soon as she opened the front door and hefted her luggage in, she heard voices in the lounge. She struggled in. There were Sukie and Jon sitting companionably on opposite sofas. Sukie's eyes lit up on seeing Katie.

'Aha! The wanderer returns!'

Jon smiled a greeting as Katie collapsed on to the sofa. 'Next time I decide to take the car instead of the train,' she said weakly, 'someone chain me to my bedroom.'

'How long have you got before your date?' asked Sukie.

Katie shut her eyes. 'Do you know,' she said, savouring the stillness. 'I don't even know his surname. Or what he studied at Oxford.'

'Your family all well then?' smiled Sukie.

'How could I possibly go on a date with someone if I don't even know his surname?' continued Katie. 'Haven't I heard of date rape?'

'Cup of tea?' asked Jon.

Katie smiled and nodded.

'Did you tell your mum,' asked Sukie, 'that after a snog like that you wouldn't care if his surname was Marmaduke?'

Katie grimaced. 'Nobody snogs that well,' she muttered. She sat up and grinned at her friend. 'This is a nice surprise. How was your weekend?'

74

'Absolutely terrible. That's why I'm here.'

'You can tell me all about it while I try on my entire wardrobe and then decide to wear what I wore last week.'

Which is exactly what they did.

'So you see,' concluded Sukie, watching Katie struggle out of her third outfit, 'I needed serious CV and letter-writing help. And then I remembered that Jon is your expert CV writer.'

Katie turned to show her friend the fourth outfit. Sukie shook her head and Katie added it to her Charity Shop pile, so called because they would only accept it out of charity.

'Has he said yes?' asked Katie.

'I'm still trying to persuade him. He says he's busy, what with writing his book and all your CVs.'

'Don't terrify him into it,' said Katie, 'he's easily terrified.' She suddenly gasped and then came and sat next to Sukie on her bed.

'I know what you can do for him in return!'

'I'm not that sort of girl.'

'He keeps getting invited to meet agents who love his writing, but he's too shy to go.'

'Mmmm?' said Sukie dubiously.

'He needs help with pretending to be more confident than he is!'

'How can I help with that?'

'He needs acting lessons!' Katie cried. 'You're the perfect person! You *have* to help him!'

To her surprise, Sukie started nodding slowly. 'Maybe then he'll help me with my letters. I'll put it to him.'

Then Katie voiced her doubts about her date. 'I mean,' she explained to Sukie, 'Geraldine was still clearly emotionally attached to him at the party.'

'It didn't stop you getting off with him,' pointed out Sukie.

Katie grimaced. 'I know. Am I terrible? I just couldn't help myself.'

'Of course not!' said Sukie. 'All's fair in love and war. You didn't do it to hurt Geraldine. You fell for Dan.'

'I did,' nodded Katie. 'But I know how I'd feel if I was in Geraldine's shoes.'

'Tall,' said Sukie. 'And you know she'd do the same to you in a flash. Dan would be with her if he wanted to be. He wants to be with you.'

When Jon brought in Katie's tea, Sukie offered to give him free acting lessons in exchange for his CV and letter writing.

'And I'll do your makeover,' added Katie. 'With both of us helping you, you'll be batting off agents with a stick.'

'What's in it for you?' asked Jon.

Katie shrugged. 'Rent reduction?'

'If I get a book deal,' said Jon, 'I should be able to afford it.'

Half an hour later, while Katie was making her final adjustments to what she'd worn last week, adding perfume, accessories and make-up, Sukie and Jon arranged their first acting lesson and CV writing session.

An hour later, Katie was waiting, wide-eyed and bushy tailed, for Dan to pick her up and take her out.

Dan was five minutes late. The first four minutes were

totally acceptable, but that last minute dangled dangerously between This Is A Man Who Cannot be Trusted and It Was All A Cruel Joke. By the time the doorbell rang, only four minutes and fifty-seven seconds after the appointed time, her stomach was one great fur-ball of fear. She gave herself a once-over in the hall mirror, smiled at her reflection and approached the door – and as she did so, her life went into slow-motion. As the door loomed larger and larger, she was assailed by the terrifying prospect that waiting outside was a mutant who only looked good at crap parties you were drunk at. She could feel her legs continuing to walk towards the door, while her spirit stretched behind her, from her chest all the way into the living room, like a cartoon pair of braces.

All too soon, she watched her hand rise up to the door handle like someone under hypnosis, while she desperately tried to think of an emergency escape plan. She could pretend she had urgent business with Jon and tell Jon to phone her after half an hour. Depending on how much Dan resembled last weekend's vision of pearly manhood or how much he resembled Frankenstein's monster, she could use Jon's call as a get-out. (The old ones are the best.)

She stared at her hand now resting on the handle, as if it held the answer, and could hear the unmistakable sound on the other side of the door, of a grotesque giant who'd got lucky at a party last Saturday night, mentally undressing her.

The evening stretched ahead of her. She took her hand off the handle. She didn't have to do anything silly. She owed this man nothing. She could just pretend she wasn't there, he never need know. She could just stop breathing until he went away and then stay in with Jon and Sukie and watch cosy Sunday evening television.

She stared at the door handle until it went out of focus. When the doorbell rang again, she jumped, offered up a McPrayer – there are no such things as atheists before a date – and imagined telling her mother from her hospital bed, 'I had no choice, he rang the bell twice,' and opened the door.

Halo of light, trumpet fanfare, choral blast. Dan was here! Dan of the cliff-face cheekbones, the crinkly cheek, hazel-flecked blue eyes, long legs and Roman nose. Dan Someone was here! Prayer, charity and goodwill fought for supremacy in Katie's singing heart, just before her mind turned to mush.

'Hi!' she probably shrieked. 'Come on in!'

'Hi,' he grinned, his dark hair even darker from the rain.

'I'll just get ready,' she said, bent down and picked up her umbrella. 'Ready!' she sang.

He laughed at her joke. A rich, deep, fruity laugh that did things to her insides.

He Laughed At Her Joke.

This thought swelled as if she'd added water to it, and expanded to fill her brain completely, rendering her incapable of thought. She didn't allow herself to speak while they walked to his car because she'd probably come out with something off the *Teletubbies*.

'Here we are,' he said, stopping by a sporty silver number.

She made a noise of approval, which she hoped didn't

sound too much like 'eh-oh' and got in. The seat was much further down than she'd imagined.

'Wow,' she said before remembering not to speak. 'I have a low-slung bottom.'

He laughed at her joke again.

He Laughed At Her Joke Again.

'Yeah,' he said. 'It is a silly car. I'll get a sensible one any day now.'

She wanted to say something about how it wasn't a silly car and it would be a shame to do something sensible, and her bottom was not low-slung at all, it was the seat, just so they'd got that clear – but her brain seemed to be completely full up with the fact that he'd laughed at her joke again.

As they set off in a silence that seemed to inflate like an airbag, Katie realised the awful truth. There was no more room in her brain. It was full up. What a crap time for this to happen. If only she hadn't worked so hard at school.

She looked out of the window, trying desperately to think of something to say.

Nope. Nothing. Total blank.

Was it possible to get Alzheimer's from nerves?

What would Sukie do?

She had visions of Sukie straddling Dan and shut her eyes to erase the image.

What would her mother do?

No, that was no help at all.

He coughed.

She froze.

He coughed again. 'So,' he asked. 'How was the weekend with your parents?'

'Oh,' she said. 'It was only one night.'

They reached some red traffic lights. She should just get out here. Run away and he need never see her again. She could live in the forest and eat berries. Oh dear God, she had to eat an entire meal in front of him. Why had she not thought of this before? How on earth had she been looking forward to this? This was torture. She mustn't eat cheese.

Or garlic.

Or any carbohydrates.

'So,' he asked, as the lights turned green. 'How was the one night with your parents?'

'Fine.'

Should she just explain that her brain was full up? He'd understand, he was a nice guy. Just as she was about to say it, he spoke again.

'Here we are then,' he said. 'My favourite restaurant.'

After a pre-dinner glass of wine, Katie was able to push her mind beyond its limits, like a boulder up a hill, and thus grew more than capable of uttering a fine collection of one-syllable non-sequiturs. Luckily, Dan was happy enough to do all the talking, and until such time as her brain was able to function, she was happy enough to do all the uh-huh-ing. Listening might take another glass of wine. Either that or not caring. She'd never realised before just how many different skills were involved in making interesting conversation: hearing the other person, making sense of their words, having an opinion – or at least borrowing someone else's – and then using your brain to make your mouth form words that will not only make sense to the other person but will make them like you, laugh with you, want to spend more time with you and wonder what you'll be like in bed. Not easy when your brain's full up.

'Have you decided yet?' Dan asked her over the menu.

'Oh yes,' said Katie, 'I think I'll eat.'

He laughed at her joke again.

But it hadn't been a joke. Should she tell him? No. She joined in the laughter with great enthusiasm, just as he stopped. To her horror, she found herself laughing loudly into an abyss of embarrassment. She stopped. My brain's full up, she explained with sad eyes, but Dan was already looking away, pouring himself some more wine.

'I'll have what you're having,' she said quickly.

Dan nodded briefly without looking up from his wine.

If she'd properly thought through what tonight would entail, she'd have backed out. Just then Dan's cheek crinkled. Maybe not, she thought. Some things were worth making a complete twat of yourself over.

After the second glass of wine and the first course of food, she felt much more relaxed. She even interrupted Dan's hot debate with himself about whether dogs dreamt with one of her anecdotes about Spartacus and Hector's bizarre sleep noises. She gave an uncanny impression of Spartacus's Scoobydoobydoo-like bleats and Hector's hiccups and Dan laughed at her silly noises so much he almost choked.

He Laughed At Her Silly Noises So Much He Almost Choked.

And she was back to square one.

Luckily Dan needed to excuse himself and go to the toilet. She watched him walk, straight and tall, handsome and confident, further and further away, past the other diners and out into beyond.

Dan walked, straight and tall, rigid and grim-faced, out to the Gents. He went straight past the urinals and into a cubicle and slammed the door shut behind him. There he stood, head against the door, his body drained.

Why the hell had he brought her to a restaurant? Why not a film? Or the theatre? Or a club? Go-kart racing, even. Sod it, a book reading would have been better than this prolonged agony.

He'd ruined it.

The journey here was bad enough, as she'd clearly changed her mind about going out with him. What had happened at her parents? Was there a long-suffering boy back home whom she'd spent long summer afternoons in the hay-loft with, who'd finally proposed? He hadn't been able to think of a single thing to bring her out of her silence. All he could do was laugh at her funnies. She was too funny for him. Too clever. Just like when he was at Oxford, and instead of finding all the girls fun and intelligent, he'd just been too daunted by their brains.

And then this bloody place.

As soon as they'd sat down in the trendy restaurant's glaring light, it was obvious that the last thing either of them wanted to do was sit facing each other and stuff a three-course meal down their gullets. She couldn't even muster enough interest to choose what to eat and had left it up to him. He'd been so thrown by that that he'd chosen bloody polenta, which was like swallowing cement. She'd spent the entire evening so far pushing it round her plate, and his throat seemed to have constricted from talking too much all bloody evening. *Dog dreams?* What the hell had he been thinking? Oh yes, that's right, he hadn't been thinking, he'd been panicking. He'd been doing conversational bungey-jumping while she'd looked on, uncomprehending, uncaring and getting increasingly pretty.

He wiped his upper lip. Oh God, but just look at her. No wonder she was unimpressed by him. In fact, unimpressed didn't touch it – when she'd opened her front door she'd looked so utterly terrified he thought maybe there were burglars hidden behind the door with guns held to her head telling her to act normal. And then she'd bent down to pick up the umbrella – in that little skirt – right in front of him – and he'd seen stars.

He must stop drinking and calm down. Meanwhile, he must ply her with drink and get her happy.

He suddenly felt giddy, put down the toilet seat and sat on it, head in hands. He'd go back in a while. He took deep, slow breaths.

Katie stared forlornly at the spot where Dan had vanished. She couldn't work out what upset her most, the fact that he'd gone, or the fact that he'd soon be back and witness her mental capacity disintegrate further. She looked at her uneaten bread roll. If someone came in and offered her £1,000 to eat that now, she couldn't do it.

Maybe she should just admit she was crap at dates. That was why college was so easy – men were everywhere: in seminars, in lectures, in the bar, in her flat. You had a chat with them every time you saw them and before you knew it you were an item. It was like buying new clothes without having to try them on because they just turned up in your wardrobe. Perfect. And so different from this ridiculous, false situation, which brought out the worst in her. Maybe she should just be watching Dan in the cinema, safe in the dark, knowing that he couldn't see her spilling nachos down her top. He must be so bored, she'd hardly mumbled anything all night. How could she explain to him that she'd suddenly lost her nerve to speak in complete sentences, when she was unable to speak in complete sentences?

She poured herself some more wine and took herself in hand.

Question: How did she feel about him?

Answer: Crazy.

Question: How did he feel about her?

Answer: He'd asked her out – it couldn't be bad.

So far so good. Keep going.

Question: How many shopping days till Christmas?

Answer: Not many now.

It was working, she was beginning to feel excited. She drank some more wine, hoping Dan wouldn't come back for a while.

Question: How much fun would they have when they could laugh about this together?

Answer: Years and years' worth.

Question: How much did she want to go out with him?

Answer: How long is a piece of string?

Question: Why do birds suddenly appear, every time you are near?

She ate some of the bread.

When he came back, she'd apologise – in a brief, pithy sentence – for her behaviour. Explain how nervous she was and tell him how much she liked him. Everything was going to be all right. Dan was the man.

Dan the man was peeing with gusto in the Gents and giving himself a firm talking-to. It wasn't over yet, there were still two courses to go and they'd be Fun. As he washed his hands, he stared at himself in the mirror, checked his teeth for stray spinach. He'd ask her about herself – that was it! He smiled at his reflection. Of course! That was what girls always did to break the ice – why hadn't he thought of that before? He'd ask her more details about her family, her weekend, her home life. Coax her out of herself, be gentle yet persistent. She'd relax and realise how much they got on. Then he'd offer to drive her to his favourite park in London where they could look over the city of lights and in the dark, cold winter air forget all about this stupid stuffy restaurant and catch up where they'd left off last Saturday . . .

Yes, it was going to be fine. He finished drying his hands, remembered that he'd brought his travel aftershave, twizzled it in place and sprayed it all into his right eye.

Katie continued to stare forlornly at the spot where Dan had vanished, like a mongrel waiting for its owner outside Safeways. Had he escaped through the window? She was just considering following him when her mobile phone rang. It was Geraldine, Dan's ex. Now was not the time. She tried to turn the phone off, but, through nerves, missed the tiny button and instead answered it.

'Hello!' sang Geraldine happily. 'What you doing?'

Katie gulped. 'Not a lot.'

'Listen,' said Geraldine. 'A little bird tells me that you're out with Dan and I just want you to know that it's absolutely fine with me.'

There was a pause.

'Just in case you thought I might be angry,' she continued. 'Or jealous.' She laughed. 'I am so not. You are absolutely free to see him. Just don't let him take you for granted, as he did me. He has a habit of doing that. And of patronising you, without you realising it, so you just end up thinking you're stupid even though you've got a PhD, that sort of thing. And he's got a foul temper. No fuse whatsoever, just suddenly flares up. And of course you'll have to start going to football matches. Every week. Rain or shine.'

'Right.'

'Anyway, I've got a good feeling about you two.'

'Have you?'

'Oh yes,' enthused Geraldine. 'I think you're going to end up sharing the same breakfast table for the next fifty years.'

Katie watched her bread roll zoom away into the distance. She looked up and blinked. 'Thanks,' she whispered, nausea creeping up from her solar plexus to her chest.

'It's so exciting!' breathed Geraldine. 'Just think, this is the man you'll get stretch-marks for.'

Katie's hand instinctively went to her stomach.

'The man you'll be watching TV all evening with for the rest of your life,' trilled Geraldine.

Katie felt a strange plopping sensation in her gut

'The man whose socks you'll be pairing into the sunset!'

Katie could hear whistling in her ears.

'The man whose snore you'll know better than your own!' Her face felt all tingly.

'The man who's gonna lose his hair and gain a paunch in your home.'

And very cold.

'And you met through me!' cried Geraldine. 'Oh it's *so* romantic!'

Katie held down a retch.

'Just relax and enjoy the evening,' said Geraldine and she rang off.

Katie stared at the table, a pulsing panic throbbing inside her. She couldn't see. She couldn't breathe. And she certainly couldn't eat. She had to get out. Get some fresh air. She managed to push her chair back and stagger to her feet. She wondered if she looked normal to everyone else; she certainly felt as if she was tilting at a dangerous angle. Without catching anyone's eye, she focused all her mental energy on walking in such a way as to prevent the floor from rushing up to smack her in the face. Somehow she found her way out of the cloying heat of the restaurant.

Cold air hit her like a slap on a new baby's bottom. She floundered away, trying to get her bearings, trying to breathe. Across the road was a bench and she ran blindly to it. Once there, she sat down with her head between her knees, counting to three – the highest number she could manage – again and again, over and over.

She heard her phone ring and turned it off. So she never heard Sukie's message: 'Turn your phone off. Geraldine just phoned here and Jon told her you were out. She wheedled out of him where you were and I wouldn't put it past her phoning you. Hope you're having a fab time, sweetie.'

The next thing Katie knew, a taxi was driving past with its light on and she jumped up, yelled, and got inside. It wasn't until she got home and landed on her bed, covered in a film of cold sweat, that the pounding faded into the distance and the panic subsided.

It wasn't for another full ten minutes that she even thought about Dan, alone in the restaurant.

6

In the corner of the sixth form college common room Matt slouched with his mates, pretending to find them as hilarious as they found themselves because some of the blondest, cutest girls had just come in and sat near enough to hear. It was such a rare event that it might never happen again in his lifetime at this college.

Matt had been amazed at how much harder it had been to make friends across the sexes at this college than it had been at school. As a bloke here, you could only be one of two things: a top-of-the-tree second-year or a bottom-of-the-shit-heap first-year. The girls' story was the other way round. They had one year of being toasted and feted as the new hottest things, and then wham! second year came and they were last year's news. There were younger, lither girls than them now, all the second-year boys had gone and all the boys in their year, who'd been shat on from such a great height the year before, turned their charm offensive (offensive being the operative word) to the ingenues who hadn't witnessed their humiliation. And so it went on in an unbreakable rhythm.

He'd also been amazed at how unoriginal everyone was

here. He'd assumed that the freedom of a sixth-form college would create an atmosphere of fashion anarchy and he'd been eagerly anticipating looking and learning. But it wasn't to be. All the girls mixed religiously with friends who looked like them. It was an unspoken rule. Not one dark, curly-haired, buxom girl went around with a straight-haired, skinny blonde. Just wasn't done. It was as if they wanted to make it easier for you to spot them from a distance. Let you know what you were getting. Then, just in case you needed a bit more help, they started to dress like each other. The most way-out girls would all come in one Monday with the same purple streaks in their hair and identical eyebrow piercing. They would all buy the same pencil cases, even grow their nails the same length, and gradually create an instant gang gauge for you and your mates. He wasn't sure what he felt most let down by, the girls' total lack of individuality or the fact that they all ignored him the same amount.

But here, today, when he'd least expected it, was one of the prettiest of the A-grade gangs, all turquoise eyeliner and pearly lipstick, sitting in prime position. Just waiting. From here, the boys could see their juicy prey well enough, but knew to their own cost that the risk could be too great, the effort too exhausting, the humiliation too deep to do anything about it.

Outclassed, his mates did the only honourable thing. They acted like they didn't care. Then, to show the girls that nothing in this sorry world was above contempt, they stopped moving their tongues to the top front of their mouths every time they needed to pronounce a 't', making do with a lazy half-closing of the back of their throat. They went phoney Estuary, and almost felt a rush of testosterone surge through their veins. Then they rolled their shoulders, squared their chests, swore like troopers and dissed their Saturday jobs.

'I was pu' on fuckin' bog rolls the ovva day –'

'Ah, man, tha's the wors' –'

'An' then this old cow comes uppa me and goes –'

'Why's i' always the old ones?'

'Yeah!'

'Yeah!'

'She goes, "You've moved the ca' food!"'

'Ah no!' Eruption of guffaws.

'Wicked, man!'

'An' then tha' bastard tried to pu' me on nights. Fucker.'

'Good money though, nights.'

'Yeah, but no' enough for wha' I need, man –'

Matt tried to tune into the high-level girls' low-level conversation. He was only able to catch snippets and kept shuffling round slightly to get better reception.

'. . . put on two pounds last week . . .'

'. . . calories in a Crunchie?'

'. . . being sick in the bogs –'

'. . . maybe she's pregnant . . .'

Matt glanced over at them. One was checking her split ends, another her nails, another her shoes and another her reflection in a tiny mirror, but there was something self-conscious about their smallest movements. Even Matt, amateur though he was, could sense that each one was on full alert, their antennae jutting sensually out, twitching hopefully into the air. Matt's loudest, bravest mate, Daz, could clearly sense it too.

91

'Oy!' he called across to a girl.

The room went quiet.

'Your name's Sara, innit?'

There was an awkward moment. All boundaries had been crossed. The boys held their breath. Then, slowly, the girls, one by one, turned to them.

The Chosen One, Sara, gave a fraction of a nod and two of her friends inched forward. Matt felt heat rising up his neck. Daz continued.

'D'you 'ave Wickford for English?'

Sara nodded and her friends gave a knowing grin. The rest of Matt's gang was now officially entitled to turn and look. The two gangs faced each other across the divide of faded old couches. Daz sauntered slowly forward – still in the enclave of his pack, but near enough to the girls. One of Sara's friends stepped forward too. Sara arched her back slightly, as if willing the boys towards her with an invisible energy from her sternum.

'Is it true,' continued Daz gravely, hands in pockets, shoulders rolling, 'that 'e sells 'is dandruff as crack at parties?'

A moment's pause and then the delicious sound of girlish laughter, followed by excited boyish laughter that shifted gear quickly into manly guffaws.

'I wouldn't put it past him,' said Sara, standing up and kneeling on the one last couch separating the gangs. Slowly, she raised her hands to put her (long blonde) hair up in a ponytail. Her tight sweater bunched up just where it was meant to and the boys watched in silent awe, just as they were meant to.

'Mind you,' quipped one of Matt's other mates, Si,

lounging forward suddenly, identity bracelet jangling, "e does use 'Ed and Shoulders, so the effec's pretty much the same.'

More girlish laughter! And on the laugh, the girls all moved to join Sara on the couch, short skirts riding up over gazelle legs.

Daz and Si perched on the back of the couch, their roles as Alpha Males established. Tony, tall but not good-looking enough to be an Alpha, contented himself with slouching nearby, arms crossed, easy smile on his face – and Matt, accepting his fate as an E-minor, leaned forward. Without a moment to lose, Daz and Si now lunged for the kill, court-jestering their way into a communal invitation to a party that Saturday night.

'Sound,' said Tony, as the girls picked up their bags and sauntered, loose-hipped, out of the room.

'Watch out for the crack though,' called out Daz and they stared at the door as the sound of more laughter was drowned by the lunch bell going off.

The quiet of the college was disrupted. Matt's mates whooped and suddenly the common room was full to bursting. Matt got out of there. He had an afternoon shift at The Café. It was a bright, cold day and he hurried, trying to think more about his syllabus than this weekend's party, taking extra care crossing the road today. It would be a really sick joke if he got run over just before he got himself a girlfriend.

He was glad to see Katie. Katie, however, wasn't particularly glad to see him. It wasn't personal, she hadn't been glad to see anyone that day.

She'd woken an hour before her alarm this morning,

having been roused into consciousness by the sensation of a knot being double tied in her stomach. She curled up in a ball and prayed that one day she'd wake up knowing that she had the right job, was in love with the right man, knew exactly how much money she had in the bank, had exercised the day before and had a tidy socks drawer. Until then, she was probably doomed to waking up every morning feeling like this.

She thought of last night and Dan, and her stomach prolapsed. Before she had a chance to start catastrophising, she jumped out of bed and performed numerous prevaricating tasks that she suddenly found energy for. Before her shower, she went for a jog and enjoyed the secret beauty of the winter morning, but, when her body almost vomited halfway home from the shock of it, she decided the secret beauty of a dark bedroom was good enough for her.

On the walk into work, she started to fear for her sanity. Her thought processes were fixating on her appalling behaviour last night. No matter how hard she tried to move on, she couldn't. It was like being stuck in a maze. For the first time in her life, it was dawning on her that she might actually have a problem. The alarming fact was that her dismal attempts at relationships were starting to take on a theme and that theme was only now revealing itself to her, thanks to her first date with a man she actively liked.

Until now, she'd been able to console herself with the heart-warming fact that she would still chuck every single man she'd ever chucked, were she given the choice again. She had always known that the simple reason that she was single was because she hadn't met the right man yet. But not any more. Dan had been right and she hadn't been able to cope with it.

What did it all mean? Was it only possible for her to go out with men she didn't care about? And if so, why? Would she ever be able to go out with someone she actually liked or was she doomed to end up on her own? Or worse still was she doomed to end up with someone like Hugh, someone who couldn't hurt her? And if so, who could she blame for all this? Had her parents not loved her enough as a baby?

As if that wasn't enough to worry about, she had no future career plan. She was stuck in a dead-end rut. It was amazing how life could suddenly turn from being full of potential to full of nothing. How come everyone else could work out what to do with their lives except her? Why didn't she have some burning, yearning vocation, something that she'd wanted to do ever since she was out of nappies? Had her mother actually been right about her all along? That was just too harrowing to contemplate.

There were so many new, shiny neuroses to consider now. It was hardly surprising that by the time she got to work that morning, she couldn't remember how she got there and was almost vibrating with negativity.

If that wasn't bad enough, Alec was early. He barely looked up when she came in, he was so busy scouring the worktop. Then, instead of making himself the first of many espressos and wandering over to his corner, he hovered behind Katie as she put out all the freshly cut vegetables for today's salads, wiped all the tables clean, got the milk out of the fridge for the coffees, opened the window shutters and turned on the ovens, and as he hovered, he wiped down every single surface she had been near, tutting just loud enough for her to hear. Refusing to give him the satisfaction of asking why he had a sudden interest in cleanliness, Katie simply got angrier and angrier and so they continued for half an hour until Alec suddenly announced that he had to go somewhere and would be back on the dot of three, by which time he expected the place to be as clean as it was now.

By the time the café opened, Katie was in no mood for serving coffees. Her belly was on fire.

'Two black coffees, please,' said the first commuter. 'No sugar. Oh no. No sugar at all. No siree.'

'Right,' muttered Katie. 'No sugar.'

'Actually,' corrected the commuter. 'Make that *with* sugar. Oh God, I don't know.'

'Tell you what,' said Katie sharply, 'don't have any sugar, but have a slice of toast with your coffee.'

The woman brightened. 'Of course!'

'It's a win-win situation,' said Katie firmly. 'You don't feel guilty, we get more money.'

The woman laughed.

'And of course,' said Katie, head tilted, 'we don't have to listen to you.'

They stared at each other. Katie's lips were thin. The woman smiled uncertainly.

'Cappuccino,' clipped the man next in the queue. 'No toast.'

'Large or grande?' asked Katie, before Sukie got a chance to start making it.

'What's the difference?' he asked, irritated.

'About a pound,' said Katie, hands on hips. 'Quick quick, there's a queue behind you.'

'Oh sod it,' said the man. 'I'll have the bigger one.'

'Right,' said the next man in the queue. 'A large latte. And a slice of toast – if you're making.'

'You asking?' asked Katie.

There was a pause.

'I'm asking,' said the man, a hint of a smile on his lips.

'Then I'm making. You sweet talker, you.' As she went to the toaster, she called out, 'Who else wants toast? I'm not coming back here again, I've got better things to do with my morning than rush to and from the bloody toaster.'

She was beginning to feel better.

Four people decided toast would be perfect this morning. When the queue died down, she and Sukie stared at each other. Neither of them spoke. They didn't want to spoil the atmosphere. By the time the next rush started for the 7.44, Katie decided she really couldn't be bothered to do any more coffees. Sukie did the first three, while she stood there, arms crossed, staring at the queue.

'Excuse me,' said a man tightly, at her. 'I'll have a coffee please. If you're not too busy.'

'Oh, I'm not too busy,' she smiled sweetly.

'Good.'

'I'm just too bored.'

The queue suddenly became very English: some blushed, some looked away and some pretended they hadn't heard. Katie wasn't having any of that. She was on a roll.

'Right,' she said. 'It's about time you lot learnt how to make your own coffees. This is the coffee machine.' She waved theatrically at the coffee machine and Sukie got out of the way. 'Can you hear me at the back?'

The woman at the back of the queue made a soft guttural sound which Katie took as a yes.

'Now, in case of emergencies,' she explained, 'such as when Sukie or myself are suddenly struck by how tedious our jobs are and piss off to get a life –'

'Or there's a fire,' added Sukie, 'and you lot need coffee to have the energy to run.'

'Thank you, Sukie.' Sukie bowed. 'Sukie Woodrow ladies and gentlemen . . .'

The queue clapped.

'You lot, said Katie, pointing at the queue, 'will have to know how to make your own.' She started making them their coffees. 'Do Not Panic,' she said. 'Rule Number One. It's not that scary. It may look it, but you will soon learn that any fool can do it. Yes, even you sir.'

The queue laughed as they were handed their cups.

'Did you two come together?' asked Katie, to two commuters who were wearing similar coats. They shook their heads. 'Did you phone ahead and work out what to wear so the other children wouldn't laugh at you? 'Cos it hasn't worked, has it? Here, have a coffee.'

When Matt arrived at the end of their shift, all three of them ended up in the kitchen to help him as he started to sort out the backlog of washing-up.

'Right,' said Sukie, rinsing the cups and saucers before passing them to Katie, relay-style. 'How did the date go?'

'Hell on earth,' said Katie, grabbing the stuff out of Sukie's hands and filling the dishwasher as fast as possible. 'I don't want to discuss it.'

'Oh dear,' said Matt, trying to be sorry for Katie and not just relieved that he wasn't the only loser in the world.

'What happened?' asked Sukie.

'I abandoned him and went home,' said Katie, turning on the dishwasher. 'I don't want to discuss it.'

'You *what*?'

Katie wiped her hands on a tea-towel and looked at Sukie in mock surprise. 'Oh don't make out you haven't done it a hundred times. I left him on his own in the restaurant.'

'You're exaggerating, aren't you?' asked Sukie. 'You just mean you didn't kiss him goodnight?'

'I mean I left him on his own in the restaurant.'

'You – you walked out on him while he was eating?' asked Matt.

'No!' exclaimed Katie. 'I'm not an insensitive bitch.'

'I knew it,' said Sukie. 'I knew you were exaggerating.'

'I waited until he was in the toilets,' said Katie. 'And then I left.'

There was silence.

'Jesus,' whispered Matt. 'And I thought I was in trouble.'

Sukie frowned. 'Let me get this straight – you waited until the man of your dreams was in the Gents and then you walked out of the restaurant?'

'God. You make it sound like I'm weird.'

'Before or after dessert?' asked Sukie.

'Before.'

Sukie shook her head. 'I'll never understand you.'

'I know,' sighed Katie. 'I don't want to discuss it.'

'Was he awful?' asked Sukie.

'Nope.'

'Did he smell?'

'Nope.'

'Did he grope you?'

'Nope. I don't want to discuss it.'

'Have you phoned and apologised?' asked Matt.

'Nope.'

Sukie and Matt sucked in air and shook their heads.

'Are you going to phone him?' asked Sukie.

'Nope. And I don't want to discuss it.'

There was silence again.

'So, what are you going –' began Sukie.

'Nothing,' said Katie, her voice starting to crack. 'My life is shit. It couldn't get any worse. And may I say that I'm really grateful to you both for respecting the fact that I don't want to discuss it.' She went back out front, leaving Sukie and Matt in the kitchen. Quickly, quietly and without fuss, Sukie went to the dairy fridge and moved the A-4 sheet that had the photo of Dan and Katie to the top of the display of 'The Ones Who Got Away' on the meat fridge. Then she joined her friend out front.

She found Katie, frozen to the spot, staring at the café door.

Sukie followed Katie's eyes and there saw Hugh, Katie's ex number three, approaching, a big grin on his face.

'It just got worse,' said Katie.

*

Hugh was wearing a pin-stripe suit and blue shirt. His eyebrows shot up in surprise at seeing Katie there.

'I hadn't realised this was the café!' he exclaimed.

'I hadn't realised you wore suits,' she replied.

'Thanks,' he blushed.

'It wasn't a compliment,' said Katie bluntly. 'Coffee?'

Hugh almost laughed loudly enough to hide his blush at the insult and said yes to coffee.

As Katie made him his drink, he explained that he and Maxine had completed on their house purchase yesterday and had moved in last night. The builders were starting tomorrow to re-wire, re-plumb, re-open all the fireplaces, knock down a couple of walls and enlarge a window or two in their lovely Victorian house.

'Maxine's taken the day off work to unpack the kitchen things,' he explained, 'I was only able to get a couple of hours off this morning. It's wonderful, you must come round. We feel like we've finally come home.'

'I couldn't be happier for you!' exclaimed Katie, so loudly it was almost a shout.

He grinned and half-saluted her with his paper cup. 'I guess I'll be seeing you in here regularly.'

'Excellent!'

'Excellent!'

She watched him leave and then turned to Sukie.

'Am I evil?' she asked.

'No.'

'Then why am I being punished?'

They stared at each other as the sound of a strangled animal announced more customers. They stayed staring at each other.

'Did you just eat a budgie?' Katie asked Sukie.

'No,' said Sukie. 'We're saving that for the customers.'

'I can't look,' said Katie. 'I just can't look. It's my old maths teacher isn't it?'

'No, it's worse,' said Sukie, looking. 'It's Alec.'

They stared as Alec chatted animatedly – more animatedly than they'd ever seen him – to two tanned men in cheap and flashy suits, one of whom had an expensive camera. When he spotted them watching from the back corner, Alec raised one eyebrow half an inch and held up three fingers, to represent three espressos. Sukie and Katie both held up one finger back, to represent what he could do with his three expressos.

Then, mumbling, Katie made the drinks and took them over. As she reached the table, she overheard Alec boasting about the café's popularity. One man then started waxing lyrical about Porter's Green's popular future and the other man joined in about the restaurant business being very popular at the moment. She tried to stop her hands from shaking as she placed their cups and saucers down on the table.

Alec stared at her.

'Yeah?' he asked. She'd obviously outstayed her welcome.

She turned and walked away, her life crumbling around her ears. When she reached Sukie and Matt, they were frowning at the men, one of whom had started taking photographs of the café, the other using a flashy looking electronic device to measure it.

Alec turned to them, gave them a sick smile and traced a line across his neck with his hand, his eyes fixed on them.

'Why's that man pointing a ray-gun at the wall?' whispered Sukie.

'Why's Alec doing that?' whispered Matt.

'We've been shafted,' whispered Katie.

'Why?' asked Matt and Sukie.

'Those are estate agents,' she said. 'Alec's selling up. So I guess we're all out of jobs.'

7

That night, Katie sat at the bar where Jon worked and systematically got herself drunk. She squinted across to where Jon was serving another customer. Bloody customers. She needed him more than they did. Her bowl of peanuts had got all empty again. She started licking out the bowl.

'I like a woman who knows what she wants,' came a voice behind her.

She sat up and turned round to find some aftershave wearing a man.

'That's nice,' she blinked at him. 'What's her name?'

'You tell me.'

She frowned. 'Crap name.'

'What are you drinking?'

'Peanuts.'

The man smiled. 'That's unusual.'

'That's nothing,' she beamed. 'I can fart Dancing Queen.'

The man's smiled wavered and he sidled away. Tsk, thought Katie. Men are so predictable.

As soon as Jon returned, handing her a new drink, she started where she'd left off.

'It's hopeless,' she moaned, gulping down her drink. 'I'm hopeless.'

'Phone him,' repeated Jon.

'And say what?'

He shrugged. 'That you're hopeless, that you like him and you'd like to give it another go. I'd find it incredibly endearing if a girl did that to me.'

'Even after she'd left you in a posh restaurant by yourself the night before?'

Jon grimaced. 'We-ell,' he started.

'And I'm going to lose my job.'

Jon sighed. 'But you hate your job.'

Her face crumpled. 'I know!' she started to cry again.

'I have to serve customers.'

'Don't go!' whinged Katie, gripping his arm. 'Stay with me.'

'Katie!' Jon unattached himself. 'Do I come to The Café and stop you from working?'

'No,' sobbed Katie. 'You bastard.'

Katie watched as he served customers for a while until Sukie arrived.

'Thank God you're here,' cried Katie, putting her arms round Sukie's neck.

'I'm only here because you begged me to come.'

'Did I?' she said, surprised.

'Don't give me that,' said Sukie. 'You begged me to be here by ten.'

'Did I?'

'Oh God,' said Sukie. 'You're pissed.'

'Am I?'

During the next hour, Sukie managed to persuade Katie to phone Dan.

'That way,' she explained, 'you take control again.'

'Control,' murmured Katie.

'You've got to have control in at least one area of your life.'

'Have I?'

'Look,' listed Sukie, 'you can't take control of finding yourself a career –'

'No –'

'– or of Alec making you redundant –'

'No –'

'– or of your family trying to rule your life –'

Katie looked at her friend. 'Let me know when this is going to start making me feel better –'

'– or of Hugh turning up out of the blue to see your final humiliation –'

'Gosh, you're really helping –'

'– but the one thing you can do is phone Dan and just explain.'

Slowly Katie burped. Everything Sukie was saying was true. Thanks to Jon explaining how hard the evening had probably been from Dan's point of view (it was so useful having a male friend) she'd realised that there was a fair chance Dan was feeling as wretched as she was. Yes, she would phone him. They could start again. And then everything would feel so much better. She was glad she'd talked it over with her friends. Now all she had to do was get home, be sick and go to bed. Preferably in that order.

Although Katie was petite, Sukie and Jon point blank

refused to carry her home that night. Jon insisted he still had back pain from the last time and Sukie had high heels on. Instead, they forced her to drink four espressos and a pint of water before letting her leave the bar. This meant that thanks to them she was physically able to walk home unaided, but couldn't do it too fast for fear of having an accident.

Suddenly she stopped. Her body was full to bursting with love for the whole wide world. She wanted global peace and no more starvation almost as much as she wanted to wee. And that was a lot. She squeezed the arms of her friends.

'I love you,' she whimpered.

'Thank you,' they said.

'I do,' she insisted, squeezing them both harder. 'I love you both. Even when you really piss me off.'

'Thank you.'

'And you know what I'm going to do?'

'Wet yourself?' asked Sukie.

'I'm going to phone him.'

'Excellent,' said Jon, starting to nudge her into walking again. 'There's a phone in the flat.'

'I'm going to phone him!' Katie started trumpeting, as they walked home. 'I'm going to phone him!'

And then she stopped again.

'Oh not again,' whined Sukie. 'We'll never get there at this rate.'

'Katie,' implored Jon. 'Please keep walking. I've got to finish Chapter 10 tomorrow.'

But Katie couldn't talk. She just stared straight ahead of them, a strange sound coming from her mouth. They both followed her eyes and just as she started to whimper, realised why she'd stopped this time. It occurred to both of them that they could try and hide Katie, but then realised that it was too late. They'd been seen.

For there in front of them, walking towards them was Dan. And he was not on his own. He was with a woman. Arm-in-arm with a woman. And if they all weren't very much mistaken, that woman was Geraldine. They were still quite a way away, but approaching fast. So far, it was only Geraldine who'd spotted them, but it wouldn't be long before Dan did.

'Ubum Dan,' whispered Katie.

'Act normal,' whispered Jon.

'Ug, hide.'

'Let us do the talking,' whispered Sukie.

'Egg,' whispered Katie.

Dan spotted them. They all smiled in greeting, Dan and Katie looking at everyone else but each other.

'Oh my God!' cried out Geraldine shrilly. 'How funny! Oh my God. We were just . . .' she turned to Dan and turned quickly away again. 'Isn't this hilarious?' She shrieked with hysteria.

'Somebody stop that noise,' murmured Katie.

'Did you enjoy the party?' Geraldine asked Jon and Sukie, as if her life depended on it.

They nodded. 'Yes thanks,' said Jon keenly. 'Nice kitchen.'

There was a pause.

'Yes, well,' said Geraldine. 'I've been invited for a "coffee" back at Dan's place – say no more.' She winked at them. 'Whoops!' said Geraldine suddenly, looking cheekily at Dan. 'I haven't given anything away, have I?'

'I doubt it,' said Dan quietly.

'Yes, you're right,' said Geraldine. 'It's probably impossible to hide, isn't it?'

There was more silence.

'Right,' said Jon. 'See you around then.' And they made their goodbyes.

As soon as they turned the corner, Katie stopped.

'Do you think all they're going to do is have coffee?' she asked in a small voice.

'Yes, of course.'

Katie stared in front of her sadly.

'I'm not going to phone him any more am I, Sukie?'

'No, I don't think so.'

Katie started sobbing silently, while Sukie rubbed her back.

'I've ruined my life,' she whimpered.

'No you haven't.'

'I'm going to kill Geraldine.'

'No you're not.'

'You're right. I'll hire someone.'

'No you won't.'

'I hate myself.'

'No you don't.'

'I have a shit, dead-end job.'

There was another pause.

'Yes,' said Sukie, 'but you're going to be made redundant.'

Katie started crying again.

'Let's get you home,' said Jon.

*

The next day, a rather important lunch-time meeting had been arranged between three men in a large chain restaurant just south of Porter's Green. Two young men sat in the dark corner waiting for their meeting to start.

The restaurant was practically empty at this time of day, its extensive menu, expensive lighting and exquisite-looking staff an empty stage in front of an echoing auditorium. A waitress appeared from a recess in her uniform of long white apron, black trousers, white shirt, black tie and surly expression. She took their order without a glimmer of humanity and left them alone again. They glanced at each other and shared a moment of mutual understanding.

Eventually, they took out their copies of the accounts for one last look before the meeting began.

'I'll leave all the talking to you,' said the shorter, fairer of the two men, whose face even in this dim light, resembled an anxious mule.

'You sure?' asked the other.

'Yeah yeah. This is your baby.'

'Hardly. You've been there much more than me. I've only seen the place once and that was at the weekend.'

'That's only while you've been training your replacement,' said the mule. 'I won't be able to pop in at all once the partnership's up for grabs and the bonuses get underway. As long as you know you'll be doing it mostly on your own after that.'

'Of course, as agreed,' nodded the taller, darker man. 'I'm just grateful you trust in me enough to help with this investment.'

The mule smiled. 'I trust you like a brother. And believe

me, you're definitely primary carer.' He lifted his coffee cup.

'All right, but you're the donor father.' They clinked cups. 'You still have rights.'

'Yeah, well. I hereby call on my right to let you do all the talking.'

'OK, if you're sure.'

'I am.'

Bang on time, ten minutes later, another man entered the restaurant. Had anyone cared enough to observe him, with his body-built shoulders packed into a costly over-coat, his year-round tan and signet ring consciously donned to play the part, they might have guessed he was part of the local Mafia.

He approached the men in the corner, greeted them with the single word 'Boys', and shook hands firmly with them, his jaw clenching on his chewing gum at each downward shake. He called the waitress 'darling', pulled his trousers at the thigh before sitting down, stroked his tie, flashed his teeth and began.

'Right, well,' he said, rubbing his hands. 'It's good news all round. I got the call first thing this morning. As you know, you are one of the few who've been asked to put in an offer.'

The two men grinned stupidly, and the man immediately raised his hand, like a policeman halting traffic.

'But let's not get carried away.' A shadow appeared at his right shoulder. He looked up at the waitress as she placed his espresso on the table. 'Thanks, darling,' he said softly. She turned to go. 'Er!' he called out. She stopped and executed a slow 180-degree turn. He stared at the table, his hand still up.

'Some sugar please, good girl.'

She barely registered that she'd heard him, before turning away again. He delicately put the tip of his index finger against his mouth, as if deep in thought. The men waited in silence. Then the waitress appeared again out of the shadows, placed the sugar quietly down beside the coffee and disappeared again. The man nodded slowly and took his finger away from his lips. He tore open the packets and added two sugars, stirring thoughtfully, then tapped the spoon several times on the edge of his cup, straightened his tie and took a sip, pinkie out. He looked at the men.

'Where was I?'

'We mustn't get carried away,' repeated the nominated speaker.

The man nodded slowly, as if the thought had only just occurred to him. He placed the cup back in the saucer, signet ring flashing.

'In the end, only two other people have been asked.' The men raised their eyebrows in surprise. He nodded again. 'I know. After all that fuss, only two. One is a rival from this neck of the woods, owns that new French café up the road, and he's trying to start a small, local chain. The other is a very big chain.'

The men both grimaced.

'Now, now. Don't give up on me. I think we're in with a chance.'

'How come?'

'I'll tell you for why. Because of one, very important, very big factor, which we must at no cost, underestimate the importance of.'

'What's that?'

'The cause of many men's downfall.' A dramatic pause. 'Pride.' He sat back in his chair. 'Doesn't always serve our cause, in fact in some cases, it is the very scourge of our entire business, but in this case, I think it might be just what we need.'

'How come?'

'Well, let me explain.' He pondered his explanation for a moment before speaking. 'This guy,' he said slowly to his rapt audience, 'is a moron.'

The two men grinned.

'This man,' he continued, 'could not find his own arse in a blackout. And that is no small arse.' The men grinned again. 'The truth of the matter is,' went on the man, 'that he has basically made a mess of his business. As you yourselves have pointed out, he has consistently failed to make key improvements to it and failed to jump at the market's movements. Which is why his accounts are so shit and you two shmucks, excuse my French, can afford to buy him out.'

The two men nodded. This much they knew.

'But,' the man leant forward in his chair, 'history has shown us over the years that having the brain of a dishcloth does not stop someone from being proud. He is, in fact, your dream come true. A proud shmuck. Excuse my French.'

Another pause.

'Sorry, I don't understand,' said the appointed speaker, finally.

'What I'm trying to say, in plain English, is that this is a man who will not, to my mind, want to sell his business –

his failing, pathetic business – to any chain, particularly –
particularly – to a growing, local one.'

'You think –'

'Unless,' he interrupted, 'unless they make it impossible
– even for a moron like him – to say no.'

'Right.'

'Which means we have to think very, very hard about
our offer. It can't be too low, it can't be too high –'

'Well, it really can't be too high –'

'I know, I know. You have a "ceiling". But,' the man sat
forward. 'I want you to do something for me.' More nods.
'For us.' He eyed them under short, thick, straight eyelashes. 'You think you can do that?'

They nodded.

'Here's what I want you to do. Two things. One' (he
held up a short finger) '– I want you to re-think your
ceiling and, Two' (he held up two short fingers) '– I want
you to have a meeting with this guy, quick. Before the
others get in there.' He let this sink in for a moment. 'You
see, the truth is, he's impatient. He wants to get out fast.
The others may have the money and the know-how, but
you two have the one thing that may swing it – the
personal factor. You've got good faces. Not my type if you
get my drift, but it works for him. You're polite, you're
clean, you're keen. So! Keep yourselves in the picture.
And move fast.' He let the pause linger for a moment.
'Meanwhile,' he cut in, when it looked dangerously like his
silence might be interrupted, 'let me remind you that
businesses like this do not grow on trees. Especially in an
area like this.' He spoke over their nodding, 'and I would
hate for you two to miss out on this opportunity just

because the chain has more money than it knows what to do with.'

The estate agent had finished. He drained his coffee. He looked at his watch.

'Right,' he said, standing up. 'And now I must love you and leave you.'

The two men stood up too and shook his hand and watched him put on his coat and saunter out of the restaurant. Then the shorter, fairer of the two turned to his partner, his mule-like face now registering some concern. 'Shit.'

'Yeah.'

'What shall we do?'

'I haven't got time to go to the café now,' said his taller friend. 'I'll pop into the bank on my way back to the office. You'll have to go to the café.'

'Right,' said Mule. 'What's your plan of action at the bank?'

'I thought I'd beg.'

'Excellent.'

'What are you going to do at the café?'

Mule scratched his head. 'Be charming.'

'Good luck.'

'Thanks.'

Meanwhile, Katie, Matt and Sukie were having an emergency meeting. Sukie had important news to impart. They all knew that Alec had a soft spot for Sukie. Most men did: there was not one straight line on Sukie's body. There had been a stage a while back, when Alec had pestered her – not sexually, he was far too big a coward for something

115

like that, but just for inane pleasantries. A nice smile from her, the odd bit of physical contact; that was enough for him – and now, as his parting shot, instead of a fumbling grope at a farewell party, he had given her a handy hint. He had asked her, in a cosy little chat on their own in the kitchen, if she wanted to keep her job. When she'd told him that she did, but only if her friends kept theirs too, he had replied that all everyone had to do was treat him with respect, especially when he was with potential buyers, and he'd put in a good word for his staff.

They took this in.

'I don't think I can do it,' said Katie.

'Of course you can,' said Sukie.

'I'm too young to lose my ideals,' said Matt.

'And I'm too beautiful,' added Katie.

Sukie sighed. 'Don't say I didn't try to help you both,' she warned and went to get on with her work.

They exchanged grim glances. The sobering truth was that it had taken the possibility of them losing their jobs to realise just how much they wanted them. There was only one thing worse than having a shit job and that was losing it, so Matt and Katie promised to help each other in pretending to respect Alec. Luckily he was hardly in all day and Katie discovered that it was far easier to respect Alec if a) he wasn't there and b) she could disrespect everyone else – and anyway, she was having fun being rude to all the customers. It was a new perk. By that afternoon, after two full hours of being respectful to Alec while he was there, she was nearly at bursting point. She needed to be rude, and fast. So when a regular came in with a friend, she was ready for action.

'Don't you have a home to go to?' she demanded as soon as the regular got near.

The woman gave a brave smile. 'I thought you could do with the custom.'

Katie opened her eyes wide in mock astonishment. 'Bloomin' cheek!' She turned to the friend. 'Is she always like this?'

The friend smiled. 'Oh yes,' she said. 'She's mad, her.'

'You see?' the regular grinned, 'I told you it was hysterical in here.'

Blimey, thought Katie. You should get out more. She started making the regular her favourite drink and told them to sit down and behave while she got them a menu.

Just then, the sound of a strangled cat announced a new customer. Everyone looked round as a young man came warily in. He carried a leather portfolio under one arm. Katie watched him walk slowly towards her and wondered where on earth she'd seen him before. He looked strangely familiar, in an almost bovine way, and yet she was fairly sure she'd never talked to him. He must be an actor. That was happening more and more nowadays. The area was up and coming, so up-and-coming actors loved it. But because it hadn't quite arrived yet, it was only actors with bit parts on *Casualty* or *Holby City*. It meant she kept bumping into people she was sure she knew from somewhere but for the life of her couldn't place.

He was still looking vaguely round him.

'Are you lost?' she asked.

'Pardon?' asked the man, giving her a quick shy glance, as if from behind a veil.

'You look lost.'

'This is The Café, isn't it?'

'I'm afraid it is.'

'Why do you say that?'

'Because it is.'

The man looked puzzled.

A commuter chose this minute to arrive.

'What time do you call this?' asked Katie, looking at her watch.

The commuter smiled. 'Day off.'

'So you thought you'd ruin ours?'

'That's right,' grinned the commuter. 'Wanted to see if you were this rude all day long.'

'Of course I am,' said Katie. 'Why should you get preferential treatment?'

The earlier regular who had sat down was now a bit over-excited in front of her friend. She called out. 'She was horrid to me too!'

'Were we talking to you?' demanded Katie. The woman and her friend laughed uproariously. Jesus, thought Katie. They're all mad.

'Now look,' she told them all firmly, 'I'm busy trying to serve this poor man who's lost.'

'I'm not lost,' said the young man.

The commuter turned to the man and grinned.

'She's like this to all of us,' he explained.

'Is she?' said the man.

'Oh yes,' said Katie. 'No extra charge.'

The commuter laughed even more and gave her a two-pound tip.

'Why thank you sir,' said Katie, taking it and biting it.

'Now I can put my children through school.'

More laughter.

After the commuter left, she turned to find the young actor studying her with a disturbing intensity.

'Have you decided what you want now?' she asked.

He nodded.

'Would you like to tell me or shall we do *Twenty Questions*?' she asked pointedly. 'I warn you though, I'm good.'

'What do you recommend?' he asked.

Ooh, this was her favourite question. 'I recommend you buy yourself a cafetière,' she said. 'The coffee's rabbit droppings, you know. And I'd change that suit.'

The man's face lengthened in surprise and she gave him a big wide beam of a grin.

'I'm only teasing,' she confided. 'It's a lovely suit. C&A have really found their niche haven't they?'

His jaw dropped, while behind him the sound of laughter from regulars and non-regulars was now filling the café. She gave him another smile, not so wide this time.

'Shall I do you a nice latte?' she whispered sympathetically. Teasing time was over.

He nodded.

'Anything else?' she asked.

'Yes,' said the man. 'Can you tell me if . . .' he looked at a piece of paper inside the portfolio, 'Alec's here please. We're having a meeting about the purchase of the café. I'm a little early.'

Katie stared at him.

'Well?' asked the man. 'Is he here?'

She shook her head.

'Oh. Right. Well, when he comes back can you tell him I'm here?'

She nodded.

'I'll have that latte while I'm waiting. Thanks.'

She nodded again. When she took his latte over to him, she couldn't help but notice that the regular was talking to him. The regular beamed up at her. 'I was just telling him how you're always like this.'

Excellent.

Twenty minutes later, when Alec came in, she watched them from behind the counter. They shook hands and Alec was all smiles. She went into the kitchen, where Sukie was on her ten-minute break. Technically, she wasn't meant to have a break at the same time, but she didn't see what she had to lose any more, seeing as tomorrow she'd be spending the first day of the rest of her life under her duvet. She explained to Sukie and Matt what had happened and they did their best to convince her that all wasn't lost. He could be another estate agent – or a buyer who failed to go through with the sale. Or the meeting could be totally unrelated to the sale of the café and he just wanted to get his own back for her teasing. She was just beginning to believe that possibly, just possibly, she wasn't the most unfortunate person in the world, when the kitchen door opened and they turned to see Alec standing proudly in its centre.

'I thought I'd find you all in here,' he said, his thin lips forming the widest smile they'd ever seen. He could barely suppress his glee. 'You'll be pleased to know I've just shaken on the sale of the café.'

There was silence.

'I asked him to save your jobs,' he was almost laughing, 'but I can't promise anything.' He turned to Katie. 'Especially for you, Katie.'

'Why?' she croaked.

'Because your new owner asked if the obnoxious waitress was always this rude to everyone.'

'What did you say?' asked Sukie.

He shrugged. 'I told him the truth,' said Alec. 'Not when she wanted to go home early.'

He laughed at his joke for a while.

8

There were now eight whole shopping days to go before Christmas, which, considering Matt had only one present to get for his mother, was plenty of time. More than a week to build up to Christmas Eve shopping.

The only thing Matt liked about Christmas was that life was put off until the new year. It was a procrastinator's paradise. College had gone mad on this last day of term and, quite frankly, he was glad to see the back of it. If he hadn't been depressed before, he really was now. Two of his friends, Daz and Si, were dating two of the most fit girls in college. This should have helped his status as, by proxy, he had now leapfrogged most of the boys in college, but it hadn't. It just made him feel self-conscious every time the girls came and sat with his crowd, humiliated that he was still single when the girls seemed so much more experienced than he, excruciated when his mates showed off in front of them, and downright angry at the looks of utter surprise at the girls' choice from the rest of the college. It had just added extra piquancy to the normal bleakness of his world.

Not only that, but what on earth did these girls see in

Daz and Si? They were tossers at the best of times. He only tolerated them because beggars couldn't be choosers. But these girls? They could have their pick. He just didn't understand it. Times had changed since the days of eternal loyalty towards one's fellow boyhood companions and, a man of his time, Matt was the first to point out that his mates lacked a *je-ne-sais-quoi* in the eligible male department.

In fact, he had done so with great alacrity to his mother on many a cold winter's night, and she had listened like the kindly soul she was. Until one night she'd stopped him mid-flow, to say, in a most annoying manner, 'You know what your problem is, don't you?'

Still to discover the correct answer to this, Matt fell into the trap and replied, 'What?'

Sandra looked at her son. 'You,' she said with a firmness which left neither of them in any confusion over whom she meant, 'are a misanthropist.'

Matt blanched. 'I am not!' he replied, livid. 'Rescind that statement!' he ordered, standing up.

'Shan't.' She returned to her sewing.

'I am *not* a misanthropist,' he insisted. 'I *hate* misanthropists.'

He saw no reason why his mother should find this as amusing as she did.

'All right then,' she said finally. 'Prove it.'

'How?'

She looked up from her mending. 'Do something nice over Christmas.'

Matt was just about to launch into his patter about Christmas being nothing but paganism cynically remoulded, first to fill the churches and now to fill the coffers of commercialism, when he realised this would only prove her point.

'Such as?'

'Invite your hopeless friends over when college breaks up, and get them to help me put up the Christmas tree – I can't do it alone – *and*,' she pointed a thimbled finger at him, 'have a laugh while you're at it.'

Matt stared at her. What was the matter with her? Did she have a book upstairs called Ten Easy Steps To Embarrass Your Teenage Son that she pored over every night?

'I'll make hot mulled wine and mince pies for you all,' she said, returning to her sewing. 'From scratch.'

He kept on staring.

'And you might even find what you want under the tree on Christmas Day.'

He mumbled something. His mother understood Matt's mumbles and grunts like no one else. In exactly the same way that she had always understood his toddler mumbles and grunts – which conveyed complete concepts and were a complex language in themselves – so she understood his adolescent version. And she treated it exactly the same; she pretended she didn't, giving him no choice but to talk in her language.

'Pardon?' she asked, clearly.

'Hmuite.'

'*Pardon*?'

'All right,' he said, defeated.

So, here he was, on the bus, on the last day of term, surrounded by his gang of idiotic mates who seemed to find it a great lark to be on the way to his house. He was the only one who was treating the entire expedition like a trek to Hades, but then, he was probably the only one who was going to be teased about his mother for the rest of his life. The only hope he was holding out was that she had been asked to work late and had forgotten her side of the deal, namely the wine and pies. He hadn't mentioned this part to his friends, knowing that they'd only mock him severely for it. He was amazed, quite frankly, that they had chosen to do this instead of hang around the mall with their girlfriends, or go to the cinema in the gang or hit their own heads with a mallet, but they had all seemed dead keen to come and have 'a larf' at his place. He dreaded to think what was to ensue.

His heart sank at the sight of the twinkling lights in the front room of the little terraced house. His mother had been to Woolies. He put the key in the lock, and as the hall filled with his mates, he became acutely aware of her standing at the kitchen door, beaming at them all.

'Hello boys!'

'Hello Mrs Davies!' Matt heard them chorus in a mockingly polite tone.

'You must be freezing! Take off your shoes and coats and there's hot mince pies just out of the oven for you.' She turned briskly and went into the kitchen.

Coats and shoes were abandoned around Matt as his mates rushed down the hall.

'NEATLY!' came his mother's voice from the kitchen.

The boys returned, piled their belongings in neat piles around him and scarpered back to the kitchen.

Matt stood with Daz, Tony and Si, somewhat

emasculated in their socks, in his tiny kitchen, watching his even tinier mum take mince pies straight out of the oven, place them on a large plate, and add brandy cream to each one. He didn't know where to look. He saw the kitchen through his mates' eyes and felt ashamed at its smallness and shabbiness. Then he saw his mother through their eyes and felt humiliated by her girlish ponytail and low-slung, New Look trousers. Why couldn't she dress like a proper mother? Tony's Mum lived in velour tracksuits and Si's mother hung her girdles on the garden washing line. He could see his mother's flesh in the gap between her fitted top and trousers. He wanted to die.

Then he felt ashamed that he felt ashamed. He tried to work up from double shame, through indifference, to pride, but just got confused somewhere in the middle.

'There's more where they came from,' she said, holding out the plate.

Gingerly, each mate stepped forward, took a mince pie, then took a plate and serviette and thanked his mother. Some of them even pronounced their 't's properly. They were taking the piss. He'd never hear the end of it.

'Right,' she said. 'I'll show you the tree.' And off she marched into the front room. As the boys dutifully followed her, she called behind her briskly, 'No crumbs, thank you.'

Matt listened out for strangled laughs.

The small front room seemed even smaller than usual. Against the far wall, in the corner between armchair and window, leant one of the largest trees Matt had ever seen. On the floor lay familiar boxes of lights and icons that immediately transported him back to his childhood. While being assaulted by memories, it occurred to Matt that his mother was a genius. This job usually took the two of them the better part of a day and was tedious and harrowing in the extreme. At least now it would be quick, and maybe that would be worth the lifelong shame.

'Right,' she said. 'We need to push the armchair over so that there's room for the tree in the window, then put the tree in the base and then hang all the crap on it.'

Jesus, thought Matt. Now she's trying to be cool.

'Why don't you play that nice band, Matthew?' she was now saying. 'What are they called, Poop?'

'Pulp.'

'Oh yes, Pulp. Silly me.' She shrugged her shoulders and seemed to giggle internally. Did she actually hate him? The thought had never occurred to him before, but now that it did, many things made sense.

'I saw them at Glastonbury,' said Si. 'They were ace.'

'Really?' his mother asked.

'Mm.' Matt watched as Simon blushed. Oh God, he thought. He was watching his own mate die a hundred deaths of embarrassment at having to have a conversation with his mum.

'Did you all go to Glastonbury then?'

They all nodded mutely. Matt almost breathed out. His mother sat on the arm of the sofa, her ponytail swinging as she did so.

'And did you all get good reports this term then?'

He stopped breathing. Daz actually hung his head down. 'Shouldn't think so. We've been a bit busy you see.'

'Ah really?'

'Yeah.'

'Too much sex, eh?' she asked.

The boys snorted with uncontrollable laughter. I'll just kill myself now, thought Matt. No one will notice.

'And so . . . these girls,' asked his mother slowly, 'are they also getting bad reports?'

'Oh no,' piped up Si. 'They work hard.'

'It's all right, explained Daz. 'Nobody expects us to do as well as the girls.'

'Don't you want to do well?' asked his mother. 'Do you want all the girls to do better than you? Do you all want to have female bosses?'

'Oh that won't happen,' said Si keenly.

'Nah, we'll be all right,' added Daz.

'How do you figure that then, eh?' his mother asked.

'Well, they all end up having babies, don't they?' smiled Daz.

They all beamed at her proudly. She stared at them, eyes wide. Matt forced himself into action. 'Right then!' he almost shouted, having found his voice. He hurried his mother out. 'You just leave us to it.'

'Yeah, with pleasure,' said his mother, the change in her voice tone only audible to him and dogs.

The boys practically fell over themselves to assure her that her Christmas tree was safe with them. He shut the door behind his mother and turned to face them.

He waited for the barrage of insults and mockery.

'What you do that for?' asked Daz. 'We were talking.'

'Yeah,' said Si. 'Toss-head.'

'Oh –' he started. 'I –'

'Right,' interrupted Daz. 'I'll put the music on. Si, you

and Tone put the tree in its base. Matt, you untangle the lights.'

'But –' started Matt.

Daz stared at his watch. 'Let's synchronise watches. It's now seven minutes past five.' They synchronised watches. They all looked at Daz, who said, 'Let's GO.'

And go they did.

Jon sat cross-legged on the rug in the lounge and stared in disbelief at Sukie, who was sitting opposite him. He had not helped her re-write her CV for this sort of behaviour.

'Pardon?' he asked deliberately.

'I,' she repeated slowly and clearly, 'am going to get inside your body.'

'No you bloody aren't.'

'Not literally, Jon. I'm not a witch.'

'Right.'

'I'm talking metaphorically.'

'Thank God for that.'

'We've done your breathing. It only took four weeks which is not a bad start. Now we need to work on your voice, the way you sit, the way you walk, the way you move your head when you talk, basically everything.'

'Would you like to see me go to the toilet too?'

Ignoring him, she then did the oddest thing. Jon watched as she moved her arms into a shielding position across her stomach, sank her shoulders, curved her spine and lowered her chin. Then she spoke to him in a rather tinny voice.

'Who do I look like?' she asked.

He blinked. 'My mother.'

'Interesting.'

'Uncanny,' he agreed.

'Notice anything about the way I'm sitting?' she asked.

'You look constipated.'

'And?'

'Uncomfortable.'

'And?'

He frowned. 'Young.'

'And?'

'Shy.'

'And?'

'Unhappy.'

She nodded.

'I have something to tell you,' she said.

He took a deep breath. 'Go on,' he said.

'I'm mirroring you.'

He blanched. 'Piss off,' he said weakly. 'I don't look like that.'

'You do. Without the curls and to-die-for body.'

He was speechless. He looked at her body and then slowly down at his own and realised that she was, indeed, sitting in exactly the same position as he was. Everything was the same, from the position of her fingers to the expression on her face.

'So!' she said brightly. 'What's the next step?'

'Buying a gun,' he whispered.

'Nooo!' she exclaimed. 'This is good! Don't you see? We have so much to work on!'

Jon could only nod, his head sinking with the effort.

'It's easy!' Sukie continued. 'You only have to be told how to change and you'll look like James Dean.'

Jon's head sank even lower. 'Before or after the crash?' he murmured.

Oh dear, thought Sukie. When she'd had this class at drama school, everyone had found it fascinating – but then, she supposed, none of them had moved, sat and talked like a suicidal mole.

She reminded him to breathe properly from his diaphragm and then made him focus his attention on making his voice come from where his breathing was coming from.

'I can't,' he said immediately, from his throat.

'Yes you can,' she coaxed.

'I hadn't realised breathing and talking was multitasking,' he groaned. 'What if I need to walk at the same time? I'll be fucked.'

'Don't be silly, Jon. Just focus.'

He did, and he spoke, very slowly at first, from his diaphragm instead of his throat. To his amazement, his voice came out lower, with more expression and more depth. He even sounded more manly.

'Oh my God!' he cried – in a deep voice. 'You're amazing!'

Sukie beamed. He beamed.

'Right,' she said. 'Let's see if we can have you walking like Clint Eastwood by Christmas.'

'But that's only a week away.'

'OK,' she conceded. 'Burt Reynolds.'

Jon jumped up.

'Okeydoke!'

Sukie held up a warning finger.

'From your diaphragm.'

Jon breathed deeply and spoke with a base timbre that

made him blush. 'Okeydoke,' he said and they both laughed.

After teaching Jon how to sound as sexy as she always knew he could, Sukie felt on a real high. Surely this should help her with today's audition, she thought, as she walked from the bus stop to the casting studio.

She hadn't been told much about the part; all she knew was that it was a medium-sized role in a costume drama. She'd worn her hair up, with ringlets falling around her cheeks, and a tight velvet bodice-style top over the most A-line of her skirts, finished off with lace-up ankle boots she'd borrowed from Katie.

She followed the signs for the audition and walked into a tiny office that was acting as a waiting room. It was completely empty. She had expected to find it brimming with women, all with that same unmistakable look of tired fear on their faces, but there was no one. The casting director's assistant suddenly appeared.

'Hi!' beamed Sukie. 'I'm Sukie Woodrow.'

The girl looked at her list, ticked off her name and then handed her a script.

'You're a prostitute from Lancashire, turn of the six-teenth century,' she said.

'Right.'

Sukie didn't know what to panic about first. Her mind raced through all the people she'd ever known from Lancashire, then all the parts she'd ever seen from there. She had no idea what the accent was. If she'd had warning, she'd have practised. Phoned up contacts and asked for help. As it was, she'd have to wing it.

She sat down and started reading the script. With a

photographic memory, the least she could do was get to know some of her lines.

'Ready?' asked the girl.

Sukie stared up at her. 'I assumed I'd have to wait.'

'No, we're ahead of schedule actually. They've already been waiting for you for ten minutes.'

'I'm not late am I?' she asked, suddenly mortified.

'No,' said the girl, over-patiently, 'they're *ahead* of schedule.'

'Right. Ready then.'

The girl nodded to the door to Sukie's right.

'Through there.'

Sukie walked to the door. She could do this. She would wow them all. She would walk in there and they would gasp in astonishment that the real thing – a real prostitute from Lancashire circa 1600 – should actually be standing in front of them.

She opened the door in the same way a prostitute from Lancashire would open the door. She stared at five people sitting behind a desk, in the same way a prostitute from Lancashire would stare. They stared back at her. And then, before she'd taken a step, she heard, like a passing bullet, the word, loud and clear – 'No.'

She stopped, half-in the door.

Five people, intensely bored, looked away from her, some shaking their heads, others tutting, the rest seemingly too depressed to do even that. Silently, she backed out of the room and made a quiet exit. She stared at the door for a while and then turned round. She smiled at the casting director's assistant and handed back the script.

'Thanks,' she smiled.

The casting director's assistant sighed, disappointed, and Sukie walked out of the studio into the winter's night.

The two young men sat in the chain restaurant, which had become their office. Both were excited and wanted to talk first.

'OK,' said the mule-like man. 'How did the bank go?'

'Great,' said his good-looking friend. 'They've upped the loan and actually looked impressed when I said that we were in with a chance – and then when you made that call mid-meeting, it clinched it.'

They both laughed.

'Well, he just suddenly said, "It's yours!"' rushed his partner. 'I couldn't believe it! I thought I'd really shot myself in the foot by insulting his staff.'

They discussed what to do with the exceptionally rude staff – they were both in complete agreement – and then moved on to their next point.

'I know this wonderful chef. Absolutely fantastic. Works in that gastro pub at the back of Hampstead, you remember?' said the mule-like man.

'Oh yeah, delicious,' replied his good-looking friend.

'Right. He's a young guy, good-looking, very dedicated, full of energy.'

'Let's go and eat there, meet him together.'

'OK. So it's just him and a new waitress and we're sorted.'

'New waitress?'

'Oh yes, just another thought.'

'Hmm.'

'You know my niece? The one I told you about the

other day? My older brother's daughter. She's nearer my age than I am his?'

His mate nodded slowly. 'Big boobs, no brain?'

'That's right! You remembered!'

'How could I forget?'

'Exactly! Just think how many more customers she'd be getting in!'

'She needs a job, does she?'

His mate sighed. 'Yes. But I do genuinely think she'll be a worthwhile addition at the café.'

His partner nodded slowly. He was eternally grateful that his mate had stumped up 50 per cent of the deposit, but he had not ever envisaged Patsy being part of his staff.

'If she doesn't work out,' said his friend, 'you can always sack her.'

He smiled. It was nice to be working with someone who could read his mind.

They shook hands.

'Congratulations, Mr Crichton.'

'Congratulations to you, Mr Brown.'

Then they discussed their plans for the café itself. It had to be redesigned. They wanted a completely new look for a completely new beginning.

'Thank goodness the bank was OK about us taking two weeks to renovate,' said Mr Crichton. They looked at the plans laid out on the table in front of them. 'We'd never have been able to completely rewire, rebuild and repaint it in only one week.'

They frowned hard at the plans a bit more.

'But there's absolutely no way we can survive if they

135

take longer than two weeks,' he continued. 'Especially if we're giving all the staff holiday pay.'

'Two weeks it is, then.'

'So we start on the day we complete, April the fifth.'

'And we open as Crichton Brown's Café/Bar/ Restaurant on April the nineteenth.'

They lifted their beers and made a toast.

'To Crichton Brown's.'

'To Crichton Brown's.'

They finished their beer and grinned at each other over the table.

'Merry Christmas,' said Mr Crichton.

'And a Happy New Year,' said Mr Brown.

9

As soon as she reached her parents' village, Katie found herself driving through dense fog. Great white swirls of it danced into the beam of her fog-lights and all she could see was the few feet in front of her. She gripped her steering wheel and drove at a steady two miles an hour, blinking rapidly at the thick mist ahead. When it cleared, she realised she'd quite liked the experience – she had no longer been the only one on the road who hadn't known where the hell she was. And for the first time in the journey she hadn't dwelt on the fact that since she'd last seen her family she'd probably lost her job and had cocked up the big date with Dan.

To the accompaniment of increasingly hysterical Christmas DJs, she'd spent her journey inventing different possible stories to explain the Great Date Disaster. Over the phone she'd been able to fob her mother off with evasive answers, but she knew that face-to-face she would be unable to manage it. For the past two hours she'd been finalising her favourite. It was simple, it was neat, it was clean: Dan had turned out to be a socialist. It was perfect. Her family wouldn't require any more details.

Christmas was two days away. Usually, by now, it had worked its magic on Katie until she was longing to get home to the bosom of her family, but not this year. She knew that the level of bonhomie that usually turned her family's bizarre idiosyncrasies into endearing quirks was just not in her, and there was little chance of it seeping in during the last ten minutes before she arrived.

In every other way though, she was ready for Christmas. She'd bought everyone's presents, she'd wrapped everyone's presents, she'd even put bows on everyone's presents.

Having spent three Christmas seasons working at the café, Katie had had no false expectations about it raising her level of festive goodwill. She'd known that Alec would put up his usual decorations – a tangled mess of paper that managed to make the place look more depressing than usual; she'd known that he would bring out the old muzac tape of Christmas ditties; and she'd known that she would end up exhausted and depressed. Yet, amazingly, it had still disappointed.

But this year, on top of all that, Alec had been in a repulsively happy mood throughout December because he had managed to sell the café to two men 'who had more money than sense', one of whom, he'd kept reminding Katie, thought she was obnoxious. On a bad day she had found herself replaying the conversation she'd had with her future boss until she just wanted to end it all in case she ever spoke again. Unfortunately, she knew she was far too banal for suicide and, as of next year, she would have three months to find a new job.

Late December had hit the café hard this year. It suddenly lost most of its daily custom in the seasonal hurly burly, with few people having time to stop and enjoy coffees and chats, fewer still wanting to come into a place that stank so much of cheap failure. They could get that in the shops and at work.

Things hadn't been much better in the kitchen.

Matt had spent his entire Christmas holidays in the café this year. In keeping with the festive spirit of the place, he had become an oppressive presence who, at every opportunity, reminded them in great detail of the hypocrisy of Christmas. Sukie had not been much better. This time last year she'd been performing in panto, the year before in rep at The Old Vic. This year she was continuing to fail at television auditions. And the chef had been his usual self.

So, Katie could hardly believe her luck when, on the day before she was to go home, a piece of Christmas cheer had entered her life. An exhausted-looking woman, who'd just finished her Christmas shopping and needed a quick pick-me-up, had also needed a good old moan. She was amazed, absolutely amazed, she told Katie, that there were no proper florist's in the area. She'd needed some nice flowers to take to a dinner party tonight hosted by a woman who had specifically requested that no one bring her chocolates.

'And not a single florist's in the whole area,' she explained, exasperated. 'I've walked the length and breadth of the entire area. Can you believe it?' Katie shook her head sympathetically. 'I mean, I can't very well take flowers from the supermarket, can I? I wanted something special.' Katie shook her head again. 'Not a single one,' continued the woman.

Katie stopped shaking her head.

By the time she had gone to the coffee machine, made the woman her pick-me-up and brought it back to her, she was decided. She, Katie Simmonds, would open up the first florist's in the area. It didn't blow her skirt up, but it was probably the obvious career for her. She waited for the familiar bubbles of optimism to start plop-plopping like hot sulphur within her. When they didn't she told herself it was because she was finally maturing.

And lo, finally, it happened that on a cold night in late December, in a little town north-west of London, Katie's last shift of the year did actually come to an end. And she was to enjoy a whole week's holiday while the café closed during the festive season and Alec visited his mother in Stoke. No more coffee orders for irate commuters for a whole week. No more dishwashing for an entire seven days and nights. No more boredom, no more aching back, no more stinging feet. Just seven days of over-eating, family politics and TV repeats. Yeeha. She tried to imagine how different she'd be feeling about it all if her date with Dan had gone well.

'So,' she said over-buoyantly, as they finished the final tidy. 'Nothing left but to celebrate the birth of our Lord.'

'Who was born in February,' muttered Matt.

'We *know*,' snapped Sukie. 'And Father Christmas is only red and white because of Coca-Cola advertising.'

'And the yule log was actually used as part of a pagan ritual,' added Katie.

'We know all of this,' finished Sukie.

'And we can beat you hands down at being Scrooge,' concluded Katie.

'Well, doesn't it annoy you?' insisted Matt.

'Not half as much as you reminding us every ten minutes,' said Katie.

'Fascist,' muttered Matt.

Katie sighed. 'Well, hard as it is to leave you all –'

Alec suddenly appeared in the kitchen, holding a carrier bag.

'A token,' he announced, 'for my dedicated staff.'

There was silence.

He held up a bag. 'Chocolate coins for all!'

There was a moment's hesitation as they all took this in. At first, they were too gobsmacked that he'd even bothered, then they were gobsmacked that he'd only bought them chocolate coins for their last Christmas with him. Then they realised that chocolate coins were still chocolate coins.

And so, here she was, driving home again, surrounded by presents, luggage and sweeping fog, trying not to think about the mess that was her life. As she turned into the driveway, only four hours after she'd left London, after only one frantic phone call with her parents at that round-about again, her mother came out to greet her, flanked as usual, by her two trusty Labradors and silhouetted against the hall's welcoming lights. Katie practised her smile. Her father and brother came to help her unload the car while Bea and Maurice finished the washing up from dinner.

Although Bea was now eight months pregnant, Katie still couldn't believe how big her sister's stomach was and, naturally, she feared the worst: that most of Bea's bump was the baby's chin, inherited from Maurice's side. She pushed the thought to the back of her mind as she was enveloped by the warmth of her family. She couldn't help but smile. Here was a place where she didn't need to explain anything, a place where she could just be herself. Perhaps it was all going to be all right.

'Now,' said her mother quickly. 'Come and have something to eat. You must be starving.'

'Ooh yes,' joined in Bea eagerly. 'Dinner was delicious.'

They nattered about everything, filling Katie in on the village gossip and Bea's latest pregnancy symptoms. Nobody mentioned her date with Dan. Yep, thought Katie, they'd discussed it. If they hadn't, Bea would have asked by now. She ate another mince pie.

Despite this, if she hadn't felt Christmassy up until now, the vast tree in the hall would surely have done the trick. It was a specimen Queen Victoria herself would have been proud of, and it cast its silent spell over Katie. After placing all her presents under it and revelling in the intriguing shapes of the presents there for her, she stood back and looked up at it, remembering all the Christmases past, savouring the realisation that at this moment, there was nowhere else she'd rather be. Then she started wondering if, perhaps, she should by now have found something else in her life that gave her this much contentment. It wasn't a particularly good sign if the happiest moments you could recall from your twenties were of remembering your past, was it?

Thankfully, Deanna chose that moment to call her to come and help. Within the hour, the women had discussed their complex cooking rota – no mention of Dan – the men their somewhat less complex log-chopping rota and Katie had had a hot bath. There was little time to waste – tomorrow, Christmas Eve, Deanna's parents and Sydney's mother would be arriving for lunch and staying until the day after Boxing Day.

'So,' said Katie eventually, unable to put it off any longer. 'Don't you want to know about my disastrous date?'

There was a pause.

'Only if you want to tell us, dear,' said her mother.

Katie shrugged.

'What happened?' asked Deanna softly. 'Did you mess it up?'

Katie's eyes widened. 'I love the way you assume it was my fault.'

'Well, I just wondered . . .'

'How do you know he wasn't a murderer?' Katie demanded. 'Or a serial rapist? Or a paedophile? London's full of them.'

'Oh sweet Lord,' mumbled Deanna, sitting down.

'Was he?' asked Bea.

'No,' said Katie. 'I messed it up.'

'Thank God,' whispered Deanna.

'And then I saw him with someone else the next night,' mumbled Katie.

'Ouch,' said Bea.

'I don't want to discuss it.'

'Neither do I,' said Deanna. 'Have some eggnog.' And the subject was never broached again.

Later, Katie decided to announce her dramatic career news – a seasonal gift for her parents. Given the choice, she'd have waited until she was more settled, but she was fully aware that these were the last few moments of sanity in the Simmonds household.

It appeared she was mistaken. Completely unintentionally, she had seemingly unleashed the dogs of hell.

'A *florist*?' Deanna had exploded, almost spilling her mulled wine. 'Have you finally gone out of your deluded mind?'

Katie felt her eyes sting.

'You want to be a *flower* girl?' Deanna spluttered.

'Um,' pondered Katie huskily. 'No?' Perhaps she should change the subject to something more positive. Like her date with Dan. She stared at the fire.

'*You want to be the next Eliza Doolittle?*'

'Darling –' attempted Sydney.

'Don't "darling" me,' snapped Deanna. 'You worked your fingers to the bone to pay for her education and this is how she repays you. By becoming Eliza bloody Doolittle.'

Katie had made her mother swear. On Christmas Eve.

Sydney sat back and gave Katie a look. You're on your own girl, it said.

'Not a flower girl, Mum –' started Katie.

'What is wrong with you?' Deanna turned her attention back to her youngest daughter. 'Do you think I don't have enough on my plate? What with your father's mother coming first thing tomorrow –'

'Now that's unfair, darling –'

'Your mother,' shot his wife, 'is a foie gras short of a hamper and you know it.'

Sydney glanced apologetically at Katie, and then he sat it out with the rest of them and hoped for the best.

They all stared as Deanna gulped back her wine in one.

As she eyed the decanter somewhat glassily, they looked feverishly at each other across the living room. This was not good. Upsetting Deanna just before Christmas Eve was not good. It was one of the great family no-nos. It was like teasing Sydney about his golf handicap. It simply was not done.

'I'm sure Katie didn't mean it,' attempted Bea.

'Oh, are you?' asked Deanna sternly. More warning glances shot round the room. This was worse than bad. Not only was Deanna turning on her own young, she was doing it when they were eight months gone. Something had to be done.

'Never mind, Mum, I'm sorry,' urged Katie. 'Please don't get upset.'

Deanna's face seemed to crumple and all the tension ebb out of it. This would have been fine had it been the day after Boxing Day, but it wasn't. As she sank into her armchair, the family glimpsed the truth and the truth was terrifying. Deanna was exhausted and it wasn't even Christmas Eve yet. She needed bucking up and fast.

'Right,' said Sydney, poking the fire. 'Enough talk, your mother's tired.'

The fire crackled against the deafening silence that followed this statement, and the family grew more scared still. They waited, breath-baited, for the silence to be broken, for Deanna to insist that she wasn't tired, but no sound came. Instead she took a deep, long sigh and eventually turned to Katie, a look of melancholy on her face.

'Do you remember,' she began throatily, 'performing in a school concert when you were eleven?'

Oh God, thought Katie. Not this. I can't take it.

'You played the triangle.'

Katie nodded.

'We drove fifty miles, through horizontal sleet, to see our baby play the triangle in the school orchestra.'

Katie held her head down.

'And then when we got there, we sat through two hours of piercing hell waiting for your piece to come up.'

Katie stared at the parquet floor.

'And then,' Deanna's voice was a whisper, 'there you stood, at the very back of the orchestra, triangle aloft . . . and we sat, breathless, waiting for you to transform Rhapsody in Blue from a cat-fight into something worth waiting for.'

Katie achieved a nod.

'And we waited.'

Katie breathed hard.

'And we waited.'

Silence.

'And then, suddenly,' whispered Deanna, 'we heard clapping.'

Katie nodded and sniffed.

'It was over. And you hadn't played a single note.'

'I lost count of the bars,' croaked Katie. 'Percussion's harder than it looks –'

'*Three years* of percussion lessons,' interrupted Deanna, leaning forward in her chair, 'a 100-mile round trip and a rendition of Rhapsody in Blue that still keeps me awake at night. And for *what*?'

Katie didn't move. Deanna sank back into her sofa.

'The truth is, I don't blame you,' whispered Deanna.

'How can I? I understand you far too well. You are as unable to make a decision as I am. Thankfully for me, your father came along and made mine for me, but I fear for you.'

Katie stared enviously at the Labrador curled up at her mother's feet.

'And that is why,' concluded Deanna, 'your mad Great-Aunt Edna refuses to change her will until she is convinced you know exactly what you want to do with your life. Her mother did not fight for the vote for you to be a bloody flower girl.'

'I know.'

'She refuses to watch you choose the bloody triangle and then not play it.'

There was a pause.

'Have I made myself clear?'

Katie nodded.

'Good.' Her voice softened. 'Do you still want to own a flower shop?'

Katie shook her head.

'Good.'

Sydney poked the fire about a bit and the family swapped reassuring looks. Deanna shut her eyes and Katie sat motionless, paralysed by such a performance.

Christmas was everything it should be. Apart from when Bea complained of pubic-bone ache at the table, there had not been a moment's awkwardness or silence. The food was delicious, the presents were all instantly forgettable and the TV repeats were utterly predictable. Even Sydney's mother, a woman who had reached the grand old age of ninety-two, mainly out of spite, had found nothing to complain about. And while they were in the kitchen, Deanna had given her youngest daughter a sudden bear-hug that had made both of them wipe their eyes furiously before getting on with the tidying up.

By New Year's Day, Katie was ready to get back to London.

10

Three months later, the novelty of the new year had more than worn off. In fact, it had worn off in the first week of January when the entire idiot nation had been depressed to discover that, yet again, the new year had failed to deliver them a new life. Now all they were left with was grey weather and repeats of *The Good Life*. Not even the changing of the clocks had helped. All that had produced was more daylight to be disappointed in.

Life at The Café had gone on this year much as before. There were two new photos of Katie on the fridge door. One was taken by Sukie at a drunken works do where Katie chatted to a lovely bloke all evening about what a failure they both were at relationships. Funnily enough, neither of them had wanted to take it any further. The other photo was of her enjoying a great night with a bloke at Jon's bar. Jon had taken the photo before the bloke had showed her his tattoo of the ship he was on at the moment.

Sukie was finally getting somewhere with TV auditions because she had learnt how to play the part. Her latest audition was for an adaptation of Dickens's *A Tale of Two Cities*. They'd asked her if she'd read the book and she'd said, 'Oh no, I don't read the classics. I find it spoils the adaptations.' They'd laughed and then asked her to read it. To everyone's joy, she had got through to the last ten for the part of Lucie Manette, the genteel heroine. She was now grateful for last year's Anusol advert because it was still going strong and she was still getting money from it.

Alec had hardly been at The Café at all and when he was there, he hadn't acted like a boss. He'd acted like an arse. Once the contracts were exchanged he didn't care any more, encouraging Katie to be rude to the customers, chain-smoking all day and telling anyone who'd listen how glad he was to be leaving. He was determined that by the time The Café was sold, it would be worth less than its price.

And finally, that time had come. On Friday April the second, he made his farewell speech. In it he managed to insult everyone who had ever worked for him and tell a bad joke that created a silence so pure Katie shut her eyes and pretended she was on an alp.

That evening Katie and Sukie went to Jon's bar where they got plastered, knowing they didn't have to get up early next day to do a Saturday morning shift. At six o'clock Saturday morning, Katie woke with a headache and spent the day in her pyjamas, drinking water and bemoaning the fact that she would lose her job, while Jon tried to cheer her up by offering to re-write her CV. She had spent February wanting to be a film director and it had been his favourite CV yet. Totally inventive.

'Come on,' he coaxed. 'You name it, I'll write the CV. You can time me.'

Katie looked up at him from the sofa. This hurt her eyes.

'Single mother,' she croaked.

'Hmm. I don't think you need a CV for that.'

'Typical. It's only the hardest job in the world.' She smiled. 'Have I told you how beautiful my nephew is?'

'Yes.'

'He's got chestnut brown hair.'

'I know.'

'Well, brown.'

'I know.'

'He's beautiful. Just started smiling.'

'I know.'

They watched the repeat of *Friends* for a bit longer.

'I want to be a mother,' said Katie.

'I know.'

'Then everything would be all right.'

'I don't think it works like that.'

'I love babies.'

'I know, Katie.'

'I'm going to lose my job.'

On Sunday, Sukie came round for an afternoon session with Jon. He'd nearly finished his novel and had sent his first three chapters to five more literary agents with a very confident covering letter. It had been easy to write, he'd just pretended he was someone else. Then they all decided that it was not the right day for a session, so they went to the local park and sat on the swings till their bottoms went numb.

'If I don't get this part, I'll kill myself,' Sukie said.

'If I don't get an agent, I'll kill myself,' Jon said.

'If you kill yourselves, I'll kill myself,' said Katie.

'Aaah!' said Sukie. 'That's so sweet.'

Katie smiled benignly.

'Don't flatter yourself,' said Jon. 'Her life's crap.'

As they swung forlornly, none of them could possibly have guessed how things were about to change.

On Monday morning Katie was the first one at The Café. She'd hardly been able to sleep all night. The only few minutes she'd had, she'd dreamt she was running down lots of dark corridors. She'd opened a door and found herself in a classroom. Dan was taking a lesson and there was a diagram on the blackboard which somehow she'd known was of hepatitis in rabbits. She'd backed away before he'd been able to speak, turned round and found herself under the sea.

She woke to the sound of rain. She looked over to her clock and saw how early it was. Then she remembered what today meant. Today was the first day with the new owners. Today was the first day of the rest of her life. Today she would be fired.

She rolled over. And then, oh joy, she was unable to move. She was, quite unexpectedly, more comfortable than she had ever been in her life. She focused on it so as not to forget the feeling. Yes, her body had chanced upon a position that made all other positions a nonsense. Her limbs felt light with the luxury of it. The spaces between them were perfection. There was probably an equation for it. Every feather in her duvet had found its optimum position, and as for her pillow, it was a cloud. Her head seemed to be cushioned in cotton wool. All thoughts were clear here. All emotions profound. Was this what heaven felt like? Why, she thought, had this not happened ten hours ago? Why had she spent an entire night trying to get this comfortable? Why had she not tried this position? It was hardly complicated. Her body almost hummed with happiness. She was the closest she'd ever come to purring. It felt as if time had stood still.

Unfortunately it hadn't and when she next looked at her clock she almost jumped out of her blissed-out skin. She had ten minutes to get to work and it took fifteen minutes to walk it, let alone shower and dress. She was going to be late.

'Excellent,' greeted Sukie, already at the coffee maker when she arrived. 'Start as you mean to go on.'

'I overslept.'

'You're fired.'

'You're ugly.'

When she arrived at Sukie's side, they exchanged glances.

'How nervous are you?' asked Katie.

Sukie turned her hands upwards. 'My palms are sweating.'

Katie closed her eyes. 'I couldn't sleep.'

The café door opened and they both jumped. Hugh beamed at them.

'Hello!'

As Katie made him his usual, she and Sukie tried to remember what their new boss looked like.

'He had blond hair,' said Katie. 'I remember thinking

he might be an actor. I think he was good-looking, but sort of like a sad horse.'

'Oh God,' prayed Sukie. 'Please don't let me fancy him.'

'No sense of humour.'

'I always like men with no sense of humour. Much more of a challenge.'

The door opened again and they jumped. It was another commuter.

'We're too nervous today,' greeted Katie. 'You'll have to make your own coffee.'

'Double espresso please,' said the commuter, approaching the counter.

'Our lives are about to be ruined and all you can think of is coffee.'

'Why, what's up?' asked the commuter. 'Not that I care, I'm just being polite to get my coffee.'

'Our new boss is coming today and he's a gormless twat.'

'With no sense of humour,' said Sukie.

'Who thinks I'm obnoxious!' cried Katie.

'*No!*' cried the commuter.

'*Yes!*' cried Katie.

'Where could he have got that idea from?' asked the commuter.

'Oh,' came a new voice behind them. 'Just from watching her.'

Katie froze. Sukie froze. Even the commuter froze. He looked past them both at the man standing behind them and his mouth twitched into a nervy smile.

'Hello,' he said. 'I-I just wanted coffee. You must be the new boss.'

'That's right,' came the voice. 'Gormless twat to you.'

Katie closed her eyes.

'With no sense of humour,' continued the voice.

'Oh shit,' muttered Sukie, turning round.

'Hello,' grinned Paul Brown happily. 'I'm Paul.' He held up some keys. 'I let myself in through the back.'

'I didn't know you could open that door,' said Katie.

'I didn't know there was a door,' said Sukie.

'It's behind the Busted calendar,' said Katie, trying a smile. 'Hello,' she said.

'How's it going?' asked their new boss.

'Oh, you know,' answered Katie.

'Not really,' he said. 'I'm new to all this.'

'Oh,' said Katie.

'You look absolutely terrified,' he said quietly.

'I am.'

'Why? I'm the one who doesn't know what I'm doing.'

She blinked. 'Yes but I'm the one who was rude to you.'

'I know,' he laughed. 'Priceless. Can't wait for you to meet –'

'*Double espresso please*!' repeated the commuter. 'I hate to get in the way of a lovely reunion, but I have a train to catch.'

'All *right*!' shouted Katie, sweeping back to the commuter. 'Keep your wig on.'

She made the commuter his coffee while, to her astonishment, Paul chuckled and repeated, 'Priceless.' The commuter looked at him. 'I trust the first thing you'll do is sack this one,' he said.

'Wouldn't dream of it,' said Paul.

'It's like being at home,' muttered the commuter. 'Except at least the wife cooks for me.'

'Maybe she could make you coffee in the morning too.' Katie slammed his drink on the counter. 'Keep you out of my hair.'

'What and miss this delightful exchange every day?' He picked up his coffee, grinning happily. 'It's what keeps me going.'

'Talking of which,' Katie looked at her watch, 'shouldn't you be?'

'Don't worry,' he said, paying Sukie. 'I'm on my way.' He looked at Paul and gave him a cheery wink. 'Best of luck mate. You'll bloody need it.'

As the commuter queues continued throughout the morning, Paul introduced himself to all the staff. At nine-thirty, as the last of the queues died down, he asked them all to convene. As he did so, a girl of tender age, glowing skin and splendid breasts arrived. She beamed happily at everyone.

'Coffee?' asked Sukie.

'Ooh,' she squealed. 'Don't mind if I do.'

'Enjoy it,' said Paul. 'It'll be your last one on the house.'

'Oh hi, Uncle.'

The staff looked at him.

'Yes,' he told them, 'you're looking at the newest addition – another waitress.' He walked out to the front of the café where his niece stood and put his arm round her. 'Everyone. I want you to meet my eldest niece Patsy.' He took in their expressions. 'My brother's fifteen years older than me,' he explained.

'Hello,' said Matt.

Patsy gave them all a big smile.

'Hiya,' she said and gave a little wave.

'The daughter I never had,' grinned Paul. Patsy giggled. 'Thanks,' he added, 'to contraception.' She giggled again, before stopping suddenly.

Within half an hour, they all discovered that Patsy was living proof that aesthetics and function rarely mix.

'Oh,' she said sadly, staring at toast she'd just burnt. 'How did I do that?'

Katie shook her head, tutting. 'It's a puzzler and no mistake. Sukie? Any ideas?'

'I can only assume you put it in for too long,' said Sukie.

'Yes, but how?' frowned Patsy.

Sukie and Katie exchanged glances. 'I think it's going to be a long day,' muttered Katie.

Paul had shut the café and asked everyone to wait in the front, showing Patsy the ropes, while he had a one-to-one with them in turn in the kitchen. He had started half an hour ago with the chef. It didn't take them long to work out the genius behind employing Patsy. With her here, they couldn't discuss Paul. Or so he thought. Katie had other ideas.

'So,' she started. 'What's your uncle like?'

'Which Uncle? I've got three.'

'The one talking to the chef,' said Matt.

'Oh he's not the chef any more.' She gasped and clasped her hand to her mouth. 'I wasn't meant to say that.'

'He's *sacking* the chef?' they all asked.

'I didn't tell you,' rushed Patsy.

'You're right,' said Katie. 'He'll never guess how we know.'

Just then Paul arrived. They all stared at him in silence.

'Right,' he said quietly. 'Matt. You're next mate.'

They all watched, bug-eyed as Matt followed Paul down into the kitchen.

Sukie and Katie stared at each other.

'So,' said Patsy from the other side of the counter. 'How do you do this toaster again?'

Five minutes later, Paul was back.

'Sukie.'

'Yes?'

He raised his eyebrows. 'Kitchen please.'

They exchanged glances and Sukie followed him down.

'So,' said Patsy again. 'Never turn it higher than two?'

Katie could only nod. He was clever, this Paul. He'd separated her and Sukie and left her with Patsy. After what felt like a year, she heard Paul's footsteps approach. She turned to him and he gave her a tight smile.

'After you,' he said, opening the door for her.

'Shall I wait here?' asked Patsy.

'Yes, I'll be back in a moment.'

Katie opened the kitchen door with trepidation. There sat Matt and Sukie on the counter. There was a moment before Paul followed her in, but their expressions gave nothing away.

'Right,' sighed Paul. 'This is all a lot more harrowing than I thought.' He checked his watch. 'My partner should be here right now, but he's been delayed picking up the new chef.'

Katie gasped. The others gave her grave expressions.

'That's right,' said Paul. 'I'm afraid there were a few things we wanted to change and the cooking was one of them. The other one was you, Katie.'

She nodded.

'I had hoped I wouldn't be alone to do this, but so be it,' said Paul. 'Katie –'

'I can be nicer.'

There was an awkward pause.

'Pardon?'

'I can be nicer. It won't be easy, but I can try. Please.'

She glanced at Sukie for help, but Sukie was shaking her head.

'God no,' said Paul. 'We don't want you being nice, this place would lose all its charm. No, we'd like to make you manager.'

Katie heard the words, but didn't get the meaning. She heard Sukie breathe in sharply and felt herself being hugged by Matt. As Paul continued, she grew overwhelmed with emotion.

'We have great new plans for this place.' He was now pacing the kitchen, slaloming round bags and ovens. 'We've hired a new chef – he's fantastic and will be here any minute. A new menu. Totally new design, new outfits and new look.' He turned to them suddenly. 'Porter's Green is up and coming,' he declared, 'and this place is gonna be up and coming with it.' Just when Katie thought he was going to break into a rendition of Oklahoma, he satisfied himself with a beam. He opened his arms to his new team, and Katie, drawing on all her reserves of self-control, managed not to run into them sobbing with joy.

She could do that later. 'We have every faith in you lot.' Paul went on. 'You coped with Alec – we think you can cope with everything. Any ideas you have will be gratefully received. You're the experts – we have a lot to learn from you.'

'I have lots of ideas,' rushed Katie. 'For recipes and menu design and waitress outfits and children's meals. And, and . . .' She stopped and looked round at everyone. They were looking back at her. She decided not to suggest organising a parade and designing a float for it. They could do that next year.

She turned back to Paul. 'You know,' she shrugged with a smile. 'Just some ideas.' She'd have to remember not to act as if her inner core had just been pumped full of light and air. It might annoy the others.

'Good. We're going to change the menu completely, and the name of the place.'

'What's it going to be called?' asked Sukie.

'Crichton Brown's. That's our surnames, my partner and me, and it's all going to be re-painted coffee and cream. Soothing yet trendy, fresh yet warm, smart yet casual. The menu will have organic everything, rice milk, soya milk, you-name-it milk, wholemeal, unrefined flour in the pastry and quinoa in the salads.'

'What?' asked Matt.

'Salads,' said Katie.

'What will we give people who want stuff that tastes nice?' asked Sukie.

'I think it's brilliant!' said Katie excitedly, trying not to bounce.

'And here's the best part,' said Paul, 'you've all got

two weeks' paid leave – yes, paid – while we totally refurbish.'

There was a pause.

'Don't all cheer at once.'

'But what will the commuters do during those two weeks?' asked Katie.

He shrugged. 'I'm sure they can cope for a fortnight.'

'No no no!' said Katie. 'They might cope for one week. For two weeks they'll settle into a new routine and never come back.'

Sukie nodded. 'And then Crichton Brown's would be a bit trendy yet empty.'

'How about we just do coffee,' suggested Katie quickly, 'while the rest of the place is being done up? All you'd need is the coffee machine, milk, coffee, paper cups, and one of us, of course, to make the coffees and serve the regulars. I'll do it. Then I can work with you on the new menu ideas at the same time.'

'Right,' said Sukie. 'I'm glad that's all been decided then. Well done Paul. You're doing a cracking job.'

Paul swallowed. His mobile rang. He turned away and whispered frantically into it, the shirt on his back a darker colour due to sweat. All Katie heard was 'already a fucking coup' before he rang off. He turned back round and gave them another smile.

'That was my partner and the new chef. They're just parking. Traffic's been lousy apparently.'

'It always is this time of day,' said Sukie.

'Right.'

They heard a high-pitched voice from the café.

'I think the toaster's broken!'

'Ah,' said Paul. 'Patsy. Who'd like to bring her in?'

'I'll go,' said Matt, moving faster than Katie and Sukie had ever seen him move.

'So,' said Paul. 'Everybody happy?'

'Yeah,' said Sukie. 'I think it's brilliant, Paul. And on behalf of all the staff, I'd like to say how much we're looking forward to working with you.'

'Thank you, Su—'

'I feel I can talk on behalf of everyone,' continued Sukie, her smile rigid, 'because, as you may know, I'm the longest serving member of staff here.' Paul nodded slowly. 'By quite a long way I think,' she went on, turning to Katie. 'How long had I been here when you came to do part-time shifts?' she asked. 'You remember, when I had to show you how to use the coffee machine?'

Katie stared at her friend. It was only the pain in Sukie's eyes that stopped her from asking what the bollocking hell she was playing at. 'Er,' she spoke softly. 'I'm not sure.' She turned to Paul and gave him a resigned nod. 'It was quite a considerable while, I think.'

Sukie nodded. 'Mm. It was two years actually.'

There was a pause and Paul started visibly sweating. He licked his lips, swallowed hard and turned to Sukie. 'You're an actress, right?'

'Hmm,' allowed Sukie, crossing her arms.

'Well,' said Paul. 'After careful consideration and of course, Alec's opinion taken into account, we finally decided that we couldn't possibly have a manager who might have to go on tour suddenly. After I've finished my sabbatical from my job, I'm going back to work full-time and my partner has absolutely no restaurant experience, so we needed a manager who was one hundred per cent committed to this job. No other commitments at all. No other priorities. No other career goals. And, if I'm honest, for a while, no other interests at all. Being manager is going to be a hugely responsible, largely thankless job at first, with longer hours and only a little more pay.'

Paul stared intently at Sukie, while beside them Katie felt her inner core slowly shrivel up and topple over. She stayed motionless, hoping the others might not have noticed the subtle implication that her promotion was actually a public declaration of failure. That might have been embarrassing.

Sukie nodded, convinced. 'I didn't mean to be funny or anything,' she explained kindly. 'I think Katie will be absolutely fantastic. But you know, I just wanted to know.'

Paul smiled uncertainly, wiping his forehead with a handkerchief. 'Blimey, I hadn't realised it would be this hard,' he joked with his new staff.

'Well, what did you expect?' Sukie asked with a big smile. 'You come here with your "smart yet trendy; bijou yet bollocks" and expect us to just take it.'

Suddenly Paul walked to the kitchen door, muttering about Patsy. He called and was answered by the sound of giggling. Patsy was holding a mug of coffee as she came in with Matt.

'I was just showing her how to fix the toaster,' Matt explained. 'And I made her a coffee.'

'Ooh! That would be lovely,' said Sukie. 'Mine's an espresso.'

They heard the strangled sound of the café door opening.

163

'Did someone just kill a cat?' asked Sukie. Everyone laughed and Katie managed a smile.

'Aha!' cried Paul almost ecstatically. 'That'll be my partner in crime.'

They waited, Sukie, Katie and Matt all watching Patsy sip her coffee.

'Ooh,' she enthused, licking her lips. 'It's lovely coffee.'

'Yeah,' said Paul thinly. 'We'll be changing it.'

Ignoring their response to this, his face lit up at the sight of a tall, broad blond Adonis who had appeared in the kitchen doorway. All eyes left Patsy.

'All right?' nodded the Adonis to the room in general, grinning from evenly tanned ear to evenly tanned ear.

'Ah! Nik!' called Paul. 'Everyone! Meet the new chef!'

The two men bear-hugged, thumping each other so much on the back it looked like part of a ritual slapping dance.

'Sorry we're late, guvnor,' said the new chef, slouching one muscle-bound shoulder higher than the other, hands in denim pockets, 'but I had a nasty hangover. He had to wait till I got showered. He's just parking the motor.' He gave Patsy, Sukie and Katie their own individual cheeky grin from under long eyelashes. A giggle escaped from Patsy.

'No matter,' said Paul. 'You're here now.' He gave a little cough and then began the introductions. 'This is Katie, your new manager.'

'Respect!' exclaimed Nik and winked at her.

'Thank you,' said Katie primly, 'same to you too, hopefully.'

'And this is Sukie,' said Paul. 'Head waitress.'

'Nice one,' nodded Nik, giving her a thorough once over. 'Nice one.'

'I'm an actress,' said Sukie. 'This is just my part-time job.'

He nodded again. 'Nice one,' he repeated.

'And this is Patsy,' said Paul. 'New waitress.'

'Hello gorgeous,' he said. Sukie went visibly rigid and Katie hoped very much that Nik was a good chef.

'And this is Matt,' continued Paul. 'Chief washer-upper.'

'Nice one mate,' Nik smacked his hand into Matt's and shook it firmly. 'Nice one.'

'Ow,' murmured Matt before explaining that he was doing his A-Levels and when he wasn't here, they'd all just have to pitch in.

'Where the hell is the man himself then?' Paul asked Nik. 'Don't tell me he's done a runner and left the country.' He laughed nervously.

Just then they heard the sound of the café door slamming shut and the cat being throttled once and for all. 'We'll get rid of that for a start!' shouted a male voice from the café.

'We're in here!' shouted Paul. 'Move your arse!' He started pacing. 'Right. You're all about to meet Dan. You'll love him, he's –'

'Pardon?' interrupted Katie. 'What did you say his name was?'

'Dan.'

She swallowed.

'It's not going to be the same one,' tutted Sukie, examining her nails. 'There are other Dans you know.'

'Same one as what?' asked Paul.

'Nothing!' squeaked Katie.

'She had a hilarious date with someone called Dan,' explained Matt. 'We'll tell you about it some time. We've got a photo of him actually –'

'He doesn't need to see the photo –' said Katie, blocking the fridge.

'You're right,' said Sukie, staring at the man in the doorway. 'Because he's standing right here.'

They all stared as their new boss stood on the threshold, beaming at them: chiselled cheekbones, blue eyes – one with a hazel fleck – and a face they all knew well from the fridge door. He was looking at Paul and hadn't seen Katie yet.

Then he came into the kitchen.

He looked at Sukie and frowned slightly before stepping towards her and shaking her hand. He still hadn't seen Katie. She stood, stuck to the floor in fright, as if she'd just been caught naked in someone's living room, knowing that there were only seconds before they caught sight of her. He was saying something to Sukie and still had his back to her. Now he was shaking Matt's hand and saying something to him. He was only inches away. She tried to think of something to do but her brain cells were too busy running round her head screaming. He turned slowly towards her and she watched as his face went from side view, still side view, nearly front view, nearly front – front view. He started to give her a polite grin. Then stopped. Then stared. Then blinked and tried to grin again. Then swallowed almost audibly. Then glanced away and then back again. Then started to speak. Then stopped. Then gave a little cough.

'Hello,' she probably shouted.

'Hello,' he said, his face frozen.

She held out her hand. He looked at it as if it was a plate of live octopus.

'Oh,' he said and eventually shook it. 'Yes.'

'Katie,' introduced Paul proudly, as if he'd made her himself, 'Crichton Brown's new manager.'

'Oh!' Dan repeated. 'I never . . . what was the surname again?'

'I don't remember,' said Paul. 'What was the surname again?' he asked Katie.

Katie turned deliberately to Paul. 'The surname is Simmonds.'

'It's Simmonds,' Paul told Dan.

'Oh,' said Dan. 'Excellent.'

Paul laughed nervously again. 'Am I missing something here?'

Katie decided now would be the perfect time to explain her behaviour last time they'd seen each other.

'I-I-I-it-you . . .' she explained.

Dan turned to Paul. 'Can we have a word outside?' They left the kitchen, closing the door behind them.

Sukie looked at Katie. 'Well done!' she said. 'Pithy yet pathetic.'

11

The nightclub's low ceilings, uneven walls and interminable bass made Katie feel like she was pot-holing in hell rather than out having fun with friends. She was scrunched up between Sukie and Matt, which would have been fun were Sukie not chatting up the new chef Nik, and Matt chatting up the new waitress Patsy. Dan and Paul hadn't come. She hadn't wanted to come either, she'd wanted to go home and write up her menu ideas or failing that, jump off a high building, but when she'd suggested getting an early night, Sukie had thrown her a look that said 'manager' all over it.

She decided to go back to the upstairs bar, where she could chat to Jon, eat bar nuts and feel her own heartbeat again. She shouted to Sukie that she was going up, making enough sign language for her to understand. She squeezed out and felt Sukie and Matt lean back into her space as she tried to step over legs and feet. She pushed her way through a mass of junkie-garbed teenagers with piercings and tattoos. She felt as if she was looking at the world through the wrong end of binoculars. As she climbed the stairs, she wondered when she'd got so old. What was the point of thinking like a parent if the nearest she got to having children was half a first date? And then, naturally, she thought of Dan and felt sick again. Was she living a hideous reality show? Was God switching the channel back from some worthy wildlife programme in Africa to titter at the comedy that was her life?

She was in shock, that was all. It was understandable. She'd been given wonderful news and received a bolt from the blue in the matter of one hour. Everything that was happening to the café was a dream come true. It had reminded her exactly why she'd wanted to go into the restaurant business in the first place. All the enthusiasm that she'd thought had died within her had in fact just been latent, like a volcano ready to explode. And today when she'd been made manager, it had exploded, red, hot steamy lava everywhere. Then she'd been told that her new role as manager was because she was the only one of the staff who had nothing else in their life. Then, after it had taken this long to finally forget Dan, he was suddenly very much back in her life, instantly turning her insides to compost. Not only that but he was angry, which turned her insides to rotting compost. And the final icing on today's cake was the new, totally unexpected ugly in the form of Sukie. It was only now that Katie was able to appreciate fully how great their friendship had been when they'd both just been waitresses. Would it ever be the same again? Or was Sukie too angry with her and was she too hurt by Sukie's stunning display of disloyalty? Ah yes, yesterday, she'd had no prospects, no boyfriend and a shit job. Today, she had an even shittier job, an angry ex as her boss and she felt like she'd lost her best friend. She should place bets on catching flu first thing tomorrow.

Thankfully, by now she was approaching the bar. She wondered if the music in here was the newest craze to hit London or if it was her ears just ringing so loudly it was a sound in itself. It was much emptier up here. It was too posh for the teenagers and the after-work drinkers had started drifting away, having put off going home for as long as possible. She'd been here once at a weekend and watched in amazement as Jon rushed to and fro serving drinks to a queue that, like some mythological beast, just grew longer and longer until suddenly daylight robbed it of its powers. Tonight was different though and he and his colleagues were chatting easily together. He was the only bar staff without acne, and even though this was because he was the only bar staff in his mid-twenties, it was a fact Katie felt almost maternally proud of. She went and sat at her corner of the bar, picking up a bowl of nuts on the way. Jon raised his eyebrows in greeting, stopped chatting to his mates and met her there.

'Having a good time?' he asked loudly.

'Am I shite.'

He grinned and nodded. 'Have I told you my amazing news?'

'You're buying the café?'

'Pardon?'

'Is it me or is there a monster dancing under the floorboards?' asked Katie.

'You get used to it after a while.'

'I feel like I'm wearing a pacemaker.'

He shook his head apologetically and pointed at his ears.

'Get me a bloody Mary and tell me your news,' she shouted.

'Two agents want to meet me,' he shouted.

'That's amazing!' she yelled. 'Where's my drink?'

He nodded and grinned again. Katie mimed drinking and then took a pen from Jon's pocket and wrote down her order on a napkin. He read it and then wrote something underneath it. She read 'Coming right up madam.' She raised her eyes to heaven.

Over the next half an hour, she managed to hear enough to glean that this time he wanted to meet them, and the only thing helping him contain his excitement was his blank utter terror. He'd never known two emotions battle so valiantly before and he felt both deserved to win.

'Where's Sukie?' he asked. 'I need to tell her. I need advice.'

'Downstairs trying to get the chef naked.'

He frowned. 'Jamie Oliver?'

'I'm going home now,' shouted Katie, 'to learn sign language.'

Jon's face lit up and just when she was about to congratulate him on hearing and getting the joke, she got jabbed in the waist from behind. She turned round to see a sweaty, grinning Sukie beside her. Sukie waved. She waved back.

'What do you think of Dick?' asked Sukie.

'Dick who?'

'*Nik!*'

'Fine.'

'Vile?'

'*Fine.*'

Sukie nodded.

The three of them didn't talk properly until they were walking home an hour later.

'Are your ears ringing?' began Katie.

'*Singing?*' asked Sukie.

'RINGING.'

'Nope,' belched Sukie. 'Pardon.'

'I didn't say anything,' said Jon.

When they dropped Sukie off at her place, she offered to make them a cup of tea and they refused. Katie had to get up early tomorrow.

'Ah yes,' said Sukie. 'First day as manager.'

'Fuck off,' Katie said, banging her ear with her palm.

'Ooh,' said Sukie. 'Get her.'

'Gimme a break,' said Katie, her ears finally popping. 'You don't want to be manager and you know it. So don't spoil it for me.'

They stood for a moment in the cold, getting used to the silence slowly coming back.

'Yeah,' said Sukie quietly. 'You're right. Sorry. And I will enjoy my lie-in tomorrow while you're working through things with Dan.'

Katie groaned at Dan's name. 'Oh my God, my life is shit.'

'You can help me prepare for my interviews,' Jon told Sukie.

'OK,' said Sukie. 'Lunch is on you.' She waved as they sauntered away.

They walked down the hill, up their road and to the front door. Katie grunted half-heartedly as they approached, so Jon found his key. They walked up the stairs to their flat door and she waited as he opened it. He dropped his jacket off his shoulders by the coat pegs and she picked it up and put it on the hook. He yawned. She yawned. They walked to their rooms and each slept as badly as the other.

12

The next morning Katie's hangover was bigger than her body. As she shuffled down Asherman's Hill, she was convinced it must be throbbing or pulsing or glowing. Possibly all three. How could this much pain be invisible? Her joints were competing for Most Pain Award. She had taken pain-killers but they'd probably got lost working out where to go first.

Maybe this wasn't a hangover, maybe it was flu. Maybe, she thought slowly, just maybe, the hangover was masking some type of malarian killer flu that she'd caught at the nightclub from someone and they'd already died. When they did the docu-drama about it, after her tragic death, Sukie would play her and a Hollywood scout would spot her and she'd marry Tom Cruise. Maybe then Sukie would like her again.

She really was in a kind of hell. There she was minding her own business despising her job and then wham! She loved it and didn't want to lose it. Two minutes later, wham-bam! Boss from hell. If only she could explain to Dan what had happened to make her run out of that restaurant, but it wasn't that simple and she didn't have the money for therapy to work it out. She had no choice, she was going to have to be adult about this situation. Big poo. Because that meant she would have to apologise. Ever since her first apology at the age of three to her best friend Manda, for sucking her toy cowboy till he frayed, she'd found apologies difficult.

It would hurt, but she'd have to say sorry to Dan for running out on their date. She decided she'd do it before Dan even said hello. She wouldn't let that stupid male pride get a grip (hers, not his), she would humble herself endearingly, naturally and winningly. Suitably won over, he would then explain that he and Geraldine had been a hideous mistake – one of the worst nights of his life – and she would go on to prove to him that she was indispensable as a manager and had a very cute body. Then she'd start dating a self-made millionaire she'd met at the gym and he'd cry into his business strategy.

Well, it was a plan.

As she walked out of the newsagent's, opening today's much-needed sugar rush, she glanced at the café. She was early, thanks to only being able to sleep for four hours last night, and The Café was still unchanged. She crossed the road and stood in front of its doorway, watching her reflection as she finished her chocolate bar. She stepped forward and looked in. She leant closer and shielded her eyes with her hands against the glass of the door, squinting to see inside. She tried imagining the faded décor with a new look, failed and stepped away again. Then she turned round and leant heavily against the door. To her amazement, she fell in.

She looked up to see Dan standing by her head.

'I see you don't need a key,' he said.

'The door was open.'

'Well spotted. You may find you're too intelligent to be a manager.'

She crawled up and watched him walk behind the counter. From there he explained how, now she was here, they could move the coffee machine and the cash-till to the front of the café before the builders arrived.

'Right,' he said, taking off his jacket. 'Ready?'

Her eyes widened. 'I'm not moving that thing.'

'Why not?'

'I'm five-foot tall and weigh eight stone.'

He gave her a look. 'I thought women wanted to be treated equally.'

'Yeah pound for pound,' she retorted.

'What's that supposed to mean?'

'It means find someone your own size to treat equally.'

He gave a scornful laugh. 'Haven't you heard of feminism?'

'It's funny how men only say that when there's something heavy to carry or one seat left on the train. That's where all male feminists are. In trains. Sitting down.'

'We don't have time to discuss this,' he said, approaching the coffee machine.

'*You* don't,' she muttered hotly, walking past him to the kitchen. 'You've got a coffee machine to carry.'

She slammed the door, went straight to the sink and ran the cold tap over her head. She wasn't going to be able to do this. She was already close to tears and she'd only just got here. She came up from under the water. Right. Get a grip. Start again. She would apologise to Dan. She would humble herself endearingly, naturally and winningly. She would not cry or punch him in the face.

When she came back into the café, pinny on, hair wet, she found him standing in exactly the same position he'd been in when she'd left him. Not a thing out of place. She felt a bit like Doctor Who coming out of the Tardis. The only difference she now noticed, on second glance, was that his face looked like thunder. A Constable thunder, all intensity and impending doom.

She took a deep breath and prepared to humble herself endearingly, naturally and winningly when he suddenly spoke.

'I can't bloody move it on my own, can I?'

She blinked. 'How long have you been standing there?' she asked.

'Look, who is the boss here?' he asked.

She looked round the café and then back at him. 'Did you move it at all?'

'I said, "Who is the boss here?"'

'You didn't, did you? Bloody hell, you just stood there.'

'Right,' he broke in suddenly. 'Remind me to put you forward for Employee of the Year.' He pushed his sleeves up further and approached the coffee machine as if he was about to kick-box it.

She ran in front of it and blocked it. 'Don't move this coffee machine.'

He stepped back in surprise. They stood like that for a moment. Then he spoke quietly. 'Will you please get out of my way?'

'What time are the builders getting here?' she asked.

He thought for a moment. 'Eight. Why?'

'Well, we don't need to move it till then, do we? We can serve an entire commuter queue before they get here.'

Before he had time to answer, she walked past him to the café door and opened it.

'We tend to leave this open,' she told him briskly, 'so the customers know we're ready for business.' As she stood there, wondering how on earth this was the same bloke from Sandy's party, a commuter walked past her into The Café. 'See?' she said, giving him a look so sweet it came with fillings.

Dan watched an instant queue file in as if they'd been waiting behind the door all night. Most of them asked Katie the same questions: What was happening to the café now? What the hell had she been drinking last night? Where was Sukie? What were the new owners like? What did she mean crap?

He pretended to busy himself collecting the menus.

'Any time you want to help,' she called out to him, 'feel free.'

He didn't answer.

'Just jump right in,' she called out again.

'I'm waiting for the builders.'

'Ah yes! They'll be punctual and want to start immediately, I expect.'

She finished the queue and came out from behind the counter. 'Right. Let's move it ready for the next queue.' She looked at her watch. 'The 7.44 will start arriving in about ten minutes.'

She looked up at him. His arms were crossed.

'I think,' he said, 'we need to have a little chat about our manners.'

'OK,' she said. 'You're a bit brusque, but you are new, so –'

'Yours.'

She blanched. 'Let's sort out the customers first shall we? The later they are, the more they panic.'

No,' he said. 'Let's sort this out first.' He took a deep breath and spoke slowly and quietly. 'I do not like being talked to as if I'm an idiot.'

'How would you like to be talked to?'

Dan spoke lightly with a pause in between every word, as if she was a bit dim and he was her remedial teacher. 'Like I'm your boss.'

She felt blood rush to her cheeks. 'You are kidding, right?' she whispered.

'I am not kidding,' he said. 'Because I *am* your boss.'

She stared at him and he gave her a simple smile. No crinkle this time. 'No clever answers to that, are there?' he asked eventually.

'No,' she muttered. 'There are a few that would be very satisfying though.'

'I don't doubt it,' he said. 'It just depends how much you still want a job afterwards.'

'I'll let you know at the end of the day.'

'I know the feeling,' he said.

'So do I.'

'Good.'

'Good.'

Right.

That was good then.

'Now,' said Dan. 'Let's move this coffee machine to the front of the café.'

As they manoeuvred it, they both became aware of a man standing watching them from the doorway. He wore a T-shirt and jeans and looked about eight months pregnant. When they looked at him, he gave them a brief wink and a knowing grin.

'More exercise than you've both had in a while, eh?'

'Ah!' cried Dan. 'Harry. Excellent.' He turned to Katie. 'The builders. You'll note they're punctual and ready to work.' He turned back to Harry. 'Let's get cracking shall we?'

Harry clapped his hands. 'Not till I've breakfasted, mate. Just came to tell you the lads are down the other caff and will be back here in about half an hour, bright n' breezy n' ready to start.'

Dan started saying something, but Harry wasn't listening. Dan and Katie watched him saunter out, whistling a merry tune.

'You were saying?' grinned Katie.

'I don't know what you're so pleased about,' said Dan. 'You're helping me shift it back.'

'What?'

'You heard.'

She stood up and stared at him over the coffee machine.

'What the hell is your problem?'

'I don't have a problem,' he said.

'Yes you do, and you know it.'

'I'll remind you –' he started.

'No, *I'll* remind *you* –'

'One cappuccino,' said the first of the commuters for the 7.44. 'And a slice of toast. If that's OK.'

180

They stared at him.

'One cappuccino –' he repeated.

'Does it look like it's OK?' asked Dan.

The commuter stared and then looked at Katie. 'What the hell's his problem?'

'I was just finding out,' said Katie. 'He's the new boss.'

'What's he like?'

'Crap.'

'What do you mean crap?'

'Well, he unplugged the coffee machine.'

'Jesus. What next? Shut up shop while you refurbish it into some posh toff's place?'

'Oh no!' she said. 'Only an idiot would do that.'

'Right!' interrupted Dan. 'Let's get this machine back where it was. Katie?'

Katie turned to the commuter. 'Pete, would you? Only, I'm a feminist and I'm making a stand.'

The commuter threw down his briefcase. 'Of course, pet. Right. After three, one, two, three . . .'

By the end of the 7.44 queue, Katie was exhausted. She sat on the counter, letting her legs dangle limply. As she was wondering how to get to an apology from where she'd left off, a man entered the café. He wore overalls and a sorry expression.

'Hello,' she said. 'Can I help you?'

The man seemed to have trouble registering thought.

'Um,' he started, his lips opening and closing slowly. He licked them thoughtfully.

'Coffee? Tea? A seat?' asked Katie.

'The others,' he said slowly, mostly to himself.

181

'Pardon?'

'Where's everyone else?'

'Hmm,' pondered Katie. 'I often wonder that. I just thought I was unhappy in my work.'

A large sigh came from Dan. 'They're at the caff.'

The man nodded and turned away.

Katie looked at her watch, kicking her heels against the counter. 'Well,' she said. 'It's all going according to plan then, eh?'

Another sigh from Dan. 'You think you're very clever, don't you?'

She stopped kicking. 'Not really, no.'

'You like taking the piss out of people, don't you?'

'No.'

'Is that why you walk out on men in restaurants? Did you have a good laugh about that with your mates? I bet you all had a –'

'I was going to phone you, but . . .'

Dan let her finish, but her voice trailed off into nothingness. She had hoped that she'd just open her mouth and explanations would parachute out, but they seemed to have lost their nerve at the last minute.

'But what?' he asked. 'Forgot how to use a phone?'

'No,' she said indignantly. 'I saw you out with Geraldine and I went off the idea.'

He looked unimpressed. 'What the hell did she have to do with it?'

'Well, you hardly took long to get over it, did you?'

His face registered amazement, and then he started laughing. It was a nice laugh, but that only made her feel worse. 'You have got to be kidding,' he said. 'You think you've got some sort of right to be indignant about me going out with an old friend after you dumped me mid-date!'

'Geraldine did not look like an old friend to me. She looked very much like a date.'

'Well, she *was* very much like a date actually,' he said, mirroring her tone. 'And she still very much is.'

It was Katie's turn to register amazement. 'You're dating Geraldine again?' she asked, eyes wide.

He started to laugh to himself. 'I don't believe I'm having this conversation,' he told the empty café. 'It's like having a girlfriend without any of the perks.' He turned to her suddenly. 'You walked out on me, no explanation, no phone call, no nothing.' He started counting on his fingers . . . 'I chose the restaurant, I booked ahead, I collected you from your flat, I drove you all the way there, I chose the bloody food,' he stopped. 'What did I do wrong? Forget to wipe your –'

'I was going to phone and explain, but then I saw you with her and –'

'Go on then.' He crossed his arms.

'What?'

'Explain. Did you suddenly remember you were married with three kids? Or that you weren't an educational psychologist but a waitress in a shitty café?'

Katie took an intake of breath. 'That was uncalled for,' she choked.

'Uncalled for! I take you on the worst date in history where I have to talk so much I lose my voice –'

'I was nervous!'

'What of?' he shouted. '*Dessert?*'

'Look. I said I'm sorry.'

'No you didn't.'

'I did.'

He did an exaggerated double take. 'Was I out of the room?' he asked.

'I *explained*.'

'No you didn't.'

'I said I was nervous.'

'What *of*?' he repeated.

She thought about it. He deserved the truth, even if she was beginning to go off him.

'Of you going bald,' she said finally.

'What? *On the date*?' he shouted.

'No, just –'

'Because by the main course, *so was I*.' She didn't answer. 'Very mature. Very nice. Very *attractive*.'

The man had a point. Maybe now was the time to apologise.

'Well,' she allowed, 'when you put it like that . . .'

'You are one crazy woman,' he said. 'Thank God we didn't make it to dessert.'

Katie balked. She'd apologised. She'd explained. She did not need to be humble any more.

'Well,' she scoffed, 'if it was as bad as the starter, I couldn't agree more.'

His eyes opened wide. 'Oh don't worry. I'd lost my appetite too. I thought I was on some freak reality show. I kept expecting Linda Bloody Barker to burst out of the toilets with a camera crew and tell me I was on Worst Dates of Our Lives.'

She gasped. 'You bastard!'

'You think that was a *good* date?'

'NO! It was horrible and I wish I'd never met you, you arrogant . . . excuse . . . for a turnip –'

'Pardon?'

Katie gasped. She hadn't meant that.

He burst into sudden laughter.

'I meant . . .' she stuttered.

He was still laughing.

'I meant . . .'

He couldn't stop laughing. Despite her fury she had to try not to laugh herself, which was almost impossible every time she caught the glint in his eye.

'I didn't mean turnip,' she shouted. 'I got confused.'

He really couldn't stop laughing. She decided now might be a good time to apologise. Now that she felt a bit closer to him again. Which was why she was very surprised when she threw a dishcloth at him. It did the trick though. He stopped laughing and slowly peeled the wet cloth off his face.

'Sorry,' she said sadly.

He turned away so that his back was facing her. She held her breath. Was she going to be sacked? He turned back to her.

'There is every chance,' he said finally, working hard at controlling his face, 'that you are the maddest person I've ever met.'

'Thank you,' she said genuinely.

He held up his hand. 'Don't speak,' he said. 'Please. Don't speak.'

She decided now was a good chance to attempt an apology. Now that he was weakened.

'I'm not mad actually,' said Katie quickly. 'I'm just . . . quite intense and . . .'

He held his left side. It looked as if he might be getting a stitch.

'But I did want to apologise,' she rushed.

He nodded, unable to answer.

'I took fright. I accept I have issues where dates are concerned.'

He took a deep breath.

'Something bad happened while you were in the toilet –'

He shut his eyes and a squeaking noise escaped from the back of his throat. She rushed on, 'I got a nasty phone call and it made me have a sort of panic attack. I'm sorry. I'm really sorry. I just . . . I fled. I didn't even realise what I'd done until I got home. It's never happened before and I'm really sorry.'

Dan finally stopped laughing.

'It's all right,' he managed.

They stood for a while in silence. He wiped his eyes and finally looked at her.

'It was a bloody awful date,' he said.

She achieved a smile. 'It was,' she said.

'Let's just draw a line under it,' he said, 'and start again.'

'Line drawn.' She bit her lip.

'And now we're in a new, entirely different, situation.'

'We are indeed,' she nodded rhythmically.

'We have to work together. For at least three months.'

She made assenting noises. 'Well, hopefully more.'

He stopped and gave her a look. 'You don't want to

stay, do you?' he asked, not unkindly.

'Of course I do.'

He frowned at her for a while.

'I love my job,' started Katie, 'and I'm good at it. I've worked here for three years. Anyway, you won't find another manager with my brain and know-how for this cheap and you know it. The customers love me, the staff respect me and your business partner thinks I'm wonderful. Which I am.'

Dan paused.

'You know I'm right,' said Katie.

'Hmm,' said Dan. 'Looks like we're stuck together.'

Katie looked away quickly, stung by this after she'd thought they'd just made friends.

'Could I have a cappuccino please?'

Katie jumped and stared at a customer.

'What?'

'Cappuccino,' repeated the customer slowly. 'If it's not too much trouble.'

'Of course it's too much trouble,' said Katie. 'Do I look like a servant?'

The customer looked at Dan and shook his head.

Katie didn't see Dan's reaction, but she thought she could hear laughing as he went to the kitchen.

Jon's eyes were half-glazed as his fingers tapped on the keyboard, his mind's eye watching a film inside his head. At the ring of the doorbell, his organs jumped. He stayed sitting perfectly still as the film slowly faded away, the moment over. He could only hope there'd be another showing when he next sat down to work.

He saved his file and closed it before returning to the real world where crockery waited to be washed up and post to be opened. He pulled open the front door.

'Hi there, future famous novelist!' beamed Sukie.

'Hi . . .'

She brushed past him into the hall.

'It's a goddam beautiful day out there.'

Jon nodded, following her into the flat.

'Now,' she said, standing proud in the middle of his lounge, 'show me how you walk.'

He frowned.

'I use the one-foot-in-front-of-the-other method. It gets me by.'

'Behave.'

Jon turned his back on her and slung his hips low, expanded his chest and shoulders, pulled up his vertebrae and walked – not too fast, not too slow – across the room. Sukie observed him carefully.

'Is this literary agent a woman?'

'No.'

'Shame. Let's just hope he's gay.'

Jon let out an abrupt laugh and Sukie flinched. She started looking round the room. 'What the hell was that noise? Has a whale just surfaced?'

'No. I-I have a funny laugh.'

'Well for Christ's sake don't laugh in the interview then.'

'OK.'

Then she sat on the floor.

'Today we are going to start with the Circle of Attention.'

'The Circle of Attention.'

'Yes,' said Sukie. 'Now. Sit down opposite me.'

Jon sat.

'Now. Imagine I'm the agent.'

'Right.'

'Have you done that?'

'Well, I don't know the guy,' mumbled Jon, 'but I doubt he'll be dressed as Beach Barbie.'

Sukie's throat blistered.

'Ignore the clothes, Jon,' she shot. 'Just pretend they're not here.'

Jon found this didn't really help.

While Sukie closed her eyes and took a long, deep, cooling breath, he rubbed his face furiously with his hands.

'Now,' she instructed. 'Imagine I'm someone else.'

'Like who?' asked Jon.

'I don't know, you're the one with the imagination, Mr Manly Booker. Anyone. Me, for example.'

'But you are you.'

'No I'm not, I'm the agent.'

Jon frowned.

'Okaaay,' said Sukie, opening her eyes. 'It appears I'm going too fast for you.'

So she explained to him how the Circle of Attention works.

'It's all in the imagination,' she concluded. 'Which should be easy for you.'

'Yep.'

'So, tomorrow what you're going to do is pretend that the agent is not an agent, he's someone who admires you, someone who thinks you're fab, who's interested in what you've got to say, someone who is 110 per cent on your side.'

'I don't know anyone like that.'

'Well use your imagination!' she told him.

Jon nodded, concentrating hard.

'Right,' said Sukie. 'Imagine I'm the agent. I'm a guy. Imagine I'm tall, with short black hair, glasses, a beard and slight BO. And I'm wearing jeans.'

'What, nothing on top?'

'Jesus, Jon. No wonder this book's taking you so long.'

Jon took a deep breath. After a while, he muttered, 'OK I see him.'

'Now open your eyes. Do you still see him? Jon. Do you see the agent? Jon. What do you see? Jon. Talk to me. First thing that comes into your head.'

Jon's eyes re-focused.

'Chocolate Digestive and a cup of tea.'

Sukie nodded. 'Thought you'd never ask,' she said.

A few minutes later, they were eating biscuits at the kitchen table.

'It's not that I mind her getting the job,' Sukie repeated, 'it's just that it's already changed her.'

'Yeah, that's Katie. Power mad. She wants to rule the world, you know.'

'You know what I mean.'

'Give her a break, Sukie. She's wanted something like this for years. It's like you getting your dream part.'

'I wouldn't suddenly start acting as if I were Queen.'

'Anyway, if it's any consolation,' said Jon, draining his tea, 'she'll be having a horrible time with Dan today.'

'No she won't. She'll be absolutely fine.'

'Why?'

'Because she'll wrap that poor bloke round her little finger and have him eating out of her hand.'

Jon nodded sagely. 'Yeah, you're probably right. She has a knack of doing that.'

Sukie took another biscuit. 'She'll be joint owner by next week.'

Back at the café, Katie was deciding whether to resign now or wait till the end of the day. After the morning queues died down, the café closed for the day. The builders erected a temporary wall separating the coffee machine and cash register from the rest of the café and set to work replastering, screeding the floor and playing Capital Gold too loud.

Meanwhile, Paul and Nik arrived for their first menu meeting with Dan and Katie. It turned out, to Katie's great disappointment, that Nik may have the body of a god but he had the brain of a wombat. To her even greater disappointment, it turned out that Paul liked him – probably because he had hired him. All this disappointed her. But not as much as the fact that the only person who agreed with her was Dan. All morning since their decision to make peace with each other, Dan had acted completely indifferently towards her. She found this so painful that she'd taken on a disdainful air with him, like the mature manager she was. So to suddenly find him an ally was most disconcerting. Did this mean he was changing his mind? Did he fancy her after all? Or was he just being professional? And if so, what a bastard.

Oh dear, she didn't think she could do this. She wanted to do her job properly, but she didn't seem to be able to put their date behind her.

She sat through the meeting, half listening, half deciding when to tell them that she'd have to leave. She began to doodle on her serviette, the sound of Dr Hook warbling through the temporary wall and the louder sound of a builder's accompanying whistle drowning her thoughts.

'What do you think, Katie?' she heard suddenly. She turned to Paul.

'What do I think?' she responded.

'Yes, you know the market more than any of us. None of us know the punters like you.'

She blinked. Dr Hook was in love with a beautiful woman.

'I think you've got to hold your ground,' she said. She felt Dan watching her.

'So you think fricassee chicken with lavender polenta is a good idea or a bad idea?' frowned Paul.

'You know what I think?' she said. 'I think we need to explain more.'

'Explain more?'

'Yes.'

'What do you mean?' asked Paul.

'Could you . . . explain more?' Dan asked her, smiling.

She gave him a look. 'All right. What does fricassee actually mean?' she asked.

The men looked at her. Nik laughed.

'Some of our customers think latte means Coffee for Homosexuals,' she explained. 'And now you want them to eat fricassee chicken and lavender polenta.'

'Do 'em good,' said Nik. 'Narrow-minded oiks.'

'They'll think it's the name of a ship,' pointed out Katie. Dan snorted.

'And anyway,' she added, 'I thought we wanted to make money out of them, not educate them.'

'Ooh,' said Paul. 'Good point.' He made a note.

'Oh for . . .' said Nik. '*Everyone* knows what fricassee means.'

'Oh good,' said Katie. 'What then?'

'Well, it's the cooking method isn't it? It's how it's been cooked.'

'And how has it been cooked?'

'It's been *fricasasseed*.'

'Oh, I think there's been some misunderstanding,' said Katie, bristling. 'I'm not deaf. I just think we need to explain ourselves more.'

Nik suddenly brightened. 'You don't know what it means, do you?' he asked, pointing an accusing finger at her.

She sighed. 'Yes, I do,' she said. 'It means stewed in a thick white sauce.'

'There!' exclaimed Nik, looking at Dan and Paul. 'Told you! Everyone knows!'

'I didn't,' said Dan.

'Neither did I,' said Paul.

'Yeah, but you don't have to!' he cried. 'You're not the experts.'

They all looked at him and he realised his mistake. He turned to Katie. 'All right then, Miss Clever Clogs. You give us some of your ideas.' He crossed his arms and sat back.

'Yes, go on Katie,' said Paul. 'I'd love to hear your ideas.'

How could she tell them that she didn't want to give them her ideas because she was going to leave?

'Or don't you have any?' asked Nik.

'OK then,' she said. 'Here goes.' She launched into her ideas. All-day-breakfast – full English and Continental, plus a fat-free version (grill instead of deep-fat fry) which would be very popular with those who don't want to put on weight but can't be doing with bio-yogurt and muesli. They'd need an extra hob in the kitchen to keep the oil ready all day, but she knew where you could buy individual ones. Fat-free version of everything to start off with to see if there's a market for it. And yes, that included fat-free chocolate cake. That would become their unique selling point, or USP. All food available all times of day, there was nothing more annoying than deciding what you wanted to eat, only to discover that you were half an hour later than the cut-off time. Live music Sunday mornings, and, on the walls, work by local artists, on sale. Kiddies corner with smaller tables and chairs, games, paper and crayons. Once a week storytime for parents and babies.

'Wait a minute!' interrupted Nik. 'First of all I'm not cooking all bloody day. Second of all is this a crèche or a restaurant. Third –'

'I hadn't finished,' said Katie.

Nik swore under his breath.

'And then finally,' she said, 'I thought it might be an idea to put a suggestion box on the counter. Ask the punters what they'd like to see. Obviously we don't go for everything, but if there's a clear majority vote for a need we're not providing –'

'Oh! That reminds me!' cried Nik suddenly. 'I forgot this one! You'll love this.'

'Go on,' grinned Paul.

'And then we'll discuss Katie's ideas,' said Dan. Paul nodded.

'Right,' said Nik. 'Well, you know the Naked Chef?'

They nodded. He leant forward, staring at Dan then Paul then back at Dan.

'Well, we *really* give them the Naked Chef.' He grinned wider and wider. 'Geddit? We give them The . . . Naked . . . Chef.'

'You're not suggesting –'

'I bloody am!' laughed Nik. 'I've got a *fantastic* body. The chicks'll love it.'

'Hmm,' said Dan. 'Interesting.'

'Wouldn't it be dangerous?' asked Paul. 'I mean with all the knives.'

'And against health and safety?' asked Katie. 'You have to keep washing your hands, God knows what you'd have to do with your . . . you know.'

'What about chip fat?' asked Dan.

Nik winked. 'I'd wear a sock, wouldn't I?'

They thought about this. Katie glanced up quickly at Dan. She knew that look from this morning. He was trying not to laugh. He was doing OK until he glanced at her.

Nik turned to Katie. 'Well it's better than her idea of asking the bloody customers. They don't know anything about food.'

'It was only a suggestion,' said Katie quietly.

'Yeah, well. So was me being the naked chef.'

'Well, thanks for that Nik,' said Dan. 'We'll discuss it at our next meeting.'

'Right,' said Nik, springing up. 'I'm gonna look at my kitchens.' As he walked away, Dan turned to Katie. 'I don't think it's a great idea to be quite so rude to the chef.'

'Sorry,' she said innocently, 'but I had no idea he had some of his brain missing.'

'He's an amazing chef,' said Paul defensively.

'Do you mind if I ask you something?' asked Katie.

'Go on.'

'Have you ever eaten his food?'

'Yes of course,' said Dan. 'We're not quite as green as you think.'

'And it was exactly the kind of food you wanted here?'

Paul and Dan looked at each other. 'We assumed so.'

'He was working in Hampstead wasn't he? In a gastro pub?'

They nodded.

'With all due respect,' she started, 'that's a very different clientele from a Porter's Green café.'

'Yes, but that's exactly our point,' said Paul. 'We're up and coming. We're going to lead the way. And we're a Café/Bar/Restaurant now.'

'Right,' nodded Katie. 'And short of providing a free bus to bring Hampstead village diners here you're going to have to start with what people *here* know and love.'

'Mm,' said Paul. 'All right, we'll all have a rethink of the menu.'

Nik walked back into the café. 'Nice kitchen,' he said. 'Only one flaw.'

'Most kitchens only have one floor,' said Dan.

'Except Hampstead kitchens,' said Katie. 'They have two. Don't you know anything?'

'What the fuck are you two talking about?' asked Nik.

'What's the flaw?' asked Paul.

'Well,' said Nik, 'the diners can't see me cooking. There's a wall in between me and my people.'

'Why is that a problem?' asked Dan.

'And not a plus point?' added Katie.

'Well, what's the point of me being naked,' said Nik slowly, 'if there's a great big fucking wall in-between me and them?'

There was a pause as they all stared at their new chef. Katie turned to her new bosses.

'Dan? Paul?' she asked. 'What *is* the point of him being naked if there's a great big fucking wall in between him and them?'

She didn't need to ask again. Nik left the room, and, once he'd recovered himself, Dan followed him to make peace.

13

Richard Miller, hotshot literary agent, sat back and looked across his shiny new desk in his shiny new office, at the shiny new potential publishing sensation: a client who could confirm his reputation in the literary world, who was so near his grasp he could feel his fingertips tingling. Jon stared back across the vast desk at him, taking deep breaths from his diaphragm and concentrating on not dribbling. He swallowed as if he had meant to.

'Gosh, sorry,' said Richard Miller politely. 'I never asked, would you like some water?'

'Thanks.'

'No problem.'

While Richard Miller popped out of his office, Jon wiped his brow, loosened his tie and continued his deep breathing.

It was going well, he thought. Surely it was a good thing that Richard Miller was the same age, same height and same colouring as him and pretty much came from the same background. Surely it had been a good thing that Richard Miller had identified so strongly with his anti-hero Henry Logan ('we both love Häagen Dazs!') and that they'd both loved *Pulp Fiction* but hated *Fight Club*?

'So,' smiled Richard Miller, returning and putting a plastic cup of cold water on his desk near Jon, 'are you seeing any other agents at the moment?'

'Well,' hesitated Jon. 'Obviously I have to keep my options open . . . I am seeing someone else this afternoon, but . . .'

'Of course,' smiled Richard, sitting back down behind his desk. 'Very wise. Well,' he lifted his hands in a despairing conclusion, 'all I can say is . . .'

Richard paused and Jon held his breath.

'. . . that I . . .' he blinked slowly, '*love* your voice, and, more importantly, I think there's a market for your voice.'

Richard held his gaze.

'Obviously, I can't make any official deals unless there is a finished manuscript,' he continued, 'but as soon as there is one, I would very much like to hear from you. My plan of action would be to auction you. In fact, I already know who I think would be interested, and I know we'd be talking big bucks.'

Jon stared at him.

'And I mean . . . *big* bucks,' Richard gave a laugh.

Jon wanted to drink the cold water very badly, but knew his shaking hand would give him away. Likewise, he wanted to say something polite and grateful, but knew his shaking voice would give him away. He felt keenly that the moment required him at least to smile, but he seemed to have lost control of his lips and he knew that the slightest tremor would give him away.

He gave a slow, repetitive nod.

Richard Miller scratched his head. God he was cool,

this one. Very cool. He could see him now on *Shooting Stars*, or in fact, any of the post-modern quiz shows that offered kudos and pay without the client having to do anything except pretend to be in on the joke.

'And I can already see the dust jacket photo – that's always a good sign,' winked Richard.

Jon laughed abruptly and then stopped more abruptly.

Whoa, thought Richard. Almost broke the ice there.

'So,' he said, 'when do you think you could finish this book for me?'

'For you?' asked Jon, amazed.

'Sorry, I mean, obviously you haven't committed yourself.' Big smile. 'A turn of phrase.' Shit.

'Well,' Jon cleared his throat. 'I'm about two-thirds of the way through, so . . .'

Richard looked expectantly at him, puppy dog eyes. 'A month?' he tried.

Jon licked his lips, braved a quick grin and nodded.

'I'm still very keen to receive it,' Richard said with a cautious warmth, 'if you're still keen to send it to me.' He stood up and shook Jon's hand. 'It's been a real pleasure to meet you.'

Two hours later, Jon found himself in a penthouse flat in Soho, 'interviewing' Dick Higgins. It was much easier than interviewing Richard Miller because Dick Higgins didn't expect him to speak.

'I was having lunch with Graham Highson yesterday,' said Dick. 'Best editor in the country. I mentioned I was seeing you today. Talked about your character, Harry Logan –'

'Henry Logan,' said Jon.

Dick Higgins stared at him with large bulbous eyes. Jon almost expected him to call for a nurse.

'Pardon?'

'My anti-hero. He's Henry, not Harry.'

Dick Higgins turned briefly to the manuscript on his table. 'Yes, well, we can discuss that. Anyway, where was I?'

'Graham Highson.'

'Ah yes! Graham.' He sighed. 'Gray. I mentioned your style, the genre, etc etc. He was very interested. Very interested indeed. Of course he also publishes Xavier McDonald, who's one of mine too.' Dick Higgins sat forward. 'Xavier's having troubles at the moment, shocking stuff with his ex-wife and children. She wants money and he simply hasn't got it. Going to turn legal any minute. All blocking him terribly as you'd expect. We have morning chats trying to unblock him. He's a *trouper*.' He tapped his nose with his finger and sat back again. 'You see, as an agent, I'm 100 per cent involved in your life, twenty-four seven. You'll have a friend as well as an agent. Been invited to three weddings, five barmitzvahs and six christenings. All part of the job.' Dick paused.

Then the phone went and twenty-five minutes later, Jon had heard a superb example of how involved Dick Higgins would be in his life.

Dick put the phone down and looked triumphantly at Jon.

'Jeffrey Daniels,' he explained, shaking his head and smiling to himself. 'Six-figure deal, contracts ready to sign and he wants to talk golf. I ask you.' He shook his head some more and gave a fond tut to illustrate the madness of writers and the fund of stories he could tell if only he had the time.

'So,' he concluded eventually, through cigar smoke. 'I can give you till five this evening.'

'What? To finish the book?'

Dick roared with laughter. 'No, no.' He laughed again and Jon envisaged him telling this hilarious anecdote in an after-dinner speech. 'To decide.'

'Decide what?'

'Who you're gonna go with!'

Jon blinked. 'You mean –'

'This business is all about decisions, Jonathan.'

'Jon.'

'Hmm,' he murmured, stroking his chin. He ripped off a piece of paper from a pad and picked up a fountain pen. He wrote down Jonathan and Jon several times. Then he looked up and gave Jon a brief working smile. 'You see, Jonathan has more gravitas, but Jon fits better on one line of the cover.' He gave a little shrug. 'We can discuss that later.' He snapped his fingers suddenly. 'No, I need to know *now*, so I can get on the phone to the most important editor in the country *now* –' he snapped his fingers again, 'so he can get on the phone to the most important director in the country *now*.' Another finger snap. ' So he can get on the phone to the most important actor in the country now. Who do you see as Harry?'

'Henry.'

'Christopher Eccleston? Shit, he's Doctor Who. Rufus Sewell maybe? Hmm.' He went off into an elaborate daze. Jon took a breath and Dick pre-interrupted him. 'We need to get going. Publishers need to know your name. Booksellers need to know your name. Broadsheets need to know your name. You know why?'

'Why?'

'So the *readers* get to know your name.' He pointed at Jon and started a slow, clever laugh. 'You beginning to get the picture?'

'Oh yes.'

'Good man.'

'Thank you,' said Jon.

'Thank *you*,' said Dick Higgins. 'You got the talent, I got the experience, contacts, know-how. Teamwork, see?'

'I see.'

'Call me by five,' said Dick standing up and putting his hand out.

'I can tell you now if you want,' said Jon standing up and shaking the hand.

Dick paused, keeping Jon's hand gripped in his.

'Think about it.' He winked conspiratorially. 'You know what they say. Act in haste, repent at leisure.'

Jon gave him a wide smile. No repenting here mate, he thought, and left the interview.

Later that day, sitting in a casting studio in the middle of a vast, dusty, echoing room on a wooden chair, her hands on a pretend steering wheel, Sukie was having less success at the Circle of Attention than Jon.

'I want you to imagine,' the casting director told her, 'that you're looking out of the window and suddenly, you see the image of your loved one. And you smile. Inwardly.'

The woman looked at her watch.

Sukie rested her hands on her lap.

'Won't I crash?'

The casting director looked up. 'Hm?'

'Well, if I'm driving,' said Sukie, 'and I suddenly look out of the window . . .'

'Well just imagine you're at the lights then.'

'At the lights. Right.'

'Oh and it's raining.'

'Raining. Right.'

Sukie turned back from the casting director. She imagined the straight-backed wooden chair was a comfortable driving seat. She imagined the vast empty space in front of her was a car dashboard. She imagined the sun throbbing into the room was sheet rain. She imagined there was a loved one in her life who phoned her regularly just to tell her he loved her. She imagined that the six-foot tall, eight-stone-heavy models sitting in the waiting room outside wouldn't be able to smile inwardly like her. She imagined she was a successful actress at the RSC and the casting agent had bought tickets just to see her give the famous inward smile critics had been raving about. And then, to finish the picture, she imagined she wasn't wearing a Beach Barbie outfit.

Slowly, she turned to her side, imagined seeing the face of a loved one (for some reason the image of Bo Peep popped up, which meant more acting than the casting agent would ever know) and she gave an inner smile of love, warmth, reflection and contentment, hoping to God that the inner scream of despair wasn't peeking through. And she kept smiling. And then, she kept on smiling.

'Can we have it a bit more inwardly please.'

She stopped smiling.

'And now a little bit more.'

She tried to smile somewhere in the middle. She could hear birdsong in the nearby park and decided to take a stroll there after the audition. Oh, and maybe she'd do some shopping.

'Are you thinking of your loved one?' asked the casting agent.

'Yes,' smiled Sukie, inwardly.

And silence again.

'OK,' sighed the casting director, 'You can stop smiling now.'

'For good?' murmured Sukie, but the casting director didn't hear her and she left the audition, grimacing, inwardly, all the way home.

That evening they all met at Jon's flat. *EastEnders* was on telly with the sound off and Katie knew she would always remember this moment. She stood in the kitchen door-way, her hand on its frame. Sukie held on to the other side, and they squeezed hands in the middle. In the living room in front of them, Jon stood with his back to them, concentrating on the conversation he was having on the phone. They watched, unmoving.

'My only concern,' he said into the phone, 'is the percentage.'

They held their breath.

'I confess,' Jon said – and they squeezed hands tighter – 'that 15 per cent feels like an awful lot of money.'

'Right. Right. Right. Right.' Jon nodded into the

phone, treading a spot in the carpet with his left foot on every nod which made him look like a nervous chicken.

Sukie loosened her grip on Katie's hand but Katie, the optimist between them, the café manager, held fast.

'Right. I see,' said Jon. 'Obviously.'

Pause.

Sukie closed her eyes and turned into the kitchen. Katie watched Jon alone. She would not miss this. She would one day say to her grandchildren that she had witnessed the world famous novelist Jon Barrister getting his agent.

'I appreciate it. No. I understand. Thank you.'

She joined Sukie in the kitchen. They made a cup of tea and agreed that they would be positive with him. They would show him the Blitz spirit. They would not let him get downhearted. They would get him chocolate and beer.

He walked in. They looked at him. He ran his hands through his hair and over his face, as if washing under a shower.

'Well?' asked Sukie.

'I . . . I . . .'

'*Well*?' asked Katie.

'I can't believe it.'

'For Christ's sake,' shouted Sukie. 'What happened?'

'I've got an agent,' whispered Jon. 'Richard Miller. Richard Miller is my agent.'

Katie whooped and then cheered. Then she cheered and whooped. She hugged Jon and then slapped him on the face to make him join in. She resented doing it all alone. He whooped and cheered. Then she turned to Sukie, who remembered she was with people and joined in too.

'He said everyone's on fifteen per cent,' said Jon, taking some of the wine Katie had just poured, 'even Dylan Edwards.'

The girls squealed. Dylan Edwards! Would there be parties? Would they be invited? Did this mean he was now a member of Groucho's?

This continued until Jon had to go to do his shift at the bar and the girls found themselves in the kitchen drinking their wine alone.

'Shit,' said Katie shaking her head.

'Mm,' smiled Sukie.

'It's unbelievable.'

'Mm,' said Sukie.

'I mean I don't mean it's *unbelievable*, I mean . . . it's UNBELIEVABLE.'

'I know.'

'He's going to do it.'

'Mm.'

'He's bloody well going to do it.'

'Yes, I know.'

'Do you think he'll remember us when he's famous?' asked Katie.

'He'll remember me,' said Sukie.

'Cheers.'

'Because I'm going to tattoo my name on his face.'

Katie laughed.

'And then,' finished Sukie, washing up her glass, 'maybe I'll get a job.'

Katie stopped laughing. 'You know,' she said suddenly, because the thought had only just occurred to her. 'I never realised my twenties would be this hard.'

14

Two hours and two bottles of wine later, Sukie and Katie had put the world to rights. The reason their twenties felt hard, they decided, was because they had never had to fight political oppression, famine, drought, earthquake or flood, genocide or even very severe weather conditions. They would not live their lives in service, in poverty or pain; their lives would not be full of – nor foreshortened by – relentless pregnancies. Television would entertain them when they did not have the energy, time or money to entertain themselves. Medication would help them should they find themselves not in a constant state of happiness. Their twenties were hard because, they concluded, they were so damned lucky.

Sukie tutted and shook her head. 'Typical,' she said. 'Too many choices. Too many expectations. Too much . . .' she searched for the right word.

'Mm,' said Katie.

'You know what I *really* want?' asked Sukie suddenly. 'To make me *really* happy?'

'A pink duffle coat?'

'I want life to be easy.'

'Mm,' smiled Katie. 'Easy.'

'Like it is for some people.'

'Mm.'

'I mean there are some people in this world who literally have nothing to worry about.'

'Like who?'

'The Duke of Edinburgh.'

Katie frowned. 'He's got family worries, and he's not getting any younger.'

'All right. Dan Crichton.'

Katie made a sort of growling noise.

'Yes,' said Sukie. 'Life's easy for the likes of him.'

Sukie was right. Life was easy for some. Some people had no money worries, no health worries and no relationship worries. They didn't borrow trouble by fearing an uncertain future, they didn't blight the present by dwelling on the past. They didn't compare themselves with others. They didn't ponder life's conundrums nor regret its mistakes. They believed in fate and horoscopes and they thanked their lucky stars. They accepted whatever life threw at them and lived for the moment. And they stayed in a lot.

While Sukie and Katie drank themselves into a fuzzy blur, Dan Crichton drove himself to Geraldine's. He parked and walked to her door without noticing. Should he ever be in the unlucky position of having to give a statement as to how he got from the car to his girlfriend's flat, he would not be able to do it without the assistance of video evidence.

He had a key, but never used it if Geraldine was in. He pressed the buzzer and massaged his temples while he waited, realising that every facial muscle was tense. The entrance mechanism buzzed and he pushed open the heavy door and walked up the communal stairs. As usual, her front door was ajar and, to the sounds of her finishing off her toilette, he entered the haven that was her flat.

Cream sofas perched, as if only temporarily, amidst desert-like stretches of real oak floor, and in the background Vivaldi violins pranced recklessly as if the adult violins had left the room.

It was strange coming back into Geraldine's life. At times it felt like he'd never left, and at others he wondered if he'd ever feel part of it. After he'd finished their relationship, during a particularly unpleasant Gerry mood which had lasted a week and had made him feel as if a metal door had slammed in his face, he'd only been to the flat once, and that was for Sandy's engagement party. Then, when they'd started dating again, it had become the flat they spent most time in. Gerry didn't enjoy staying over at his place and he understood. Her flat was bigger, trendier and more comfortable, and it had all her cosmetics in it.

He looked over to the far corner where a Bang & Olufsen television stood. That was where he'd met Katie. He picked up the remote lying on the sofa and turned on the set.

'There's wine in the fridge!' called out Geraldine.

'Right.'

He walked into the kitchen where he poured one glass for her, knowing his ulcer wouldn't let him drink until he'd eaten.

She entered the kitchen and smiled radiantly at him.

'Hello, MD!' she greeted and gave him a big hug.

'Hello,' he said, wondering if an MD should feel better than this.

'I've booked the table,' she said, pulling away and finishing her hair. 'We either had to see the film at six or eat at seven, so I plumped for the latter option.'

'Fine.'

'I assumed you'd be hungry first and then we could see the film later.'

'Perfect.'

'Right. Let's go then.'

Switching off the television, Dan, feeling slightly lighter already, followed as Geraldine led the way.

At dinner Geraldine gave a tale of woeful budget-pinching at the large furniture store in central London where she worked as a buyer, with much dissecting of her boss Bryan, whom she admired and resented in equal measure. Dan fell asleep during the film, which in his books made it a good one. It wasn't until much later, when they were lying in Geraldine's kingsize bed, that the conversation turned reassuringly familiar.

Geraldine had spoken to her mother, who lived in Sweden with her new husband, earlier today.

'It's so funny,' Geraldine murmured into the dark, 'Mummy keeps going on about your intentions.'

He gave a lazy chuckle. 'You make me sound like some Victorian suitor.'

He knew immediately that the silence emanating from Geraldine was not a good silence. She had not fallen asleep. She was not smiling. She was sending over an Active Silence, made more active by the surrounding

212

pitch-black. It was a silence only Geraldine could do and it squeezed his heart with its usual icy hand.

'It's not like we're in our thirties is it?' he asked, pretending he hadn't noticed the icy grip.

'Hah!' laughed Geraldine, feigning delight at this answer. 'We wouldn't be together in our thirties if you hadn't made your intentions clear by then, I can tell you that for nothing.'

'Who's that talking?' asked Dan. 'You or your mother?'

'Oh that's me,' said Geraldine lightly. 'No point in wasting time if it's not going anywhere. Not this time anyway. It's not the same relationship, remember? Same people, different relationship.' She repeated her mantra, and then turned away from him on to her side, her back a barricade. She couldn't have had more of an effect if she'd whisked the mattress from under him, thrown him out of the window and left him lying on the pavement.

He thought about the months he'd spent without her. How he'd ended up on a date with someone who'd walked out halfway through. How he'd never felt so alone as that night and had actually cried before falling asleep. And how when Geraldine had phoned the next morning, completely by chance, just to say hi, he'd felt like he'd been saved from drowning.

'I suppose,' he whispered into the dark, still pretending he hadn't noticed the ice and the barricade, 'it's nice to know how it's all going to end.'

The sheets rustled and he felt Geraldine's warm body curl up into him. He buried his hand in her hair.

'Mm,' she said, sliding a leg between his and uncurling. 'It must be.'

'And this,' he murmured, as he stretched the length of his body against hers, 'must be the perfect way to end it.'

The next thing Dan remembered was his alarm going off at 6.45 a.m. sharp. He felt himself shift from unconsciousness to consciousness. He could hear the ensuite shower going. He could sense the duck-down pillows round his head. He could now tune in to the bass of Geraldine's ensuite radio. She was back. He was safe. No one could hurt him again. At the thought of Katie on that date, his body immediately went into mild panic, yet again. He forced himself to think of Geraldine. 'Listen,' he told himself. 'She's in the shower now.' And then, with that thought uppermost in his mind, he allowed himself to picture Katie now: Katie from the café; Katie who was powerless to hurt him because he had Geraldine. God he'd been stupid to think he could go back to the hell of single life. He scrunched his eyes shut and imagined Geraldine in the shower, tall and powerful. All was right with the world, he told himself. Katie could not hurt him. Life was good.

What would the builders have done by this morning, he wondered suddenly. And his eyes were open. Would they have finished the floor? And the new counter? When would that arrive? Would that artist remember to come today? And the guitarist? And the organic supplier? When his stomach started to feel as if it was eating itself, he got out of bed.

An hour later, he was at the café. The builders weren't there yet, but in fairness he could see that they were progressing quite well. As he wandered round the shell of a room checking tiny details – sockets, skirting boards and such like – he heard Katie arrive, the coffee machine being filled and the milk being steamed. It was a weirdly reassuring noise.

'Morning!' he heard a male voice.

He couldn't help a smile when he heard Katie give the man what for because he'd made her jump, and tuned out of the conversation. He truly didn't want to overhear anything. Then he heard his name. He froze.

'. . . all right,' he heard Katie say. 'Doesn't know his arse from his elbow, but that's OK because neither are on the set menu.'

'Do you think he'll ruin the café?' came a male voice.

'Nah,' said Katie. 'He'll have a steep learning curve, but he'll be fine.'

'What makes you so sure?'

''Cos he's insanely bright – and you lot haven't got the wit to find somewhere else to go.'

Dan jumped at the sound of Harry arriving behind him.

'All right boss?'

Dan gave him a broad grin back. 'Morning Harry! And isn't it a fantastic one?'

'I'm more of an evening man myself actually.'

'Excellent, excellent,' said Dan, feeling better than he had all day. He got out his notebook for today's snagging list.

Two hours later, after the last of the commuter coffees had gone on their merry way, the new menu was unveiled. As the Beachboys harmonised about the quality of their vibrations to the sound of buzzing, sawing and thumping, Katie and her new bosses, Dan and Paul, entered the future world of Crichton Brown's. Nik, the new chef, presented them with his finished menu and they read it slowly. Katie concentrated on not looking up at Dan. Dan concentrated very hard on the menu.

'Well?' beamed Nik eventually, nudging Dan, who was seated next to him, opposite Katie. 'Eh? Eh?'

'I'm not sure it's an "A",' said Paul kindly. 'But B-plus for effort.'

'Eh?' frowned Nik.

'What's "Lightly Whipped Organic Eggs Abed Softly Toasted Rye"?' Dan asked the table, his eyes resting on Katie for a moment.

'Scrambled eggs on toast,' she said. They smiled briefly at each other.

'That's all right mate,' said Nik, 'that's just what you do nowadays. It's spin, isn't it? All the rage.'

'But isn't spin about rendering the truth opaque?'

'Eh?'

'Exactly,' grinned Dan. 'Not nice is it?'

'What's not nice?' asked Nik. Katie looked down.

'I think what Dan's trying to say,' explained Paul, 'is that, like the government, we need to be transparent.'

'*Eh?*'

'People have got to be able to understand the menu,' Katie told Nik. 'So they know what to order.'

'But it's bloomin' obvious,' said Nik, picking up his again.

'How can a mushroom be elegant?' asked Paul. Dan and Katie both laughed.

'A*ha!*' cried Nik. 'I'll show you how. They don't call me Nigella for nothing.'

'What makes a chicken proud?' asked Paul.

'Crossing the road?' asked Katie and Dan in unison. Dan gave a little cough and stared hard at the menu, so Katie stopped laughing and didn't say 'jinx'.

'I just think,' began Paul slowly, 'that the style isn't quite right. As to the content . . . Dan?'

'Hmm,' Dan was concentrating. 'Not sure.'

'Why?' asked Paul. 'You think it's a bit too Hampstead?'

'No,' said Dan. 'Because I can't understand it.'

'I think I can,' said Katie.

'Well?' asked Paul. 'What do *you* think of the content?'

'I think it's as good as the style.' She stared very hard at Paul.

Dan and Paul nodded.

'Eh?' asked Nik.

'It's just not very Porter's Green,' explained Dan.

'Yes but we are up and coming, remember,' said Paul.

'Yes,' conceded Dan, 'but this is like a different language. I mean,' he looked at the menu again. 'What's a shy turnip?'

'It's a turnip that's only just been shown the oil,' cried Nik. 'What are you? Amateurs?'

'Yes,' shrugged Dan.

Nik stood up. 'Excuse me,' he said. 'I have to go to my kitchen now.' And he walked out, his dramatic exit being hampered by having to squeeze out of half a doorway and climb through builders' polythene, instead of being able to get a good slam in.

217

'I wouldn't call you amateurs,' started Katie.

'Thank y—'

'So much as complete novices.'

'Thank you.'

They sat in silence, apart from the pearly sound of Cliff Richard and the occasional thud of mug hitting floor.

'So tell us, oh expert,' Dan looked at Katie, 'what you think of this menu.'

'In its favour –'

'Yes?'

'I must say –'

'Yes?'

'It's a fantastic font.'

And Dan gave her a smile that took her straight back to Sandy's party. They both looked down quickly.

15

At the end of a fortnight, the builders, polythene doors and Capital Gold were all as a dream and The Café was no more. Long live Crichton Brown's.

The day the builders left, Katie was given the afternoon off, so Messrs Crichton and Brown could finish the final transformation on their own. The next day, the day before its official opening, they decided to keep the Café/Bar/Restaurant – for such it was now – closed, so as to give their staff a chance to acquaint themselves with the new equipment and teach Patsy the ropes. Only the coffee queue would stay open as usual. Tomorrow was to be the first day when everything was up and running. Initially, Katie had disagreed with their decision to keep the food section closed for another day. She thought it should open as soon as possible, before the customers forgot that once, a long time ago, they used to be able to buy food here. It was, after all, now into the third week of closing. However, after ten minutes with Patsy she saw the wisdom of her owners. For Patsy was an oaf. With a capital 'OH F . . .'

That morning, Katie was the first in. As she walked down the road, she glanced laconically over at the café and gave an audible cry. It looked as if The Café had been plucked out by a vast hand from the sky and replaced with a new, sparkling restaurant. It was unrecognisable. Shiny new lettering glistened across the street at her. The colour was an almost golden coffee against soft cream. The font – a smart italic – somehow conjured up a feeling of cosy finesse. She could almost see the waiters in their long white starched aprons carrying tiny espresso cups and speaking French while the clientele lounged in cushioned seats. On the window, in the same font and colour was written *Cappuccino, espresso, latte, Americano, tea and herbal teas. All-day-breakfasts, pastries, meals* and then, *All organic, soya milk, gluten-free options.* Oh well, thought Katie. Nothing diet then.

She sped up. As she approached she could see so much more of the inside from the street than pre-renovation. She hadn't realised how dirty the window must have been. She ran across the road and pushed open the door. A delicious sound of tinkling bells, like laughing fairies, announced her arrival. She stopped and stared, taking everything in.

The tables were shiny steel – very modern, very fresh – and all small squares to seat just two. There was nothing, not a saltcellar, nor sugar bowl, nor flower, on them – and yet the room didn't feel cold because the seats were big, comfy square tub sofas, each one a different vibrant colour – turquoise, purple, fuchsia or yellow – and on the walls hung vast mirrors and artwork. Here, not a single line was straight – the mirrors curved into witty shapes, the artwork swooped in elegant bends. The space was full of movement and warmth, like a smiling invitation. In the far corner, nearest the counter, was a white-gated children's section like a mini-crèche, with tiny chairs, tables and toys. On the wall in jaunty lettering were the words 'Mini CB bees' (the C for Crichton, the B for Brown) and prices of mini-meals, milk shakes and juices. There was a toy till and even a toy coffee machine. Genius. It was so good she wanted to have a baby.

She took a step in and realised she was standing on a vast mauve mat. To the left of it, small, brightly coloured steps beckoned children to their section. Where the mat finished, a honey-coloured stone floor began which led her to the counter. She rushed towards it. What a counter. She placed her hand on it, almost to prove that her eyes weren't lying. Was it marble? Was it stone? Was it tiles? It was warm to the touch, mottled and honey – almost the same as the floor except gloss. It curved round to the side of the restaurant where four vibrantly coloured bar stools nestled below it like sleeping punk flamingos. At two of the stools, on the counter, sat two glistening state-of-the-art Applemacs, one purple, one cerise.

The coffee machine now glistened in contrast, resplendent in its black and chrome stateliness. The back wall was mirrored and the shelves were glass which more than doubled the size of the place. She realised she was now staring at herself, and that she was gawping. She started to laugh, then put her hands over her mouth and turned back to the café to take another look. I'm the manager of this, she told herself, a deep throaty laugh escaping from the base of her throat. I am Manager of Crichton Brown's.

'Morning!'

She jumped and turned. When Dan saw her

expression, a grin almost split his face. He started speaking and then stopped. There was that crease again, just where she'd left it. His eyes were luminous and he looked like a little boy who'd just found Santa. She wanted to hug him. She made do with laughing out loud. He returned the complement. They stood there laughing at each other. It seemed the only thing to do. Her laughter had a life of its own and just when Katie expected it to makes its excuses and leave, it chose to stay. She let go of all her reserves and roared till it hurt. Dan returned the compliment. This Katie found very funny and her laughter, only recently ready to wend its way, found new energy and made to stay with vigour. So they stood there having hysterics at each other for a while.

'I said "*Hello*".'

Paul was staring at them, bemused.

'Hello,' she grinned.

Ten minutes later, the three of them were sitting at one of the new shiny tables.

'So Katie,' said Paul. 'What do you think?'

She gave a big sigh. 'Oh Paul,' she breathed finally. 'Dan.' She tried to find the right words. 'I think it's absolutely wonderful.'

There was silence. Paul grinned happily at her and Dan looked down. But the glimpse of a deepening colour in his cheeks gave her a sudden surge of confidence. 'And I'm honoured and excited to be your manager,' she said keenly. Dan looked up at her, his deep blue eyes focused on hers completely. She gave him a slow, wide smile. 'Thank you for trusting me,' she said softly. 'I won't let you down.'

They stared at each other until they heard a little cough from Paul. He raised his espresso cup. They raised theirs in the air and clinked Paul's.

And then Sukie arrived.

She stopped still. She stared at everything in turn, pointing and gasping and then turning back to them.

'Oh. My. God,' she breathed, open-mouthed. They all laughed. 'Oh my God,' she repeated, pointing at the artwork, and they laughed again. 'Oh my *God*, oh my *God*.' She whirled round, pointing at the counter and the mirrored back wall.

'I feel like I'm watching *Big Brother* live,' mused Katie happily. 'When do I get to vote?'

'Oh my *God*.' Sukie was pointing at the children's area.

'You did this,' Katie told the boys. 'How does it feel?'

'Oh my *God*,' they heard Sukie in the distance. She was running round, sitting on every chair in the place.

'Good,' Paul confided. 'Although most of it was Dan's idea.'

'No mate –'

'*Yes*,' interrupted Paul. 'The café-style crèche . . .' he began listing.

'Well –'

'The Internet sites –'

'Yeah, but you said to make them Apples –'

'The artwork – it's a local artist,' Paul told Katie, 'they're all for sale.'

'That was Katie's idea,' rushed Dan. 'I thought it was brilliant. And the café crèche. She suggested having a kiddies' section. I just took it one further.'

Katie was speechless.

'Oh my *God*.' Sukie again, now waving at a monitor in the top corner above the till.

'The colour scheme, the mirror at the back, the footsteps to the crèche, the interconnecting tables: everything. I'm just money. He's money and brains.' Paul gave Dan an English bear-hug – a sort of teddy-bear-hug – over the table.

'Thanks mate,' coughed Dan.

Sukie grabbed Paul and Dan from behind in a Sukie bear-hug and almost winded them.

'What can I say?' She joined them. 'I-I'm speechless.'

'Congratulations,' Katie told the boys. 'You should be very proud.'

By the time Patsy, the shiny new waitress, joined them, Katie and Sukie were already at the coffee machine; Paul and Dan with Nik, going through the new menu.

'Oh my *God*,' gasped Patsy, almost swallowing her chewing gum, stopping in her tracks.

'I know,' grinned Sukie and Katie.

Patsy gasped again, her hands clasping her face. 'Does it show?'

'What?'

'I left my make-up at home. Does it show? 'Cos I can go back home and get it.'

Within half an hour, the first commuter arrived. Katie and Sukie grinned at him from behind the counter and started preparing his takeaway coffee. Thanks to the new brightly-coloured paper cups, even this now seemed more fun. He stepped in, did a double-take and then stepped out again, pretending to check the lettering.

'Oh my *God*,' he said as he came in.

'Right that's it,' muttered Patsy, flinging down her tea-towel. 'I'm going home. I can't do a whole day without mascara.'

With a little explanation, the three of them managed to persuade Patsy that the complete renovation of the café would take most people's attention away from her naked face. She nodded vigorously, trying not to blink.

'You see, it all looks so different,' said Katie. 'Do you remember?'

Patsy shook her head. 'I can't believe it's my first day and everything.'

'Good girl,' said Katie. 'That's the spirit.'

Commuter one was joined by number two.

'Bugger me,' said commuter two.

'With or without sugar?' asked Katie, as Sukie started to make his usual.

'It's like a completely different place.'

'Yes,' smiled Katie, 'but with the same charming staff.'

'So I see,' said commuter two, eyeing up Patsy.

'This is Patsy,' said Katie. 'Today's her first day.'

'First day, eh?' grinned commuter two.

'Yes,' said Katie, 'in the community. Be gentle with her.'

'Oh,' giggled Patsy. 'You are *so* funny.' She shook her head, 'I *swear*.'

In the lull between the 7.44 and 8.14 queues, Katie decided to show Patsy how to use the coffee machine while Sukie prepared the vegetables for Nik's experiments in the kitchen.

Patsy nodded firmly at each instruction, chewing her gum with renewed concentration, watching every nozzle Katie twizzled and staring as Katie demonstrated the difference between steaming the milk for cappuccino and latte.

'Do you think you've got that?' Katie asked after every new move she made.

Patsy blinked. 'Hope so,' she said.

When the first customer came in asking for a cappuccino, Katie let Patsy make it.

Patsy leapt to the challenge. She stood in front of the machine, chewing furiously, high heels astride.

'Right,' she said firmly and chewed a bit more. 'OK.'

Katie touched the espresso handle. 'Every cup starts with espresso.'

'Oh! That's right!' said Patsy and pulled the espresso handle towards her so vigorously without twisting it that she almost brought the coffee machine down on top of her.

'Twist it,' rushed Katie, lunging forward. She turned to the customer. 'You're not waiting for a train in the next half hour, are you? Only it's Patsy's first day.'

Patsy snorted loudly into the coffee machine. She turned to the customer.

'Hi,' she grinned. 'I'm Patsy. It's my first day.' She shook the woman's hand.

Katie rolled her eyes. The customer smiled at Patsy.

'Hello Patsy,' she said kindly.

'Please, don't overdo it,' warned Katie. 'It'll give her the wrong impression. Would you like to sit down? We'll bring your coffee over to you. At this rate, with the coffee machine.'

The customer was fine with that.

'In about an hour,' said Katie, as the customer found herself a table. Patsy took both hands off the espresso handle and clasped them to her mouth, to aid the process of laughter. 'Oh!' she gasped, shaking her head. 'You are so funny!'

Katie returned to the task in hand, giving Patsy a re-run, step-by-step of the cappuccino process. She stepped in at the milk steaming stage so that no one in Porter's Green got scalded. She allowed Patsy to sprinkle the chocolate over the cappuccino and stopped her with a sharp jab in the ribs just before it started to look like a cow-pat. Then she packed her off to the customer with a parcel of serviette, sugar and teaspoon like a mother packing off her little one to nursery with a snack. She came over quite emotional.

In the kitchen with Nik, Sukie was also coming over all emotional.

'I mean – "all-day-breakfast".' He hit the menu for the third time. 'It's *so* done to death, you know what I'm saying?'

Sukie nodded. 'God yes.'

'I'm not being funny, but that Kate babe doesn't know what she's on about. Y'know what I'm saying?'

'Yes,' said Sukie. 'You're not being funny at all.'

'I'm telling you, tofu bangers and mash is *it*, mate. It's the dog's bollocks.'

'How about Tofu Dog's Bollocks?'

'That's the way forward. Not bloody all-day-bloody-long breakfasts.'

'There. That's all the potatoes done.'

'Cheers.' Nik picked up the potatoes and put them in a bowl, while Sukie noticed that his forearms were kissed with blond hairs. 'I mean what experience has she got?' continued Nik, while Sukie watched him flick his hair out of his eyes. She followed the line of his jaw. He turned to her. 'Y'know what I'm saying?'

'Mm.'

'You know what I think?' he said urgently, leaning in.

'No. What?'

'I think you understand me.'

'Mm.'

'*You* know that cooking's an art form.'

'Yes. You're right.'

'I'm an artist, me.'

'Mm. A bit like my acting.'

'And I have to be in control of my art.'

'Yeah, well, that's right.'

'Otherwise I might as well be a bloody – I dunno – *plumber* for all I care.'

'Would you like me to have a word with Katie?'

He stared at her. 'Would you?'

She blushed. 'Course mate.' She found herself going Estuary. 'We're mates.'

'You're a star,' he said and gave her a hug. To her joy, she felt a pulsing down below, but it turned out to be Nik's mobile phone vibrating. 'Bollocks,' he said, and took the call.

By the time Katie and Patsy had joined them – the new video camera with its monitor in the kitchen making that possible when the café was empty – he was still on the phone. They all stood staring up at the new monitor in the top corner of the kitchen. They could see Dan and Paul having a meeting with their organic fruit and veg supplier in the café, and the monitor was so state-of-the-art the staff could almost lip-read the conversation. They started playing with the remote. Now they could see behind the counter. Now they could see front of house again. Now they could see the till. Now they could see the panic button with direct access to the police station.

Nik rejoined them and asked which lucky bird was going to fetch his peppers and courgettes from the store cupboard for him. Patsy jumped down from the counter and pulled her ponytail. 'I'll go.'

He winked at her. 'Beautiful.'

Five minutes later, she came back.

'Where's the store cupboard?'

Katie explained while Sukie demonstrated where the bunch of keys were kept and which key was the right one. Patsy chewed vigorously. She turned to Nik.

'I'm having a stressful day,' she explained. 'Left my make-up bag at home.'

'You don't need make-up, beautiful.'

Patsy gave him a smile.

'I don't think you understand,' Katie told him. 'It had grey cells she needed in it.'

Patsy collapsed with laughter. 'You are *so* funny!'

While she went to find the store cupboard, Sukie gave Nik a guided tour of the fridge photographic gallery that was Katie's love life. Thankfully, he barely batted an eyelid at the photo of Dan and Katie deep in chat.

Patsy appeared. 'They didn't fit the lock.'

'Top lock?' checked Katie.

'I thought you said bottom lock.'

'No. I said top lock.'

Patsy looked at Katie and Katie looked back at her. Eventually, Patsy turned and went back down again.

'So,' said Nik, 'you snogged the boss, eh?'

Ah, so he had noticed.

'Yes, but that was before he was in the business.'

'Is that what got you the job?' asked Nik.

Katie let out a splutter of shock.

'Hardly!' she said. 'We had a disastrous date and weren't even talking when he bought this place. If he'd known it was me, he'd never have hired me.'

Patsy appeared. 'Top lock doesn't work.'

'You have got the right door, haven't you?' checked Katie.

'Yes, the black one.'

'The blue one.'

'You said the black one.'

'I said the blue one.'

Patsy tutted and went back down.

'I got the job because I'm good at it,' Katie turned back to Nik, 'and have years of experience. Like you.'

'That right?' asked Nik.

'Yes.'

Patsy appeared. 'Top lock, blue door. This key does not work.' She held it up to illustrate her point.

'That's because,' said Katie approaching, 'it's the wrong key. I told you it was the Yale one.'

'I thought you said yellow one.'

'Yale one.' Katie smiled. 'Try again.'

Patsy went back down.

'And just like you,' she turned back to Nik, 'I want this place to be as good as it can be. Nothing more, nothing less.'

Patsy came back carrying a bag of vegetables and plonked it on the counter. Sukie and Katie clapped.

'There,' she said huffily. 'Courgettes.'

'And peppers.'

Patsy almost started to cry. 'He said courgettes!'

'And peppers!' said Katie. 'Courgettes and peppers!'

Patsy sighed wearily and pouted her lips.

'Wouldn't it just be better if *you* went?' she asked.

'Not for me, no,' smiled Katie.

Patsy stared at the floor for a while. When Katie and Sukie turned back to Nik, she wandered back down to the store cupboard.

'Don't forget the bag!' called out Sukie. Patsy clomped back into the kitchen, picked up the bag and clomped out again, muttering something about taking the piss.

'There's no need to take it out on the girl,' Nik told Katie, after Patsy had gone.

'I do not have anything to take out on anyone,' said Katie.

Patsy appeared. 'There are your frigging peppers,' she said tearfully, throwing them on the counter. 'I'm having a break.'

By the end of their shift, Katie and Sukie were exhausted. When they had first seen Patsy they'd resented her because they didn't need any extra help. Now they resented her because, thanks to her, they needed all the help they could get. Their job had become the stuff of nightmares. Patsy had to sit down every half hour due to

231

her aching feet and she made more mess than the customers. She burnt the toast, took so long to make a cup of tea that customers waiting to be served left quietly, and she followed Katie and Sukie round like a kid sister on a shopping trip. The men didn't seem to notice any of this, which made Katie and Sukie feel like her two ugly sisters. It took them till noon to realise it was a waste of time to moan about Patsy's global incompetence to anyone with testosterone. Thank God they had each other.

The next day was the Grand Opening which meant a free glass of wine with every order, delicious canapés, new outfits for the staff (neat little skirts and tops in black, turquoise, purple, fuchsia or yellow with little white starched aprons), visits from local press and MP, Geraldine taking a day as holiday to be in the photographs, and David Gray on a loop, which, by the end of the day, was exactly where the staff wanted to hang him. Dan wore a beautiful linen cream suit with tan shoes, a tan tie and a green face. Paul had been unable to make it as something bad had happened in the office – 'A footsie player has collapsed which has upset a market in the city', Patsy had explained – and from then on Dan's cool had vanished. He seemed unable to process the most simple of thoughts and incapable of hiding the most base of them. He rushed around making sure everyone was happy out front chatting to customers, laughing with the MP and smiling for the photographer. Then he rushed into the kitchen, shut the door and leant against a counter, massaging his temples. Katie handed him a glass of water and some headache pills. She didn't even look at him, but just said, 'Take them,' and went back. She had no idea if he did or not. When he came out front, she saw Geraldine approach him and felt wrong-footed. Had she acted like a girlfriend in helping him before he'd asked for it? She watched Geraldine take out a tissue from her bag and, with her back to everyone, so shielding Dan, wipe his brow and upper lip. Yes, thought Katie, she had. She kept watching and saw that as the couple turned back round to the public, Geraldine's face was locked in grim disapproval and Dan's brow, neatly wiped, was now creased in – what was it? Katie's heart clutched. It was shame. She saw Geraldine say something to him under her breath, hand him the tissue and then turn sharply away from him towards her public. Katie looked away quickly, knowing the expression on her face would give her away.

When the local press turned up, Dan was charm personified. Katie watched as he worked the reporter and buzzed around confidently and expertly. In seeing him with Geraldine, she felt as if she'd glimpsed a secret she shouldn't have and she watched his public persona guiltily. She suddenly felt exhausted – maybe her adrenaline had stopped pumping – and went into the kitchen to see if Nik needed any help. He was busy creating another tray of canapés, while two more trays cooked in the oven. Suddenly Dan burst in.

'*Chips!*' he shouted.

Nik and Katie jumped round and stared at him.

'CHIPS!' he repeated louder, sensing that the message had not hit home.

'WHERE?' shouted Katie.

Dan tutted angrily. 'The *Gazette* guy wants chips!' he clarified. '*Five stars* if we give him chips.'

'I'm not gonna be bribed –' spluttered Nik.

'Thick and gooey!' shouted Dan wildly. 'Like his dead mum used to make! She died when he was ten!'

Nik and Katie stared at Dan and he stared back at them.

'Right,' said Katie. 'We need oil. It's in the store cupboard. Come on Dan, it takes two to carry it.'

She picked up the keys and led him downstairs. The store cupboard was a long, dark, cold and very narrow room with shelves on either side stacked with raw vegetables, layers of raw eggs and enormous tins of tomatoes and tuna. In the far left corner was a fridge and freezer, leaving just enough room for one person to open it, and on the right, almost halfway in, a vast can of frying oil. The light-bulb needed changing, so Katie had to keep the heavy door open with one foot while they tried to look in the dark without treading on each other. Dan was in front of her, and stretching her body in front of him, she pointed the oil out to him. Unused to the room, he couldn't see it. She took a step forward, squeezing in between him and a large sack of potatoes to point it out more clearly. She almost stumbled and he had to hold her so she didn't fall back on top of the potatoes. As soon as she realised she'd made the mistake, she gasped in shock and horror. Dan turned to her and was about to ask her what was wrong when the heavy door behind them swung violently shut, leaving them in pitch-black darkness. She let out a cry of fear and instinctively clasped Dan by the arms. The last thing she saw before there was complete darkness was him being pulled towards her, looking concerned.

She froze. There was silence. Pure and utter silence. She felt wretched at what she'd just done, but more than that, she felt terrified of the darkness, which seemed to thicken with every second. She could hear Dan's breath quicken. Was he angry with her? Would the darkness fade? Would it help if she shut her eyes? She tried. When she opened them again, a dart of panic shot through her body at the complete darkness.

'I'm sorry,' she whispered, gripping Dan closer. 'I forgot –'

'It's OK,' he whispered back, soft as a caress. She closed her eyes again and muffled herself into his body. That way she could pretend the darkness was him.

'It-it,' she whispered. 'It really is dark, isn't it?' She tried to laugh, but it came out more like a whimper.

'Did you bring the key with you?' he whispered.

'Yes,' she managed, her voice beginning to rise and tremble.

'Good,' he soothed.

'I'm a bit scared of the dark,' she confessed.

To her surprise, he then gave her a full-body hug and told her in a warm voice that everything would be all right. She became instantly exhausted and gave in, relaxing her body and allowing herself to be held up by him. She pressed her face against his chest so he didn't hear any stray whimpers.

'Right,' he whispered. 'Where's the key?'

'It's in the door.' Her voice was high.

'Good.'

There was a pause. 'The other side of the door.'

There was silence again. Neither of them moved.

Then suddenly Dan let go of her.

'Oh my God,' he said. 'The chips.'

'Don't worry,' she whispered, eyes still firmly shut, hands grappling in the dark for a shelf to hold on to. 'The chips will get made. Don't panic.'

'OK,' he said. 'OK. I won't panic about the chips if you don't panic about the dark.'

'Oh God,' she wobbled. He hugged her to him again.

'Right,' said Dan. 'Where were we? Now. We're two intelligent people. How do we get out of here?'

'Um,' murmured Katie, focusing all her attention on not thinking of the dark. 'Um. I-I can't really think at the moment.'

'No, me neither.' She could hear his smile. 'Let's just stay in here forever.' Katie forgot about the dark as a firework went off in her body.

There was a long pause while she wondered what on earth to say. She heard Dan give a long, melancholic sigh. 'That way,' he said sadly, 'I've got the perfect excuse when the café doesn't work.'

'Don't say that,' she said, squeezing his body tighter, keeping her eyes shut. 'It's going to be a massive hit. And more than that, it's going to be fun making it a hit.'

'You think?' He sounded suddenly vulnerable.

'I'll eat my hat if I'm wrong,' she told him.

'Thanks,' he said. 'That means a lot.'

'It's made of chocolate,' she whispered. 'With toffee swirls on top.'

He laughed a deep throaty laugh which travelled all along her collar bone to her shoulder and down her

236

spine. It lingered around her pelvis and then drifted downwards to her thighs. If there hadn't been a sack of potatoes at her feet, she'd have been on the floor by now. His laugh died a slow death and was followed by a silence that was even longer than all the other silences. It just kept on going.

It was the kind of silence that made a girl examine a situation and ask herself some rather stern questions. Such as, where exactly were all the components of her boss's body, for example? Which begged the next question; where exactly were all the components of her body? This automatically led on to another tough question to answer: how would her boss's girlfriend – and her friend, for they were one and the same – feel were she to come in and see this, minutes before a perfectly reasonable explanation were given? (Not that she could, of course, because the door had very firmly slammed shut.)

But it was a question that should be answered. She could feel both Dan's arms firmly round her body and the palms of both hands stretched round her frame. No, no, that would not do at all. It would look highly inappropriate. Not only that, but the length of one of his thighs was nudging the outside of one of hers while the other acted like a tripod between her legs. Nope. When all was said and done, this would probably look very suspect. Thank goodness the door had slammed shut. (But there was a key on the other side, which meant it could open any second.)

She jumped away suddenly. 'And,' she added with forced jollity, 'of course, now that we've got Patsy, there's no stopping us.'

She opened her eyes. Yes, the darkness was fading. And the room seemed bigger than she remembered.

There was a little pause and then Dan laughed some more, stepping away from her too.

'I'm joking of course,' she said kindly. 'About the hat.'

'Of course,' he said.

'I have every faith in you.'

He didn't answer.

'So,' she ventured, suddenly desperate for something to say. 'I take it this was the new business you worked so hard in the city to be able to buy?'

She cringed in the dark. This was the first admission that they'd confided in each other before and, if she remembered rightly, just before a rather intense kiss.

'Yeah. That's right.'

He obviously didn't want to go there. Fine. Stay with the hat jokes. Then he surprised her by saying, 'I thought you were an educational psychologist.'

'A what?'

'You said you were an educational psychologist.'

'Did I?'

'Yeah.'

She laughed. 'Oh no! I thought I wanted to be one then. I tend to get carried away when I think I've found the dream job.'

'Ah.'

'I can't decide what I want to be.'

'Ah.'

'So I'm just waiting tables till I decide.'

'Ah.'

'Oh God! You must have thought I'd lied.'

'Something like that,' he admitted.

'No. That weekend I really thought I was going to be an educational psychologist.'

'I see.'

There was a pause. She suddenly felt ashamed of her job, as if she was reading his mind.

'Why are you –' he began,

'I don't want to make a mistake,' she blurted.

'Pardon?'

She gave a big sigh. 'I've got friends who work ridiculous hours in their chosen profession photocopying or making the tea,' she heard herself garble, 'and it's like watching the life blood drain out of them. They absolutely hate it, but already, in their early twenties, they can't get out of it because they're too busy or tired to look for a new job and it would make them look fickle if they changed their minds. I've watched them get worn down by it all and I just don't want to get into that. This way I get to do easy hours while working out what I want to do. Well, they used to be easy hours. But I don't mind now because I'm getting experience, because I always wanted to be a restaurateur –'

She was interrupted by the sounds of a submarine going off.

'Oh we're saved!' Dan cried. 'My mobile!'

She made happy sounds and heard a lot of sudden movement followed by the sound of a mobile phone crashing to the concrete floor.

'Damn!' cried Dan. 'I've missed the call.'

'It's OK,' said Katie. 'You can make a call out.'

'I would,' said Dan. 'Except now I can't find it.'

Katie gasped. Of course! Why hadn't she thought of this before? She squeezed past him and opened the fridge and freezer to give them a bit of light. After a few minutes he found the phone in-between the carrots and potatoes. Dan phoned the café. No answer. He turned to Katie, as they stood in the fridge light.

'No bloody answer.'

'Well they're busy. It's a big day.'

He shook his head. 'Bloody hell,' he muttered at the phone. 'Answer!'

He smiled sheepishly at Katie and she smiled back.

'Ah! At last. Patsy! It's Dan. I'm in the store cupboard. Can you come and get us? . . . Because I'm in the store cupboard . . . The door slammed shut . . . The door to the store cupboard . . . No, I'm *in* the cupboard. Oh, for f— Come downstairs and open the store cupboard. *Now!*'

Every second that Patsy took to find them felt more amusing than the last. Eventually they heard her outside.

'Patsy!' shouted Dan.

There was a pause.

'*Patsy!*'

'Who – who's there?' came Patsy's voice from outside.

'We're in the store cupboard.'

Another pause.

'Why?'

Katie giggled. '*Because it's where the oil is,*' she yelled.

'Oh hello, Katie!'

'Hello Patsy!'

'Why are you in there?'

'Because it's where the oil is,' she repeated.

'Oh,' said Patsy. 'Right.'

'*Patsy, listen to me*,' shouted Dan.

'Hello Dan.'

'*Hello! Listen to me.*'

'Right.'

'*Are you listening?*'

'Yes.'

'*Right. Open the fucking door.*'

'Oh, OK. There's no need to shout.'

It took Patsy two full minutes to manage the key the right way and by the time she opened the store cupboard they were weak with laughter.

'Hi guys!' she squealed.

'Hi Patsy,' grinned Dan, allowing Katie out ahead of him. Patsy followed them upstairs with a sage running commentary. 'We wondered where you were! And you were in here all the time! We had absolutely no idea! That is *so* funny! That is the funniest thing I've ever heard. That is *literally* hilarious. Why were you in there?'

Dan and Katie stopped on the stairs.

After they'd gone back down and got the oil, there were thick and gooey chips just like the *Gazette* reporter's dead mother used to make. That Thursday, Crichton Brown's got five stars in the local paper, and the photo of all the staff smiling by the coffee maker was put up in the kitchen. If the local paper had used colour photos and expensive printing techniques, people might have noticed that two of the staff had an extra inner glow. But the paper didn't, so no one did. And anyway, that was not of prime importance. What was important was that Crichton Brown's was officially on the map.

16

The next fortnight saw everyone adapt, in their own time and in their own way, to the new status quo. Patsy was still being shown the ropes and, after much thought-provoking discussion, Katie and Sukie had finally agreed on a nickname for her. She was, they decided, the teletubby that everyone forgot because she'd got lost in the shopping mall on the way to the television studio. She was called Ditzy and on her head she had a fluffy question mark with sparkly bows on. This kept them happy for a day or two. Nik, however, now called Patsy 'Beautiful' all the time. Katie and Sukie, in response to this, agreed that should the two ever have children together, there might actually be a reversal of evolution and they would be the first humans to ever give birth to a live ape. This kept them happy for a week or so. They were friends again, although Katie felt constantly mindful of how quickly Sukie could turn.

They soon realised that Paul was not going to be anything more than a financial patron and figurehead. Unlike Dan, he had not resigned from his job in the city and had only taken a month-long sabbatical to get the new restaurant off the ground. From now on, his only involvement was being on the other end of Dan's mobile phone. Dan was on his own and coped by being as hands-on as he could be without physically cutting up the customers' food and feeding them – and Katie coped with his constant presence by pretending they'd met at a party and become friends. This was actually easier than it sounded because, since their store cupboard experience, it felt as if they'd started again and really were friends.

Geraldine popped in occasionally and Katie and Sukie analysed every physical movement she made with Dan like tabloid editors at a premiere, only with less compassion. As far as they were concerned Geraldine had more hidden issues than hidden cellulite and they gave the relationship a month, tops. This kept Katie happy.

Nik was doing well in the kitchen. His food was truly delicious; the man could make a meal out of mould. This kept everyone happy, until he stopped being on his best behaviour and showed his true colours. He had a habit of losing his temper, shouting a lot and then collapsing in an exhausted, artistic heap, from which he could only stir with the help of female coaxing. Patsy called this his male ego and found it part of his charm. Sukie called it acting like a child and found it strangely erotic. Katie called it acting like a prime tosser and told him to be more like a woman. However, deep down, she knew that the reason she was so intolerant of this flaw was because she fought the very same tempestuous flaw in herself on an almost daily basis. She understood him and therefore, unlike the others, was not in awe of him and knew exactly what would get him out of it most easily.

He found an uneasy respect for her, she liked him for this and the two gradually formed a grudging alliance.

Unlike all the others, Matt did not like change. Like most teenagers he talked rebellion but acted like an old reactionary. For the first week he moaned about everything. By the second week he had forgotten how it used to be and was fine. One thing he definitely preferred was the change in clientele.

The day now looked like this: the usual commuters still came in every day, but were now much more eager to take a biscotti with their daily fix or even a homemade crostini that Nik had rustled up first thing – hot bacon and Emmental or melted cheddar and roasted peppers. Thanks to a brainstorming between Katie and Dan one morning, trying to get inside the heads of their customers, they decided that the key thing about commuters was that although they moaned about it, they actually thrived on routine. Katie should know – she needed her visit to the greengrocer's and newsagent's before work, just as they needed their coffee. So they sat Nik down and asked him to devise some portable, easy-to-eat mini-breakfasts to go with their coffee. And faster than you could say 'One Skinny Latte to go' the plan had worked. Once those commuters had taken the first leap of faith by giving Katie a £2-coin for a morning snack and coffee instead of a £1-coin for just coffee, that was it. They were hooked into a new routine. They began to crave their crostinis as much as their Americano almost as soon as they woke. Nik started making individual ones for individual regulars and within days, complaints were heard if he hadn't made them their favourite – a favourite they hadn't even known existed before.

After the commuters faded away, the mums came in for elevenses, beside themselves with an almost hysterical joy that their toddlers didn't mind making new friends while their mums actually spent time doing exactly what they wanted to do, instead of the other way round. Patsy proved to be very much at home in the mini-crèche and a firm favourite with all the littl'uns. Some would even cry if she couldn't play with them, which suited everyone, because Sukie and Katie were often close to tears for the same reason.

To everyone's surprise, a whole new range of customers loved sitting at the counter, thanks to Dan's inspired idea of providing internet access on the two computers – at a cheaper rate than at the run-down internet café down the road. People would lose themselves in the internet world while downing three lattes and a brioche.

The lunch-time clientele was almost completely new. Trendy home-workers came out of the woodwork like ants to take their lunch at Crichton Brown's, and then stayed on with their laptops to finish their afternoon's work surrounded by gentle background music and staff who let them stay as long as they liked. Writers, actors and theatrical agents were beginning to lunch in here – and the old regulars still came: all the staff from the local job centre, banks and offices traipsed in during the hour around nine a.m., with lists of orders for coffee and snacks, and then for another hour around four p.m. when the afternoon sag took hold and they needed a fix to see them through the rest of the day or just wanted to get some fresh air.

One clientele addition in particular had caused a change in Matt's life that he liked very much. For he had fallen in love.

She had started coming in for lunch regularly and, boy, was she a sight for bored eyes. She must have been about his age – maybe a bit older – and she put the A-gang girls his mates now hung around with to shame. Her hair was like spun silk (not that he'd ever seen spun silk, but it was exactly what he imagined it would look like), her complexion soft as morning dew (he'd never seen dew, in the morning or not, but it was exactly what he imagined it looked like), and her bare midriff was like that of a children's TV presenter, maybe even an American one (and he'd seen plenty of those).

She was a glossy fox in a world of battered mongrels and, more importantly, she was now here every day – so regularly in fact that Matt's body had started to react on the dot of one o'clock. She came in at ten past one every day with a friend and had lunch till ten to two. Matt surmised that she had a local summer job and this was her lunch-hour. He also surmised that it wasn't a fun summer job. The biggest give-away was the friend she brought in with her. Instead of being the obligatory carbon copy, she couldn't have been more different if the two of them had decided to make some sort of wacky social statement. Her hair, unlike that of the glossy fox, was like wire wool from a black sheep. Her complexion was nondescript and her midriff was well hidden, which could only mean that she must be hideously scarred or something. All this told Matt, the expert on the social habits of teenage girls, that both of them had very little choice when it came to lunch companions in the temporary environment in which they now found themselves. Neither would have chosen the other – the glossy fox because the wiry sheep ruined her image and the wiry sheep because the glossy fox made her invisible to the male human eye.

For the first half of the first week, he was content to eye his new obsession from the safety of the hatch in the kitchen, but by the Thursday he was growing impatient. A week was a long time in teenage love. What if her holiday job was only for a fortnight? He started to find excuses to come out and collect dishes from the tables, chat to Katie and Sukie, and generally loiter. To his amazement, he often found, when his eyes sought out the girl, that her eyes were fixed on him – and not shiftily either: confidently, squarely, like a real woman. Each day he ventured further forward into the café and each day he got further proof that it was not his imagination – this girl knew he existed: on the Friday of the first week they cast a glance at each other at the same time; Monday of the second week, it was most definitely more than a glance, it was a look; Tuesday, she was smiling at the same time as looking at him; on Wednesday, it was a look and a very definite smile of recognition, and on Thursday, a lingering smile. And Friday, oh sweet Friday, it was the same smile and look, again and again, only these looks lingered into an immense ocean of time – probably about five whole seconds – and all the while she was wearing the skimpiest top he'd ever seen. It was practically a bikini. It had taken every ounce of his self-composure not to send the crockery flying.

After lunch on the second Friday, while he was finishing

247

off the cutlery wash, exhausted from an entire forty minutes of long looks lingering into immense oceans of time, he was, naturally, feeling a bit down. What if she wasn't going to come in next week? What if the bikini top and long looks had been a coded message – come and get it now or not at all? And he, like the great pillock he was, had completely failed to respond. That was it. The greatest opportunity of his life – let's face it, the only opportunity of his life – and he'd let her walk out, unapproached and unmolested.

Something must be done. If only she'd come in again next week.

Meanwhile things were changing elsewhere too. Back at home, Jon had signed on with Richard Miller and had finished his book. His dream had come true. Then he was auctioned and asked by Miller to come up with a synopsis for book number two and some ideas for future works. His dream was over. To his surprise he discovered that he had never thought beyond being published and guesting on *Parky*. Now he had to think of another idea and turn it into another completely new book. It dawned on him that it had taken him twenty years to come up with the first one and he'd put all his best lines and profundities in that. He coped with this by drinking and being morose.

Sukie had more auditions and was being asked to more and more final auditions. Perhaps Greta had been right after all. She was now adopting the persona before entering the audition and was initially astounded at the difference it made to how the panel responded to her. It was like dying your hair blonde and visiting a male prison.

Everyone gave her the benefit of the doubt. Greta was right. The audition was just another extension of the job – it had suddenly clicked. She could tell a prime job was going to land in her lap any time soon.

Katie was feeling more positive too. She loved her job. She didn't mind that working with Nik was like working with a temperamental bear with a sore head. Every morning she told herself that today she would prevent one of his mood swings by gentle sensitivity. Every day she failed. And every day it didn't matter because his food was a dream. She didn't mind that Patsy was driving her into an early grave. Every morning she told herself she would not lose her temper with Patsy. Every day she did. And every day it made no difference because Patsy didn't notice, remember, or care. Katie didn't even mind that sometimes Sukie gave her a look which made her feel more management than friend. (Yes she did, but she'd have to cope. Life was like that. That's what growing up was all about.) She didn't mind that sometimes her job felt like a glorified waitress, sometimes like a mother hen and sometimes like a slave, rather than a manager. (Well, yes she did, but she could see that Dan had no time or energy to deal with that right now. It was something she'd bring up at an assessment. Meanwhile, she'd enjoy it when it felt exactly like a manager, which did happen every now and then.) She didn't mind that sometimes when Dan was at his most frazzled, he lost his temper with her because he knew he could. She didn't mind that he hadn't finished with Geraldine yet. (Yes she did, but she knew it wouldn't last.) She didn't mind that she didn't have a boyfriend to prove she was over him. (Yes she did, but what could she do?)

She didn't mind that she had to get up an hour earlier and leave work an hour later. She didn't mind that she was so knackered at the end of the day she could barely flick over from one soap to another. She didn't mind that she hadn't visited her parents in a while because she wanted to supervise the weekend shifts. She didn't mind any of it because on her CV it said Manager of Crichton Brown's and that was something to be proud of.

Slowly, after a month on choppy waters, she began to feel on terra firma again. It was a May morning and the air felt lighter than it had done for months as she walked down Asherman's Hill. She could feel summer beckon: cool dresses, flip-flops, birds, the sun on her skin, pink-skyed evenings, open windows, barbecues, strawberries, shimmery lipgloss and espadrilles. Katie's heart seemed to expand with anticipation. She popped into the grocer's to pick up a banana (healthy option), and then the newsagent's for a chocolate bar (happy option). And then she entered Crichton Brown's. She called out to Nik, who was always first in. No answer. She wandered into the kitchen. No one there. She frowned. That was odd. He was usually chopping vegetables and ranting by now. Hmm, she thought. She put down her bag, then realised she didn't know Nik's phone number. She picked up the pen she'd fixed to the wall by the pad of paper under the phone. *Make contact list* she wrote. She'd collect everyone's phone number today and put them up on the fridge and in her mobile phone. She reprimanded herself for not having done it sooner, but for now, she'd just have to get cooking until he got in.

Nik had still not arrived by the time Sukie came. Katie

was starting to feel edgy and decidedly understaffed. Matt wasn't in all day because of a coursework deadline. As she cooked, Sukie started making the commuter coffees and was as fast a draw as the best of them, but Katie could see the queue lengthening. There were just too many for her. However, she decided it was worth the risk of making them wait a few minutes longer, rather than tell them their new breakfast fix was off today.

'What are you doing in there?' shouted one of her regulars, as she brought the results of her efforts from the kitchen.

'Highland fling,' she shouted back. 'What does it look like?'

He smiled and looked at Sukie. 'Always a pleasure.'

By the time Dan arrived, Katie was feeling concerned. Tetchy even. Where was Nik? What if he never came back? What was his contract? How were they going to cope today?

'Hello, where's Nik?' asked Dan.

'How should I know?' she answered. 'You're the boss. I don't even know his phone number.'

Dan assessed the situation quickly using his newly honed powers of management know-how.

'You're angry,' he said, taking off his jacket. 'We'll put Patsy with Sukie on coffee duty this morning.'

Katie snorted.

'You're right,' he said. 'I'll go on coffee duty with Sukie.'

'I didn't know you could make coffee.'

'I can't,' he said, putting an apron on, 'but at least I don't do it in heels, chewing gum.'

Left alone Katie raised an eyebrow. So he *had* noticed Patsy was less than a pretty face.

Dan reappeared.

'That was management speak,' he said. 'You tell anyone I said that and . . .'

'I won't.'

'Good. Thanks.'

Blimey, thought Katie, realising that meant she couldn't tell Sukie. This management business was tough.

Nik phoned at nine. He had food poisoning and had been sick all night. He gave such lurid details over the phone and complained so bitterly about how the café would go to rack and ruin without him that Katie believed him. She went to tell Dan, who was making someone an espresso and sandwich. His little white starched apron suited him. She waited till he'd finished, then guided him back into the kitchen, so as not to let the customers know that their chef had food poisoning.

'You're kidding,' he said, ashen faced.

'I'm not.'

'Bollocks.'

'Yes.'

He tried some lateral thinking.

'Bollocks,' he concluded.

'Yes,' said Katie. There was no faulting him.

'So,' she said. 'What's Plan B?'

He stared at her. 'I don't have a Plan B. I hadn't worked out Plan A yet.'

'Look,' she said, 'just tell the customers there's a limited menu and I'll carry on cooking.'

'I've got a lasagne I can make,' he said.

'And I've got a chicken breast,' she said.

'Oh I wouldn't say that.'

'Very funny.'

'No, let's keep it simple.' He started rolling up his sleeves. 'I'll do my lasagne. We need you out front.'

"Really, I could go and buy a few more chicken breasts and do a quick –'

'Katie.'

She looked at him. He gave her a look that said *I'm the Boss* and she gave him one that she hoped said *You're A Twat, That's What You Are* and went out front to help a frenzied Sukie.

Twenty minutes later, Dan appeared by her side.

'Hello Boss!' she cried. 'Everyone's asking for lasagne.'

'Are they?' asked Dan.

'No.'

Dan sighed. 'Very funny. Can you come out back please?'

They stood in the kitchen, mirroring each other with hands on hips.

'The oven's broken,' announced Dan.

Katie looked at it.

'No it's not,' she said.

'*Blimey!*' spluttered Dan. 'Can you tell just by *looking* at it? The girl's a *genius*.'

'Yes,' said Katie. 'Because the light's on.' She turned to go.

'So why isn't it cooking my lasagne?' asked Dan, opening the oven door.

Katie crossed her arms. 'How often have you opened the door and looked at it?'

Dan shrugged. 'Dunno,' he said. 'Every so often.'

'Well, what do you expect?' Katie tutted. 'It's like taking the kettle off the hob to see if it's boiled.' Dan stared at the oven. 'Leave it alone and do something else,' said Katie. 'And put some oil on for chips.'

'Chips?'

'Yes, then you can do something simple like egg and chips. Some people might even order just chips to take their mind off the fact that there isn't actually a main dish yet,' she looked at her watch, 'at noon.'

Dan thought about this.

'Or,' suggested Katie, 'you could stuff a pepper with some of the roasted veg from the fridge plus some rice – or make a tart with the veg and cheese. We've got peppers and pastry cases in the store cupboard. Then in half an hour there'll be a choice of three lunches.'

Dan looked at her for a while, then looked back at the oven.

'I'm not sure,' he said. 'My lasagne'll be ready in a minute. Don't want to overdo it.' He opened the oven door again.

'Don't keep opening it!' cried Katie. 'And it's summer – people don't want lasagne in summer. Any idiot knows that.'

Dan slammed shut the oven door. She couldn't tell if his face was flushed by the heat or what she'd just said to him.

'Well that's what they're getting,' said Dan firmly.

'Not if you keep opening the bloody door they're not,' she replied, just as firmly.

'Is there salad outside?'

'Yes. And sandwiches as usual.'

'Right.' Dan was pacing. 'And later there'll be lasagne.'

'Excellent,' said Katie. 'Just in time for supper.'

They dared each other across the worktop with their eyes. Dan chewed his lip thoughtfully.

Katie counted to ten.

'You know,' she whispered, 'it takes a very big man to admit he's wrong.'

'Jesus Christ,' cried Dan, running his hands through his hair. 'It's like working with a bloody mind-reader.' Katie smiled and then stopped. 'Get me twenty pastry tins and all the peppers we've got,' she said. 'Plus ricotta cheese and eggs. And don't forget the oil.'

'At least say please,' muttered Dan as he left.

She laughed and as he went further away, she was able to hear the sound of her own happiness. She stopped suddenly. She stared at the counter. She'd heard that laugh before. Oh dear. She was in trouble. What to do, what to do, what to do. She looked up at the monitor and saw Hugh enter the café. Thank you, she thought, and went out to be rescued.

When she reached him, Sukie had already asked him if he wanted a coffee and he was mumbling something about needing Katie.

'Hi Hugh!'

He turned to her and she was quite taken aback. He looked terrible.

'Hi,' he managed.

'You look like you need a coffee.'

'Have you got time for a little chat?' He was even speaking differently. Quieter and lower.

'I'm really busy, Hugh,' she said gently. When she saw

255

his eyes well up, she instinctively touched his arm. 'A quick chat,' she said. 'Take a seat. I'll just check everything's OK in the kitchen. Don't go away.'

After she'd got Dan started on simple preparations in the kitchen, she popped back out to Hugh. Maybe this was good timing; it would show Dan how important she was.

She sat down and gave Hugh her full attention, safe in the knowledge that she had delegated wisely in the kitchen and they could cope without her the next five or ten minutes.

'Everything all right?' she asked.

To her horror Hugh started crying. She'd never seen him cry before and it didn't take a genius to work out that he didn't do it often. In fact he seemed not to know how to. He was making a squeaking noise and almost sneezing out his tears. She would have found it funny had she not found it so disturbing, and she put her arm round him. To her further horror, he turned to her and gave her a hug so fierce she could hardly breathe. She looked at Dan over his shoulder. He had started doing a little dance purely for her benefit, and after a moment, she worked out that he was in fact trying to semaphore to her, using his entire body, that he'd got a bit stuck and would be most appreciative if she could help. She tried to semaphore back to him, using only her eyebrows that she would be one moment and if the worst came to the worst, there was always his frigging lasagne.

Hugh unclasped her.

'Sorry,' he mumbled.

'Don't be daft.'

'I just don't know what to do.'

'What's happened?'

He started squeaking and sneezing tears again. She could still see Dan and started feeling desperate.

'Hugh,' she said calmly. 'I'm going to be two minutes.'

He nodded through his squeaks.

'Don't go anywhere,' she said urgently. 'I'll be back in two minutes. Here,' she handed him a serviette, 'blow your nose.'

She rushed into the kitchen where Dan was now standing by the oven and he spun round when he heard her. She knew the signs.

'Have you opened the oven again?' she demanded.

'No.'

'Oh for pity's sake,' she muttered. 'I'm going to have to leave you for just a few minutes, but here's what you do. Cut the top off the peppers and seed them. Peel the veg and put the rice on to boil. Meanwhile put the pastry dishes in the oven for ten minutes. Ten minutes, not a moment longer. And start boiling the oil. Got that?'

'Yes,' nodded Dan. 'Peel the peppers –'

'No!' She glanced back at the monitor and saw Hugh getting up. 'I've got to go,' she said. 'I'll be back in a minute.' She tore back out into the café.

Hugh looked up at her. 'Sorry,' he mumbled. 'Don't know what came over me.'

'Sit down and have your coffee, y'daft beggar,' she said, 'and tell me all about it. No squeaking.'

Hugh let out a snotty laugh and sat back down.

It turned out that he and Maxine were over. It also turned out that this was not the only reason he was crying. He was crying because the builders had given him a new estimate and the work on his new house was going to cost double what he thought it would. *And* she'd taken all the new furniture. *And* the whole house was painted in magnolia because she'd wanted magnolia when he'd preferred almond white. *And* she'd had a fling with the carpenter. He was called Dave.

'I'm broken,' he finished. 'Broken. I'm squatting in an empty, magnolia-coloured house, in debt up to my eyeballs and no Maxine to make it all better.' He started squeaking again and Katie decided not to tell him the obvious paradox in his thinking. Instead she turned to a shadow behind her. She smiled up at Dan.

'Hello,' she said. She turned back to Hugh. 'Hugh,' she said softly, 'I am working and we're a bit short-staffed today. I'm going to have to go for now, but –'

Hugh started nodding furiously while making odd guttural noises. She watched in alarm and then looked up at Dan. To her surprise, Dan sat down.

'Hi there,' he said to Hugh. 'I'm really sorry about this, but I'm afraid I need Katie in the kitchen. Perhaps you could come back at a quieter time.'

Katie nodded at her boss, turned to Hugh and held his hand over the table.

'Hugh –' she started.

'Go out with me!' demanded Hugh suddenly.

'Hugh.'

'Please. I just need to be with you.'

She heard an exasperated sigh from Dan and bristled.

'Of course Hugh. It will be my pleasure. I was going to suggest it myself.'

Hugh managed an impressive beam. 'It'll be just like

old times. You and me,' he said, his eyes shining almost as much as the viscous tear nudging out of his nose. Hard to resist.

'Call me,' she said as she followed Dan into the kitchen, where she found frozen chips sprayed all over the counter.

'What's this?' she asked.

'Pity dating, eh?' asked Dan. 'Nice motive.'

She registered shock and flick-flacked through her database of fast retorts but none seemed to match the moment, while Dan tutted and picked up a knife and put it down again. 'Just don't run out on him in a restaurant,' he said. 'He may be a danger to himself.'

'Hugh is an ex-boyfriend, of whom I'm still very fond,' she said.

'Really?'

'Yes.'

'How long did it last? Two courses?'

Her jaw dropped.

'Ten months,' she said.

'Ten months!' He spluttered, and then started nodding a lot. He looked at the monitor at Hugh who was now blowing his nose on a napkin. 'Perhaps I should have played the loser card then. That's obviously more your type.'

Katie was stunned into silence. She flick-flacked again through her database of pithy one-liners but it kept stopping at 'It takes one to know one,' but that did her no justice at all.

'So anyway,' she said, turning away, 'what are all these chips doing on the counter?'

'We've had four orders for chips in the last ten minutes,'

said Dan, 'and the lasagne's probably going to be another half hour.'

'Hmm, she said slowly. 'And your point is?'

'My point is,' he spoke to her like she were a child, 'that I'm your boss and I'm telling you to come in the kitchen and cook what you said you were going to cook instead of flirting on my time.'

She felt her eyes sting. 'Right,' she said. 'Point taken.'

Good, she thought. Hugh had done the trick, she told herself grimly. There would be no more laughing. Dan was a prick. He treated her with disrespect when she was clearly better at the job than he was. He was rude and selfish and knew nothing about food or about keeping the regulars happy. And he resorted to playing the boss card every time he felt outdone. She did not like him. She was safe.

17

That day, between the two of them, Dan and Katie prepared and cooked everything available on Crichton Brown's restricted menu. When they finished making the food, they helped out front and when they finished helping out front, they cleared everything up and cleaned the entire restaurant until it gleamed. It was impressive, but not as impressive as the fact that they did all of this without saying a word to each other. This may have been usual for Dan, but for Katie it was a new experience. She paid scant heed to her customers or Sukie that day, for she was indulging in a competition with Dan and she was going to be victorious.

When Nik called, she answered before the phone had rung twice. He told her that he was definitely coming in tomorrow, if he got any sleep that night. They chatted for a while until he thought he was going to be sick again. She was willing to wait, but he hung up. She was doubly grateful for the call, first because she'd had someone to talk to and second, because she didn't think she could survive another day without saying whatever occurred to her out loud. It was giving her a headache.

'Girls aren't meant to do things in silence,' she told Jon that night. 'We're not made that way. That's why men beat us at sulking.'

'Mm,' grunted Jon.

At the end of the day, Katie sat waiting for Sukie to finish putting on her make-up for the walk home, her feet numb with pain. Dan came and sat down next to her.

'Well done,' he said finally, looking round the restaurant that they'd both just finished cleaning, silently. 'You should be very proud of yourself.'

Katie gave him a long look. So, he was making peace. She had won. She let out a satisfied sigh. It would be nice to talk again.

'I don't need you to tell me how to feel about myself, thanks,' she muttered.

She heard him say, 'I'm –', then they both started at the sound of Geraldine's voice.

'Hello!' she said and came and sat down next to Dan. Katie got up and went to find Sukie.

'Ooh,' said Geraldine. 'Was it something I said?'

'No,' said Dan. 'She's had a hard day, that's all.'

'You weren't too much of a taskmaster were you?' she asked eagerly.

Dan managed a laugh.

'So, how's it going?'

Dan could barely focus his eyes. 'Fine.'

'Good! I've had a wonderful day.'

'Good.'

'I went window shopping in my lunch-hour for rings,

and I think I've found just the thing. We'll go at the weekend.'

'Hmm?'

'I said we'll go at the weekend.'

'Fine.'

Geraldine looked at her watch. 'Right,' she said. 'I'm off home to make you dinner and run you a hot bath. I'll expect you in an hour.'

Dan closed his eyes. 'Perfect.'

After she'd gone, he sat gazing into space for a while, until Patsy, Katie and Sukie trooped past him with their coats and bags on.

'Bye,' they chorused.

'Bye,' he replied, and watched them go, feeling envious without knowing why.

That night, Matt made it home from college in record time, dashing across the roads as if he had nine lives, without even looking left then right then left again. By the time he got there, he and the girl who'd spent oceans of time looking lingeringly at him were losing control together in a red Porsche. He didn't own a red Porsche or even know anyone who had one, but it was a lovely dream.

'Wipe your feet!' greeted his mother in the hallway.

He gave her a quick kiss before asking what was for tea and dominating the kitchen with his presence.

His mates and even the A-gang girlies who sometimes joined them had noticed a difference in Matt, but he wasn't telling. He wasn't telling that, while they were whiling away their pathetic lives, he was planning a weekend away with all the trappings, and that while they were playing a stupid game of pool, they were in the company of someone who this time next year, might be having his girlfriend – his girlfriend – up to stay with him at university. Oh no, he wasn't going to tell them why he was in such a good mood, tease though they might. They were children and he, he was a man.

By eleven that night, the female staff of Crichton Brown's had fallen into bed, exhausted. Sukie dreamt of being on stage with Jon and Katie in the audience, who were married. Patsy dreamt of the cosmetics section at Boots, and for some reason Katie dreamt of Orinoco, who wasn't even her favourite Womble. They all woke early the next morning.

Nik was still off sick, ringing to explain that now the poison had moved down his body and he'd been awake again all night. He was exhausted. His mate had also got it and had been told by his doctor to take two days off. Katie and Dan set to immediately. He fetched all the necessary ingredients from the store cupboard that she'd needed the day before, and, in a casual aside, told her he'd get some more chicken breasts if she wanted to do something with the ones from yesterday. She told him, just as casually, that it was too late, they had now been in the fridge for two days. He nodded and she turned quickly round, confident he'd got the message. They worked quickly and almost silently together, although now there were the odd and necessary one-liners, such as 'Where are the cucumbers?' which yesterday they would have both have hunted for rather than lower themselves to ask. The cold war was slowly thawing. Still, Katie found it hard to believe that only yesterday morning, they'd been giggling together like teenagers. It seemed like weeks ago now. Amazing that only one day later, they were barely talking. The fact was that however much of a prick Dan might be; however rude, selfish or disrespectful he might be, or however often he played the boss card when he felt outdone, she missed giggling with him. Which made her confront the fundamental truth that she liked him and being stand-offish with him only hurt herself. This fundamental truth piqued her so much that she decided to be even more stand-offish with him.

Then she decided she'd be much better at her job if less of her energy was spent thinking about Dan and her. Then she wondered if Dan felt the same way and started replaying all of their conversations to date.

As soon as Matt arrived, he promised to give anyone his share of the tips if they called him when the hot chick came in so he could take her order. Not that he needed to be called. His body told him exactly when it was one o'clock.

Sukie and Katie frowned heavily at him.

'Hot?' repeated Sukie, shaking her head. '*Chick?*'

'I'm so sorry,' said Katie, 'I don't remember there being any fowl on the premises, heated or otherwise.'

Suddenly Sukie gasped. She turned to Katie. 'He means a *woman!*'

'Oh I *see!*' said Katie. 'Oh, how *sweet.*'

Matt grunted, blushed and made his exit.

As it happened, Katie gave him the nod, but she didn't hold him to his promise – she could tell from his pasty expression of determined fear that he hadn't needed her prompting. He left the kitchen and stood, as nonchalantly as he could, against the restaurant counter, pretending to chat to Katie as he felt the girl walk towards him, closer and closer. He turned. She was even more beautiful close up.

'Hello,' she said.

'Hi there.'

'You taking our orders today then?'

'Yeah, that's right,' said Matt, focusing hard on getting the right syllables in the right order in the right words.

'Well, I would like a –'

'Oh, we haven't got any hot food today,' he rushed. 'Our chef's still away. Only sandwiches and salads.'

'And chips,' said Katie.

'And chips,' Matt told her.

'And tartlets and stuffed peppers,' she reminded Matt.

'And tartlets and stuffed peppers,' he repeated.

'But no lasagne or pies or anything big,' Katie said, heading for the kitchen.

'But no –'

'Yeah thanks,' cut in the ugly friend. 'We can hear her too.'

If the beautiful girl hadn't blinked her large brown eyes at him in such a kind way, he'd probably have gone back to the kitchen too and never come out again.

'Oh dear,' she said to him ever so sadly. 'I would have liked lasagne.'

Matt felt the pity of her situation thoroughly. In the nano-second before he was about to offer to go and buy her one, or failing that learn how to make one, her friend broke in with, 'So you're not really taking proper orders then.' He turned to her and concentrated on her for a moment, reminding himself who she was and where they all were. 'Are you?' she demanded. 'Strictly speaking.'

'No,' he answered slowly. 'No.' He turned back to the fox, hoping that none of what was happening inside his body was showing on the outside. 'I'm so sorry, but I can't take your order today. We've got a restricted menu.'

She stared at him.

'Will you have lasagne tomorrow?' she asked.

His eyebrows leapt up hopefully, like two Yorkshire terriers whose owner had just come home. 'Are you coming in tomorrow?'

She leant forward slightly. 'I will now.' And then she gave him another grin. He grinned back.

'Good,' he said, wiggling his sweaty toes inside his shoes. 'I'll look forward to it.'

The ringing in his ears almost deafened her parting 'So will I.' He remembered to nod at the ugly friend before turning back and giving the fox another smile, just so she got the message, before she turned round and walked out.

He watched them make their way down the road, and took in every little bit of the fox's perfect proportions. He only just heard the wolf-whistles coming from the kitchen hatch. He turned to see Sukie and Patsy holding up score-cards. Apparently, he'd got an average of 8.5 out of a possible 10.

'You weren't there the whole time, were you?' he mumbled, nausea creeping up his body.

'Only from when you started talking,' assured Katie.

'Tell me you're taking the piss.'

'They're taking the piss,' said Katie, looking at Patsy's 8 score-card. 'You were a nine. Easily.'

'You were so cute back there,' said Sukie. 'Like a little puppy.'

'Oh shit,' moaned Matt.

'Of course they weren't!' rushed Katie.

'We had the hatch closed,' added Sukie.

'Katie kept closing the hatch!' concluded Patsy. 'She's so mean!'

Next day, Matt was in the kitchen washing up when the girl arrived. He walked out, wiped his upper lip and brushed his hand through his hair. Now he knew why some men grew moustaches. It stopped the sweat showing. There she was, sitting facing him, opposite her nasty friend, her eyes flitting round the café. As he came level with Katie, he heard Katie say in his ear, 'No one's taken her order yet, Big Boy. Go get it.' Sukie handed him a pad and pen but his hands felt numb and cold.

He walked onwards, ever onwards, his eyes fixed firmly on her. Just as he reached her table, she looked up at him and gave him a dazzling beam.

'Hi there!' she said. 'We were just wondering where you were.'

His insides galloped at the word 'you'. One simple syllable, just a consonant and a couple of vowels, and yet, oh so full of glorious meaning. They had wondered where he was. These two grown-up women had discussed him enough to actually wonder where he was. They had actually –

'Are you all right?' The nasty one was staring at him.

'Yes,' he said.

'Only you look ill.'

He let out a strangled laugh to give him time to think of the perfect response. Then he laughed some more.

'Want to join us?' asked the fox.

'I can't,' he replied. 'Too much to do out back.'

'Oh.'

'But –'

'That's a shame.'

'But . . .'

'Yes?'

'We could meet up some other time if you like,' said someone from inside his head.

'That would be great,' grinned the fox. 'Where?'

'The Gnat and Parrot? Wednesday, eight o'clock?'

'Great!' she laughed. 'It's a date.'

'Oh, what a shame!' cried her friend. 'I'm busy.'

The fox smiled across at her and then looked back up at Matt.

'Looks like it's just you and me then,' she smiled. 'I'm Jennifer by the way.'

'I'm Matt,' said Matt cautiously, only too aware of the significance of the moment. He didn't want to get it wrong and say Pat or something.

They smiled at each other.

'I'm Eva,' said the friend.

He looked at Eva and she looked back at him. Then he looked back at Jennifer.

'Right,' he said.

'Next Wednesday,' said Jennifer, with a big grin on her face. 'Eight it is. The Gnat and Parrot. See you there.'

'Well, I'll see you here first,' he said. 'Unless you stop coming, coming here, I mean, but I'll see you there too.'

'Great.'

Matt turned slowly and walked back to the kitchen a different man from the boy who'd walked out. He was on cloud nine. He was king of the world! He pitied everyone else for their small, inconsequential lives.

He grinned a little shakily at Katie and Sukie.

'Well?' asked Katie.

'Gnat and Parrot,' he whispered. 'Next week.'

They waited until they were in the kitchen to do high-fives. Then Matt took a beer out of the fridge. His hands were shaking. This would go down in history as the day his life changed. He had to be careful not to get run over before next Wednesday.

When Dan arrived back from the store cupboard, neither Sukie, Matt nor Katie took much notice.

'What are we going to do about next weekend?' he asked after a while.

Sukie and Katie stopped tousling Matt's hair. They frowned over at Dan who didn't elaborate.

Eventually Sukie shrugged. 'I say we just let it happen,' she said.

'Yeah,' agreed Katie. 'Chances are we can't stop time, however hard we try. I go with Sukie's suggestion.'

'I second it,' laughed Matt. ''Cos that means I'm even nearer my date.'

The girls started tousling his hair again and he pretended to bat them away.

Dan rolled his eyes. 'I mean,' he said, 'what are we

going to do about the personnel situation that morning?'

'What do you mean?' asked Matt.

'Well, I'll be at a wedding all weekend,' said Dan, 'as will Katie.'

'Eh?' she asked.

Dan looked at her.

'Sandy's wedding. I take it you're going. You were at her engagement party.'

Katie felt for a moment as if Dan was speaking in another language. Then slowly it all fell into place, and her jaw fell into what felt like a ravine. She had completely forgotten Sandy's wedding. How on earth could she have? After all, she'd met Dan at Sandy's engagement party! The hen party had been last weekend, but she'd been unable to go because of work duties. She'd even bought an outfit for the wedding which usually helped her visualise, and therefore look forward to, an occasion – and she'd even bought a present off the wedding list (but because that meant making one phone call to the store, it was very easy to forget). She just hadn't thought any further about practicalities such as how to get there, or where to stay overnight. It had felt so far off. And now the horrible truth was dawning. It was next weekend. And Hugh would be there. As would Maxine. And Dan would be there with Geraldine. And she'd be on her own. It would be the first time she'd be in enforced proximity with Geraldine and Dan since her aborted date with Dan. Would Geraldine keep her distance? Or would she wear Dan like a medal? 'In fact,' said Dan, 'Geraldine's going to call you and ask if you'd like to travel down with us. There'll be plenty of room in the back.'

271

Excellent. She mumbled something about not being able to wait and felt all her will to live seep out of her body. She couldn't remember much about the following discussion except that everyone around her finally managed to work out suitable cover for the weekend and she said 'mm' a lot. Where the hell would she stay? Inside the invitation Sandy had given out details of the hotel where the wedding was, but that would be far too expensive for her and was probably booked by now anyway. She told herself she'd sort it out first thing tomorrow and felt better immediately.

By the time she was ready for her date with Hugh that night however, she was probably more depressed than he was, especially as Hugh was doing the man thing and pretending all was normal. They met at a local Greek restaurant where their mezzes sat uneaten for three hours because they were too busy finishing the wine to remember to eat. Katie found it surprisingly pleasant being with Hugh, like searching through an attic full of childhood memorabilia and finding all her favourite toys in one box. She found herself watching his lips as he spoke and remembering how it had felt to kiss them. And whenever he sat back she remembered nestling into his Aran sweaters and sniffing their Hugh-smell. She didn't want to now, but it was unexpectedly comforting to remember. She started wondering whether she'd felt like this when she'd been with him and had just forgotten because she hadn't felt that level of comfort for so long.

When she'd left her flat that evening she'd been

prepared for lengthy, in-depth discussions of all-things-Maxine, but she couldn't have been more wrong. Hugh was not indulging in self-analysis; quite the opposite. He was determined to stick firmly to small-talk. The only problem was that, due to the depression he was pretending he didn't feel, he kept plying Katie with questions but was then completely unable to process the answers, so he would either just ask her another question, or more frequently, the same one again. It was like being on *Mastermind*, with her chosen subject being Katie Simmonds, The Surface, 1990 to the present day.

'So how's The Café?' Hugh asked again.

'Café/restaurant/bar,' she corrected again.

'Café/restaurant/bar.' Hugh bowed his head reverentially again.

'It's good thanks.'

Hugh nodded. 'And working for the new owner? What's that like?'

'Oh you know, like most bosses. Good points and bad points.'

Hugh nodded. 'Good,' he said.

'And bad,' helped Katie.

'Where do I know him from?' he asked suddenly. 'Haven't I seen him before?'

'Dunno. More wine?'

'Thanks. Absolutely positive I've seen him before. What's his name again?'

'Dan.'

Hugh shook his head. 'Could have sworn it.' He drank some more wine, while Katie tried to see what time his watch said. It appeared to be quarter to three. Did that mean quarter past nine? Or was it three in the morning and she'd been answering the same questions for nine hours? Difficult to tell.

'Are you going to Sandy's bloody wedding?' asked Hugh.

'Oh God.' Katie slumped. 'Yes.'

'I know. All those bloody people,' said Hugh, with more genuine emotion than he'd shown all evening long, 'being so . . .' he waved his arms about, trying to find the right words, 'happy.'

Katie slumped some more.

'*Bloody* . . .' he paused for thought, '*hell*.'

Katie couldn't agree with him more.

'Bloody *Maxine*'ll bloody be there.'

It was the first time he'd mentioned her all night. Then, suddenly, he sat bolt upright, his eyes focusing the most they had all evening. He had either had a fantastic idea or sat on something sharp. 'Oh my *God*!' he screeched. Possibly both. He started clapping his hands and pointing at Katie and then pointing back at himself. She winced and frowned at him but she still couldn't understand what he was getting at. He pointed at her again and then at him again, while making a strange, excited sound.

'You and me!' he finally managed. 'It's perfect!'

'What is?'

'Let's go together!' he cried, staring at her fanatically. 'I've got a suite booked in the same hotel as the wedding, Maxine insisted. I'll sleep in the lounge on the sofa and you can have the bed. My treat! You'd be doing me a favour. It's a four-poster!'

Ooh, thought Katie. Beats sleeping on a park bench, which was probably where she'd otherwise end up.

'You *have* to,' said Hugh, filled with a sudden determination to win her over. 'You *have* to agree,' he insisted, 'You *have* to. You just *have –*'

'All right!' cried Katie.

Hugh started laughing. 'Fantastic!' he almost sang. 'That'll piss her off!'

'Oh Hugh, how kind!' laughed Katie.

Hugh joined in the laughter until it sounded as if he was dangerously close to tears. Then he suddenly got all serious again. 'I'll pick you up first thing on Saturday morning and we'll pootle down there in good time, maybe take in a spot of lunch.' He started laughing again. 'Maxine will be absolutely livid.'

'Hold on a minute,' said Katie, 'I don't want her to think we're a couple or anything.'

'No, no, of course not.'

'Good.'

'Mind you,' reminded Hugh, 'she did paint my whole house the colour of old wee and then take all the furniture.'

'No, Hugh.'

'OK.' He held up his hand, as if swearing an oath. '"Caran D'Ache" will not think for one minute that we are an item,' he said. Katie had to bite back a sudden tear.

'Promise?' she coughed.

'Promise,' he said and then belched to close the deal.

He gave her a shy glance. 'Just like old times, isn't it?'

She had to agree, it did feel somewhat cosy.

And then the whole evening shifted gear, Katie's subject changing to Katie Simmonds, Beneath the Surface,

1997 to 1998. He asked her why, after ten happy months and without warning, she had finished with him all those years ago. 'Don't get me wrong,' assured Hugh, 'I'm not having sleepless nights about it or anything, but it *was* rather sudden.'

And Katie found herself rewriting the past and her personality to fit his bruised ego.

'It really was more about me than you,' she finished, 'and the proof is in the pudding.'

'What do you mean?'

'Well, I haven't had a long-term relationship since then, so I clearly have relationship issues to iron out, but you and Maxine have been together forever.'

Perhaps it was not the best thing to say. Not only did it catapult them straight into the danger zone, but once she'd said it out loud, the truth of the situation suddenly hit Katie with some force. She hadn't just said a cliché, she had just told him the truth: her finishing with Hugh really had been more about her than him. Jesus. While Hugh collapsed into squeaky, sneezing tears, Katie wondered if she was perhaps, the first person ever for whom that cliché was actually true.

18

The next morning was deceptive in its lazily beautiful start. Katie woke up to sun streaming in through her curtains and the reassuring sound of the kettle softly boiling. She found Jon pacing the kitchen, yawned a hello and joined him at the kettle.

'I have *got* to get on with my work,' he muttered to the wall.

'I have *got* to stop drinking,' she muttered next to him.

They stared at the wall together.

'I'll help you if you help me,' said Jon suddenly.

'OK.'

'So far,' he said, 'there's a very clever twist with a parrot and a dwarf, but I need another twist.'

She ran through yesterday's customers and remembered the woman with unfeasibly large hands.

'Why not put in a transvestite?'

He gave her a sideways look. 'Why?'

She shrugged. 'Because you can have someone thinking the murderer's a woman until you realise one of the characters likes dressing up in women's clothing.'

Jon started nodding slowly. 'Hmm,' he said, pouring boiling water into their mugs.

'OK,' said Katie. 'Your turn to help me.'

He gave her a long look. 'Stop drinking,' he murmured, and left the kitchen.

By the time she'd walked to work, the sun was already burning hot. She opened the café door and once inside opened all the windows, which let in a delicious through-breeze. Then she offered up a prayer to the ceiling and crossed her fingers before calling out to Nik. After two beats, she got the response she was hoping for, thanked the ceiling and went into the kitchen to find him. Nik must have lost half a stone, most of which was tan, and Katie had to hide her shock at his pale, wan appearance. She also had to hide her shock that they hugged.

Everyone else got in early today too, just in case Nik wasn't in again, and the first commuter queue and menu preparations were well under way by the time Dan arrived. In fact, all seemed to be going extremely well until mid-morning, when Katie and Sukie were sorting out the last of the morning queues and Patsy was helping Nik. Dan noticed a puddle by the freezer. His eyes doubled in size and his breath shortened. He pointed wildly at it.

'What the hell's that?' he demanded in a voice that stopped all chatter. Patsy and Nik followed his finger and stared.

'The . . . floor?' asked Patsy.

'What's that *on* the floor?' cried Dan.

'The . . . freezer?' she asked.

'Oh *no*,' breathed Nik slowly. He had seen what Dan had seen. 'I hope that's not what I think it is.'

'Not as much as me,' said Dan.

'What's going on?' asked Patsy, eyes wide. 'You're frightening me.'

'Are you going to open the door or am I?' Dan asked Nik.

'You are mate,' replied Nik. 'You're the boss.'

Patsy started whimpering while Dan slowly opened the freezer door. She stepped back slightly towards Nik who instinctively grew an inch taller. Dan squinted in and slowly started to take out Tupperware boxes to put them on the counter. It took him a while to decide that all the food was defrosted, then much less time to have a nervous breakdown. He started pacing while Nik inspected all the food and Patsy rushed out to tell Katie and Sukie. After the last of the commuter queues had left, they all congregated in the kitchen.

'Right,' said Dan, 'it's all *perfectly* solvable.'

They looked at him.

'It's perfectly solvable, so no one needs to panic.'

'Oh my God,' wailed Patsy at the word panic.

'It's all right,' said Katie. 'All the stuff that we need for today is fine, so Nik – you just keep cooking like the star you are, while we worry about tomorrow.'

'Excellent, yes,' said Dan. 'Nik, keep on cooking while we worry about tomorrow.'

'Let's get some chips going,' said Katie.

'Excellent,' nodded Dan. 'Let's get some chips going.' Nik started pouring oil into a pan.

'Right,' said Katie. 'Now we need to deal with the freezer.'

'Shall I buy a new one?' Dan looked at Katie.

'No!' she said. 'It's still under guarantee, I'll phone the manufacturer.'

'Excellent,' said Dan. 'You phone the manufacturer while Nik gets some chips going.'

'What shall I do?' asked Patsy.

'Er, the chip fryer's broken,' announced Nik.

'*What*?' cried everyone except Patsy.

'*What*?' cried Patsy.

'I think the chip fryer's broken,' said Nik, his face level with where the flame should be. He tried again and then stood up. 'Yep,' he said. 'It's broken.'

'Right,' said Dan, pacing. 'OK. The chip fryer's broken.' He looked at Katie.

'That's important, but not urgent, so I'll call the repairers after I've called the freezer guys,' she said, looking at the fridge door. 'Their number should be up here.'

'I'll just keep on cooking till then, right?' asked Nik.

'Yes,' said Katie and Dan at the same time.

'Yes,' said Dan. 'Carry on cooking while Katie makes the calls and the rest of us just get on as normal.' He looked up at the monitor and saw four people waiting to be served. 'No,' he said, 'scrap that. I'll make the calls, Katie and Sukie serve the customers as usual and don't let on anything's up. For God's sake don't be polite or they'll rumble us.'

'Dan, what shall I do?' asked Patsy.

'Um,' Dan was at a loss. 'What do you normally do?'

'Um,' Patsy was at a loss. 'Um . . .'

'Help anyone who asks you,' said Dan. 'You can be the general sous.'

'What does that mean?'

'You're under whoever asks you.'

There was much laughter at this which, credit to Patsy, she took very well as soon they'd explained it.

Katie and Dan spent the rest of the day phoning up the repairer and manufacturer on the hour every hour, which was why it only took until 3 p.m. for them to come and fix the problems, and by 4 p.m., Crichton Brown's Café/Bar/Restaurant had a fully functioning kitchen again.

At the end of the day, when Crichton Brown's had closed and the rest of the staff had gone, Katie and Dan sat down together and counted the day's takings. Then they counted again. They dared smile at each other and, without a word, Dan went to the wine bottles and took out a good chardonnay.

'Dan!' she protested, laughing.

'We bloody deserve it,' he said, finding the corkscrew. 'And we can afford it.' The bottle uncorked and they both laughed. He came over, sat down opposite her, poured out two glasses and handed her one. They grinned again and clinked glasses.

'To us!' he toasted.

She only hesitated for a second. 'To us.'

'One hell of a team.'

'One hell of a team.'

They both drank down too much wine. Then he held up his glass again.

'To Katie Simmonds.' She laughed. He held up his

hand to stop her. 'I don't know what I'd have done without you,' he said, softer. 'And I'm sorry for being an idiot the other day.'

She pretended not to be as touched as she was. 'It's all right. And you'd have coped,' she smiled.

'I wouldn't,' he contradicted. 'And I'd have had a bloody heart attack trying.'

'Well, it is my job.'

He nodded and lifted his glass in the air again. 'A toast! Thank God for Katie's job!'

'I'll drink to that!'

There was a little lull and Katie asked if now was a good time to make some suggestions.

'Always working,' murmured Dan, a lazy smile on his lips. 'Always working.'

She started by suggesting her mother's unique recipe, a delicious frittata – a special Spanish omelette – that she had learnt how to make before she was out of ankle-socks. She didn't know anywhere else where it was done and felt it would satisfy both healthy eaters and pie lovers. Then she decided to broach two subjects that had been concerning her: Nik was having trouble keeping up with the demands of a bustling Café/Bar/Restaurant now that the clientele had grown so significantly, so couldn't be asked to do more, but she felt that the place had an obvious gap in its repertoire.

'Nik's so busy, so is there enough money to find some local cook – maybe a stay-at-home mum – and ask her to make us two, maybe three, choice desserts throughout the week? Each slice will get us back more than the entire ingredients.'

Dan nodded thoughtfully. 'Good idea. I'll put an advert in the local press and see if anyone fits the bill.'

'The local council has a free magazine that's a lifeline for mums in this area. I could see about putting an advert in there.'

'Brilliant.'

'And . . .'

'Yes?'

'It might be nice if there was room for customers to sit outside, especially with summer coming. But you know how mad the English are, they'd even sit out there in the winter. We can look into finding out if we need a licence.'

Dan looked unimpressed. 'We haven't got enough room have we?'

She shrugged. 'There's enough for two tables, that's all you'd need. You'll get more money and it will show passers-by that there's a café here. Just an idea.'

Dan nodded slowly. 'Hmm. I'll talk to Paul.'

Katie forced herself not to push it further. Instead she changed tack and asked how Paul was. Dan gave her a vague reply and she gave him a vague nod in return.

'OK, my turn now,' he said. 'Can I ask something?'

'Am I allowed to say no?' she smiled.

'Of course!' He put his arms up in mock-arrest.

She shook her head. 'Go on then.'

'It's not a boss thing, it's a . . . friend thing.'

She gave him a long look. 'I don't let many friends tell me what to do all day.' He gave her a small smile. 'Or remind me that they pay my wages.' She took a sip of her drink. She looked up and saw an endearingly apologetic expression. She took another sip of her wine, so as not to hug him.

'OK,' he said quietly. 'I deserved that. You're right. I can't have it both ways.'

'No,' she cut in. 'Go on, ask the question. As a friendly boss.'

He took a deep breath. 'I know you're waiting . . .' he started.

She froze. 'Waiting?'

'Yes. For the right job.'

'Ah.'

'And I just wondered why?'

There was a pause.

'And?' she asked.

'That's it.'

'That's it?' she repeated.

'Well, what I mean is, what are you doing wasting your time and your considerable talents, skills and brain-power, being a waitress?'

'I'm a manager,' she said in a hollow voice.

'Of course,' he said quickly, '*manager*.'

'Don't patronise me.'

'I'm not!'

'I'm either a manager or a waitress. You're the boss, so you tell me.'

'You are most definitely a manager. What I meant to say – and I don't know why I'm suddenly sweating so much –' he gave a quick laugh, 'is that you could be a manager of somewhere massive. Or . . .' he trailed off into an uneasy silence.

'Are you asking me to leave?'

'*No!*'

'Are you telling me my job's crap?'

He gave a big sigh. 'I thought I was telling you I think you're worth more than this job, but that does not make this job crap.'

'Hmm,' said Katie. 'Have you met my mother?'

'No,' said Dan.

'Shame. I think you'd really get on with her.'

He grimaced. 'That was below the belt.'

'I'm fine with this job,' Katie told him. 'I'm good at this job.'

'I know –'

'And I will stay doing this job until I decide to leave this job. Unless you don't want me doing this job.'

Dan shook his head furiously. 'God no, I'd be lost without you.'

There was an uneasy silence. 'You know . . . In this capacity.'

'I know perfectly well what you meant,' Katie gave him a long, kind smile.

Dan looked at her seriously, then looked down at his feet. Katie felt suddenly deeply depressed. Oh God, what the hell was she playing at? When they started making friends, she pushed for more. When they rowed, she behaved like they were having a lover's tiff. It was not a good working relationship. She would start to look for a new job. The thought made her feel instantly even more depressed. No, she'd stay. No need to over-react. They were a good team. This was a celebration. She felt better. Not as good as before, but not depressed.

Dan suddenly gulped down the last of his wine and

sighed. 'Excellent,' he said. 'Perfect. Right. That's all good then. I'm so glad we had this little chat.'

'Was there anything else?'

Dan shook his head.

'Oh and by the way,' she said, getting up. 'I'm going to Sandy's wedding with Hugh, so I won't need a lift, thanks all the same.'

He looked up at her. 'Oh,' he said softly. 'OK. That's a shame. I mean,' he looked down, 'Geraldine was looking forward to it.'

Katie gave him a very sweet smile. 'I bet she was,' and turned and walked away.

Wednesday morning, the day of his date and first day of the rest of his life, found Matt staring in wretched disbelief at his reflection in the mirror. Here was proof that his worst fears were true. There was no longer any doubt: God – if there was one – really, *really* hated him. Maybe in another life Matt had killed His favourite pet or something. Eaten His favourite baby. Maybe, due to the Chaos theory, he had inadvertently started a natural disaster and thousands of innocent people had died senselessly. Whatever it was, Matt now knew with absolute certainty, as he stared in the mirror, that whatever he'd done was celestially unforgivable. He would not know redemption. For behold, there in front of him, clear as a pillar of salt, radiant as the sun, glossy as Pegasus's mane, shone a spot on his nose the size of a frigate.

He closed his eyes (which hurt) and then slowly opened them again. Same face, same nose, same overnight mountain on it. It was practically waving at him. What the hell was he going to do?

There was no way round the problem. He would have to cancel his date with Jennifer. She was not a girl who should know such things in her life. She was a creature of love and beauty and light. Not of infected pus.

Yes, he would cancel, he told himself as he squinted painfully at the spot, revelling in its revoltingness. It had its own sick beauty; a Saturn-shaped ring of boiling scarlet throbbed round a rigid white planet and at the pinnacle perched a black hole the size of a pin-prick. Right on the top of his hooter, like a flag. He might as well wear a placard that read Danger, Testosterone.

He tried rearranging his nose, ignoring the pain and stretching his face out of all recognition. He knew from bitter experience that the nose was the worst place for this to happen. It was nothing less than a bull's-eye from up above. He could almost hear the archangels chanting out 'One hundred and *eight*-eey.'

He perched on the edge of his bed, trying to work out what to do, but instead merely sank into depression. Why the hell didn't old people get spots, people who didn't need to find lovers any more because they were too busy shopping for thermal underwear? Why give it to adolescent boys, the only members of the human race for whom spots could literally mean the end of all their hopes and dreams? Sometimes he had so many spots he wouldn't have been surprised if his forehead spelt 'virgin' in braille.

Yes, he would cancel. It had all been too good to be true. Life stank and he would die a virgin. Thank you, God.

Then he realised that he didn't have Jennifer's phone number. He didn't know where she lived. Or even what her surname was. He sat in an increasingly panicked daze hoping an answer would come to him soon.

Eventually, he realised there was only one possible solution. It was simple, effective and left him with some dignity. He would turn up at the Gnat and Parrot at the appointed time in a balaclava, tell Jennifer he had a summer cold and go back to his room, never to leave, dying a long and lonely death. But first, he had to sort out a convincing way to avoid her at the café. He'd ask Katie for help. She was always full of good ideas.

He leapt up off the bed and found the only scarf he had, a thick red number – perfect for the mid-summer heat. Deftly, he wrapped up half his face and then left for work.

Half an hour later, he passed the coffee queue and beckoned frantically to Katie.

'Hi Matt,' she said, hardly glancing at him. 'Another spot?'

Matt furiously yanked down his scarf, careful to hide his nose with his hand.

'I need to talk to you,' he hissed.

He ran into the kitchen, followed by Katie while Sukie kept Patsy away from them with her arm.

Truth to tell, Katie wasn't fully sympathetic to his situation until she realised its gravity, when she saw Matt's nose. Her eyes widened. Nik took a look too. They both stared at him in awe.

'I *think*,' said Katie slowly, 'don't get too excited, but I *think* this one is even bigger than the Summer of 03.'

Matt leant heavily on the dishwasher. 'Leave me alone,' he snivelled. 'Just leave me alone.'

Katie examined a picture on the fridge. 'No, maybe not,' she said.

Once Matt had explained that tonight was his first date with Divine Jennifer and his life was doomed to failure, he finally felt they understood his plight. Nik started laughing and Katie let out a long low whistle and shook her head sympathetically. 'You are stuck, my friend,' she whispered.

'I know.'

'I mean, if it was just another spot and she was just another girl, there might have been some hope.'

'I know.'

'But it's an alien life form hatching its young on your face and she is the Goddess of Light.'

Matt frowned, which hurt his nose, so he stopped. 'You're not helping.'

'Matt,' Katie said quietly. 'It's just a spot. And she's just a girl.'

'Nobody understands,' he groaned and opened the dishwasher.

Nik swung round suddenly. 'Nutmeg or parsley?' he asked Katie.

'What's this?' she asked. 'Naming the children?'

'In the pasta?'

'Nutmeg.' She turned to Matt. 'Would you like me to have a word with Jennifer? Ask her to postpone. Say you're off sick?'

Matt stared at her. Would she? Could she? Was it that easy to save his life? He nodded frantically (which hurt) and they worked out his story. Thank goodness for that – now he wouldn't have to buy a balaclava. The story was that he had caught the bug that Nik had had and was off today. Nik was only too delighted to provide Matt with every gory detail of his food poisoning, should he need to know.

At lunch-time Jennifer and Eva came in together as usual and Katie went to take their orders.

'Lover boy not here then?' Eva asked her.

'No, he phoned in sick this morning.'

'Oh,' said Jennifer, more surprised than sorry. 'OK.'

'He asked me specially to say sorry to you. He won't be able to make tonight. It's some 24-hour bug thingie. Can he call you?'

Jennifer shrugged sweetly. 'I'll be in again tomorrow.'

'Is he really bad?' asked Eva.

'Nah,' said Katie. 'Just some up-chucking and stomach pain.'

'My kid brother had that last week,' said Eva. 'There's something going round. Was he sick all night?'

'Um, not sure really.' Katie was surprised at how bad she felt lying. With any luck Matt would get the bug. She turned to Jennifer again. 'Does he have your number, so he can call you.'

Another sweet shrug. 'No need,' she smiled. 'I'll be in again.'

Katie had just finished taking their order when Hugh almost ran up to the counter to check she was still going to the wedding with him. He'd found a great pub to stop at on the way there, and wanted to show her the write-up in his national pub food guide. Katie didn't know why, but she wanted to get him far away from Dan, who had obviously heard this. She sat him down at one of the tables furthest from the counter, but was disconcerted to find Dan approaching, and unnerved not to know why.

'Hello there,' said Dan.

Hugh looked up at him, surprised.

'Dan Crichton,' Dan put his hand out and Hugh shook it. 'We met briefly when –'

'Yes. Hugh Penrose.' They nodded at each other.

'So,' said Dan. 'You off to the wedding too?'

'Oh! Are you going?'

'Course!' said Dan. 'My life wouldn't be worth living if I wasn't there. I've known Sandy for years. My girlfriend was her flatmate all the way through Oxford.'

Hugh suddenly clapped and laughed. 'That's where I know you from! You were at the party!'

'Yep,' said Dan swiftly. 'So which way are you travelling up?'

Hugh was only too delighted to fill Dan in on his choice of A-roads and motorways while Katie tried to work out what Dan was playing at. She listened to their conversation as tense as a poised Slinky on a top step. Hugh suddenly stopped mid-sentence. 'I've got an idea!' he said. 'Why don't we all go up together?'

'I'm sure Dan and Geraldine will be leaving later than us,' said Katie, her Slinky collapsing at the bottom of the stairs. 'I mean, we are making a day of it.'

'Yeah, actually you're right,' nodded Dan. 'Geraldine might need to work Saturday morning, so we were going to leave in the afternoon.'

'Ah,' said Hugh politely. 'Yes, we were planning to go earlier in the day.'

Dan gave them both a one-move smile and nod.

It occurred to Katie that if Geraldine was working most of Saturday, Dan could have done his Saturday shift too and hadn't really needed to sort out weekend cover quite as urgently as he had. Musing on this, she went to collect Jennifer and Eva's food and let Matt know how well Jennifer had swallowed the lie. But when she walked into the kitchen, she spotted the problem immediately.

There stood Eva, smack bang in the middle of the floor, hands firmly on waist, staring questioningly at Matt. Matt was staring back at her in blank terror as if he'd been caught with his hand down his trousers. Which for all Katie knew, was exactly what had happened.

'Hello,' said Katie. 'Anything wrong?'

Eva swung round. 'Oh hello!' she cried. 'Here's the liar.'

Katie was about to refute this, but then she realised this was a fairly accurate description.

'It was only a white lie,' she tried.

Eva pointed at Matt, still staring at Katie. 'You call that up-chucking with stomach pain? What's white about that lie?'

'Have you seen his spot?' asked Katie.

'Katie!' cried Matt.

'I mean look at it!' Eva looked. 'It's like he's got two noses,' helped Katie.

'*Katie*!' Matt screamed.

'You are *so* lucky I'm not going to tell Jennifer,' Eva told Matt.

'Yes, please don't do that,' urged Katie. 'There's no need to hurt her.'

Eva let out a scornful laugh. 'Excuse me,' she said haughtily, before walking out of the kitchen.

Matt and Katie stared at each other.

'Oh dear,' said Katie. 'It's rather humbling to be scolded by someone wearing sparkly platform boots, isn't it?'

' "Two noses"?' repeated Matt, his face distorted with anger (which hurt).

It wasn't until later, when she was making her way up Asherman's Hill with Sukie that Katie voiced her confusion over why Dan wasn't working on the Saturday morning of the wedding and why he had introduced himself to Hugh. It wasn't because he wanted Hugh to know he had got off with her at the party, because he'd changed the subject so sharply when Hugh realised where he recognised him from.

'Why do you think there's a reason for it at all?' asked Sukie.

'I don't know. It all just seems odd.'

'Oh dear,' said Sukie. 'I have a really bad feeling about this. You want there to be a reason, don't you? You want to discover that Dan is somehow trying to engineer it so that he and you can go to the wedding together where he can confess that he's in love with you.'

Katie gasped, swallowed and then gasped again. 'Do you mind?' she spluttered.

'Good,' said Sukie. 'Because it's not going to happen and I don't want you to be disappointed.'

Katie gave a sad little whimper. 'You could at least pretend you're on my side.'

'I *am* on your side, that's why I'm being cruel to be kind.'

It wasn't until they had gone their separate ways and Katie was walking up the hill on her own that she realised Sukie really was on her side. Because in the cold light of day, if she was really honest with herself, she knew that part of her had been hoping for exactly what Sukie had said.

It appeared she still had some of the Dan Crichton Virus in her bloodstream. And from past experience with DCV, she knew what that meant. Short of getting a blood transfusion she would just have to wait until it made its way out of her system naturally.

Matt wouldn't show his face in the restaurant until Friday. Gradually the Alp region of his nose diminished to one of the least dramatic Lake District areas. It became less angry too, more resembling a Barbie tutu than a raging planet, but nothing could induce him to move from his place at the dishwasher, especially since Patsy had pointed out to him that the hot steam would help it reduce at a greater speed. If he could, he'd have put himself in a short cycle. By Friday afternoon, however, he knew he would have to brave the restaurant to ask Jennifer out again, otherwise their love might never be consummated.

He took a deep breath and went to their table at lunchtime. Thankfully, Jennifer didn't seem to notice the spot, but then that was probably because she didn't really give herself the chance to. She seemed unable to look him in the eye and instead looked at Eva when she was answering him.

'I'll make it up to you,' he said. 'I promise.'

Jennifer looked at Eva. 'Whatever,' she said in a pleasant sing-song voice.

'So?' he said. 'Saturday night?'

Both girls spluttered with laughter.

'Er, I'm busy!' Jennifer told Eva.

'Sunday?'

Jennifer gave Eva a nod and Eva drew her eyes to his for the first time in the entire conversation. He fought the urge to hide his nose. She didn't pay any attention though because she was far too busy looking haughtily unimpressed by him.

'Mhm,' she said curtly before looking away.

'Same time and place?' he asked, beginning to feel smaller than the spot, which wasn't too difficult.

Jennifer nodded at Eva and Eva said 'mm', this time without looking at him. Then the girls started talking about something else and he wandered back to the kitchen where he hoped he'd find a knife sharpener, so he could sharpen a knife to fall on.

He stood leaning on the counter with his face deep in the dishwasher steam, not knowing whether his tears were from heat or mortification. He would never lie again. Whatever the consequences would have been from telling Jennifer the truth, they could not be worse than this feeling. Had Eva told Jennifer the hideous truth? Or had he already hurt Jennifer? If only she'd given him a chance to explain his 'illness' properly – but he knew it was not an explanation, it was a fabrication, a story, a concoction. She deserved better. She hadn't even gone out with him yet and he'd already lied to her. Women were right: men were bastards. He felt ashamed to be one of his own kind. It was moments like this that belied the Bible's claim that God made man in his own image. He was willing to bet good money that no other creature had ever felt such burning humiliation and yearning regret. (Except perhaps for Barney, his nan's dog, who'd eaten the entire double chocolate Victoria sponge cake she'd made for Matt's third birthday and while being scolded by his beloved owner reproduced it for her on her favourite rug.)

His wretched musings were interrupted by Katie. She had no time for his dilly dallying today. There was far too much to do. She was having a late lunch-break to squeeze in a leg, underarm and bikini wax for tomorrow's wedding, and now deeply regretted such a rash decision. For a start, there really wasn't time. Secondly, why on earth was she having a bikini wax? She'd never yet seen wedding photos where the guests showed their knickers. And finally, she was paying money to have her body hair ripped out from its follicles without the aid of general anaesthetic.

At two o'clock, she hot-footed it down to the local hairdresser's where a tiny, dark, airless corner had been separated off by an MDF wall and turned into a high-class beauty parlour. The heady aroma of fear and damp sweat hung in the air as ten minutes later, she lay, waiting for the warm wax on her leg to be ripped off by Loretta.

'You watching *Big Brother*?' asked Loretta. She mixed some more wax. 'It's so good this year. I'm addicted.'

And *rip*.

Katie's body went into minor shock, small quivers of relief rippling through it.

'And just bend your leg there and – that's right – and that one there – that's right.'

More hot wax.

'It's much better than last year. I can't even remember who was on it last year.'

And *rip*.

Katie's body went cold.

'I hate Damian. I *love* Jimmy.'

And *rip*.

Katie held her breath.

'My mum's the opposite. She hates Jimmy and loves Damian.'

And *rip*.

Katie stared hard at the ceiling.

'But I don't. I hate Damian. And I love Jimmy.'

And *rip*.

'Can you just turn over a bit? That's it. And whasisname? That gay one. He's *so* funny.'

And *rip*.

Katie started taking long deep breaths.

'Ooh look!' said Loretta. Katie was scared to. She didn't want to see her own skin in someone else's hand. She looked. Loretta was holding out her fingers.

'Chipped a nail. That cost me £15!' Sigh. 'I'll go back, they don't mind.'

Katie sank back down on the bed.

'And that girl, whatsername? Debbie. She's meant to be engaged. If I was her boyfriend I'd chuck her.'

And *rip*.

Katie clenched her fists. Her wet eyelashes were squeezed shut but still leaked.

'Ooh, sorry,' said Loretta. 'Didn't get it all. I'll just . . .'
And *rip*.

Katie lay back exhausted.

'Right then,' said Loretta sweetly. 'All done. If you just want to get yourself ready, I'll be out front.'

Katie heard the door shut and lay on the bed listening for the sound of her follicles weeping. Half an hour later she was standing back in the hot café, plucked like a chicken and roasting nicely.

When Sukie got the phone call from Greta her agent, how was Katie to understand the massive implications? She had no reason not to be excited for her friend.

'Another audition!' she repeated, clapping her hands in girlish glee.

'For *A Tale of Two Cities*!' sang Sukie.

'Wow!' sang Katie.

'Down to the last five!'

'Fantastic!'

'Tomorrow morning!' rejoiced Sukie.

Katie stopped dancing. 'Oh,' she said.

Sukie stopped dancing. 'Oh,' she said.

'Damn,' Katie said. 'You mean I'm going to have to work Saturday morning instead of setting-off early to go for a pub lunch with Hugh?' She smiled.

Sukie gave her a hug and went out to tell Dan.

When Hugh popped into the café on his way home from work to check yet again what time tomorrow morning he would be picking her up, she broke the news gently to him. 'Oh, I see,' he said, a few times.

'I'm really sorry,' she said. 'Can't be helped.' She

turned to Dan. 'Dan would come in but he doesn't like to use the coffee machine.'

Dan smiled. 'I'd love to come in but Geraldine isn't needed at work after all, so we're setting off for the wedding early, make a weekend of it.'

Katie nodded and then turned to Hugh. '*And* he doesn't like to use the coffee machine.'

'You must show me some time,' Dan called out to her. 'And I'll show you how to invest all your money in a new business and employ staff.'

Geraldine wasn't going to let it spoil her evening out with Dan and his parents. In fact she wasn't going to let anything spoil her evening out with Dan and his parents. She'd just confirmed that she wouldn't have to go into work tomorrow morning. When Dan picked her up from her flat, she almost flew into his arms.

'Wow,' he said, letting her hug him hard. 'What's all this about?'

'Nothing,' she said, kissing him again. 'I'm just happy, that's all.'

'That's good.'

'Yes,' she smiled, giving him another kiss. 'It is, isn't it?'

They sat in the car in silence, Dan wondering how on earth he'd keep up the conversation with his parents tonight. Thank goodness for Geraldine.

'I booked The Avenue,' she yawned, 'Asked for a corner table.'

'Excellent.'

'Had a complete bugger of a day.'

'Oh yes? Why?'

'That line of Retrouvez sofas I ordered turned out to look like The Pier cast-offs. Bryan nearly killed me.'

'How come? Didn't you see them in Paris?'

'Yes, after a week of fourteen-hour days, and with half an hour to make a decision.'

'Well tell Bryan that. He'll understand.'

'I can't,' she tutted.

'Why?'

'"Oh sorry Bryan. Turns out I'm not good at snap judgments after all. Maybe you'd like to give someone else sixty grand a year plus bonuses."'

Dan chuckled.

'What?' asked Geraldine.

'I was just thinking about your snap judgments. First thing you said about my father was "I bet he doesn't suffer fools gladly."'

Geraldine smiled. 'How are they?'

'Don't know. Haven't had time to speak to them.'

'You are terrible,' admonished Geraldine fondly. '*I* speak to them more than you.'

'Perfect.'

She stroked the back of his head, looking approvingly at the odd silver hairs at his temples, which she felt added dignity.

The Avenue was packed and as soon as they arrived Dan realised that spending several hours in a restaurant was the least relaxing way he could possibly spend an evening, second only to spending an evening in a restaurant with his parents. From the moment he walked in, he was unable to shake himself out of a creeping awareness of every last detail, from the waiters' trendy outfits to the pianist in the corner. He decided to use his stop-watch for the time it would take for their orders to arrive.

His parents had been there for half an hour, his mother, Harriet, in soft fawn cashmere and soft fawning mood. His father, Albert, must have been having one of his days.

'Hello darlings,' cooed Harriet, raising her softly powdered cheek for a kiss from both, resting her gentle, veined hands on their arms.

'Geraldine!' greeted Albert, his face creasing into a warm smile and the lines round his eyes stretching all the way to his hairline. He turned to his son and heir. 'Daniel,' he said fondly, giving him a firm handshake.

Geraldine and Dan sat in the appropriate seats, Geraldine next to Harriet, Dan next to Albert, the women with their backs to the restaurant. As Albert gave his menu opinions in a commanding voice, Harriet whispered her approval of Geraldine's choice of restaurant and table. After the food decisions were made, the wine approved by Albert and all journey tales exchanged, they got down to business.

'Well?' demanded Albert. 'And how's my son the restaurateur?'

Dan achieved a weary smile. 'Fine thanks,' he replied. 'It's tiring, but I think it's going to be OK.'

'Not regretting it?' his father frowned.

'God no, of course not.'

'Good. Nothing ventured, nothing gained.' They all nodded, having heard Albert Crichton's favourite sayings many times before. 'One day you'll be running a place like this.' They all followed his eyes round the smart

Hampstead restaurant. 'Only with a better hors d'oeuvres selection,' he added.

'You can always have some of mine if you don't like yours, dear,' remarked Harriet. 'You love moules.'

'And why would I prefer yours to the one I chose?' asked Albert in mock surprise.

'It's just an option,' she said quietly, 'should you so decide.' She turned to Geraldine. 'And how is my favourite couple?'

Geraldine smiled at Dan and laid her hand over his on the white tablecloth.

'We're absolutely fine thank you, Harriet.'

'Oh *good*,' said Harriet. 'Good.'

'In fact,' Geraldine squeezed Dan's hand and looked at him. He looked back at her. She raised her eyebrows in a question. He gave a little frown. She did it again. He gave her a relaxed smile and she then gave him a little shrugged grin. 'Shall I tell them?' she half-whispered.

'Tell them what?'

'*You* know!'

'Tell us what?' asked Harriet quickly.

'Search me,' shrugged Dan. 'I haven't got a clue.'

'Oh *you*!' cried Geraldine, trying to hide her disappointment. She turned to Harriet conspiratorially. 'He's no fun at all.'

'Oh,' said Harriet, crestfallen.

They all leaned back one-by-one as their hors d'oeuvres were placed in front of them.

'What's this, my boy?' winked Albert. 'About to make an honest woman of her?'

'Oh Dan!' gasped Geraldine with delight.

'What?'

'Well we have to, *now*!'

'Have to what?' he asked.

'Oh Daniel!' complained Harriet. 'You're determined not to let us have any fun.'

'I am not!' he cried. 'I just don't know what's going on.'

Geraldine turned to his parents.

'Well,' she said. 'If your only son won't let you in on our delicious secret, I can't.'

She started attacking her moules with gusto, hardly tasting anything. Dan looked at his parents for support but they both frowned their disappointment at him. How had this all turned sour so suddenly? He had to rectify the situation; there was a whole meal to get through. He gave a little cough and turned to Geraldine. 'Go on then,' he said. 'Tell them whatever you want to tell them.'

'Oh goodie!' cried Harriet. Dan unclenched his buttocks and listened to what Geraldine wanted to say.

Her face lit up. 'It's nothing official,' she prefaced quickly, wiping her hands on her serviette. 'And this is strictly between us four . . .' she looked round at them all before whispering, 'I've been looking at some rings.' She said 'rings' as if it was a magic word, and so it appeared to be, because suddenly Dan found himself watching his life unravel before him. Harriet and Albert jumped to their feet quicker than if royalty had arrived and started exchanging hugs and wiping lipstick marks off cheeks. It felt like an hour of this went on before he found his voice and started insisting that Geraldine was just *looking* and instructing them not to get too excited, but it was just doggy paddle in the face of an incoming tidal wave.

303

'Oh darling!' insisted Harriet. 'Don't spoil the moment!'

'It's not a moment,' Dan said in a shrinking voice and he was absolutely right; it wasn't 'a' moment, it was 'the' moment. It was the moment his mother had been waiting for ever since she'd met Geraldine. And the moment his father had hoped for ever since they'd packed him off to Oxford. And the moment Geraldine had dreamed of ever since she first saw Dan. Everyone was having the moment of their lives, and there he was, not realising it was one at all. How wrong could you be?

Albert ordered champagne, and in the meantime poured more wine for everyone.

'A toast!' He announced. 'To the happy couple.'

Dan downed his wine in one and when he glanced at his father found himself basking in his proud beam. He felt a fork of lightning momentarily light up his insides, and then, when his father looked away, all was dark again. The next ten minutes passed in a blur, but by the end of the hors d'oeuvres he was sure of one thing. It was official.

And by the end of the main course, he was sure of another thing. Geraldine had eaten a dodgy moule.

19

Dan had not noticed his wife-to-be disappear to the Ladies because he was in a bit of a daze, but after his parents had finished their main course, and hers still lay untouched, he began to suspect. This had happened once before at a May ball. She hadn't been able to resist eating the oysters and then her body hadn't been able to resist bringing them up again. Her ball dress, which had impressed 250 drunk Oxford students, had then made an impressive £7.50 for Cancer Research. He excused himself and found the Ladies. He waited outside for a while until he was fairly sure no one else was in there and crept surreptitiously inside.

He could hear very feeble sobbing.

'Gerry?' he whispered.

One of the cubicle doors moaned.

'Dodgy moule?' he asked it.

Another moan.

'Do you think you'll be able to get to the car?'

Silence. Then a large sniff.

'I can't bear it.'

'Hey hey,' he coaxed gently. 'We'll get you home in no time.'

'No!' she cried. 'I mean why me? This was not how I pictured celebrating the news about my engagement.'

Dan couldn't agree more. 'Come on,' he said, 'you'll laugh about this one day.' Geraldine responded by being violently sick and Dan took her point: He didn't believe it either. In the silence that followed, he found he had absolutely no idea what to say to make it all better. Then, after the briefest pause, some slightly different noises from behind the cubicle door began all too vividly to convey that the moule was not only affecting his chosen one's upper digestive tract and he decided he had to get out of there before they were both sick. He told Geraldine to come out as soon as she could and they'd go straight home. She groaned an agreement.

He joined his parents and told them what had happened, trying very hard not to remember the noises. Harriet was devastated. She'd had the moules too, but hers had been fine. Albert pointed out that it usually only took one. But if only they'd swapped bowls, Harriet explained. It was just too bad. It was more than too bad, it was very upsetting. *Very* upsetting. She was devastated. Poor Geraldine, was she *very* bad? Albert snapped at her not to get so upset which upset her. This upset his equilibrium, so he started demanding to talk to the maître d'. Dan hoped that Geraldine would come out of the toilets before the maître d' came out of the kitchen. He'd rather see her projectile vomit across the restaurant than see his father lose his temper.

To his relief Geraldine appeared. He jumped to his feet

and collected their coats as she approached. Her face was grey and her hair hung in damp, limp strands. She couldn't even speak to his parents but just gave a pathetic wave goodbye and followed Dan out. She was sick twice on the journey home and from the way she ran upstairs Dan suspected that more was going on than she'd let on. He didn't know legs could do that.

She rushed straight to the bathroom while he got undressed and lay in bed waiting for her to join him.

Two hours later, he woke up and looked at his clock. It was midnight. He looked over to Geraldine, but the bed was empty. Oh no, she hadn't been sick again, had she? He would go and make her a hot drink, or just be with her . . .

Four hours later, he woke up and looked at his clock, then looked over to Geraldine, but the bed was empty. Not again? Blimey, that was one bad moule. It had probably been a druggie and alcoholic. He chuckled to himself and then stopped. Poor Geraldine. She was going to feel awful at the wedding. He wondered if Katie would be staying at the same hotel as them. His eyes opened wide. Was Katie actually going 'with' Hugh? He heard a sort of low bellowing noise from the bathroom. Ah, Geraldine must be feeling better now. He'd check that she was OK when she came back. He turned over and plumped his pillows.

Four hours later, he woke up and looked at his clock. Eight a.m. Bloody hell. Time to get up. He wondered if Geraldine would be up to it or if she'd rather have a little lie in. He looked over to her, but the bed was empty. Poor thing. She must have been sick again. He got up and took a shower. He'd make her a nice strong cup of coffee. He checked his post while waiting for the kettle to boil. Then he pulled down Geraldine's favourite mug, made her a pot of coffee, made her some plain toast as well – good for the stomach – and went to find her.

He opened the bathroom door and stopped. Geraldine was sitting on the floor, still in last night's clothes, her back curved against the bath, eyes staring at the floor. Her dress was damp with sweat; her lips were white; her face was green. It was an ugly sight and Dan was suddenly very afraid.

'Bloody hell,' he whispered. She gave a flicker of recognition. 'I-I brought you some breakfast,' he tried. Another flicker. 'Come on,' he knelt down beside her. 'It'll do you good.'

She whispered something inaudible.

'What's that?'

'Go,' she breathed hard, 'away'.

'Why?' he asked. 'What have I done?'

She bent her head down and started crying. When he put his arm round her she shrugged it off.

'I have been sick –' she managed.

'I know –'

'*All*,' she whispered, 'night.'

'Oh my God! I had no idea –'

'No. You were too busy sleeping.' She took a breath. 'Bastard.'

'You should have woken me.'

'I couldn't stand up!'

'Oh my God.'

Neither spoke for a while.

'Shall I call a doctor?'

She shook her head.

'Good way to lose weight for Sandy's wedding, eh?' he whispered. 'You'll be thinner than the bride.'

She moaned. 'I can't go to the wedding.'

'Why not?'

She looked at him. He inched away and looked back at her.

'Do I look ready for a wedding?' she asked.

'Not at the moment, but you've got make-up, haven't you?'

She dry-retched and immediately shuffled down into a foetal position, moaning. She let him stroke her hair, then he helped her sit back up again.

'God,' he said, 'I'm really sorry, I had no idea.'

She managed a weak nod.

'I won't go,' he said suddenly.

She looked up at him with sudden focus. 'Oh no,' she said. She took a piece of toast and gave it a tiny bite. 'You are *going* to that wedding,' she breathed, after the toast had gone down. '*And* you will explain exactly how bad I look *and* you will take the present I spent four hours hunting down and wrapping.'

'But I can look after you,' he implored.

'Hah!' even without any bile left of her own, she could still fill the word with enough of it to unnerve him. 'I needed you last night. Not now.'

Dan scrunched his eyes shut, waiting for the feeling of wretchedness to go. 'I'll never leave you alone again,' he said. They both started at the sound of the phone. He jumped up. 'Back in a mo.'

309

When he came back, she had finished the toast and started the coffee.

'Great news,' he said. 'That was my mum. She's coming right round. She said it's only what your mum would have done if she lived in the country and she's going to be your mum too now.'

Geraldine started really crying.

'What's wrong?' he asked.

'I'm so happy,' she replied.

When Dan appeared in the café kitchen later that morning, Katie was so surprised to see him that she asked what the hell he was doing there. The weather was so good today that the café was exceptionally quiet. They were overstaffed as it was, so even with Sukie at an audition, Katie could easily have taken the day off without Dan being here. She'd been feeling more and more frustrated as the weather had got more and more glorious and the café more and more empty. So seeing Dan unexpectedly – now making the ratio of staff to customers an impressive five to one – was the icing on a cake made of spleen.

Even so, she hadn't intended to sound quite as aggressive as she did, and would have happily apologised if Dan hadn't answered her back quite so sharply. Her only possible response to that was to up the aggression and add knobs, and before she knew it they were rowing. The row took a turn for the better when she found out that Geraldine had been ill all night while he had slept, and was now laid low at home. Now she really had something to stick her teeth into. She was appalled on behalf of women everywhere. Poor Geraldine. How would he have felt if Geraldine had slept through an entire night of him being sick? (But if she'd woken him –) She shouldn't have *had* to wake him (But he wasn't bloody psychic –) And why on earth was his poor mother having to travel across London to look after his girlfriend? (Because she had volunteered to –) Would Geraldine's father do the same for him? Dan was momentarily bamboozled. Hah.

'My mother and Geraldine are very close,' he said, 'especially now.'

' "Especially now"?' repeated Katie. 'What, now that Geraldine's vomiting from both ends? Your mother sounds fascinating.'

'You wouldn't understand,' he said.

'Well, I am only a waitress.'

'Talking of which, don't you have work to do?'

'Ah yes,' said Katie, looking round the near-empty café. 'I'm here instead of being driven down a winding country lane in a convertible to a gastro pub.'

Dan slapped his forehead. 'I forgot!' he cried. 'You had a date with Hugh! But you're covering Sukie because I wasn't going to be here. I thought we'd be understaffed! And now I'm here anyway!' He scrunched his eyes shut, to stop the feeling of wretchedness that was beginning to feel a part of him. He opened them again and looked at Katie. 'What can I do to make it up to you?'

Katie drew herself up short, wondering how Geraldine ever kept sane.

'It was not a date,' she said primly, 'and you can't make it up to me.'

'There *must* be something, oh Always-Right-One.'

311

Katie gave him a wry grin. 'Ah, but if I let you make it up to me I shall lose all my power.'

Dan stopped suddenly and Katie chose this moment to walk past him and out of the kitchen. When she came back five minutes later, she had Hugh with her. She was hoping she might get away early. Hugh was wearing his weekend outfit – pleated-front chinos, a stripy shirt under a round-necked sweater. On his feet, Hush Puppies.

'Look who I found!' said Katie. 'Dressed to party! Lock up your daughters!' She took an appreciative look at Hugh, before turning back to Dan. 'And your wildlife,' she added.

He was looking pensive and barely acknowledged Hugh.

'I was just wondering,' started Katie, 'as most of Porter's Green seems to be at a park instead of here, could I go now?'

'I think I'm going to go back and look after Geraldine,' he said quietly.

'Oh,' said Katie.

There was a pause as she realised this meant she couldn't go early.

'Oh,' said Hugh, 'that's a shame. We were going to ask you if you wanted a lift to the wedding.'

Dan blinked. 'Were you?' He gave Katie a surprised look. She gave one to Hugh. Hugh gave it straight back to Dan.

'Well,' Hugh shrugged, 'seems mad for us all to go up separately. If we collect your stuff on the way we'd be there in a jiffy.'

Dan looked at his watch. 'Hmm,' he said. 'I have

definitely overstaffed. And the weekend staff do know what they're doing.' He looked outside. 'And the weather is lovely,' he sort of muffled to himself. He stood for a while, seemingly weighing something up in his mind; something that was tricky to get on the scales.

'Well,' said Katie, 'we'll let you think –'

'No,' cut in Dan. 'Let me just call Gerry.' He nipped out the back.

Katie turned to Hugh. 'What did you say that for?' she whispered.

'I was only being polite,' he whispered back. 'I thought he'd say no and let you go. How did I know he might say yes?'

When Dan came back into the kitchen he was grinning broadly. He laughed and clapped his hands.

'Gerry's managed some porridge and my mum's going to make her boiled eggs with soldiers for lunch. She told me to have a fab time and report back on everything.' He didn't add that Geraldine had especially wanted notes on Hugh and Katie's 'dalliance'. Or that she was thinking of making an appointment with that amazing local wedding dress shop while his mother was with her, if she was up to it later this afternoon. He knew that Geraldine was far happier being looked after by her future mother-in-law than going to the wedding of her former flat-mate.

And so they set off. Dan and Hugh wanted to do the boy thing and take the front seats, but Katie pulled rank. She was, after all, the only one in the car with a uterus.

'What's that got to do with the price of fish?' asked Hugh.

'What's him having *testicles* got to do with it?' she spluttered.

'What has anyone's testicles got to do with the price of fish?' asked Dan.

'It's nothing to do with his testicles –' said Hugh patiently.

'Oh good –' said Dan.

'– it's because his legs are longer because he's a man,' finished Hugh.

'That's an absolutely *ridiculous* argument,' cried Katie. 'If I'm in the front, I'll have the seat forward so he'll have loads of leg room. We're the same two people, so it doesn't make any difference which one of us sits in the front or back. Except that I'm shorter so if I'm in the back, I get to see much less because he'll be blocking my view and I'll be all squashed up.'

Hugh thought about this. Katie hadn't been a champion debater at Oxford for nothing. 'So why did my mother always sit in the back when we went on family holidays?' he asked.

Katie shrugged. 'I don't know,' she said. 'Because your father drove like a maniac?'

Hugh's eyes widened. 'Oh my God, I think you're right. I was always car sick in the front.'

Dan started laughing and Katie and Hugh turned to him. He crossed his arms and gave them both a big grin. 'Oh boy,' he said, shaking his head, 'this journey is going to be such fun.'

The journey was a lot of fun, although only in retrospect. Living through it was hell. After they had picked up

314

Dan's bag then Katie's bag, struggled to open the roof of Hugh's car, packed their bags in his boot and draped the creasable outfits beside Dan in the back, they were all sweating. Katie waited eagerly for the car to pick up enough speed so that the wind could blow through her hair and into Hugh's face, making it impossible for him to talk. But he didn't drive that fast, partly because he had a lot to get off his chest and partly because he firmly believed that speed limits were there for a reason. Hugh needed to talk about the builders. This Katie understood. Dan joined in too. They all had their share of builder anecdotes to last them to the motorway. Then Hugh decided to regale his passengers with hilarious tales from his and Katie's past. This she could not understand, but she could enjoy. To her surprise she found it a nice trip down memory lane and before long was giggling with Hugh at shared reminiscences. Yes, that had been funny when she'd gone to a lecture after an all-nighter and only realised it was the wrong one when it slowly dawned on her that everyone was speaking French.

'I just thought they were talking fast. Anyway,' she said, 'this must be very boring for Dan.' But he insisted it was fascinating. 'Always good to know the truth about your staff,' he said, which riled her from so many angles she didn't know where to start. So she just sat back and reminisced with Hugh until his driving rendered her no longer able to talk.

'Have you ever had to go on a journey with her?' Hugh asked Dan, and before Dan had a chance to answer or Katie to shut him up, he went on, 'Un-bloody-believable.' He was already starting to laugh. 'She couldn't find her way out of her own toilet. She needs wallpaper that's a map with "You Are Here" on it.'

'Do you mind?' tried Katie.

'We had more rows about that than anything else.' Hugh turned to her. 'Do you remember when I was waiting in that café for four hours?'

'The map was out of date.'

'It was two streets away from your flat!'

'But –'

'And have you ever asked her to make a decision about something important?' he asked Dan. He could hardly talk for laughing now. 'It's like watching a cow with CJD.'

'Right,' cut in Katie. 'Stop the car. I'm getting out. On behalf of cows everywhere.'

Hugh finally shut up and the three of them sat in silence for a while, Hugh to enjoy the drive, Katie and Dan to focus on not being sick. It had turned out that Hugh thought the way to drive was to exert minuscule pumping movement after minuscule pumping movement on the gas pedal. After half an hour she wondered if she could convince Dan to sit in the front. After an hour she wondered if she could convince Hugh that travelling in reverse used less petrol. After an hour and a half, she wondered if she'd ever feel normal again. She'd never before been glad to hear twelve songs from Celine Dion in a row, but at least it meant she could moan without anyone being able to hear, often in tune.

'So!' said Hugh so suddenly and loudly when the tape finished that she would have jumped if she'd been physically capable of moving. 'How's the famous "café" going?' By now, Katie was frightened to open her eyes, let alone her mouth. She decided to let Dan do the talking. He was in the best seat, after all.

'Dan?' Hugh turned to look at him, swerving the wheel as he did so. Katie felt her breakfast lurch up into her chest.

'Mm?' said Dan weakly.

'How's the wonderful café going?'

'Fine thanks.'

'I think you've done a marvellous job,' Hugh said. 'Absolutely marvellous. You've shown real balls.' He let out an enthusiastic burst of laughter. 'You know what I mean? Real *balls*.'

'Thanks,' managed Dan.

'Mon plaisir, capitaine,' smiled Hugh, 'mon plaisir.'

Now Katie felt really sick.

'And it's a lovely little café,' continued Hugh. He suddenly sat bolt upright, and leant over to the glove compartment in front of Katie. He pulled out a map-book and threw it on to her lap. 'Right,' he said. 'I need directions from here.'

'Hugh,' Katie sat up. 'You know I can't read maps.'

'I know!' cried out Hugh. 'It'll be just like old times.'

'But we'll end up in Wales.'

'Right, there's a roundabout coming up soon,' said Hugh patiently. 'Do I go right or left? It's easy, right's the one on the right. Left's the one on the left.'

'And Pillock is the one behind the wheel.'

Hugh laughed good-naturedly. 'You see?' he said. 'Just like old times.'

Katie turned round to Dan, who gave her a wobbly smile. She pleaded silently with him, but he raised his

317

eyebrows in mock ignorance. 'We'll get there faster if you do it,' she mouthed. He sat up and grabbed the map from her.

When they arrived at the hotel, they had just over two hours to get ready before the wedding was due to start. Or in Katie and Dan's case, one hour to be sick, one hour to recover and ten minutes to get ready.

As they drove, jerkily, up to the hotel they were momentarily hushed. Ahead of them stood a fourteenth-century castle, turrets stretching up to the aqua sky, swans floating round it in the moat below. They pulled themselves out of the car rather unsteadily and crunched over the gravel to the entrance where they were signposted to the cosy reception desk.

Had there been any doubt in anyone's mind that a wedding was taking place here this afternoon, all doubt now vanished. Had there been any doubt that daisies were the theme of this wedding, all doubt now vanished. The hotel was adorned with daisies: the imposing oak-banisters that spiralled from entrance hall to dining room and beyond were bedecked with them; every low, oak-beamed door (complete with attached cushion for those who might forget to bend) was smothered in them; in the small, private lounges, the vast fireplaces were festooned with them. There was a summer wedding here and daisies were the theme.

Hugh became jittery with excitement. He unwrapped one of the boiled sweets in the bowl on the check-in desk and popped it into his mouth and then took a quick look round the place, while waiting for the receptionist to

318

confirm their details. Some of the other wedding guests were also checking in and Dan and Katie smiled at people holding overnight bags and carrying creaseable outfits over their shoulders. Old college friends who had not been seen since the engagement party were greeting each other with whoops of delight, claims of great excitement and then uncomfortable silences.

'Right,' the check-in receptionist smiled briefly at them both and held up a key. 'Suite Number 121. Luxury four-poster bed as requested.'

'Oh no,' said Katie quickly. 'We're not together.'

'No,' said Dan half under his breath. 'She's with the buffoon in the lounge eating the Murray Mint.'

Katie gave him a haughty glance. 'You mean the buffoon who gave you a free lift all the way here?'

'You're right,' said Dan mildly. 'I meant the "bastard" in the lounge.'

They stared at each other until the check-in receptionist gave a practised little cough, and Dan started giving his details. It turned out that he was in Room 120 opposite, so after Hugh had found them again – 'I've just seen Todd Jackson! He's completely bald!' – they climbed the thickly carpeted main stairs and then a narrower winding stairway.

'You've got the four-poster you requested,' Dan informed Hugh.

'Excellent,' beamed Hugh, which hadn't been quite the response Katie had expected. 'Have you got one too?'

'Don't know yet,' said Dan.

'What a shame Geraldine's missing all this,' said Hugh.

'Yes,' said Dan. 'She'd have loved the drive down.'

Katie had to stifle a smile. They reached their doors and Dan turned on his heel to face them both. He was holding his uncrushed dinner jacket and shirt behind him on its hanger, his hair slightly ruffled, his cheeks flushed, his head slightly cocked to one side. Katie looked away, stared at her closed door and then looked back.

'Well,' said Dan. 'Enjoy the four-poster.' He gave Hugh a boyish wink and then turned to unlock the door to his room.

Katie stood looking at the suite, feeling suddenly glum. It was spectacular. The windows did not merely have curtains, they were garlanded with them. The bed did not merely have a quilt, it was swathed in fabric. The bathroom did not just have a bath, it had a small swimming pool. She was standing in the middle of the bathroom, performing a 360-degree stare, when she heard Hugh curse loudly. She came back into the bedroom to find him sitting on the four-poster, his travel bag beside him, holding an envelope. She was about to remind him that he had promised he'd sleep on the couch when she realised he was pale. She walked nearer.

'Hugh?'

He waved the envelope dismally at her.

'It's Maxine's writing,' he said. 'She's here already.'

Katie hadn't given it a moment's thought that Hugh had been driving towards a confrontation with Maxine. No wonder he'd wanted Dan to join them. Safety in numbers. He'd probably have asked the rest of the café if they'd been invited. She sat next to him on the bed and looked at Maxine's writing. She wasn't giving much away. Smack bang in the middle of the envelope was the letter 'H'.

'It was her nickname for me,' said Hugh, miserably.

'It might be nice,' she said hopefully. 'Come on.'

He opened it and while he read it, she held his hand, looking away. He sighed heavily. 'Oh God.'

'What?'

He gave her the letter.

H,

I thought it best to let you know that I'm here with David, my boyfriend. I didn't think he'd get a late invitation, but Sandy called this morning to say that Geraldine wasn't coming, so she had a spare space. It means swapping a few people around, but she did it. She just wants everyone to be happy on her big day. As do I. I hope you can find it in yourself to be happy for me.
See you at the altar. I'll be the one in lilac.

M.

They sat in silence until eventually Hugh said, 'He was my carpenter.'

'I know.'

'He's a good carpenter.'

'Oh.'

'Not very punctual.'

'Mm.'

'That'll annoy her after a while.'

'Good.'

'Our bedroom's lilac.'

'Oh.'

'It's the only room in the whole bloody house I like.'

Katie smiled. 'I'm surprised she didn't wear magnolia.'

He gave a half-hearted chuckle. Then he held her hand and thanked her for being there with him. She squeezed his hand and told him it was her pleasure. Then he hugged her and said he didn't know what he'd have done if he'd been there on his own. She hugged him back and said it was her pleasure. Then he rested his head on her shoulder, and she got up to quickly unpack her outfit.

They arranged that Hugh would get ready first because Katie's dress was so tight she wanted to get in some extra breathing before putting it on, but as the length of Hugh's baths had been legendary at uni, she asked for the bathroom first for a quick shower. At this he promised her that he didn't mind if she wanted to share bathroom time with him, and she told him to quit while she still felt any sympathy. Then he gave such a heart-wrenchingly sincere apology that she felt sorry for him all over again. When she came out, she lay on her bed in an oversized towelling robe, channel flicking, while he submerged himself for so long she thought even his internal organs must have gone wrinkly.

As she heard a bold knock on the door she assumed Hugh had ordered some drinks and jumped up eagerly. 'Ooh,' she called to him, as she opened the door excitedly. 'Is this what I think it is?'

'Doubt it,' grinned Dan, leaning nonchalantly against the door frame.

They both stepped back, Katie's hand instinctively jumping up to her robe.

'Hello,' she said in a small voice, the towelling feeling suddenly very thin.

Dan glanced behind her into the room before speaking. It transpired that Sandy had set off a phone chain round the hotel to all her friends, pleading with them to pop up in turn and see her before the ceremony.

Katie's eyes widened. 'But I've just found *Big Brother Live* on Sky TV.'

'Wow!' said Dan. 'Hard to resist. Or we can go and see Sandy before she gets married.'

She gave a squeal and a little jump before instructing him to wait outside for two minutes while she got dressed back into her travelling clothes. When she opened the door again, he went off at some speed down the corridor, only talking to check if she'd told Hugh and left the name of the next person on the chain for him to call. Of course she had.

Sandy's door was ajar and, as they approached, the moment suddenly overcame them. They gave the door a tentative knock and pushed it slightly.

The room was vast with an enormous double bed and there were flowers and presents strewn everywhere. In the background, *Big Brother* was on and three women in big hats, flowing dresses and stiletto heels stood watching it intently. As a toilet flushed in the bathroom, the woman in the middle zapped off the television and flung the remote somewhere on the bed. Then all three turned round and spotted the newcomers.

'Hello!' said Katie quickly. 'I'm Katie.'

'And I'm Dan.'

'Aha!' said Sandy's mum, clapping her hands. 'I'm Barbara. You must be Katie Simmonds and Daniel Crichton! Table 12. By the bay window. We had a last minute shuffle after Geraldine Harris phoned in sick and Maxine White brought David Barker along. It means Uncle Bob's now near the band, but he's deaf so he won't notice . . .'

'We don't know what we're going to do with her after the wedding,' confided Barbara's older sister and they all laughed, a little too loudly.

The bathroom door opened and Sandy stood framed there.

Katie gasped. She'd never seen a bride this close up before. The dress was an exquisite tight, beaded number in ivory silk. The bride's face was magnolia.

'*Look*!' exclaimed Barbara in a high-pitched voice. 'Daniel Crichton and Katie Simmonds! Table 12, near the bay window!'

Sandy stared at them. 'Hi,' she said weakly.

Barbara nudged her sisters and they hustled past Katie and Dan, with manic grins. Barbara stopped when she got to them and in a stage whisper said that the bride had a few pre-wedding nerves, and then closed the door behind her with a resounding click.

Sandy stared at them. Her hair was up in a bun, tiny white daisies round its base and a short veil hanging down to her shoulders, with matching daisies sewn into its hem. She was about half the size she'd been at her engagement party. Her collar bone looked as if she'd swallowed a hanger and a patchwork of blue veins showed through her almost translucent skin. Her large blue eyes suddenly filled with tears.

'What the fucking fuck am I doing?' she whispered.

Katie ran to her and, stopping short of hugging her in her dress, squeezed her bare arms. Dan stood frozen to the spot as Katie slowly guided the almost paralysed Sandy over to the bed.

'I mean,' she breathed, sitting on the bed. 'For fucking fuck's sake . . .'

'You're going to be fine,' soothed Katie.

'Maybe today,' whispered Sandy, 'But what about tomorrow? And the day after that? And next year? And the year after that? I need a cigarette. They're on the table.'

'You'll be fine,' said Katie, passing her the pack.

'How do you know?' Sandy's hands shook as she lit up. 'I mean you're not exactly Commitment Queen yourself, are you?'

'Sweetheart,' soothed Katie, 'I won't take that personally.'

'I didn't mean it personally,' Sandy held her hand tightly and took a deep drag on her cigarette. 'I'm in shock.'

'I know. You're doing fantastically. You just have to take it one day at a time.'

'He doesn't shower before he goes to bed.'

'Who doesn't?'

'The man I'm about to marry.'

'Simon?'

'That's it.'

'Well, tell him to.'

Katie looked over to Dan for support. He was still where she'd left him, rooted to the spot, and staring rigidly at Sandy.

'How can I?' asked Sandy. 'I'm about to publicly relinquish all rights.'

'No you aren't!' said Katie forcefully. 'You're about to publicly declare how much you love him.'

'Same thing.'

There was a pause as Sandy inhaled deeply.

'You look stunning,' said Katie.

'Thanks,' said Sandy, flicking ash on the carpet. 'Bloody should do, it cost three grand. Every bead cost twenty pounds.'

'They are the most *beautiful* beads I have ever seen,' smiled Katie. 'I was going to say.' Sandy managed a smile too.

The door opened and Hugh bounded in, a smile on his face and a lilac bow-tie at his neck. He clapped his hands in delight.

'Here she is then!' he boomed. 'The blushing bride! Ready to swear Love and Obedience?'

A bit later, Dan sat in his suite staring at the television. He really should turn it on, but he couldn't be bothered to find the remote, and anyway, his headache was getting worse. In fact, he was still feeling a bit nauseous from the journey. Jesus, he thought. What was all this sickness? First Nik, then Geraldine, now him. Maybe there was something going round. Life, he thought bitterly. His bones ached. He kept thinking he should get up and shower for the wedding, but then he visualised

Sandy's rigor-mortis-in-ivory look and felt sick again.

Seeing her like that had hit home to him with the force of a wrecking ball: he, Daniel Crichton, was getting married. His girlfriend, whom he had actually finished with once precisely because he had thought – had *known* – she was not the woman for him, was this very afternoon flicking through photos of wedding dresses with his mother, maybe even trying some on. He was going to share his surname with her. He would be giving her a part of himself, turning them into one entity.

Why? Why was he getting married, he asked himself now, repeating the words over and over again until they lost all meaning. Was he scared of life without Geraldine? Or just scared of life without anyone?

Oh God, what had he done? He started to rock to and fro as real panic began to rise inside him. No, he would keep a grip. He would concentrate. Think this through. He stood up suddenly and started pacing.

It was OK to marry out of fear, he told himself. After all, wasn't fear what made most people marry? Fear of being alone, fear of being an outcast, fear of never being loved. Look at Sandy. She was fucking terrified. He felt cold all over. No. Get a grip. He started pacing again. It was OK to have doubts, he told himself. After all, didn't everyone have doubts? He paced a bit faster. Anyway, everyone knew marriage wasn't what it used to be. It was rarely for life any more. Divorce wasn't the stigma it used to be. He could safely be married for ten years, divorce Gerry and still be able to have a family with someone else. He stopped still. Shit. That was not the attitude to go into marriage with.

He leant against the window frame and stared out into the gardens, letting his eyes fix on the leaves of the magnificent oak tree gently swaying in the summer breeze. If that tree could talk, he thought to himself. How many men had worried about their future in its shade? How many of those doubts had been futile? He shifted his gaze to the drifting clouds behind it, their shapes fluid. He watched them for a while. Feeling a bit calmer, he told himself there was nothing he could do now anyway. Just enjoy the wedding. And get drunk. Then he looked at the clock and walked into his bathroom.

Meanwhile, Katie was standing, eyes shut, shoulders bare, the sound of Hugh's soft breath sending shivers down her spine. As she felt his fingers on her shoulder blades, her whole body shuddered.

'Nearly there,' he whispered.

He made a small, guttural noise and she let out a moan.

'One more minute,' he said. 'God I'm out of practice.'

'Shall I turn round?'

'No.'

'I don't want to be late.'

'I never had to do this with Maxine.'

Silence.

'*Aha!*' he cried. 'Done it!' He stepped away from her. 'Top button done up.'

Half an hour later, she was standing in the lounge of her suite phoning Sukie. She would not be sitting for the rest of the day unless absolutely necessary. Her dress only flowed from the hip; above the hip it clung to her small frame with the determination of a teething baby clutching its mother. If this dress could have got under her skin it would have. Her body wasn't so much wearing any underwear as eating it. Her diaphragm was wondering who'd turned out the lights. Any food that hadn't passed through her body yet only had itself to blame. This was a tight dress.

'Your voice sounds funny,' said Sukie. 'Are you in The Dress?'

'Yes.'

'Do you look tiny?' Sukie was grinning.

'Yes.'

'How tiny?'

'I'm Thumbelina.'

'Ohmygod,' said Sukie. 'You look so gorgeous in that dress. Do your boobs and bum look big and small at the same time?'

'Yes.'

'You are *so* gonna score.'

'I doubt it. I can't bend.'

Sukie's audition had gone well. This time the director had discussed his philosophy at some length and even asked her for some ideas. He asked her for ways she thought they could add humour. She'd said, 'Put in some jokes', which she thought they found quite amusing.

Then, at the sound of a long, low wolf whistle, Katie's conversation had to come to a close. Hugh was waiting. She said her goodbyes to Sukie, clicked off her phone and collected her sequinned shawl and purse.

'Right,' he said, his face suddenly grim. 'Ready?'

She nodded. 'You?'

He nodded too. She went up to him and laced her arm under his. 'You'll be fine,' she said. He gave her a smile and, together, they went down to the wedding.

20

Dan sat as near to the back as he could. He didn't want to block anyone's view and felt somewhat soothed by the thought that he was near the exit. He kept having flashbacks to Sandy in her room and felt like shit in a suit – a nice suit, but that seemed irrelevant right now. He looked down at it and gave it an almost nostalgic smile. This would probably be the last time he wore it. Geraldine hated it.

Gerry! He'd forgotten to call her and find out how she was. He looked round the room and gauged that he'd still have time to rush back upstairs and phone her – he hadn't brought his mobile down with him. He stood up and apologised to the guests shifting in their seats to let him out.

As he slowly closed the door behind him, the sound of the string quartet dimmed. He sped across the thick-pile carpet, to the sweeping stairs and then stopped. At the top, coming towards him were Hugh and Katie sharing a joke. Katie wore a golden corset with ball-gown skirt, her hair covered in glitter, skin the colour of warm honey, cheeks flushed. She was holding up her skirt and he could see flashes of gold shoes and slender, bronzed legs. He felt like an intruder.

'Hello!' called out Hugh breezily.

Katie looked at Dan and stopped. He forced himself to keep on walking up and greeted Hugh. Katie came slowly down towards him.

'Aren't you going the wrong way?' asked Hugh.

'I forgot to phone –' he stopped. He looked at Katie who was now level with him, her autumn eyes smiling.

'Hello,' she said.

'Hi.'

'Let's all sit together,' said Hugh. 'I'm bricking it. Could do with the moral support.'

'Hugh's ex is here with her new man,' explained Katie, her shoulder almost touching Dan's.

'Oh right,' he said. 'Awkward all round then.' He paced up a step or two, until he was standing above Katie.

'Did you see a woman in lilac?' Hugh called up to him.

'Er . . .' He racked his brain, noticing some freckles on Katie's right shoulder. 'Er . . .'

'Answers to the name of Mad Max,' added Katie, turning up to him.

He readjusted his eyes. 'Don't remember.'

Katie glanced away.

'You're cutting it fine, aren't you?' asked Hugh, checking his watch. 'We're late. Would have been earlier but I got a bit waylaid doing up Katie's dress, if you know what I mean.' He gave him a man-to-man wink above her head.

Dan raced up the stairs as he heard Katie give a phoney

gasp of shock. 'Save me a place,' he called back down to them. 'I'll be back in a sec.'

He ran all the way to his room and just stood there for a while.

There was no way he'd have time to phone Geraldine now. What had he been thinking? He couldn't be later than the bride. Poor Sandy was nervous enough as it was. He would just have to tell Geraldine they only arrived with an hour to spare and that he had to go and see Sandy before it had started. How the hell was she to know? What she didn't know couldn't hurt her, right? He paced to the window overlooking the oak tree. His mobile phone was on the desk there. He'd text her. Brilliant.

Got here late. Journey hell. Speak asap. Love Dan

He shut the door behind him and ran back to the wedding.

The ceremony was in a small oak-panelled room looking out on to a rose-filled garden. To one side at the front perched the string quartet, solemnly bowing their instruments, and in the guests' seats family and friends exchanged intrigued glances.

Katie and Hugh, at the back on the bride's side, scrutinised the other guests. Hugh nudged Katie and pointed to a large lilac hat about third row from the front, but Katie shook her head and pointed out a smaller lilac hat only one row ahead of them, just over to their right. Maxine turned round and gave them both a quick yet effective all-in-one glance before turning back only halfway, to half face the front. To anyone else, this would look like a guest preparing herself for the entrance of the bride. To Hugh and Katie, it looked like she was keeping them in the corner of her eye. Hugh insisted on keeping a place for Dan on the other side of Katie. Katie started trying to feel her top button. If only she was here with a girlfriend. She didn't want to ask Hugh with Maxine this close, but she didn't want Dan to sit next to her before she was sure her top button was done up. She had definitely caught him looking at her back. It was either a spot or she was coming undone. The door behind opened and all eyes turned towards it. Katie felt Maxine's eyes bore into her back. It wasn't Dan, but the next one might be.

'Can you check my dress is still done up,' she finally whispered to Hugh. She felt him lean right in and give her back a pretend nuzzle before whispering in her ear seductively, 'Perfect.'

She gave him a look. She could see Maxine in soft focus behind him.

'What,' she said in a slow, firm whisper, 'the arsing hell do you think you're playing at?'

'Have you seen David sitting next to Maxine?' Hugh smiled warmly at her, his eyes brimming with affection. 'He's got a white bow-tie on. Tosser.'

'That is no reason to look at me as if you've just proposed marriage,' whispered Katie firmly.

There was a cough behind them and they jumped and turned to see Dan standing there. He threw Katie a rather dry look. She did her best to throw it right back at him.

'I don't want to interrupt anything private,' he said, 'but is this seat taken?'

She went red to her roots. 'See?' she shot back at Hugh. 'We look like a frigging couple.'

'No we don't.' Hugh gave an affected laugh and tapped Dan on the shoulder, leaving his hand on the back of Dan's chair, so that his arm was now round Katie. It was only the fact that she couldn't bear to humiliate him in front of Maxine that stopped her from slapping it. 'Do we look like a couple?'

'*Hugh!*' hissed Katie.

'Why?' asked Dan. 'Trying to keep it a secret?'

Hugh laughed again, this time loud and long. Katie could swear she heard Maxine whisper something to David, but she couldn't see them because Hugh was now completely blocking her view. In fact, he was practically sitting on her lap.

Suddenly the string quartet started playing 'The Arrival of the Queen of Sheba' and the guests rose. Thank God, thought Katie. She turned to look at the bride, and caught a glimpse of Dan staring straight ahead. He was almost as pale and stiff as Sandy had been earlier. At the memory of Sandy, a sudden knot formed in her stomach. This was the first of her friends to cross the big divide in their big white dress. How on earth had Sandy known this was the man for her? She looked ahead to the groom, who was now turned to face his bride, a self-conscious smile on his face. Was Sandy going to be all right? She hopped from foot to foot, trying to make out the bride through the guests' heads, nervous of how she would appear.

Then she saw her. She had expected Sandy to look either rigid with fear or rigid with stoicism; either way rigid. Instead here was a glowing, radiant bride bestowing

335

sunshine smiles on all her friends and family, giving little waves to a lucky few. Where was the smoking, shaking, swearing girl from the hotel room? Sandy caught Katie's eye and gave her a smile of such love and hope that Katie felt a sudden uplifting, like a glider being carried away. She trusted Sandy's future, romance, luck and life. She loved everyone in the room, she loved her parents and her pets, she loved Sukie and her job and she wanted Hugh and Maxine to fall back in love. Weddings were life-affirming miracles. She wondered how long Sandy would wait to start having children. Sandy would be a mother! She would create a new person, a new life, a new journey, a new miracle.

Hugh handed her a tissue.

Then, Sandy approached the altar (which was groaning with daisies) and gave a modest look down before meeting the gaze of the man she'd pounced on in a drunken bet at a party. She turned and demurely handed her bridesmaid her bouquet and slowly lifted her veil. Sandy was every inch the bride. Gone was all uncertainty. Sandy was a woman now.

Standing in the rose-garden, only forty minutes later, Katie could hardly get a word out of Dan. He downed his champagne like a man dying of thirst and barely joined in the conversation that Hugh was forcing on them both, just loud enough for Maxine to hear. Everyone's eyes were fixed on the glowing bride as she flitted from group to group. Finally, she reached Katie. They screamed at each other and gave a little jump in the air. Katie asked her how she felt. Sandy felt wonderful, she was walking on air, she had never been so happy. Katie squealed with excitement. What was it like being a bride? Wonderful, it was the happiest day of her life. Katie squealed with excitement again. What was it like wearing a dress like that? Wonderful, it was like being a fairy princess, she was walking on air. Katie squealed with excitement. And-and-and what was in that perfect, beaded purse she was carrying? Sandy stopped for a moment, frowned and then opened the bag.

'Painkillers, ciggies, tampons.'

Katie stopped squealing.

'My head's killing me,' sighed Sandy. 'This bun's agony, I've got such bad period pains, and I'm *dying* for a fag.' She gave Katie a smile. 'Apart from that,' she beamed, 'I'm walking on air.'

Katie, Dan and Hugh quickly became a threesome. And then, almost as quickly, they became a drunk threesome. Champagne was served for two hours while the photographs of the bride and groom, bride and groom's family, all the men, all the women and all the cousins twice removed, were taken. Any canapés there were, were being offered too far away and never made it through the crowds to them, or else passed by too fast and they just didn't catch them in time. Katie and Dan tried to persuade Hugh to talk to Maxine, but he was having none of it. 'I'm far too busy being happy for her,' he kept saying, until eventually they found this quite funny.

When they all slowly made their way to the table plan, Katie started getting nervous, and, as she reached it, she discovered she had every good cause. Not only was she on the same table as Hugh, but she was on the same table as Dan, Hugh, Maxine and Maxine's new boyfriend David. Hugh was sandwiched between Katie and Maxine, Katie between Hugh and Dan. David was next to Maxine. The other three people on the table had no idea of the minefield they had stepped into.

Hugh, Katie and Dan stood at their table, staring at their place-names in disbelief. Just as they were wondering what could possibly be said about it, Maxine and David arrived. Everyone pretended not to see each other. Then Hugh turned to Katie, his back to Maxine, 'Thank goodness we're together,' he murmured in her ear and, one hand in the small of her back, one on the back of her chair, he guided her into her seat. As she sat down, she could have sworn she saw Maxine giving her the evil eye. Oh great, she thought. I'll be dead by Wednesday.

It was Katie who started the conversation. She thought she was doing the right thing, thought that if she broke the ice, it would all be OK. After all, this was a wedding – there were daisies in the middle of their table and everything.

'Hi there,' she called across Hugh to Maxine in a voice she hoped was open and friendly. 'Long time no see!'

Maxine gave her a level look before blanking her and looking at Hugh.

'Didn't take you long to get over me, did it?'

Katie felt her eyes sting at such an obvious rebuff. She wouldn't have minded, but from Maxine White! She of

338

the pointless questions in lectures, of the shoulder blades like pistons, of the etc. Humiliation coursed through her body.

She heard Hugh answer back: 'As I recall, it didn't take you any time at all.' Katie could feel his left foot twitching with tension under the table. 'Oh yes, I forget,' he went on. 'We'd just finished decorating the house and the carpenter had just gone.' He looked across at David. 'Hi there David! Nice to see you again.'

David nodded, coughed and looked away.

'We're just friends actually,' said Katie quietly.

'Hey,' Dan leant forward. 'It *is* a wedding, guys.'

Maxine looked at him while the others all looked at their plates. She turned back to Hugh. 'So, was she always there in the background?'

'She?' croaked Katie, her voice catching.

'Oh that's right,' boomed Hugh. 'Tar everyone with your own . . . broom.'

The band struck up and everyone was asked to be upstanding for the bride and groom. In came the joyful couple, to thunderous applause. They made their way through the room to the top table where they sat down. Delighted, everyone took their seats again.

'You mean brush,' Maxine hissed at Hugh so loudly that three tables stared at her. She sat up straight and swept her long hair over her shoulder.

'Well,' smiled Katie to Hugh. 'That told you.'

Maxine whipped back to face Katie, her eyes two thin slits of hatred. 'This is between me and Hugh, *thank you*.' Katie was about to say there was no need to thank her; it had been a pleasure, when Dan butted in again.

'Actually,' he said. 'It's affecting all of us and we're all here to enjoy a wedding. If you want to have a row, please go somewhere and have it privately.'

'Who the hell is this?' Maxine asked Hugh. 'Judge Judy?'

Katie laughed despite herself. She turned to Dan and raised her eyebrows.

'Ooh yes,' she said. 'That works.'

'Oh *look*,' Maxine pulled a sickly face that was half-grimace, half-smile. 'She's playing one off against the other. Just like back at college.'

Katie could barely breathe for shock and hurt. She waited for someone to put Maxine in her place, but the deafening silence was only broken by three loud cheers for the happy couple.

Not much food was eaten at table 12, but the wine went down in a flash. By the end of the meal and speeches, no one cared who was angry with whom. They were at a wedding and the drink was free.

Then the dancing began. Katie was not surprised when the three other people from table 12 escaped to the bar. Dan immediately left to go and chat to the bride and groom, abandoning her to Hugh, the madwoman and the carpenter. Katie squared herself up for round two, but the carpenter stood up, put his hand out and Maxine graciously rested her hand in his, stood up and they took to the dance floor. Katie and Hugh looked at each other, exchanged glassy smiles and then watched Maxine and her new man. The couple strutted out as if they were on *Come Dancing* – Hugh and Katie started to snicker – and then, to everyone's surprise, they stood opposite each other on the dance floor and were transformed into King and Queen Salsa. They were mesmerising.

'Right,' slurred Hugh, standing unsteadily and rolling up his sleeves.

'No!' cried Katie, leaping up and holding him back as much as a five-foot-tall drunk girl in a corset could. 'She's *really* not worth it.'

Hugh blinked two watery eyes at her.

'I was only going to ask you to dance.'

'Hugh,' she said, looking at the Salsa Two, 'you can't beat that.'

'Please.' He held her hand. 'Don't refuse me in my hour of need.'

And so she let herself be led out on to the dance floor where Hugh swept her up (only catching her shoe on one other dancer's heel) and held her in his arms. He couldn't salsa, but it turned out he was a pro at that well-known dance called The Throb. He rubbed himself up so close to her that it felt as if they were trying for a baby to music. She kept trying to pull away, but like a dog's choke chain, his grip got firmer each time. Halfway through the dance she was trained. She just kept as still as possible. By the end they were so close that if she did move away he'd have fallen down and never got up again. And then Maxine would have salsa'd all over him. Katie would just have to wait till the music stopped.

She had enough time during the dance to wonder why she felt she owed Hugh something, and ponder on why she felt her politeness was being abused? It was just like being fourteen again. She pulled her neck back a bit and

341

looked up at him. His eyes were closed. She called his name and he leaned back a little, giving her the most space since they'd started dancing.

'You don't really think I played you off against anyone at college, do you?' she asked tentatively.

He gazed at her fondly. 'Hmm? No!'

A lilac form whizzed past them.

'I never meant to hurt you,' she said, her voice quivering slightly.

'I know, sweetheart.' He flicked some gold flecks off her shoulders.

'I-I just got scared.'

'I know.'

The lilac form whizzed past again.

'I don't play with men's feelings.'

'I know.'

He looked down at her and gave her a deific smile. She rested her head on his chest so as to prevent the sensation of spinning and the more terrifying sensation of nearly being kissed.

After the music finished, she tried to pull Hugh back to the table, but he refused to go with the stubbornness of a mule and increasingly, the glazed look of one. She waved at Dan, who was, conveniently enough, looking at them. She beckoned him over and he slowly rose and approached. He really did look good in a suit, thought Katie, watching him make his way to them across the dance floor. Especially now he'd loosened his tie. She watched him squeeze in between all the dancers until he finally reached them.

'Aha!' exclaimed Hugh. 'Dan the Man!' He slapped

him on the back. 'Katie and I were having an intermintent moment.'

'Is that what it was,' said Dan.

Katie explained the situation as simply as she could. Hugh needed to get to bed. (On this Hugh gave Dan a big, slow wink.) But she couldn't get him there on her own. (Hugh shook his head and frowned.) If Dan could help her get him upstairs, she would open the door to their suite, they could get him on the sofa and then come back down again. 'Just as long as no one looks at us,' Hugh confided in Dan. 'We don't want anyone seeing.' It was agreed. Dan put his arm underneath Hugh's and gripped him firmly at the waist while Hugh placed his arm round Dan's shoulder and Katie ran to get her purse. Hugh looked at Dan. Dan looked at Hugh. Hugh smiled at Dan. Dan smiled at Hugh.

'She's very *very* special,' said Hugh.

'I know.'

'Very very *very* special.'

Katie arrived. 'Right, let's go.'

'I was just telling Danny boy . . .' started Hugh, before launching into 'Oh Danny Boy' which, all things considered, he sang rather well. By the time they got him out of the ballroom, across the main reception, up the grand oak staircase and to the bottom of the narrower winding stairway, they were worn out.

'Wait a minute,' said Dan, hefting Hugh into a sitting position on the bottom step. 'Let's just rest here.'

They collapsed in a small heap, Dan and Katie either side of Hugh. Hugh sprawled up the stairs. 'Ooh,' he said. 'This is *nice*.'

Katie and Dan looked at each other over his prostrate body and smiled. When he started to snore, Katie started to giggle, but not Dan.

'We'd better get him going again,' he said, getting up. 'Otherwise we'll be stuck here all night.'

They pulled him up and he put his arms round them both.

'Hello,' he smiled. 'Is it morning?'

They finally reached the door to the suite and Dan leant him against the wall while Katie found her key and opened it. She pointed where the sofa was, but Hugh launched himself on to the bed.

'No no,' she said, rushing over to him and shaking him.

'He's supposed to be on the sofa,' she told Dan. But Hugh was out cold.

'He's not going anywhere,' said Dan. 'Looks like he's in the bed.'

They sat down on either side of Hugh, who started a slow, rhythmic, almost melodious snore. It was only fair, thought Katie, as she watched him. He had paid for the suite. She'd go on the sofa, it looked comfortable enough.

'Yes,' she said quietly. 'I think you're right.'

'I'll leave you to it then,' said Dan and was gone. She stared down at Hugh in frustration and to her surprise he slowly opened an eye. Then, to her astonishment, he opened the other one. And then he gave her a broad grin.

'Ding *dong*,' he said.

21

'What are you doing?'

'Nothing!'

'Then stop moving your hand.'

'I'm not moving my hand. Look!'

'The other one.'

'Just relax.'

'Hugh, this is not Porky's, and I am not fourteen. Let me go.'

'Shhh.'

'Let me go or I will knee you so hard your doodads will give you an overbite.'

'I love you.'

'I don't care.'

'Oh.' That was unexpected.

'It is irrelevant,' she continued. 'You are drunk, you are still grieving Maxine –'

'No!' Hugh sat up. 'I love you. I've always loved you.'

'Don't be ridiculous.'

'I'm not being ridiculous! I love you.'

'I don't care.'

'You must believe me.'

'No, Hugh, you're not listening to me. I don't want to get into a debate about this because that will validate it.'

'What?'

'And anyway, I will win. Get some rest and –'

'Promise me one thing!'

'No.'

'You owe me.'

Katie gasped. 'I owe you nothing, Hugh Penrose,' she whispered hoarsely. 'Just because I ended a relationship that was no longer right for me. You have absolutely no moral –'

'Oh shut up, I meant because I drove you up here and let you stay in the suite.'

'Oh. Right.'

'Sleep with me.'

She gasped again. 'You –'

'I mean,' he rushed. 'I mean *sleep* – in the same bed. I'm so *lonely*.'

'I'm beginning to see why,' she said. 'You're not to be trusted.'

Hugh fell back on to the bed and sighed melo-dramatically. 'Katie, Katie, Katie, Katie.'

She looked at him. 'What, what, what, what?'

He gave another sigh. 'Just Katie, Katie, Katie, Katie.'

She whispered a curse and stood, but Hugh pulled her back down again. She fell back on to the bed just as he was sitting up. He gave her a hazy kiss on her cheek and nuzzled into her neck. Gently yet firmly Katie pushed him back so he was lying down

'I'm going now, Hugh,' she told him.

'Let me just say one thing.'

346

'No.'

'Yes.'

She got up. 'No.'

'Yes.'

She reached the door and, feeling relatively safe from there, decided it was the least she could do. 'All right then, go on, what is it?'

There was silence for a moment and then, from deep within Hugh's very essence, came a deep, rich, polysyllabic belch.

It was a long way back to the ballroom. All down the corridor to the stairs, Katie swished her long ball skirt, musing on what a bitch Maxine was and what a poor sap Hugh was for ever having got involved with her. As she tripped lightly down the winding staircase, she relived the venomous exchange of insults at the table, especially Maxine's horribly off-target accusation that she was some sort of tease. As she walked past the now dark reception, she relived Dan's comment 'awkward all round', at being told Hugh had an ex-girlfriend. She reflected suddenly that maybe he too thought she was here 'with' Hugh. As she stepped across the now silent room where the wedding had taken place only a few hours ago, she wondered had she, unconsciously or otherwise, been playing Hugh and Dan off against each other? And in fact, had she been doing this all her life? She slowed down as she approached the ballroom. Was that why she had a (hmm, what was the collective noun for ex-boyfriends? A 'waste'?) . . . a lot of ex-boyfriends and yet was unable to form a viable long-term relationship? Was that why she couldn't see through even one date with the first man she'd actually liked?

She stood at the ballroom door for a while before opening it. Maybe she'd just say goodnight to Sandy and go back up to bed. For some reason, she didn't want to face Dan. Then a young couple pushed the door from the other side and, smiling at her, held it open. She stood in the doorway for a while watching the drunken revellers, almost unrecognisable from the stilted guests of this afternoon. She stared straight ahead, scared of scanning the room and finding Dan. She shouldn't have come back downstairs. She should have just made herself comfortable on the sofa up in the suite.

Just then Sandy spotted her, waved as if she'd just come off a transatlantic flight and rushed to her. They hugged – Sandy was a bride! – and Sandy pulled her on to the dance floor where, Katie would later insist to Sukie, she had no other option but to do the Birdie Song with her old friend on her wedding day.

It was a moment to cherish. The other guests decided now was the perfect time to form a circle round the bride and camcorders were set to 'on'. Katie saw no other option, she would later insist to Sukie, than to really go for it. So go for it she did. It was a miracle she didn't burst out of her corset. She felt being forced to do an encore was a tad unfair, but she only had herself to blame.

After it was over, she made her way, somewhat unsteadily, off the floor. She had done her bit. No one could accuse her of being a spoilsport. A tease, maybe, a spoilsport no. As she collected her shawl, she saw Dan sitting in the chair next to it, eyes on her.

'You've been practising, haven't you?'

She held her breath. 'No. I don't know what you're talking about.'

'Yes you have,' he continued. 'In the mirror. Birdie Song all week.'

When he allowed her the tiniest leeway into a smile by raising his eyebrows, she almost laughed with relief. He pulled out the chair next to him and indicated a bottle of wine.

'I've been keeping it warm,' he said, pouring her a glass.

'Shame you didn't get to me before Sandy did.'

'Hah! Wouldn't have missed that for the world.'

She took a gulp of wine.

'Luckily,' he picked up an instant camera, 'I've got a memento for the café.'

She stared at the camera. 'Oh, you're kidding.'

He gave her that grin again, crease included for free. 'Nope,' he said. 'In fact, I finished the film.'

She tried to reach the camera, but he held it too high for her. She didn't want to land on top of him (much) so she gave in and sat back down on her chair, having to make do with giving him her best 'I dare you' look.

'Ooh,' he said. 'Nasty. Are you trying to play me along, just like Maxine was saying?'

Her face must have given her away because he fell over himself to convince her that he had been joking. She was suddenly tired and cold. When she shuddered, Dan wrapped his jacket over her shoulders.

'I am not "with" Hugh,' she said quietly and firmly, her eyes fixed on the floor.

He gave her a slight smile. 'Yet,' he said lightly.

'Oh for goodness sake, credit me with some brain.'

'So, just out of interest,' he replied, 'and not that it's any of my business . . .' He paused. 'Why the twenty-four seven flirting?'

She questioned his description of her behaviour – and allowed that instead of flirting, she had merely not put a stop to Hugh flirting with her, although not for want of trying.

'It's hard to slap a friend down when you know they're feeling desperate already.' She received a questioning look. 'People always judge the woman in these things. It's not the woman's fault if a man uses her.' She sensed she was losing him. 'Look, if the tables were turned and a depressed, vulnerable woman was using a man to help her feel better because her ex – whom she still loved and who was with their new girlfriend – was watching, would you blame the woman or the man?'

'I don't know,' frowned Dan.

'Of course you don't. Because you're a chauvinist.'

'No. Because I'm drunk.'

'Anyway,' she said. 'I'd do anything to help Hugh.'

'Why?'

She shrugged. 'He's an ex.'

'So? I don't talk to any of my exes.'

She didn't want to know. 'Maybe I'm just nicer than you.'

'Sounds a bit extreme to me.'

She thought about it. After finishing her wine and refilling her glass.

'Because,' she realised, 'I suppose I feel guilty.'

'Guilty?'

'Yes.'

'What of?'

'Of finishing with him at college.'

'Why? Did you do it nastily?'

'Not particularly. Maybe a bit suddenly.'

'Worse things have happened at sea. Did you two-time him?'

'No.'

'Three-time him?'

'No.'

'Four-time him?'

'*No!*'

'Then why do you feel guilty?'

'Because,' she said slowly, 'he started talking marriage and instead of gently letting him down, I got scared and buggered off.'

'What? Before dessert?'

'No – but before the night was out.'

Dan sucked in some breath. After finishing his wine and refilling his glass.

'In fact,' Katie was thinking aloud now, 'I did it so suddenly that, on the rebound, he ended up with someone we both used to take the piss out of.'

'What? Maxine?'

'Yeah. God, she was one of our favourite in-jokes.'

'Aha!' said Dan slyly. 'So you're jealous! This is your revenge!'

'*What?*'

'Oh come on. A tiny bit of you must have been surprised at his choice. How long have they been together?'

'Ever since.'

He sucked in a lot of breath. 'So – let me get this right – you went out with him for ten months –'

'How did you know th—'

'He said earlier – and then as soon as you finished with him, instead of him falling into a pit of despair or begging for you back – he found love in the arms of your once-shared joke. Ouch. Nasty. Who then,' he continued, 'rejects *him* – so what the hell does that say about you?'

She swallowed. 'It says that Maxine and I don't fancy each other,' she managed before turning away. She started to collect her things, hoping he wouldn't see her eyes.

He leant forward.

'Sorry.' He put his hand on her purse. 'Just getting back some revenge of my own for being abandoned during the worst date of my life and then being blamed for it by the person who abandoned me.'

'I didn't blame you,' she croaked.

'Well,' said Dan, a smile softening the words, 'you certainly didn't blame yourself.'

She sat back down and sniffed. How much wine was left? She picked up the bottle and poured the last of it into her glass, then drank it down. She looked at Dan. Or rather, both of him. OK, now was her chance to explain everything. That's what you did at weddings; you got drunk and put the record straight. You laid all your cards on the table. You bared your soul and exposed your innermost feelings. You did the birdie song.

'Listen,' she started.

He leaned in even more. 'Oh, this should be good.'

She lowered her head and focused on her hands.

'At college I found it easy to go out with people because there was no need for horrendous dates – things just happened naturally.'

'Mm.'

'I don't like dates. I mean, I'm not very good at them. I find it hard to be natural in such an unnatural situation.'

'Well,' he said softly, 'it's putting yourself out on a limb.'

'Yes, I suppose so.'

'It's a gamble.'

'I,' she took a deep breath, 'I-I-I liked you. Very much. So much so that I got into a ridiculously nervous state beforehand. Then it was so bad that I found I became completely tongue-tied and the more I didn't speak the more I couldn't speak. I almost couldn't breathe. Then, when you were in the toilet –'

She stopped. She couldn't possibly tell him that it was Geraldine who had called her, that would look like she was playing *them* off against each other. She was trying to work out what to say, when she felt him lean over the table. More wine was poured into her glass and, with a shaking hand, she took a gulp.

'Thanks.' She spoke quickly. 'Then a friend phoned me and started saying stuff that frightened me.'

'Frightened you?' His voice was quiet. 'Stuff about me?'

'It sounds so silly now. It was just stuff about the future. About our projected future. She – *they* just pushed the wrong buttons at the wrong time.' She shook her head. 'It must sound so ridiculous.'

'No, no. It doesn't. I think I know what you mean.'

'Well, the long and the short of it is that I completely

panicked. I mean I actually had what I now realise was a panic attack. It felt like I was having a heart attack. I just about made it out of the place. I thought I was going to faint. If a taxi hadn't come by just then, you'd have found me head-on-knees on a bench outside. I just about got back home in one piece. I collapsed on my bed and don't really remember much else after that.'

'Bloody hell.'

She gave a wry laugh. 'Yeah. Attractive, isn't it?' She drank some more wine. 'Now you know why I didn't want to tell you. Not so much highly strung as out of my tree.'

He gave her a sad, almost concluding, smile.

'Anyway, as you can imagine,' she continued, 'I was so ashamed and embarrassed – firstly because I knew it had been a horrendous date because I had been unable to string a sentence together, and then also because I saw you with Geraldine.'

'Which –'

She held up her hand. 'Which was totally acceptable – of course it was – she was your friend, and even if she wasn't, what on earth did you owe me?'

'Mmm.'

'But the point was it shook my nerve so much – either because you were dating her the next night which made me question how serious our date had been, or, at the very least, you'd been talking about me being the worst date of your life. I just couldn't face phoning you and explaining the truth, which would just make it all even worse. I suppose I decided that I'd rather have you think I was a bitch than a loopy weirdo you should run a mile from.'

The boulder of black granite that had been lodged in the pit of her stomach since their date finally crumbled. She braved looking up at him. Ooh. He was much closer than she'd remembered.

'Sorry,' she said. Or she would have said, if he hadn't interrupted her by putting his lips exactly where hers were. What she said in fact was 'Somph', but she felt she got her point across.

There was only one kiss on Katie's Kiss List that had ever been even nearly as good as the one she was having at the moment, and that was, coincidentally, with the same man she was kissing now. As far as she was concerned, this made him the reigning champion. Although perhaps she should insist on best of five. Then, all too suddenly, it stopped. She opened her eyes.

Dan wasn't there any more. Or at least his face wasn't. He had stood up.

'I need another drink,' he said, rather shakily, hand over his mouth, and he vanished to the bar.

She tried to call out that he might as well get a bottle when a thumping vibration started in her very soul, and then a strange low throbbing started all over her body. Oh my God, she thought. Another panic attack. Or was this a love attack? Was this what all the songs were about? Had she finally discovered the Holy Grail of kisses?

No, it was her mobile phone. Someone was texting her. She fished it out of a pocket and read it.

Found my wedding dress!!! Your mother and I had a ball! Feeling much better now! Give my love to Katie! Your fiancée! Gx

It wasn't until she was halfway through her reply that she realised she didn't know a G who was getting married, who knew her mother and who was her fiancée. Then she realised that she'd pulled this mobile phone out of a jacket pocket . . . and that the pocket belonged to the jacket over her shoulders . . . and that the jacket over her shoulders belonged to Dan. Which meant that the phone belonged to Dan . . . and that G must be Geraldine . . . and that Geraldine must have gone shopping for wedding dresses with his mother today. That meant that Dan must be engaged to Geraldine . . . and that meant that he had just kissed her while he was engaged to Geraldine . . . and that she had just confessed her innermost heart to him . . . and he had used it to get off with her, while being engaged to Geraldine.

She got up, switched the phone off, put it back in the jacket pocket, flung the jacket on the chair, picked up her shawl and purse and ran all the way back to her room.

22

It wasn't until Katie had spent a frustrating five minutes
trying to open the suite door with her Monsoon card that
she realised she'd left the key inside earlier when putting
Hugh to bed. She stood looking at the closed door for a
while, hoping for inspiration and thankfully inspiration
came. There was only one thing for it. She would have to
hitch-hike home.

Then she heard the sound of a television from inside
and banged on the door. Eventually it opened and there
stood Hugh, doing an impressive Stan Laurel imper-
sonation. Deeply sexy if you liked the dumb-shmuck look.
Which, now that Katie was a working woman with her
own Monsoon card, she felt she had grown out of.

'Ah, Katie,' smiled Hugh. 'Who is it?'

Oh dear.

'It's me,' she said, walking past him into the room.

'Excellent, excellent. *Excellent.*'

The television was on, but the rest of the room looked
very much as she had left it. Even Hugh looked very much
as she had left him, the only difference being that he was
now vertical. He was staring perplexed at the remote

control on the bed where he had been sleeping. He scratched his head.

Katie leant across the bed, picked up the remote and turned off the television.

'I'll sleep on the sofa,' she said, picking up her belongings that she'd left on the bed earlier.

'What, with me?' grinned Hugh.

'No. You're sleeping on the bed.'

He stared at the bed. 'Am I?' he said wonderingly.

Katie closed her eyes. She really was in no mood for this.

'Hugh,' she began.

'Katie.'

'Where are you sleeping?'

She could almost hear his brain clicking.

'When you *do* sleep,' she clarified, 'where will you do it?'

He frowned. Then slowly he began to cry. 'I don't know.' She went over and hugged him, hushing him like a baby. Then, when it became necessary, she pushed him, gently yet firmly, away and went into the lounge, shutting the door behind her.

Two minutes later the phone went and Katie woke with a jump. She stretched over to the table beside the sofa and picked up the phone, knocking over the lamp. 'Mm?' she groaned.

'Hello!' exclaimed someone very smug to have been awake since 5 a.m. 'This is your wake-up call!'

Katie made a heavy croaking noise into the phone to show that she was awake and then managed to put it back after only three attempts. By the time she had succeeded she was fully awake. Very clever these wake-up calls. She looked at her watch which seemed to say '8 a.m.' Goddam it. What on earth had seemed such a good idea about all meeting for breakfast with the bride and groom? There was absolutely no way, she now surmised, that the bride and groom would want to go downstairs for breakfast on their first morning of married life, and everyone else would be far too hung-over to make it down too. She turned over. Just five more minutes, she thought, drifting off into a beautiful sleep.

Then suddenly she was wide awake. Someone was pulling her blanket off her. She yanked it back. It got yanked away again. She sat up and found Hugh lying next to her.

'Hello!' he smiled, eyes shut. 'Thought we could snuggle.'

Which was why, at 8.30 a.m., Katie was to be found sitting on her own at a breakfast table for ten, reading the menu and ordering a coffee.

When, ten minutes later, Dan appeared, she felt prickly all over. He looked rough, like he'd slept on a picket fence. Typically it was a look that worked for him. They caught each other's eye and she looked away instantly. The man was engaged. When she felt him sit down opposite her, she turned back.

'Morning,' she said. She tried to say it blithely, but the blithe bit got stuck in her throat.

'Well,' he said, sharply. 'Now you see her, now you don't. Turning into a bit of a habit, isn't it?'

'I beg your pardon?' What a cheek! Mr Silently

359

Engaged! Katie didn't know what to be annoyed about most. The fact that he was engaged or the fact that to hide her horror that he was engaged she had to pretend not to be indignant. What a tragic waste of indignation. She just couldn't believe he was sitting there, bold as brass, secretly affianced, like some Austen anti-hero. She had half a mind to tell Geraldine. And she was certain she would have, if only she liked her more. Meanwhile, she could feel Dan looking at her as if she was a bad smell. She did her best to give him the most breezy of smiles.

'I thought you went off to get a drink,' she said absent-mindedly.

'I was getting us both a drink. I thought we might want to talk.'

'About what?' she asked. She put half a croissant in her mouth to stop herself from saying, 'About you being engaged you mean?'

'*About what?*' He looked at her incredulously. She swallowed half a croissant.

'Yes,' she said, as evenly as possible. 'Not our little goodnight kiss, surely?'

He shook his head. 'After all that stuff you told me. I –'

She laughed. 'Oh God, did I go heavy and intense? I have a habit of doing that when I'm drunk. Talk a load of rubbish as if I'm opening my heart. I didn't say anything embarrassing, did I?'

He stared at her.

'Don't worry,' she assured him, picking up her coffee cup to hide her reddening face, 'I won't tell Geraldine anything. I've kept much more important secrets than this.'

He just kept staring and then suddenly two hands appeared from behind his head and slammed on to his eyes.

'Guess who?' whispered Sandy in his ear.

'Who?' managed Dan.

'I got married yesterday.'

'Um . . .'

Sandy found this insanely funny and after laughing uproariously in Dan's ear, joined other guests at the table who had made the effort to come down for breakfast specially to see their new bride.

When a rather fragile Hugh joined the happy throng only minutes later, he was dismayed to find Katie quite so indignant with him. What the hell had happened between them last night? Had he made a complete arse of himself? All signs pointed to this conclusion. He knew he shouldn't have had that last bottle. When Maxine joined the breakfast table without her carpenter, he was totally incapable of using the opportunity and just sat miserably nursing a pot of hot black coffee.

The groom followed an hour later, by which time the table was full. Conversation was muted while many full English breakfasts and black coffees were slowly downed. By the end of the meal, Katie was still busy stopping herself from congratulating Dan on his engagement, and Dan was busy being grateful, yet again, that due to his engagement, he was safe from Katie Simmonds. When Hugh had finished his fourth cup of coffee, they made their arrangements for the journey home and Dan rose to get himself packed. Katie gave him a decent ten minutes before going upstairs to her room.

*

The journey home was just as nauseating as it had been out, except that now all of them felt sick all the way. Hugh dropped Dan off first and Dan got out of the car without a look behind him. Then Hugh took Katie home and she managed to do the same, which only told her how sick Hugh must be feeling, not to leap out of the car and try and beat her into her own flat.

She had a long, hot bath, followed by a long, hot cry and then, with a long, hot Sunday evening stretching ahead of her she phoned Sukie. It was at about 6.46 that Sukie discovered there had been Another Kiss, and she was round at Jon and Katie's flat by 7.01, a record even for her. Jon joined them at about 7.10, so they had almost a full two hours to put the world to rights before *Big Brother*.

23

Twenty minutes later at 7.30, Matt stood outside the Gnat and Parrot. He glanced furtively in the windows to see if Jennifer was here yet. He was early. Should he go in or walk round the block once more? Or should he use this golden opportunity to give himself some Dutch courage? He pushed open the pub door, the smell of smoke and alcohol a muggy comfort, and walked to the bar. He ordered a pint – no, half – no, a pint. Didn't want her turning up and thinking he was a lightweight, did he? On the other hand, he didn't want to get pissed. Still, there was no law to say he had to drink the whole pint was there? He wondered what she'd have. As his pint was being poured, he checked yet again that he had enough cash for the date, and had brought *Time Out* with him, just in case she fancied going a bit further afield. And he'd brought some fags. Only ten. He didn't smoke as a rule, but you know, he did it socially. And tonight was social, wasn't it?

Pint in hand, he turned round and checked out the location – no cosy nooks free. He checked the time, still early, and sat at the table nearest the only possible cosy nook where a couple cuddled up to each other, matching half-finished drinks in front of them. He started to sip his pint.

'He's *engaged*?' Jon and Sukie chimed together.

Katie nodded pensively, hunkering down further into her oversized cardi, sipping a big mug of hot chocolate. All she needed was a trendy silver ring and she'd look like a tampon advert.

'To *Geraldine*?'

Another nod.

'That girl has got claws,' said Sukie, vibrant with anger.

'It takes two to get engaged,' said Katie, blowing her hot chocolate.

'I doubt it,' muttered Sukie.

'You've only met her once,' said Katie.

'That's all you need with that type,' said Sukie.

'Yeah, well, I've met her loads,' said Jon, 'and it was always bloody obvious she was going to get Dan.'

'Gee thanks,' muttered Katie. 'Finished the book yet?'

Jon grimaced.

Ah well, thought Katie. There was one comfort; at least she could bring someone else's world down with her.

Matt wandered back rather fuzzily to the nosy cook – cosy nook – a glass of water in his hand. It was great that he'd managed to nab such a perfect place. All he needed now was Jennifer. He checked the time again. She was only half an hour late – anything could have happened. And he had blown her out the first time, hadn't he? Maybe she was trying to let him know how much it had hurt her feelings. Oh, poor girl. He imagined them, a few years down the line, laughing together in bed over how he'd pretended he was ill when really he'd been scared to let her see a stupid spot on his nose. She'd find it endearing – 'no other bloke would be so sensitive' – and then they'd have wild, carefree, abandoned sex. He gulped down the water. Maybe – just maybe – *she* had a spot tonight. Ah, but she didn't need to stay away. He'd understand. He was different from other boys. He'd find her even more attractive with it – as long as she wore a plaster when they kissed. He finished his water.

He needed a slash. But what if he lost this great seat? Or worse, what if she came in – out of breath from running because her bus had broken down – only to find that he wasn't here? He'd have to sit it out. Wouldn't be long now.

Katie and Sukie observed the change in Jon as he discussed his book. His whole body seemed to droop with anguish as he described the torment of trying to work out a new plot.

'It can't be that hard, surely?' said Katie finally.

He balked. 'Fuck off.'

'Well, sorry,' she said. 'It's just that – well you look so troubled. It's only writing.'

Jon did a fish-out-of-water impression.

'Yeah,' agreed Sukie. 'It's like reading, only different. Try going to a few auditions; you wouldn't last a week.'

'Yeah. Or try waiting tables,' added Katie.

Jon sat up, red in the face. '*You* try writing a fucking book.'

Katie gasped. Of course! Why on earth hadn't she thought of it before? It had been staring her in the face all this time, been under her nose all these years and she'd missed it. The perfect job! The ideal career! No CVs needed, no professional training, no boss, no politics, just the decision to go and do it – and she could do it while being a waitress! Like Sukie and her acting! This way she could turn the searing pain of contemporary urban dating into art! She stared at Jon. He stared back at her.

'No,' he said.

'*Yes*!' breathed Katie. 'You have got yourself a deal!'

'You won't be able to do a paragraph.'

'I'll show you!' she cried, flushed with excitement. 'Just you wait.'

She ran out of the living room into her bedroom. Two minutes later she was back.

'Jon?'

'What?'

'Can I borrow your laptop?'

Dan was glad of the opportunity to see his mum on her own. His father was at his Sunday evening Lodge meeting; it was good for him Harriet always said, and, more importantly, it was good for her – one evening a week when she got to keep the television off, listen to a radio play and do her tapestry. She'd had a lovely time with Geraldine yesterday, although she'd been glad to get home. She did have one of her heads. It was always lovely to see Dan though. As soon as he'd called her from his hotel that morning, she'd set to making one of her quiches and his favourite chocolate pudding. Now he was here she rustled up a salad and told him all about her day with Geraldine. Then she waited for him to begin.

Katie sat bright and alert, back straight, eyes wide, fingers on the laptop keyboard. Adrenaline was practically burning through her veins – and she hadn't even started yet! This was going to be amazing. This was going to be It. She would discover herself through words, she would fly, she would soar, she would *be*.

She grinned stupidly at the screen, flexed her fingers, then spread them back on the keyboard. She'd heard that the hardest thing was starting. Which was why she was just going to jump straight into the water, feet first, like some brave holidaying kid who doesn't know fear yet – there could be rocks in there, crocodiles even, but they didn't care, life hadn't tainted their every action with fear yet. She was brave, she was fearless, she was . . . she was hungry, that's what she was. Hmm. Of course, every writer needs succour. Wasn't that a famous saying? she thought, as she wandered through the living room (ignoring Sukie, Jon and the flickering television) into the kitchen in search of brain food. Or perhaps it *should* be a saying. Perhaps that would become her forte, there would be quotations from her in all the best quotation books. As the bread toasted, she saw herself reviewed in all the best literary supplements. As she spread the peanut butter and jam on one slice, cheese and honey on the other, she imagined certain crinkly-smiled married men picking up the paper and realising just what they'd let slip through their fingers. She brought her toast back to the bedroom and sat munching happily for a while. Ah yes, she thought, people would say 'I remember her from school/college/ work! She pretended she was just a waitress but all that time she was writing that amazing Pulitzer Prize-winning best-seller. And she never let on!' She finished her toast and spread her fingers on the keyboard. Look at that keyboard – just twenty-six letters – and yet, the gateway to an infinite number of possibilities. It was a miracle really, when you thought about it. Only she never had thought about it, until now. And now was the beginning of the rest of her life. Hmm, wasn't that a saying?

Sukie and Jon stopped calling Katie after the fourth time. Sod it. They'd watch *Big Brother* without her. More Cheesy Wotsits for them. Every now and then Jon muttered something about killing himself if Katie got published before him and Sukie reassured him that Katie probably would not break the habit of a lifetime and actually finish anything she started. Then they watched TV for the evening, looking up briefly every time Katie wordlessly strode through the living room into the kitchen and back into her room again.

Only forty-five minutes late, Jennifer wandered into the pub, a vision of everything that was right with the world. Was it Matt's imagination or had it suddenly got lighter in here?

'Hi!' she grinned.

'Hi!' Matt stood up and then, feeling a little unsteady on his feet, sat down again. 'Is everything all right?'

'Yeah!' She swung her silken hair across her back and sat down opposite him. 'You all right?'

'Yeah, sure,' he said, deciding to go to the toilet later. Then he remembered himself. 'Fancy a drink?'

'Oh yeah. A Grolsch, cheers.'

'Right.' He got up slowly and made his way to the bar where he ordered two pints. He didn't want another pint, but he couldn't very well order one for her and then order himself a Diet Coke, could he? And he didn't want to have to mention that he'd already had two pints (not counting the swift swig of gin at home before coming out) while waiting for her. It might embarrass her.

He walked back slowly with his two glasses, then just had to give in and go to the Gents. He couldn't help noticing other blokes eyeing Jennifer up as he made his careful way across the room, and wondered, somewhere in the dim recesses of his clogged up mind, why that didn't make him feel as proud as he thought it would.

'I do think you'll love the dress,' Dan's mum told him.

'Good.' He stared at his whisky glass.

His mum nodded. 'Frightening times,' she murmured. 'Frightening times.'

Dan looked up at her, the late Sunday sun behind her casting a coral haze over the garden. 'What makes you say that?'

She smiled. 'I just remember how I felt before marrying your father.'

'You were *frightened*?'

'Of course! It's terrifying, marriage.'

Dan couldn't believe his ears. Confusing, yes, a roller-coaster of emotions, yes. But terrifying?

His mum smiled, shaking her head. 'You do make me

369

laugh, you young people. You always assume we had none of the same feelings as you do. But you're more like me than anyone else I know.'

Dan took this in slowly. 'I thought I was more like Dad,' he said quietly.

His mum scoffed. 'Like your father? You're nothing like your father. You're all me.' Dan pondered this for some while, idly looking at the still garden. 'That's why,' his mum continued quietly, 'I thought you'd never marry.'

'Really?'

'Yes. You're a male version of me and if I'd had to do the asking it would never have happened.'

'Wow.'

'But you've done us proud.'

'I know.'

'Geraldine's a very special lady.'

'Yes.'

'And being terrified is just part of getting married. If you're anything like me. Which you are.'

'How did you get through . . . the terror part?'

His mother didn't hesitate. 'You just have to believe in fate,' she said firmly. 'This was meant to be. If it wasn't meant to be it wouldn't have happened.'

'But I don't believe in fate.'

'Well, you have to.'

'Right.'

'Just tell yourself: This was meant to be. If it wasn't, it wouldn't have happened. Repeat it to yourself in your darkest moments.'

Dan wished he'd known that before Sandy's wedding. He pictured himself back there, standing at the bar after that kiss with Katie. He'd been shaking with exhilaration, preparing to go back, open his heart to her like she just had with him, and break it off with Gerry. Again. Up till then, he'd convinced himself the kiss with Katie hadn't been as good as he'd remembered. He was right. It was better. Then, when he'd found her gone, he'd raced up to his room, thinking she must have thought he'd gone there and tried to follow him – but no Katie. Then just when he thought he'd go back down and try and find her, he'd heard voices in her room. Were she and Hugh going to sleep together? After that kiss? Would she tell Hugh? Was she with him? He had to know.

When the voices stopped, he'd started to knock quietly on their door at intervals, hoping it would only be heard by Katie, but to no avail. Half an hour later, utterly confused, he had no choice but to go to bed, his mind and body reliving her words and that kiss. He must have got about one hour's sleep. He'd told himself he'd wait till he saw Katie in the morning, get himself sorted out. He fell asleep at about 6.30, woke soon after, didn't bother shaving, just showered and dressed, and then had knocked lightly on Katie and Hugh's door again before going downstairs. No bloody answer. He'd leant his head against their door. Was she in bed with Hugh? Were they sharing that bed? He couldn't bear this. She'd done it to him again.

In desperation he'd decided to go for a fast walk round the grounds, because he couldn't sit in his room any more and he had to get away from theirs. He rushed downstairs and on his way out, to his amazement, saw Katie sitting on her own in the dining room, leisurely perusing the breakfast menu. He'd stared at her for a few moments through the glass before feeling brave enough to go in. After breakfast he'd phoned Gerry. She'd been so happy to hear from him that it was a comfort just to hear her voice and he'd completely forgot to feel guilty about kissing Katie.

His mum cut him another piece of chocolate pudding. If she was right and what was meant to be would be, it made everything so much easier. One misunderstanding could be put down to bad luck; but two? If he was meant to be with Katie, none of this confusion would have happened and they'd be together, right? They just weren't meant to be.

As he munched through his chocolate pudding, he thought back to that disastrous first date and Katie's so-called 'panic attack'. Did she really have a panic attack? He didn't know whether to believe that story or not now. After she'd abandoned him in that restaurant, he'd never felt more lonely in his life. Like the proverbial motherless child. He hadn't been able to eat or sleep properly for weeks. It was worse than any relationship break-up he'd ever known. Which was why, when Geraldine had called the next morning, he'd almost fallen into the safety of her arms again. It had only taken them a month to get back into the old rhythm. He'd hardly noticed it happen. Was that what it was like when it was The One? He had said then and there that he never wanted to go through another night like that – and, thanks to Katie Simmonds, that was just what he had done. Better to stay away from girls like her. Gerry was good for him. She was meant to be.

Yes, he was much more like his mother than he'd realised. He tried to imagine what she'd been like, a shy seventeen-year-old girl from a village coming to live with her successful new husband, almost fifteen years her senior and already a name in the city. And yet she'd done it.

'Mum,' he asked gently, 'have you ever regretted your choice?'

'Of course not, dear. I was just being a young silly.' She gave a little chuckle and whispered, 'Scared of making love for the first time.'

It was a bit like making love, thought Katie, this writing lark. It was all about letting go, allowing yourself to be utterly exposed, vulnerable, about losing yourself in the moment. Poor Jon, maybe that's why he found it so hard. She gave a tiny gasp. Oh dear! Maybe he was a lousy lover. Maybe she should tell him – in a kindly way of course. Just mention that there are some people suited to writing and some who aren't. It's like some people being able to climb Everest and some who just don't have the lung capacity. Or the motivation. Or dedication. Or they don't like the cold. It's nothing specific. Writing isn't just about writing; she knew that now. It was about a whole host of factors, and all you need is one of those vital factors to be missing and the entire edifice collapses – like a house of cards! Yes! It was exactly like a house of cards! (She should carry a notebook around with her all the time, she was coming out with pearls.) And you need every single card to make that house – and the lowest cards are as important as the top one – in fact it's probably more important. And if just one of those cards isn't in place properly, the whole lot falls down. It was tragic really when you thought about it. Poor poor Jon, she thought, as she spread her fingers over the keyboard.

Matt and Jennifer linked arms as they made their slow way back to her parents' house. Matt was glad they'd linked arms, partly because it showed she didn't mind touching him and partly because it stopped him falling on his face.

He'd been glad that she hadn't felt the need to tell him why she was three-quarters of an hour late. It showed a sense of trust, a sense of ease that proved she already felt natural with him. He'd been fascinated to hear so many details about her crappy job and her crappy friend. He'd always guessed she and Eva weren't bosom buddies. He'd been a bit shocked to discover that not only was Jennifer almost two years older than he was, but she wasn't on some gap year, or doing some temporary job to fill in her holidays, she had completely left school and was working full time. Later on, he decided – maybe when she came up to see him at university – he'd try and convince her to give education another go. She'd admire him for helping her change her life.

Going up the hill, they started singing some pub song which ended in hysterics by the time they reached her parents' road. She started giggling and shushing him as they got nearer to her home, and putting her fingers to his lips to keep him quiet. It was so nice he sang even louder. He could hardly believe it – her lips were inches away from his. Was this going to end well? Was he actually going to get a snog with the divine Jennifer? He sang louder still.

Hugh woke, dry-mouthed and bleary-eyed, to a dark, cold, empty room. He turned to his new clock, which lay on an upturned cardboard box. Almost 10. He felt crap. And hungry. He'd make himself some toast in his cheap new Argos toaster. God, it was the silence he hated most. He leaned over to his remote control and switched on his cheap new telly from the bed. Maxine had insisted they be able to watch telly in bed and he was bloody grateful now. It was some crappy reality show – did anyone really watch them? – but it was good background noise. Good to see other losers in the world. He put on his slippers and a big loose sweatshirt and went downstairs.

The kitchen was stunning, even without any of its designer appliances and furniture. It had taken them weeks to decide on the tiles and cupboard doors and he had to hand it to Maxine, she'd got it right. He flicked the switch for the lights and filled up his cheap new kettle, turning on his cheap new telly with the remote by the sink. Someone in the reality show was crying. Hugh turned to watch as the kettle boiled. Two girls comforted another girl who was distraught because she'd been called a rude name. Lucky bitch, he thought. How old was she? She looked about nineteen. He wished he was nineteen again and upset because someone had called him a rude name. Better than having your whole life crumble round your ears. The kettle boiled and he realised he hadn't put the toast on. He went to the American-style fridge, big enough for a family yet stylish enough for a young London couple. Maxine hadn't taken it with everything else because there hadn't been enough room in the carpenter's van. It had half a loaf of bread and some mouldy cheese in it. He took two slices and put them in his cheap new toaster and turned back to the telly. The girl was saying that she wanted to go home. Lucky bitch, he thought. I'm at home and I fucking hate it. He took his toast upstairs, turning off all the lights as he went. He sat in his bed, drinking tea, eating toast and watching *Big Brother*. They were now cooking together, laughing and jostling loudly for attention. Lucky bastards, he thought as he lay down in his cheap new bed and went to sleep.

Katie couldn't believe literary critics. First they put you on a pedestal you didn't ask to be on, critically acclaiming your first book and calling you a debut wonder, and then they pan your second book, calling you a has-been. I mean give a girl a break. Haven't they heard of the Curse of the Second Book? How could you enjoy the gift you've been born with when you have the whole of the country on the edge of their seats, waiting for you to fail? And anyway, she'd be willing to bet that none of *them* could do it. Oh yes, it was easy to criticise someone else, but to actually put yourself on the line? She didn't think so. You see, the trick was learning how to write without the ghosts of your readers haunting you. All those ex-boyfriends, all those potential boyfriends, all the would-be ex-boyfriends, all your old friends, your old enemies, your family, all those sad critics – all those people with crinkly smiles and hazel-flecked eyes . . . all those people *everywhere*. How could you keep sense of who you were while at the same time letting go? And all the endless questions – Are the characters fictional? Were you using your book as catharsis? Or revenge? Was that me in the book? Was that your mother? Is that Dan?

Oh! It was too much to bear. How would they like it if she started publicly criticising *their* jobs . . . *'I opened Mr Smith's reviews of this week's best paperbacks with dread and awe – could he possibly have been as accurate and fulsome as last week?'*

The truth was, did any writer actually enjoy writing? It was one of those eternal questions. She was nothing but a victim of her gift. She didn't choose it, it chose her. That's right – it had chosen her.

Katie spread her hands over the keyboard and began again.

Matt was halfway back down the street before he was even able to take in what had happened. Oh sweet Jesus, she was a goddess. And he should know; he'd felt her breasts. He looked at his hands, reliving the moment.

He'd just stood there, not expecting anything, just waiting to say goodnight and have her peck him on the cheek if he was lucky – but no! She'd swayed towards him and landed him one right on the lips, one of those kisses you know means business, leaving a boy in no doubt whatsoever of where he stood.

Then, when he'd imagined it was all over for this lifetime, it went into overdrive, like she'd suddenly sold her soul to the Devil. Talk about being in the right place at the right time. He'd lost himself totally in the moment, while trying to etch it in his mind for ever. He remembered thinking that the rest of his life didn't matter any more. None of it mattered. This was what it was all about. This was real and raw, this was life, this was death, this was –

Then he'd got her zip stuck.

Precious seconds were lost and then the hall light came on in her parents' house and she was sucking herself away from him, unclamping his hands from that body, whizzing round, opening the front door and grinning a cheery goodnight at him. He'd stood in the late summer evening, staring at the closed door in front of him, dazed, confused and so happy he wanted to live for ever and so happy he was ready to die.

'Hello!' said Jon, diving on to Katie's bed.

There was no answer. He looked up.

'You all right?'

Katie was sitting at her desk, her arms slumped to her side, her head on the keyboard. She lifted her head suddenly, like a Jack-in-a-box.

'You all right? You missed a cracking *Big Brother*. They made Bobby cry.'

'Hunugh,' she said.

'How's it going?'

Katie's head fell on to the keyboard again. 'One sentence.'

Jon lay back on the bed and laughed. Katie started moaning. 'And it's lousy,' she wailed. 'It took me four hours and it's lousy. I just re-read it after a break – you know, for some distance – and . . .' she started to weep, 'it hasn't got a verb in it.'

Jon felt his shoulders lighten. 'Welcome,' he sighed, 'to my world.'

24

Dan stared at his reflection in the jeweller's window, imagining what Katie would be doing at the café now. It had been a whole week since Sandy's wedding and once they'd both got back to work it had been far easier to pretend that it just hadn't happened. In fact, they'd hardly spoken to each other. He'd decided that the kiss really had been a drunken mistake on her part and she was now probably scared that he might come after her. The last thing he wanted to do was turn into another Hugh, so he had made a concerted effort all week to appear as indifferent to her as possible. In fact, he'd come close to telling her about his engagement just so that they could be normal with each other again, but he'd never been alone with her long enough. No, he'd wait until it was somehow relevant – maybe tell everyone at work together. Meanwhile, his wedding plans were hotting up, which was really helping to take his mind off the kiss. That and his mother's mantra.

Standing outside the jeweller's on a bright Saturday morning, he was suddenly assaulted by the image of Katie coming down the hotel stairs in that ball-gown. He let out a long, slow sigh.

'I know,' sighed Geraldine, bending forward beside him. 'It's so hard isn't it?' He looked down at her. She was staring hard at the rings in the window her neck slowly extended like a feeding tortoise.

'Hmm,' she murmured. 'You see, I love that one, but it's just like Sandy's – only of course much bigger – and the last thing I want is her to think I'm copying her. As if. But it *is* wonderful. Unless, maybe it's a bit too big. I mean I don't want to have to take it off if I'm on the tube, do I? God Sandy would be green. But then, I'm bound to find one that's similar, aren't I? I mean that is today's look. Then again, should I go for something so fashionable? Or should I go for a timeless classic instead? I mean I do have to love it in fifty years' time.'

The mantra, the mantra, the mantra.

'I never thought it would be so difficult.' She stood up tall, a thought occurring to her. 'Which one do you prefer?' she asked Dan. He looked at the trayful of rings.

'That one.'

'Which one?'

'*That* one.'

'*Which* one?'

Dan nodded violently towards a ring. '*That* one!'

'It's no bloody use just repeating yourself. Which one are you talking about?'

'The one with the wotsits.'

'Do you mean diamonds, Daniel?'

'Yes.'

She gave him one of her looks. 'They've all got diamonds and you're being a dickhead.'

He cocked his head at her. 'What does that make you,' he asked. 'Mrs Dickhead?'

'Dan, what the hell is your problem?'

There was no ignoring that tone; he'd gone and done it again.

'My problem,' he said slowly, 'is should we be buying rings at all if we can't do it without name-calling?'

'You had a problem before then and you know it.'

'What? Because I don't know how to describe the ring with four diamonds instead of five?'

Geraldine stared at him. 'I knew I should have come with a friend,' she muttered. 'You spoil everything.'

He lowered his eyes. 'Sorry.'

'Oh well, as long as you're sorry. That's fine then. Doesn't matter that you're spoiling my once-in-a-lifetime experience.'

'You're right. Let's go in.'

'Oh I'm *really* in the mood now.'

'Look, I'm sorry. You're right, I spoil everything. I'm just a bit preoccupied with the café –'

'Oh for Christ's sake, not again. This is the first whole Saturday you've had off in God knows how long. You live and breathe that bloody café. I've got a career too, but I manage not to bring it home with me. At least when you were in the city you cut off at weekends. If I'd known the café was going to take over our lives, I'd . . .' she trailed off. She'd made her point. Sometimes it was best to leave things hanging.

'You'd what?'

'I don't know, Daniel. I just hadn't realised it was going to have such an impact on our life together. One bloody

Saturday looking for the most important ring of my life and you're still in bloody Porter's Green.'

'I'm sorry. I'm crap. I don't know what you see in me.'

She half-smiled. 'Neither do I.'

'Do you forgive me?'

Geraldine gave a deep sigh before giving him the other half of the smile. 'Well now,' she said, 'that all depends on how many wotsits my engagement ring has.'

Two hours later, the wedding list assistant at Harrods handed them their forms and Geraldine giggled with excitement. Dan smiled and put his arm round her. It had taken a lot of wotsits and a two-course lunch with a classy Bordeaux at Fortnum's, but she was finally back to herself again. And he knew he could expect this familiar sensation of shell-shock from one of her bombs to have died down by this time tomorrow. They went to the china department first, Geraldine almost running up the escalators. They held hands at the entrance, took a deep breath and went in to find the dinner service of their dreams.

Meanwhile, Sukie Woodrow, tomorrow's Brit-flick sensation, watched her feet take her to her last audition for the *Tale of Two Cities* adaptation. She looked up at the people waiting at the bus queue. No one glanced her way. Was all this about to change? Was her anonymity coming to an end? Was she finally about to gain recognition? Was this where her life would begin? Her stomach clenched. Just one more audition. So near and yet so far. Greta had phoned her just yesterday and told her the good news.

'Darling, it's between you and that minx Miranda.'

'Miranda Armstrong?'

'Yes. You can do it.'

'But she's half my age. How can she be up for that part?'

'I know. It's utter madness. They'll be auditioning foetuses next.'

'Oh bloody hell.'

'Now now, my love, my Katherine Hepburn, my silver screen queen. Do not give up hope.'

'So it's just us two.'

'It is just you two. You're within a cat's whisker. The part of Sydney Carton has gone to Harry Hampton.'

'Hal!' cried out Sukie. 'Fantastic! I was with him at The Almeida – the dynamic was exactly the same, he had an unrequited crush on me. You told them that, didn't you?'

'I did,' sighed Greta, 'and they said "Where's The Almeida?" '

'Oh for God's sake.'

'But it will help you and him become those people instantly.'

'Yes.'

'That's the good news. The bad news is that they're auditioning you first. You're in the morning, Miranda's in the afternoon.'

'Damn.'

'So you *have* to make a lasting impression. You have to *inhabit* Lucie, so that when these silly TV people go to bed at night, they see you as her and not that lanky teenage gobshite.'

And so it was. Sukie Woodrow, tomorrow's Brit-flick

sensation, stared at her hob-nailed, tightly laced ankle boots, inhabiting Lucie Manette, nineteenth-century heroine. And as she walked past the bus stop she wondered if her time had finally come.

As soon as she entered the now familiar audition room, she saw Hal perched on the back of a chair, drinking tea with the cameraman. She dearly wanted to do the luvvie thing and rush up to him, throw her arms around him and launch into reminiscing about their work together, but it would look too staged. And anyway, it might be good to have some tension between them. After all, Sydney Carton and Lucie were hardly friends. She smiled at the director and screenplay writer and gave the cameraman a wave. They all acknowledged her with the polite satisfaction of knowing that they had less to fear than she did. Ooh, she thought, we're just like one big happy, dysfunctional family. She plopped her bag and little summer cardi down on a chair at the side of the room and went over to Hal. He gave her an encouraging smile and a kiss on her cheek. Good man. He hadn't had to do that.

'Congratulations,' she whispered.

'Thanks,' he said. 'Good luck.'

And that was when she remembered. Hal had bad breath. *Really* bad breath. Hal, short for Halitosis, she had privately joked during their run together. She had spent her entire time at The Almeida popping mints and offering him them on the pretext that really she needed them. How could she have forgotten? And today she had no mints in her bag. Which meant she had to remember her lines, work to the right camera, obey the twelve-year-old director's idea of direction, perform the part for the first time with an actor and make a lasting impression – all while not breathing in.

During her second try, she made the mistake of taking a deep breath and was rewarded by retching before her line. At the end, she looked at her hands while waiting for the director's version.

'SukieSue,' he said. 'I bloody loved the bit where you retched. So real. So raw. So Dickens's London. I think Lucie would *definitely* be sickened. Keep that in. But this time I want to see more physical attraction. *That's* why she's retching.' He couldn't keep the pride out of his grin. 'She's revolted not by the man – but by her *attraction* to him.'

She nodded, wide-eyed. An hour later, she was on her way back to the café, giving Greta the run-down.

'So if I get it,' she summarised excitedly, 'it will all be thanks to Hal and his bad breath.'

'Well done darling, I'll phone you as soon as I've heard.'

As Sukie approached the café, she stopped for a moment, closed her eyes and made a secret wish. Almost as soon as she went in, she knew something was up.

'Have you heard?' Patsy called out, before she'd even reached the bar.

'Heard what?'

'*Time Out*? We're good-looking!' She was jumping on the spot. "Good-looking staff"! We think it was that odd bloke with the moustache in the other day. Isn't it brilliant? Look!'

Sukie scanned the article desperately hoping this wasn't

the last review of her work she'd ever read. Suddenly, she felt very depressed.

'Wow.' She handed it back to Patsy. '*How* exciting.' She heard Patsy squealing behind her as she wandered into the kitchen.

She and Matt exchanged preoccupied greetings, Matt being almost physically attached to his mobile phone. As she nodded at Nik and considered seeing what he was cooking today, Patsy was suddenly in between them.

'She's seen the review,' she giggled to Nik. Sukie turned to Patsy. 'What are you doing in here?' she asked, her voice cold.

Patsy's smile froze on her face. 'It's OK; Katie's out front.'

'Yeah, well, if we only needed one waitress out front Dan wouldn't have taken you on, would he?'

Patsy gave Nik a confused glance before returning to the café. Sukie apologised to the room in general.

'Don't say sorry to us, love,' said Nik. 'Say it to Beautiful.'

Sukie decided not to. As she bent down to place her cardi and bag under the counter, Katie came in behind her.

'Have you seen *Time Out*?' she grinned.

'Yeah,' Sukie forced herself. 'Well done.'

'Thanks, well, it's well done to all of us,' said Katie.

'Don't be ridiculous,' scoffed Sukie. 'It's all *your* doing.'

'Fuck off!' cried Nik. 'What am I, Scotch mist?'

'Good question,' said Sukie. 'I think you're more frozen fog actually.'

Nik exploded into a rant about the importance of the

chef in a café-cum-restaurant and Katie watched them for a while before quietly leaving them to it.

As soon as his shift was over, Matt made his way to Jennifer's street. The street where the pavement had once disappeared beneath his feet. But not today. Today the pavement was horribly there. He'd had no reply from Jennifer's mobile all day. And he'd left three messages on her voicemail. And she hadn't come in for lunch since Thursday. He'd hoped she might pop in for brunch today, but no.

Had she been kidnapped? Was she still alive, even? Was she chopped up in a bin bag somewhere? Or worse, had she chucked him? Had he been too pushy? Had he felt intimidated by his desperate goodnight kisses? Oh God, he had been so forceful, but he hadn't been able to help himself. Him and his stupid libido. As he turned the corner of her street, he made a solemn oath to himself that if she was alive and still wanted to go out with him, he'd never force so much as a kiss on her again. He approached her house and offered up a prayer.

He rang the doorbell and listened for sounds. After a while, he heard movement from upstairs. He rang again. Someone was coming down. His heart was in his mouth. What would he do if it was her parents? What would he do if –

And there she was!

He stared at her. God, she looked terrible. He must have got her out of bed. This time on a Saturday afternoon? And she was in her dressing gown too. He was right. She'd been ill. Oh, Jennifer! He wanted to take her in his arms and make her well again, and then make wild, passionate love to her.

'Jennifer,' he explained. 'It's me.'

'Yeah I can see that. What do you want?'

A pair of naked feet appeared on the stairs behind her.

'I wanted to see how you were,' he whispered.

'I was fine till you turned up.'

The feet spoke. 'Everything all right, babe?'

Jennifer turned round and the feet turned into a man, also wearing a dressing gown. Was this her father?

'Hello, Mr . . .' began Matt, before realising he didn't know Jennifer's surname.

'Hello hello hello,' grinned the man. Funny, Jennifer didn't take after him at all. 'Is this one of your little fans?' said the man. Jennifer didn't seem to find this half as amusing as the man did. She turned back to Matt and spoke with some urgency.

'Matt,' she said. 'Go away.'

'W-what have I done?'

'Just go away.'

'Is it 'cos I lied to you?' he said desperately.

She stared. '*What?*'

'When I pretended I was ill? I promise I'll never lie again, but the spot was massive. It was right on my nose. I can't believe Eva told you. She swore she –'

Jennifer and the man's reactions were polarised at this: the man started laughing hysterically, but she saw red.

'You lied to me?' she barked. '*And* you told that cow?'

'Yes but –' he stopped. 'What?'

'You complete tosser!'

389

'But-but?'

'I can never trust you again!' She started to shut the door.

'It was like I had two noses!' Matt shouted through the rapidly closing gap.

'Forget it Matt. It's *over*.'

And the door slammed in his face.

Stunned, Matt stood there for a while until the hoots of laughter from inside propelled him into movement. He turned round slowly and walked, not knowing or caring where he was going. It was only when he found himself ordering a pint that he even realised he was in the Gnat and Parrot.

He stood at the bar, staring into his glass, blinking and sniffing, blinking and sniffing, blinking and sniffing until, after a while, he realised someone was staring at him. Someone who looked vaguely familiar.

As his size tens thundered on the treadmill, Hugh looked down at the clock. Bloody hell, this was amazing. He'd never run this far in his life, not even before uni. It did help being able to watch all the MTV babes while you did it. Much better than boring old countryside.

In all the years he'd been a member of this gym, he'd never come in on a Saturday afternoon and he'd been amazed to find it so full. It had been like entering another world. Madness really, when you thought about it, considering how much his membership cost, but Maxine had always wanted them to spend their weekends together: shopping or seeing friends or family, even just eating out or going to the cinema.

As he ran, he realised for the first time that being alone might actually be a liberation for him. He could start living the bachelor life he'd thought he'd missed out on. While getting fit at the same time. God, he could actually lose his stomach. This could be the best thing in his whole life. He slowed down the treadmill and got off. He sat on it catching his breath and wiped himself down. There was more sweat than body.

On his way home, he decided suddenly, he'd buy himself one of those lads' magazines and maybe read it in the pub. Or a cookery book! And a bread maker! He'd really wanted to buy one but Maxine had said they'd never use it. Oh my God – he could buy all the things for the house that she'd vetoed. He wasn't really *that* broke. Yes. That's what he'd do. He ran down to the changing rooms. First stop, the kitchen shop.

Back at the café, three full hours after her audition, when Sukie's mobile finally rang she could barely answer it for nerves. Luckily she wasn't serving anyone, and she squeezed back through the kitchen and sat on the back stairs. She held her breath before answering.

She knew instantly from Greta's voice.

'Darling, it's shitty news.'

Her tears came fast and furious.

'You were so close,' soothed Greta. 'You'll get it next time, I just know.'

Sukie sniffed loudly.

'They *loved* the retch,' said Greta. 'They've asked Miranda to put that in. The director said it suddenly made him "get" Lucie. Called it a pivotal moment.'

If Sukie had had the energy, she'd have retched now. Instead, she hung her head on her knees and allowed herself time to let this sink in. The thought of going back outside and serving customers, of pretending she cared about a bloody restaurant review in *Time Out*, of coming in day after day and doing everything again and again suddenly wore her out. She started sobbing.

'You have got to be kidding,' Dan said to Geraldine, staring at an eggshell-blue teapot with turquoise birds on it and a gold-leaf spout. 'That is grotesque.'

'I am most certainly not kidding. It is the most beautiful thing I've ever seen,' repeated Geraldine. She turned to him. 'Can you imagine having friends round and pouring them tea from that?'

'Not friends of mine, no.'

'Well it's a darn-sight less grotesque than the bloody naked woman vase.'

'That was art.'

Geraldine sighed heavily and crossed her arms. 'Why must you fight me on everything?'

'What?' Dan managed to exclaim without raising his voice above a whisper.

'You do,' hissed Geraldine. 'Everything's a fight.'

'Because believe it or not it'll be my dinner service too!'

'You don't care about a dinner service as much as I do.'

'Why not?' Dan choked.

'You're a man.'

He stared at her as a couple walked behind them, the man spluttering in sotto voce staccato, 'If we get *that*, then I get the fucking flat screen.'

Dan tried a smile, but Geraldine didn't flicker. 'It wouldn't be in Harrods if it was grotesque,' she said.

He let out a snort of laughter. 'They've got exotic pets but that doesn't mean I want an elephant.'

She stared at him like he was mad. 'You do talk rubbish sometimes, Daniel.'

Slowly, Matt turned round and faced the vaguely familiar someone who was still staring at him.

'Hello there,' she said. A slender, attractive, dark-haired woman was smiling at him.

'All right?' he mustered.

'They give you Saturday afternoon off, do they?'

He blinked at the woman. She smiled. 'Where's lover girl?' she asked. There was a pause and then she leant on the bar. 'You don't recognise me, do you?' He frowned. 'I'll give you a clue,' she said. 'You usually have eyes for someone else when I come into the café for lunch.'

His eyes widened. He gasped. He tried to remember her name. He failed.

'Eva,' she said drily.

'Eva! Of course.'

'Blimey, I knew it was bad, but I hadn't realised how bad.'

'You look different.'

'Oh yeah?' she grinned.

'Yeah. Much older.'

She gave him a look. 'Thanks.'

'No, no, it's a compliment.'

'I'm only twenty-one.'

Twenty-one? *Twenty-one?* She was twenty-one!

'Want a drink?' she asked.

He nodded.

'Well?'

There was a pause.

'Oh sorry,' he rushed. '"Yes please".'

'No, I mean what would you like?'

'Gin and tonic, thanks.'

Matt stared as Eva bought him a drink. She asked about Jennifer and he told her the extraordinary twist of the story, but to his amazement, she didn't seem half as surprised as he had been. In fact, she apologised.

'Why are you sorry?' he asked.

'Because I work with her, remember? I know the real Jennifer. I know what she gets up to. I could have warned you.'

'Yeah but you're her mate aren't you?'

Eva snorted. 'Do me a favour,' she retorted. 'If I wasn't trapped in that god-awful office I wouldn't give her the time of day. I wouldn't trust her with the lead in my pencil.'

Matt took a gulp of his drink. It was all too much for him. As if he was in a bad sci-fi film and he'd just discovered that his past had been some idealised, yet hologram, reality.

'So . . .' he began slowly, 'let me get this right. Was she really chucking me because I lied to her? Or because it was you I'd told? Or was that just some excuse? Who am I kidding – the other bloke was there in her house, in a dressing gown!'

Eva became serious. 'Matt, listen. She fancied you. She liked you. Really, she did.'

'So, why chuck me?'

Eva sighed. 'She uses everyone. She doesn't have relationships, she has temporary dependencies.'

'But why did she want me in the first place?' Matt asked, almost to himself. 'I mean what on earth could I have possibly given her that she couldn't get elsewhere? I mean that bloke she's with – he's a *man*. He must be about twenty years older than me.'

Suddenly, Eva grabbed his arm and pointed: 'Quick, table.' She darted for it, beating two blokes and an Alsatian. Impressive. Matt sat down next to her. Right, where was he?

'I bet that bloke doesn't get zits,' he moaned. 'Why was she with me when she can get a man twice her age who doesn't get zits?'

'It's hard to explain. She has issues.'

Matt looked at Eva. 'Who was he?'

'Oh, just our boss.'

'Your *boss*?'

'You see? Issues.'

Matt got the next drinks in. After which, with some persuasion and alcohol, he found out a little bit about Jennifer's issues. It turned out that the boss she'd spent the past week bedding had just announced his engagement to one of the other girls in the office – and she had once nicked one of Jennifer's boyfriends.

'Are you the other girl?' he asked in a hushed voice.

'No! Piss off!' exclaimed Eva. 'Do I look like a complete loser?'

'No.' He shook his head firmly.

*

It took Katie half an hour to find Sukie. The café closed for an hour on Saturday afternoons before the restaurant opened up in the evening. It gave them time to clear up, have a breather and then change shifts.

'Oh no,' she whispered, sitting next to Sukie on the back stairs. 'Bad news?'

Sukie sniffed and put her mobile away. 'Isn't it always?' She wiped her face with her hand. 'Same old same old.'

'No it isn't always,' said Katie gently. 'You've just had a run of bad luck.'

Sukie let out an angry laugh. 'My whole career is a run of bad luck.'

Katie nodded. 'Tell me about it,' she muttered.

Sukie looked at her. 'Oh don't give me that,' she shot. Katie blinked at her in surprise. 'You're riding high,' Sukie said. 'You're manager of a restaurant that's just got a review in *Time Out* – everything you've ever wanted. And all you had to do to get your dream job was . . .' She pretended to think for a moment, 'Oh wait! Absolutely *nothing*. What a surprise! You didn't even have to go for a bloody job interview. You just insulted everyone and guess what? The job was yours! They should write a book about you. What Katie Did Next? *Nothing*! Big, fat, round *nothing*. And she still got *exactly* what she wanted.' Katie felt too winded to speak. 'While I go to crappy audition after crappy audition,' continued Sukie, 'selling my soul for one crappy part, your ideal job trots over to you like a bloody lapdog and rolls over on its back.' Katie refused to blink. 'Even the bloke of your dreams lands on your sodding lap.'

Katie swallowed.

'Yup,' continued Sukie. 'Even after you get asked out by this man – something us mere mortals can only imagine happening – you don't even complete one single date with him. Then you don't even phone the poor bastard to say sorry and he *still* comes back begging for more! Even though he's now engaged to someone else – an old *friend* of yours no less – you *still* get off with him. Because this way *you* haven't had to take any risks and that's all that matters. That's right, as long as everyone else in the equation has everything to lose, except you. And you *still* think *you're* unlucky.'

'I-I-I,' Katie mumbled, her voice hoarse. 'It wasn't like that.'

'Katie, it's *always* like that.'

'What does that mean?'

'Have you any idea how much you hurt people?'

Katie could barely speak. She shook her head.

'Just the other night you had the bare-faced *cheek* to ask to borrow Jon's laptop to write a book when he was going through hell writing his. What kind of friend is that? Do you have any idea how shitty that made him feel? How would you like it if he tried to become a restaurateur while you were in the depths of despair because you weren't one?'

'I didn't think,' she whispered.

'You never do. Not about anyone else anyway. But don't worry. I told him not to panic because there was absolutely no way you'd finish a book.'

'Of course not. I can't write –'

'Oh it had nothing to do with writing. I knew you wouldn't because that would mean you'd have to stick your neck out; take a *risk* and face the terrifying possibility of *failure* – and unlike Jon or me or Dan or even Geraldine, you are physically incapable of doing that. So, Katie, please don't tell me that your life is a run of bad luck.'

Katie heard Sukie get up and walk back through the kitchen into the café. Two minutes later, she heard Sukie come back. Oh thank God. She turned round and looked up. Sukie was unable to look her in the eye. She put her hand on her hip.

'As Dan's away today,' she said hotly, 'it turns out I have to ask you if I can go early.'

'Yes, of course,' mumbled Katie.

All was excitement in the *Big Brother* household as someone was going to be voted out within the next hour. Hugh turned up the volume. He checked his watch. He still had forty-five minutes before he had to be at the pub. If Maxine was here, she'd be making him clean up the kitchen but sod that. He'd do it tomorrow. The satisfaction of a home-made loaf of bread was worth an untidy kitchen. Shame it tasted of brick, but he'd do it better next time, and anyway, tonight wasn't anything special. Someone's birthday. Maxine was going to be there so he wanted to be late, but not so late that it looked like he'd done it on purpose. The moment the adverts started he ran into the shower. He was back on his bed in his towel as the adverts finished.

By the time he had his aftershave on he was deeply regretting not phoning in with his vote for who he had wanted to stay in the *Big Brother* household. It would only have taken two seconds of his time and now that stupid bint was staying in and the lad he liked was out. He watched as the loser, with only an hour's warning, was pushed out of the house, waving to all the lucky ones he was leaving behind. The doors shut behind him and he was forced to walk up the white fluorescent stairs, up, up and up to the waiting crowd and camera.

It was like dying and going to heaven, thought Hugh. Sudden nothingness. No more judgments. No more chances. Was heaven going to be a tabloid frenzy? Was St Peter going to be a pregnant TV babe who cuddled you and told you you did really well with the time you'd been given, even though you'd made an arse of yourself, hadn't helped those worse off than you, hadn't tried hard enough in your trials and had ignored all your opportunities?

He looked at his watch. He had to go. Shit. He'd so much rather stay at home. He turned off the telly, picked up the birthday gift, switched off all the lights and shut his front door behind him.

Later, as dusk made its shy entrance, Matt and Eva left the pub together. She gave him a friendly punch on the arm.

'So, are you feeling a bit better?' she asked. 'No broken heart?'

'No,' he grinned, holding his arm where she'd punched it. 'Just a broken arm.'

'Sorry,' she said. 'Don't know my own strength sometimes.'

'Thanks for . . . you know,' he said.

'No problem,' she said. 'Any time you need to chat about it, just call me. I understand. Really.'

Matt wanted to ask why, and then realised he could find

out next time. This thought kept helping him every time he remembered the man laughing behind Jennifer and the door slamming in his face. He walked home at a slow pace while day turned into night, trying to make sense of all this new information.

Around the same time, Dan parked his car and he and Geraldine made their slow way up to her flat. They were exhausted. That morning his mother had told them both how jealous she was that they could just go out and choose everything they'd ever hope to need in their life together. In her day it had been so different. She and his father had had to scrimp and save and go without for decades to make the sort of collection he and Gerry were about to achieve in one afternoon.

Dan's feet and head ached as he trailed up the stairs behind Gerry. Maybe that was why marriages used to last longer, he thought as he followed her into her flat. People were too busy scrimping and saving to row over naked lady vases and grotesque teapots.

Meanwhile, Katie made her way back to the flat, absolutely shattered from a busy Saturday in the café without Dan. She was still in shock from Sukie's outburst and she could barely stand up straight, she was so worn out. She just needed to get to bed. Maybe she was coming down with something.

25

Katie had absolutely no qualms about phoning in sick on Sunday morning. In fact, she felt she had no choice. Yes, she had had close to no sleep last night, but, more importantly, she was unable to face Sukie or Dan. She didn't care what they thought about her taking time off, or rather, she cared less about it than she did about having to face them. Next Friday they were having their first summer party, and all the people who had helped make the café what it was were invited, including all their regulars, partners and friends, and of course, local journalists. She had to be able to face them all by then.

She just didn't want to get up, she realised, as she lay in bed after calling in sick at the café, and then calling Dan on his mobile. She really did feel sickened, truly sickened to the stomach, by everything. By herself, by her actions and by her life.

She hadn't had to face Jon last night because he had been ensconced in his room. So she had taken a bottle of wine and drunk herself into depression in bed, while watching crap TV. Every time she'd thought about what Sukie had said she'd started crying again. At first, she'd cried because of the venom in Sukie's voice and the injustice of how wrong her best friend could be about her. Then, gradually, it got much worse and she started crying because she realised that maybe Sukie was right. And then she started re-evaluating everything and looking at it all through Sukie's eyes for the first time. It did not make easy viewing.

It was true, she had never taken a risk in her life. She had used flimsy excuses to pretend it was more complicated – and somehow more special – than that. But the truth was all too obvious to her now. There were so many holes in her argument, it didn't hold enough water to wet a flea. OK, so she hadn't known what career to invest Great-Aunt Edna's money in. So why hadn't she thought to put it into the amazing property market? She could have put it towards a deposit for a London pad and made a fortune by now. Great-Aunt Edna would have been proud to see her do that with her money. She now realised that that was exactly what Jon was doing, while at the same time risking his life's dream by trying to write his books. Jon's parents were, in effect, giving him his inheritance by buying him a property. No wonder he was sometimes less than phlegmatic with her when she treated the flat disrespectfully. There was that time, when she'd just moved in, when she'd spilt perfume on the bathroom floor and not bothered to wipe it up till the evening. The stain was still there now. She hid her head in her pillow at how irreverent she'd been when he'd tried to confront her about it.

The truth was that she had used her job as a waitress to hide the fact that she was just a lazy, selfish coward. No more, no less. She had no more reason to wait for divine intervention to tell her what risk to take than anyone else in this world. And she was surrounded by risk-takers. Which was why they had all been able to see through her self-denial. Yes, the only person who hadn't been able to see it all was herself. Everyone else could see it as plain as day – that was why she was always having to defend her position to them.

Which led on to her next happy thought. Had they all discussed it behind her back? Had Jon and Sukie moaned about it to each other?

Then her mind turned to Hugh and Maxine – had they taken risks? Or were they cowards like her? She moved her head on to a cool bit of pillow to think properly about it.

Yes. They had taken the biggest risk one can take – they had risked setting up home together. And then, even more bravely, Maxine had risked losing it all. Oh dear God, it had come to this; respecting Maxine.

And what about Dan? Yes; he had risked everything – first in his city career and now with the café. In fact, in taking on the café, he had risked an entire decade of career – his entire past was riding on the success of the café. How terrifying must that be? She held her breath as she re-saw their working relationship through this new all-too-clear lens. There she'd been, all hoity-toity answering-back, all Miss Know-it-all, when really she knew nothing.

She shut her eyes against the painful sunlight coming through her thin curtains.

And what about Sukie? What sort of risks did she take? Katie put herself in Sukie's shoes, going to auditions, having to take time off work only to have to come back and face everyone again when she failed to get the part. And Geraldine, was she a risk-taker? Yep, the ultimate, Katie realised. She was risking her heart being broken again by the same man. And her own big sister, Bea? Risking giving birth to a child with that chin. More importantly, risking her very life – baby Edward had been born a month early and was put in intensive care for four weeks. Bea had had to stay in hospital for ten days while her body recovered after a three-day-long labour followed by emergency caesarean. She still walked funny. What about Great-Aunt Edna? Here was a woman who had risked being made a social pariah in her youth by following a career, and who was willing to give her savings – all she had to show for her entire life's work – towards helping her, Katie Simmonds. Why? Katie wondered what she must look like to her great-aunt. She who had everything life had to offer – money, support, education; and what had she achieved? Nothing. The generosity of her aunt's gesture suddenly became awe-inspiring and heart-breaking. She was unworthy.

Everyone, Katie now realised, absolutely everyone in the whole wide world was braver than she was. Those morning commuters selling their souls for the price of a mortgage, even Alec buying a café and dealing with bolshie staff every single day (no wonder he'd got out) – all of them, every single one of them was braver than her.

How could she ever face the world again?

She turned over and looked at her bedside clock. Maybe she'd just lie here until everyone she knew had died. Shouldn't take more than about a hundred years.

Was this a nervous breakdown, she wondered suddenly, the thought waking her up more efficiently than any alarm clock. The sound of Jon's morning noises from the bathroom seeped into her consciousness. Oh God, Jon. Brave, brave Jon, courageously writing his life away. He started singing Oh What a Beautiful Morning and she winced.

What did you do if you had a breakdown? (After phoning in sick, of course.) She had no idea. Should she smoke, get drunk, overeat and watch television all day? No, she didn't like smoking, felt sick already and couldn't bear daytime TV. Was that all a good sign? Or a bad sign? What the hell was the next step?

She curled up tighter into a foetal position. It was at times like these that she wished she could take off her own head as easily as taking off her clothes. She groaned. This *must* be a breakdown. She wanted to hide under her duvet and stay there forever, or at least until dinner.

Dinner. There was no food in the flat. She'd have to go out and get some in – but that would mean getting washed and then deciding what to wear for the entire day, even though she didn't know what the weather would be like later, then dressing and then being in a supermarket surrounded by people and then making decisions about what to eat . . .

So many decisions. The world was full of them. Small risks as well as big risks.

Of all the days for this to happen, Sunday was the worst. Sundays were crap. It was crap having to work Sunday and crap having the day off on a Sunday. And Sunday evening was the worst of all because, whether you worked on a Sunday or not, the evening air was laden with the doom of a working week ahead of you.

Ultimately Sukie was right, she concluded, as a great gaping ache of despair opened inside her. She would only ever be a waitress. She wasn't ever going to be a proper restaurant manager, or a writer, or an educational psychologist or a film producer or anything else. She was always going to be a waitress. And there was a very good reason she was a waitress. Because she preferred taking other people's orders to making up her own mind.

She looked across to her bedside table and her eyes alighted on the phone. Aha. Of course. The one solution that would light her way through this blackest of moments. The method to pull herself up from this pit of melancholy. She watched her own arm stretch away from her, as if it was disembodied, towards the phone. She saw herself pick it up and with great concentration dial the number correctly first time. The dialling tone soothed her until the fourth one, when the awful thought that there might be no answer kicked her in the gut. Suddenly, there was a click.

'Hello?' came the voice, clear and authoritative, yet soft.

Katie almost cried with relief. She was going to be OK. The rescue plane had seen her flare. She croaked into the phone, wiping her eyes.

'Hello Mum,' she whispered. 'Can I pop home for a day or two?'

Dan clicked his mobile phone off almost in slow motion. So. Katie wouldn't be in today. On a Sunday, their busiest day. She sounded so bad he'd told her to take as long as she needed, until she was completely well again. It was awful to hear her so low; he'd got used to her being constantly bright and perky. Rude, bolshie and unpredictable, yes, but never low. Was it arrogance to wonder if it was anything to do with what had happened between them at the wedding? He pictured her at home, all tiny and vulnerable. Maybe he'd pop round later.

'Who was that?' asked Geraldine, wandering into his bedroom, towel-drying her hair.

'Katie. She's not coming in today.'

'Oh dear. Why not?'

He shrugged. 'Didn't say, but she sounded awful.'

Geraldine threw the towel on the bed and started putting on her business suit. 'Hmm,' she said, unimpressed. 'Anyone can sound awful. You just make the call with your face upside down. Let's hope she's better soon.'

'I told her she should take as much time as she needed.'

'You what?'

'She sounded awful. Maybe it's a really bad monthly thing.'

'You are a mug, Daniel Crichton. If I phoned in sick every month, I'd be sacked and with good reason. I mean look at me, I've got a wedding to organise and *I'm* going in on a Sunday.'

'You have a great sense of sisterhood.'

'Bollocks to that,' said Geraldine. 'It's dog-eat-dog in the workplace.'

'You know, I just don't understand women.'

Geraldine smiled. 'Good. The less you understand us, the more control we have.'

'You don't think I should be concerned when my most important staff member phones in sounding ill?'

'I would have thought your chef was your most important staff member,' said Geraldine drily. 'For goodness' sake, you're her boss, not her counsellor.' She looked at her watch. 'Talking of which, I must dash.'

Dan got into work early and helped Sukie and Patsy because there was a rush, while Nik got things going in the kitchen. Sukie was in a fantastically acerbic mood today. She made Patsy cry with laughter at some of her put-downs, just as soon as she'd worked them out. Dan hadn't realised how much Katie usually stole the show.

'I think you're going to be fine without your friend,' he told her when they'd finished.

'I should think so,' Sukie told him briskly. 'We're not attached at the hip, you know.'

He turned to Patsy. 'Remind me why you're called the gentler sex again?' he asked her.

She gave him a pretty smile. 'Because we're gentler,' she said.

'Than what?' he muttered.

Patsy laughed, then stopped. 'Than men of course,' she said. 'Dur-brain.'

Hugh flicked the kitchen light on and stopped dead. Shit. The kitchen was a tip. His head was hammering. He needed coffee and a long, hot shower. He could do the kitchen tonight. He opened the fridge door and looked at the loaf of bread. It seemed much smaller than he remembered. He took out the milk and sniffed it. He almost gagged. He put it back in the fridge, slammed the door shut and leant against the kitchen counter. Bloody bloody hell. He bloody hated being alone. Maxine hadn't come to the party last night and no one knew why. Bloody rude of her. He made his instant coffee black and, without a backward glance at the kitchen, went back upstairs to bed.

It only took Katie four hours to get up, washed, dressed and packed. And only another four to 'pop' home. A good day's work, in her opinion. By the time she arrived in the bosom of her family, the bosom was heaving. Bea was there and, of course, so was her recent appendage of five months, Edward. Technically, Eddie should only be four months old and he'd always be small, but oh, he was perfect. Katie took him in her arms and looked at him properly for the first time, seeing him for the miracle he was. Not just because, as yet, he had no signs of inheriting his father's chin, but because his mother had risked her very life for his. Was motherhood the ultimate example of courage, she wondered, staring at his extraordinary, ordinary babyness.

Eddie's new Daddy, Maurice, was working away, which was why Bea and Eddie had come to stay for a few days. Katie's brother Cliffie and father Sydney were milling around at a safe distance, concerned for her, but unable to do much to help other than nod reassuringly to her from across the room.

So the job of support network was left for Deanna and Bea to fill, and fill it they did, amply, whenever Eddie wasn't doing anything cute like grinning, burping, farting, sleeping, waking or breathing. The women sat in the kitchen around the large pine table as if it were a life raft. Just sitting here gave Katie a sense of peace and inner control that she couldn't seem to find in London. She decided to take another two days off and phoned Dan immediately. He didn't ask why and she didn't care what he thought – she suggested making Sukie temporary manager and he said that was a good idea. She thought about asking him to say 'hi' to Sukie, but decided against it. She now had time to be with her family, walk in the fields and smell the cow-pats of home. Bliss.

She sighed deeply.

'Oh! What was that nasty big sigh for?' Bea asked Eddie, who was blinking pensively at them all from his grandmother's arms. 'Wasn't that a nasty big sigh? Yes it *was*. Yes it *was*. Yes it –'

'Do you want to come with me to the market tomorrow?' Deanna asked Katie, kissing Eddie's head.

'Yes please.'

'Good. I've got to get a few things, but we can treat ourselves to a cream tea in Ye Olde Tea Shoppe.'

'Lovely.'

'Oh!' exclaimed Bea to Eddie. 'Isn't that lovely? Yes it *is*. Yes it *is*. Yes it is.' She turned to them both. 'We won't be able to go I'm afraid. Eddie's got his first swimming lesson.'

'Ah, shame,' said Deanna and Katie.

'Yes you *have*,' Bea told her son and heir. 'Yes you *have*.'

What harm could a text do, thought Hugh, looking at his mobile phone. It would just be friendly interest wouldn't it? Maxine had said she'd be at the party and she wasn't there. She could be ill, or something could be wrong. Maybe that carpenter was hitting her. He'd just give her a quick text to find out how she was. After he'd tidied the kitchen. Yep. Right. He slipped his mobile into his back pocket and walked carefully down the stairs, turned on the telly and made a start on the mess.

What the hell did people do on a Sunday, thought Hugh later. He'd watched *The Waltons*, cleaned the kitchen, thrown away the bread and been food shopping. And all that with a dull hangover, so he hadn't exactly been rushing. When he and Maxine had been doing up the house, their weekends had been so busy they hadn't had a moment to themselves. He remembered commenting about how he thought he'd never have time to read a Sunday paper again. He'd read it front to back today, even the travel section which he hated, and still there were hundreds of hours left till Monday. He sat down in the living room and flicked on the telly. Absolutely nothing on. He might just write and complain. He pulled out his mobile phone. Right, he thought. Just a light-hearted text, nothing serious. He picked up the remote and checked the other channels. Nothing. Oh sod it. He texted Maxine and then finished off a bottle of whisky.

Katie always enjoyed going to the market. Whatever stage of life she was at, it always represented just what she needed. When she was younger it made her feel responsible and important because she was doing errands for her mother. When she was a teenager it made her feel adventurous and reckless because this was where the boys from all the neighbouring villages came and loitered on their motorbikes. When she was a student it made her feel connected to home again. And now it made her feel as if the world was a safe and harmless place and all her problems could somehow be sorted out.

They set off bright and early, to give Deanna plenty of time to stop and chat to most of the stall-holders. All of them seemed delighted to see Katie, asked how her job in London was going and told her how all their own family were, especially those of corresponding ages. Yet again, the market did its trick, because to each stall-holder alike, Katie's choice to up-sticks and move to London, the scariest city in the country, represented the biggest risk anyone could take.

By the time she and her mother found themselves in Ye Olde Tea Shoppe – where nothing had changed, including owner, cutlery and menu since it had opened fifty years ago – Katie was feeling a little better. She was welcomed back there with such familial warmth that she felt guilty she hadn't given the café a single thought in the years she'd been away. Now, however, she looked at it with different eyes. Would her mother consider Mrs Blatchett, owner of the shop, a woman who had wasted her life? No. She had a strong business that had seen her through her husband's early death and her son's emigration to the other side of the world. Now easily in her seventies, she was still agile and the light in her eye still shone as brightly as in the days when Katie was brought here as a reward for getting a good end-of-term report. And of course, Katie now saw, the café was a testament to the courage of Mrs Blatchett, who had taken a risk and followed through, come rain or shine. Her café, a respectable business and beloved landmark for an entire village, was her deserved payback.

'Now what can I get for you, my dears?' asked Mrs Blatchett, no need for pen or paper.

'We'll have two of your best English cream teas please,' answered Deanna.

'Lovely.' Mrs Blatchett turned to Katie. 'And how is the waitressing going in London, my dear?'

'Fine thanks.'

'Hard work?'

'Yes, but I enjoy it mostly.'

Mrs Blatchett sighed. 'I can't find anyone who wants to stay in this job any more. Not after poor Miss Abbingdon upped and left for Cornwall.'

'You've still got waitresses though, haven't you?' asked Deanna.

Mrs Blatchett lowered her voice. 'Flighty things. Work here for a summer and then they're off. Everyone wants to travel nowadays, like the world might up and vanish if they stay put longer than a week. When I was their age I was happy to go to Blackpool for the day.' She sighed. 'Lord knows what'll happen when I retire. One of those wretched coffee chains will probably snap it up.'

'Perish the thought.'

'Well,' said Mrs Blatchett, 'coffee's the thing now, isn't it? Americans are taking over the world. Came in late to the war so they think they've got a right. No, I'll probably sell up soon. Quit while I'm ahead. Anyway, hark at me. Two cream teas coming up.' And off she went.

By the time Katie's home-made scones and crustless

white cucumber sandwiches were in front of her on a plate with a doily, she was beginning to feel unfamiliar stirrings of pride in her work. And as she watched her mother pour tea out of a china teapot, another unfamiliar feeling came to her. The feeling of wanting to take a risk. She stared at the scene in front of her and could barely breathe, let alone eat, for excitement. Oh, this was a new feeling altogether. It made all the other times shrink into insignificance. This, she realised, staring like one possessed at her plate of neat white carbohydrates on a doily, was it.

She would visit Great-Aunt Edna this afternoon.

She could barely concentrate on anything until she got home. And then when she did, she was in for a big surprise. Sydney had had a busy day rounding up all the eligible young men still left in the country, with the energy and focus of a sheepdog. It was the only way he knew to help his youngest daughter. There would be six for dinner, he informed his wife. Luckily, Deanna had foreseen such a tactical move and had decided that if you can't beat them, join them. She had invited two friends from her local book club; one the owner of a book publisher's based in the nearby city centre, the other a buyer for the county's most élite furrier. Both had promised they would put in a good word for Katie, should she so desire. And she'd bought enough game to provide dinner for at least ten, just in case.

Thankfully, Katie had time to visit Great-Aunt Edna before such a trial. In the little kitchen, she was unable to wait until the tea had been poured before pouring out her own plans. Great-Aunt Edna listened with eyes alight, and none of her custard creams were eaten that day. They talked until dusk. Then Great-Aunt Edna walked her to the front door and gave her a surprisingly firm hug for someone of her small frame. Then she kissed her on the forehead, said 'Remember what I told you', and waved her off.

By the time Katie got back home that evening, there wasn't enough time to discuss her visit: they only had half an hour to get ready. Deanna hardly noticed the change in her daughter; she only knew that things seemed to get done a lot faster than usual.

And so that evening Katie found herself facing two twin-sets and earls. Or rather, earls-as-soon-as-their-entire-cousin's-families-were-wiped-out-in-a-hideous-tragedy.

'So,' Lavinia, the furrier's buyer, began over soup. 'I hear you're at a loose end, career-wise?'

'Well,' replied Katie, reluctant to embarrass her mother, 'shall we say I'm keeping my options open? For the moment, that is.'

Lavinia nodded, dabbing the corners of her mouth with a serviette. 'I see. So, tell me, what are your thoughts on fur?'

Katie was wondering whether to say that fur was great because it kept animals from looking stupid, when Eligible Bachelor Number 1 spoke up. 'Ah fur!' he murmured at Lavinia over his soup spoon. 'I hear the chattering classes have now decided it's back in fashion.'

Lavinia smiled. 'It never really went out of fashion around here.'

He nodded. 'I should think not.'

They proceeded to discuss the superior demographics

of a village unsullied by fashion and run entirely on tradition. As they spoke, Eligible Bachelor Number 2 saw his chance. He turned to Katie, as the soup plates were being cleared away.

'I hear you live in London at the moment?' he said. 'I know London very well, we have a house there. Which part?'

Katie told him and he looked at her as if he didn't quite believe she was telling the truth. 'Never heard of it. Is it anywhere near Dulwich?'

'No, it's north.'

He stared at her. 'North?' he repeated. 'Oh, I don't know that part at all.'

'I *love* south London,' chimed in Susannah, the publisher.

'Oh you know London do you?' asked Eligible Bachelor Number 2, almost turning his entire body away from Katie.

'Oh, God, yes,' drawled Susannah. 'I have to go to four meetings a month down there. Dreadfully dull, but at least it's near Chelsea, and I always pop to the King's Road.'

And so ended that evening's potential to further Katie's career and marital chances, and so began two successful relationships accommodated in four magnificent properties and resulting in five children. It turned out that that day was one of risk-taking for a lot of people.

Katie and her parents finished up in the kitchen, washing the dishes, while the others drank their port. She really was dreadfully sorry for them both, not just for this evening, but for the past few years. So it was good to know that was about to change.

26

Tuesday was mid-June perfection and Katie was woken by the sound of about three-hundred exhilarated birds announcing this happy fact. She was out of bed in the blink of an eye, showered, dressed and out of the house before anyone else awoke, catching a precious dawn hour that gave her a sense of ownership over the rest of the day. She drove through narrow, blossom-hemmed lanes and felt confident that she would see many more such mornings. For she, Katie Simmonds, Cowardess Extraordinaire, was about to change her life and take a risk. She was putting all her eggs in one big, fat, frilly basket. And to her amazement it felt good – like taking the stabilisers off a bike. After all these years, the very thing she'd been scared of had been the very thing she'd needed to do to unlock her spirit. She felt liberated.

Great-Aunt Edna met her at the door, her eyes bright and warm.

'What say you to a morning cup of tea in the garden?' she asked with a smile. They shared the bijou garden with all manner of birds proclaiming the news that the sun was hot, the grass was green, the hedges were full and the bird bath was glistening. Great-Aunt Edna smiled across her little table at Katie. 'Changed your mind?'

Katie shook her head. 'Nope. Not on your life.'

'Ooh,' laughed Edna. 'You don't want to go betting on *my* life, my dear.'

'Oh sorry,' rushed Katie, blushing. What a stupid thing to say to an old person.

Edna gave a little chuckle. 'It's far too long and full.'

Katie held up her china teacup and against the back-drop of a soft summer breeze, they clinked to each other's good health and good luck. 'Because that is all you really need in life,' Edna had said when they'd met the day before. 'Good health and good luck.'

Hugh had never been so grateful for his job. He walked along the city street, breathing in the toxic fumes, watching the other city workers all pacing to work, holding their coffee high, their briefcases low, ear-pieces stuck in place.

He'd popped into the café again today, but Katie still hadn't been in. Normally that, on top of Maxine not returning his text, would have crushed him, but he had work to go to. He had a job to do. He had a desk all his own, waiting for him. He had mates to gossip with and argue about *Big Brother* with. He had a boss who didn't take any shit. He had a bonus to look forward to. He had stuff to do. Busy busy busy.

He walked into the office. Early again. Maybe he'd get a rise. All these extra hours he was working. Blimey, that and the exercise. When Maxine next saw him he'd be a new man. Best thing in his life this was turning out to be.

He heard the lift door open behind him and turned to see who it was. Excellent! His boss.

'Morning Penrose,' said his boss. 'How's that lovely girlfriend of yours?'

Hugh managed a croak and a smile and then, as soon as his boss had turned the corner, went to the Gents. His stomach had gone peculiar.

When Katie and Edna arrived, life was stirring in the Simmonds household. Sydney and Cliffie had left for work and Deanna and Bea were in the kitchen. Katie sang out a cheery hello from the hall before leading Edna in. Deanna and Bea stared in astonishment at them.

'I thought you were still in bed,' Deanna said to Katie before turning to Edna. 'Hello Auntie. What a lovely surprise!'

'Hello my dear,' said Edna. She changed to a gleeful whisper. 'We've been plotting.'

'Oh God,' said Deanna, sitting down heavily at the table. 'Go on. Tell me the worst.'

Great-Aunt Edna turned to Katie. 'I see what you mean,' she said. 'Doesn't fill you with confidence, does it?'

Katie pulled up a chair next to her mother and placed a hand on hers.

'Don't worry Mum,' she said. 'I don't blame you for your damaging lack of confidence in me.'

'What?' asked Deanna.

'Wait!' ordered Bea. 'I'm just preparing Eddie's milk. Wait for me. I don't want to miss this.'

Edna approached the baby with her face stretched into an enormous smile and over his mummy's back Eddie laughed a delicious laugh. Bea finished preparing the milk, sat down with Eddie in record time and stuck the bottle in his mouth. He guzzled contentedly.

'Well, you see,' began Katie. 'I-I think I know what I want to be when I grow up.'

Deanna and Bea didn't bat an eyelid.

'Is it an acrobat, darling?' asked Deanna.

'A dog-trainer?' asked Bea.

'No,' said Deanna, 'no, don't tell me, don't tell me, it's, a . . . bagpipe player?'

Katie sighed and waited for silence.

'Oh I'm sorry darling,' smiled Deanna weakly. 'It's only my way of putting off the panic attack.'

Katie gave her mother a pained look. 'Do you usually get one when I say that?'

'Oh my sweetest heart,' said Deanna. 'It kicks in at the sound of your voice.'

Katie was speechless.

'Right,' said Edna slowly. 'I think that's enough unconditional maternal support. Now for Katie's announcement.'

Katie mumbled something about the time not being right, to which Edna replied that the timing could not be more right, to which Katie mumbled something about not being in the mood and she'd had a rather tough week what with work and everything. Bea and Deanna were now agog and soon Katie had all three women cajoling her to talk.

'Great-Aunt Edna and I,' she began, and Bea gave a little squeal, 'have decided what I'm going to be when I'm grown up.'

'Which means,' added Great-Aunt Edna, eyes twinkling, 'I will change my will, leaving Katie all my money.'

There was silence. Not even Eddie dared make a noise. Katie went for it.

'I am going to buy my own café and manage it myself.'

Bea and Deanna processed this information while Katie glanced at Edna. Edna gave her a quick smile which beamed across to her like a lighthouse.

'And-and,' said Katie, 'not just any café. I'm going to ask Mrs Blatchett if she'd like to sell Ye Olde Tea Shoppe to me. That's where I was when I realised I wanted to invest in a café – yesterday when we were there, Mum. In all honesty, it's – it wasn't my first choice,' she looked over at Great-Aunt Edna. Her voice lowered. 'I love working where I am and I'd love to stay being manager there. But . . .' she sighed and Great-Aunt Edna squeezed her hand over the table '. . . we've thought it all through, haven't we?'

Great-Aunt Edna smiled. 'Yes, my dear.'

'And we do think it would be a very . . . *sensible* choice.' Katie sat for a while with her eyes down, before looking up at her mother and sister and giving them a wide, if thoughtful, smile.

'So you'll be coming home!' gasped Deanna, and to everyone's surprise except hers, started crying.

'Did you hear that?' Bea asked Eddie. 'Auntie Katie's coming home!'

'Well yes,' smiled Katie. 'I hadn't thought of it like that.'

Now all she had to do was set the wheels in motion before braving her London friends.

421

'What's that look for?' asked Edna. 'It's all going excellently.'

'Yes,' said Katie. 'Yes it is, isn't it?'

When Dan took the call from Paul he knew something was up. For a start, it had been the first time Paul had contacted him for almost two weeks, and only after Dan had left countless messages on his voicemail. The last time they'd spoken, all Paul had seemed interested in was if he was getting his big city promotion – he was hoping to get the same amount as a bonus as Dan was hoping to achieve as annual turnover. Dan had hoped he might put some of it towards the café, but, from the silence, had assumed Paul hadn't got it. So his initial response was to be glad to hear from his business partner. However, it didn't take long before he was fearing the worst. Paul asked to meet up with him that evening in the café; he couldn't talk now. Then he rang off abruptly. Dan knew it was difficult to talk in an open-plan office full of lads, but why did he want to meet in the café? Why not up in town? Because it was easier for Dan? It was totally out of character for Paul to put Dan's feelings before his own.

After the call, Dan stood in the middle of the café, eyes down, hand over mouth. Was it going to be good news or bad news? Had Paul got the promotion or not? If he had, would he want to invest any of his increased salary in the café? Or was it bad news? Had Paul fallen into the classic city trap and spent money, only to find that he hadn't got the promotion and was now in debt? In which case, was he actually going to want to take money *out* of the business? Unfortunately, that sounded much more like the

Paul he knew and loved. Well, he would just have to be firm with him. This was a business, his livelihood. He was not looking forward to this meeting. He wished Katie was here for moral support.

He suddenly felt claustrophobic. He rushed out of the café, just about remembering to yell to Patsy that he was nipping out for something. As he walked up the hill, he let his mind dwell where he knew it shouldn't.

The truth was he wished Katie was here, full stop. He missed her terribly and constantly. He missed her in the morning before he got into work because he knew she wasn't going to be in. Then he missed her all day and only in the evening did he pick up a bit at the thought that she might be in the next day.

Her absence had made him realise that every time he walked out of the kitchen into the café or out of the café into the kitchen, the thought that he was approaching her was a miniature high of his day. And every time he looked up at the monitor in the kitchen and saw a grainy yet unmistakeable image of her, there was another little lift. He'd even been known, while he was on his own in the kitchen, to stand motionless and watch her, safe in the knowledge that no one could see him.

Without her, he felt he was walking with an extra weight of loneliness inside him. And it had only been two days. He had never felt like this over Geraldine, even when they'd split up. What if Geraldine had been right and Katie had had her head upside down when she'd phoned in sick? What if she wasn't ill but was really busy going for job interviews? What the hell would he do if she didn't come back?

More importantly, what the hell was he doing feeling like this about Katie when he was engaged to Geraldine? And how vulnerable did that make him, when Katie could turn her own emotions on and off like a light-switch?

Had Katie realised he felt this way about her before he had? Could she tell that he kept having dreams about the time they got stuck in the store cupboard? Was she scared by the intensity of his feelings? Or was it all just a game to her?

Why was she really off sick? Were his feelings repelling her? Frightening her? Nauseating her? Or amusing her?

He got to the top of the hill without even noticing the climb and realised he was out of breath. He turned round and walked slowly back down the hill, telling himself he was over-reacting. When he got back, he walked through the café and straight into the kitchen. He gave a little cough and then made his suggestion.

'Why?' asked Sukie. 'She'll be in again when she's well.'

'Well she's been off for three days now,' said Dan, 'and she did sound awful.'

Sukie shrugged. 'So phone her.'

'I think it's a lovely idea,' said Patsy. 'I'd like to think that if I was ill you'd phone me to see how I was.'

'He wouldn't need to phone you, Beautiful,' said Nik.

'Why?' asked Patsy.

Nik grinned. ''Cos I'd have phoned you first.' He gave her a wink that had destabilised many a woman before and Patsy responded with a laugh Barbara Windsor would have been proud of. Sukie walked past Dan out of the kitchen. 'Excuse me,' she muttered. 'I may just barf.'

They watched her go and then Patsy and Nik started wondering why she had suddenly turned so spiteful.

'It's not our fault we're having fun,' pouted Patsy, delighted.

Dan was unable to answer them. He tried to work out when the atmosphere had suddenly soured and asked them if they'd said anything to Sukie recently that might have upset her. While they tried to cast their minds back, he glanced up at the monitor in the corner and saw Geraldine coming into the otherwise empty café. Oh shit. He knew exactly where she'd been; she'd taken time off work to collect her engagement ring, and if he knew Geraldine he had to get out there fast. There was absolutely no way she'd understand why he hadn't told anyone about their engagement. He muttered something to the others about discussing this later and then –

Too late. He stood, paralysed as the grainy image of Geraldine on the screen stretched out her hand across the counter and displayed her ring to Sukie. He watched out for signs of surprise from Sukie followed by surprise then muted anger from Geraldine. He rushed out into the café to face his fiancée's wrath.

The two women turned to him and he stopped. Geraldine gave him a smile.

'Gorgeous ring,' said Sukie. 'I always knew you were a man of taste.'

'Well,' said Geraldine, 'he did pick me.'

'Exactly,' smiled Sukie.

Thank God, he thought. Sukie had thought on her feet and not let on. She had saved him a day of heartache. She deserved a rise.

Later that afternoon, Katie went to Ye Olde Tea Shoppe. She sat at the table nearest the kitchen, so that she and Mrs Blatchett could talk in relative privacy. She looked at the café with new eyes; the eyes of a future owner. She studied the layout, she looked at the view on to the street, she considered the number of tables, she scrutinised the menu and she wondered what the first changes would be. She realised how consistent and how correct Ye Olde Tea Shoppe's image was for its clientelle. Mrs Blatchett had been thorough and spot-on with her vision for this place. It had been no lucky coincidence that her business had stood the test of time. It appeared that Mrs Blatchett was more than a little old lady in sturdy shoes. She was an astute businesswoman ahead of her time. Katie suddenly felt nervous.

'Hello my love,' she greeted Katie, wiping her hands on her pinny. 'What can I do for you?'

Katie swallowed hard, fighting the temptation to ask for a cream tea and then go home. She'd never been daunted by Mrs Blatchett before. 'Mrs Blatchett,' she said quickly, before she could change her mind. Then she went quiet.

Mrs Blatchett frowned. 'Do you mind if I sit down? Only I have a feeling this is going to take time.' She sat down at the table, opposite Katie, and gave a deep sigh. Then she gave her a direct, but not severe, look. 'What's on your mind, my dear?'

Katie told her she didn't know where to start.

'Pretend you're a newspaper,' instructed Mrs Blatchett immediately. 'Give me the headline, then the first paragraph, and then the whole story. And if you can, finish on a weak pun.' She gave a little chuckle.

'Would like to buy your café,' said Katie. Mrs Blatchett stopped chuckling. She stared at Katie. Then she nodded for her to go on. 'I have excellent relevant experience,' continued Katie, 'and I have come into some money. I would like to update the café while maintaining your vision exactly. So . . . you could say . . . that I would like to *make over* your business,' a thin film of sweat lined her upper lip, 'more than *take over* your business.'

Mrs Blatchett gave her a pat on the hand. 'I was only joking about the pun,' she said softly.

Katie gave her a wan smile.

Mrs Blatchett explained that her son, Dennis, who lived on the other side of the world, was to inherit the café. If he liked the sound of Katie's offer, the café was hers. As long as Katie would not mind giving Mrs Blatchett a regular afternoon shift. She was far too old to learn how to do nothing with herself. 'Mind,' she said, pointing a knobbly finger at Katie. 'Dennis is no pushover. I feel I should tell you that.'

Katie grinned. How had she ever thought Mrs Blatchett was sweet? This woman was terrifying.

They agreed that Dennis would contact Katie through his solicitor before the day was out and then Katie left the café feeling more adult than she had ever felt before.

She went home, packed up her car and said her goodbyes. Then she popped in to say goodbye to Great-Aunt Edna and set off back to London where she was desperate to put things straight: apologise to Jon, straighten things out with Sukie and then hand in her resignation to Dan. She would work her notice. She would be there for the summer party, at the end of the week: it was an event Dan was hoping would become a regular, along with the Christmas party, so it was vital that the first one was good. In fact the whole thing had been her idea, so there was no way she'd leave him in the lurch before that.

There was no doubt about it, she told herself as she drove home, Dan had been a more than decent boss. She had been given complete carte blanche with nearly all of her ideas, despite her being bolshie and prickly to him. However, the possibility of being her own boss, of not having to answer to anyone and of being responsible for herself was proving more thrilling than she could ever have imagined. Oh yes, this was the right thing to be doing. And not just for her. She needed to leave Dan and Geraldine alone. In the cold harsh, unforgiving light of day she knew that she should leave them to their joint risk-taking. (And Geraldine was certainly taking on a risk with him. A man who could so lightly betray her.) She tutted to herself, said out loud that all men were the same and then put on her Divas album.

Sitting in the Gnat and Parrot after work, Eva took the compliment from Matt as it had been intended. Eva knew how to take a compliment. This one, though heartfelt and genuine, wasn't the best she'd ever had, but it would do. She gave Matt a warm grin and thanked him sincerely.

'I mean it,' he insisted.

'I know,' she insisted back.

'You're so easy to talk to.'

'So you said.'

'It's almost like talking to myself.'

There was a fraction of a pause before she thanked him again, slightly less effusively than before. Then she crossed one leg over the other and resettled herself. She'd worn a short floaty skirt with little navy flowers on, a strappy navy top, strappy white sandals, a funky bright plastic ring on the middle finger of her left hand and a white cardigan for later. Her dark wiry hair was up in a ponytail; carefully coiffed ringlets shaping her face, and her features were enhanced with subtle, expensive make-up. And it had all been worth it because she was, she had just been informed, the easiest person in the world to talk to.

She glanced back at Matt, who was now staring at her short floaty skirt with little navy flowers on.

'So,' he started slowly.

'Yes?'

'I was just wondering . . .'

'Yes?'

'Has Jennifer said anything to you about me?'

Eva pulled a face. 'It's all got a bit awkward at work, so she has other things on her mind at the moment.'

'What's happened?' asked Matt. 'Has his fiancée found out?'

'No! If she had, Jennifer would be sacked. You wouldn't want that to happen to her would you?' Matt was silent for a while. 'Would you?' she repeated.

He shrugged. 'If it meant she'd come crawling back to me,' he said in a dull voice, 'and force me to have wild passionate sex with her . . .' he sighed, 'I'd live with it, yes.'

'You're all heart, Matt.'

They took contemplative sips of their drinks.

'So what are the complications then?' he asked.

'You really want to know?'

'I really want to know,' he answered stoically.

'Right,' prefaced Eva. 'Well, at the moment, Jennifer's problems include trying to find a cupboard big enough for her and her boss to do it in without his fiancée finding out, but with enough people in the office to realise so that his fiancée is suitably shamed and humiliated.'

Matt grimaced as if he'd just been punched in the stomach. The thought of that old man touching Jennifer actually caused a physical reaction in his body. How was that possible? He hadn't even felt sick watching *Pulp Fiction*. He hung his head. Oh God, this must be love. Why hadn't anyone told him love felt like being sick?

'So,' Eva said. 'Let's try and talk about something else. Seen any good films lately?'

He shook his head.

'Theatre? Do you like theatre?'

He shook his head.

'How's school?'

He grunted.

'How's the café going?'

He shrugged.

'What did you think about the war in Iraq?'

Another shrug.

'What's your favourite colour?'

They sat in silence for a while.

'So,' said Eva eventually. 'When was the last time you saw Jennifer?'

'A week and a half ago. She's stopped coming into the café. Is she avoiding me? Or has she just got better things to do with her lunch-hour? Don't answer that, I don't want to know. You see, that's the thing –'

Then suddenly, as if from nowhere, another feeling, not quite as nauseating as love, not quite as spiritual as heartache but none the less very real, rose within him. Without lifting his head, his eyes shifted to his upper thigh and yes, sure enough, he found the cause. On it, *on his thigh*, as bold as brass, lay Eva's hand. He knew it was hers because of the vast plastic ring on her middle finger. And because she was the nearest person to him.

He froze. Then he heated up. Then an inner ice cracked through the heat. His body was all over the place. He could almost hear a weatherman grinning inanely into the camera, pointing out various parts of his body: 'And here we have a warm front drifting down to the groin, while in the north, I'm afraid it's a thick, dense fog.'

Matt's learning curve shot up into a vertical line.

'You're going to have to forget her,' came a voice in his ear.

Forget who? he thought.

'Come on,' said Eva, her hand – the one on his thigh – squeezing ever so gently. 'I'll get you another drink.'

And suddenly the hand was gone as Eva took it to the bar with her.

He watched her and the hand go. That skirt was short. Not slutty short – just-right short. And the top went in and out exactly where she did, as if it was meant to. No, her body wasn't like Jennifer's, but if you looked at it from the right angles you could see it had many good points. He watched it for a while from the right angles. He watched it as she stood at the bar, one leg resting on the foot-rail, strappy sandal sliding off her foot, skirt rising up her thigh. He watched it as she turned slightly to her left and eyed a bloke at the other end of the bar. He eyed her back! And then she smiled at him. He smiled back! Tosser, thought Matt.

By the time Matt looked back at Eva, she was walking towards him with a warm, inviting smile. He jumped up, taking the drinks out of her hand.

'So,' he said, as soon as they sat down. 'They're showing a new Tom Cruise film at the Odeon.'

'Ooh, I love Tom Cruise.'

'Do you? Me too! Isn't that funny!'

'Yeah. Amazing.'

'Fancy going? Tonight?'

Eva sipped her drink and gave him a little grin.

'Yeah, why not?' she shrugged.

Dan glanced across the street as he turned the Closed sign to face outwards, and Paul sat himself down at one of the tables near the counter. Dan joined his business partner and prepared himself for the worst. He could never have expected to hear what he heard. He blinked at Paul, and then smiled.

'Congratulations! Blimey! What the hell brought that on?'

Paul allowed himself a smile. He shrugged. 'I just woke up and decided she was the one for me.'

'Had enough flings on the side had you?'

Paul shook his head firmly. 'Those days are over, mate.'

'Good. So what really brought this on?'

Paul gave a resigned look. He knew he couldn't fool his

432

best mate. 'Well, all right,' he started, and then gave a big sigh. 'She just said that she wanted to know where our future lay, that sort of thing.'

Dan eyed his friend. 'An ultimatum?'

Paul frowned in concentration. 'I suppose, as it was, the relationship wasn't really fair on her. She's not getting any younger, she wants kids one day, we've been together five years. She needed to know where it was going, or –'

'Or she was going to leave you?' finished Dan quietly.

Paul nodded. He spoke quietly. 'And it made me realise that all those stupid flings were meaningless. Without her I'm nothing. New slate. New me.' Dan smiled. 'The lads at work are ripping the piss out of me, but I knew you'd understand,' continued Paul. 'You being engaged and all that.' Dan stopped smiling. 'When you've met the one, you've met the one.'

'This is wonderful news,' said Dan. 'So why the long face?'

And so Paul told him.

It was only afterwards, when Dan was sitting on the floor in the silent kitchen, staring at the dishwasher, that he realised he couldn't ever have prepared himself for the worst because his imagination wasn't that good.

Paul had said his well-rehearsed piece about how he had got the promotion. About how this and the prospect of his wedding made him realise it was time to stop gambling with money that wasn't his alone any more. About how he wanted to put a deposit on a house and he might as well put it on as big a house as he could get. He owed it to his girlfriend – no, his fiancée. And then he had waited in an echoing silence.

Dan tried to speak, cleared his throat and tried again. 'Mate . . .' he said weakly, all his breath gone.

'I know,' said Paul sadly. 'The last thing I wanted to do was hurt you.'

'Hurt me?' repeated Dan.

'Yes. You mean a lot to me. This place means a lot to me. But I just feel . . . well, like I said, "new me". I haven't got a choice.'

'You haven't hurt me,' whispered Dan.

'Oh thank God –'

'You've ruined me.'

Paul managed a laugh. 'Oh come on. It can't be that bad.'

'Of course it's that bad. I can't afford to keep this place on my own if I have to buy you out.'

'It's only a café, Dan. This is my life.'

There wasn't much to say after that. Paul left, although Dan couldn't remember how. All he could remember, as he leant back against the cold fridge door, was his father's favourite motto, 'Nothing ventured, nothing gained', and the price of the engagement ring with all the wotsits.

Katie made it back to London in good time – she took the wrong turning off that wretched roundabout again, but next time she'd get it right. During the journey, she took two calls from Dennis Blatchett's solicitor. The first was to say that Dennis was very keen: he wanted a fast sale and she sounded perfect. Name your price. She named her price. The next phone call from Dennis Blatchett's solicitor was to say that Dennis wanted £10,000 more. After she'd parked, she sat in her car for a while, wondering where on earth she'd find that much.

She decided that when she got upstairs she'd phone her mum. She'd like to phone Great-Aunt Edna and discuss it with her, but it was late – and also she didn't want her to think she was asking for more money. What she did know though was that she felt fired up with determination. She wanted Ye Olde Tea Shoppe.

From her car, she looked up at Jon's light in the flat. She couldn't remember the last time she'd got such a good parking space. It was a sign. Everything was going to be all right. Like a black cat or two magpies, a space right outside a London flat was a message. Right. It was time to go in.

She heaved herself out of the car, pulling her bag with her as she went. She couldn't wait to apologise to Jon and re-write herself. She'd worked out exactly what she'd say to him on the way home. She ran up the stairs, opened the door and catapulted herself on to the sofa where she knew he would be sitting. He nearly hit the ceiling in fright.

'Jon,' she rushed. 'You have to listen without interrupting, OK?'

He pointed at the television. It was *Star Trek: The Next Generation*.

'Call me when it's over,' she said. 'I'll be unpacking.'

Half an hour later, he came into her room with two mugs of tea.

'Right,' he said, handing her one and then sitting cross-legged on her bed. 'Fire away.'

'I am so sorry for being a completely selfish, self-centred flatmate for the past two years.'

Jon looked at her.

'That's OK,' he said. 'Did you have a nice break?'

'Yes.'

They stared at each other for a moment.

'Have I been horrendous?' asked Katie.

'No.'

'Am I an awful friend?'

'No. I think you're quite a good one actually.'

'But I've been very selfish. That time with the perfume.'

He smiled and shrugged. ''s only perfume.'

'No, it was more than perfume. It was your property and I abused it.'

He frowned. 'What's going on?' he asked. 'Have you been on some hippy retreat or something? You haven't taken any mind-altering drugs have you?'

'No,' she said. 'Sukie made me realise how selfish I've been and thoughtless – borrowing your laptop to write a book that night – and always expecting everything to be laid on a plate for me all the time . . .'

'What are you girls like?' he was shaking his head. 'You're all as mad as each other.'

'That's sexist, Jon.'

'It's true. Look at you both. Mad as March hares.'

'But Sukie said –'

'Sukie's going through hell. She's angry. She took it out on you.'

'No, it was more than that.'

'Anyway,' said Jon. 'I was dead chuffed that night you borrowed my laptop.'

'Why?'

''Cos I won a bet with Sukie. I made twenty pounds without moving my arse.'

Katie's eyes widened in surprise. 'Sukie bet money on me being able to write a book?'

Jon laughed. 'Don't be ridiculous. She put money on a literary agent knocking on the door and offering to represent you after reading the title.'

Katie tried to laugh. 'Oh yeah, that's funny,' she smiled. 'That's really funny.'

'I know,' he laughed so much he fell back on to the bed. 'So thanks to you, I won twenty pounds *and* had a good laugh.'

'Excellent. Well,' said Katie. 'I'm glad I could help.'

'Actually, there is something you could do to *really* help.'

'Yeah? What?'

'You could read the synopsis of my next book before I give it to Richard Miller. And then look at my list of future ideas for him. I've just finished it. I want to send it tomorrow morning, and I'm bricking it.'

She was overcome with emotion. 'Me?' she gasped. 'Why me?'

'Because you owe me for all those bloody CVs I wrote for you.'

Matt sat in the cinema to Eva's right, staring at the screen, his left leg close enough to her for her hand to stray, but not too close that it should look obvious. It was such an unnatural position his thigh muscles were starting to cramp. He wondered that she could eat at a time like this, let alone be so wholly preoccupied with her popcorn and Diet Coke. He coughed a little and used the excuse to move his left leg slightly nearer to her. It touched her accidentally, so he shot it away again fast. It practically rebounded off his own leg and back into hers, so he tightened the muscles again and kept it close to him. He was now sitting like a coy transvestite. He tried to remember how he usually sat. He visualised himself on the bus. Nope. He had no idea. He tried to relax his body but stopped short when he realised that this might mean knocking into Eva again. His leg was now beginning to shake. God, he wished for once in his life he was thick. It would be much less exhausting.

Next to him Eva laughed at an advert, then leant in towards him.

'Popcorn?' she whispered in his ear, offering him some.

He shook his head.

This was ridiculous. Here he was, about to watch a fantastic sci-fi thriller with an attractive, bubbly, bright 21-year-old woman who had put her hand on his thigh, and his head was ruining it.

Eva giggled at the adverts again.

He frowned at the screen.

Maybe she wasn't so bright. These adverts were crap. How could she find them funny? Maybe she had some kind of mental disorder. Maybe that was why Jennifer no longer came to lunch with her, and why she was in the cinema with a bloke four years younger than her. Maybe she had the mental age of a fifteen-year-old and he'd been so hung up on Jennifer he hadn't noticed. Maybe he was on a date with the saddest woman in the country. He almost smiled. It would figure. The saddest woman and the unluckiest bloke. Of course the film would be crap too. That would be the icing on the cake, wouldn't it?

Yep, he should just face it. The film would be shite, Eva

would reveal herself as special needs and he'd dislocate his left leg from the effort of not touching her. Excellent.

'Hey Matt,' whispered Eva.

'Hm?' he turned to her.

And then, without any warning whatsoever, she kissed him so softly and lingeringly he thought he was in slow-motion. And paradise.

Late that evening, still in the café, Dan stared at the café phone for a long time trying to decide who to call with his shit news. Geraldine deserved to be the first to know. She was going to be his life partner. She had stood by him through thick and thin. Yes, she deserved to know that her engagement ring would be his last shiny gift for a long while. And maybe she'd have some useful advice for him. Yes, he sighed loudly. He would phone Geraldine. Maybe she could come and pick him up; he was in no fit state to drive. He started to dial her number then his eye strayed to the list of contact numbers on the wall that Katie had put there. He slammed down the receiver, and then, quickly, before he changed his mind, started to call her at home.

Katie looked up at the ringing phone again.

'Please,' she begged Jon, 'let me answer it.'

Jon shook his head. 'Uh-uh.'

'It might be for you.'

'All the more reason not to answer.'

They stared at the phone.

'That's the sixth time in under an hour,' said Katie. 'It must be important.'

'Not more important than my synopsis. Where are you up to? Has the talking snake come out of the wardrobe yet?'

The phone stopped and Katie sighed. 'I haven't started it yet. I'm still on your list of future ideas. I like the new genre "lager sagas". She read from his list: ' "Say goodbye to clogs and shawls, say hello to jobs and brawls." ' She looked up. 'Very nice.'

'Does that mean you haven't started the synopsis yet?'

'Well, I'm tired.'

'Jesus, Katie. My nephew reads faster than you. I know, I'll make you a coffee.'

He left the room as the phone started ringing again. '*No answering!*' he yelled from the kitchen. Then he popped his head out from behind the kitchen door. 'I think,' he said slowly, 'it was sixty CVs in all.'

Katie began reading the synopsis.

Just before midnight, a none-too-pleased Geraldine parked her car outside Crichton Brown's and hooted four long blasts on her car horn. Five minutes later, Dan stumbled into her car and they drove off back to her flat.

At approximately 12.03 a.m., in Eva's flat, Matt Davies lost his virginity, aged 17 and seven months, and started his epic journey of sexual discovery that was to last him the next six decades of his life.

27

Dan sat on his apartment floor, clicked his phone off and flung it on the sofa. Then he turned to the pad at his feet and crossed off another name so vehemently it tore the paper. He gave his stubble a slow scratch. He was glad Katie was back at the café. He hoped she was feeling better. Perhaps now Sukie would stop behaving so oddly. He gave a long sad sigh. Only two days to go before the café's summer party. Should he tell her before or after it? He knew he should tell her before the others, although chances were they'd guessed something was wrong by his absence today. The only problem was, the longer he left it, the less energy he had and the less energy he had, the less he felt able to do it. He wasn't even sure if he had it in him to go to the party. And if Katie took the news half as badly as Geraldine had, it would still mean another hysterical banshee on his hands.

Ah dear, Geraldine. Just one more thing to worry about. It had been hard facing up to the fact that he had to tell Geraldine such bad news. Hard because he realised there was something wrong if he was this nervous to tell his bad news to the woman he was about to marry. And he'd been right to be nervous. Where he had hoped to spend the night resting his throbbing head on the forgiving bosom of his fiancée, he had spent it trying to reassure a mad harpie. Instead of helping him in his hour of need, Geraldine had just become another stress on top of all the others.

Her reaction had been the proverbial last straw on the camel's back. It made him question whether there had been other times he'd turned to her for help. He realised he never had, and that this was not a healthy dynamic for a partnership. He looked back over their years together and wondered why he had never asked her for help. He realised the painful truth: he had never thought she was able to help him: practically, emotionally or psychologically. It just wasn't in her make-up.

This made him question the kind of man she needed. He concluded that this was someone with thicker skin than he had; someone who got a kick out of looking after their woman; who felt that a high maintenance woman was a feminine woman; someone who was harder than him; who wouldn't notice her constant hammering away at the emotional bridge they'd be building together, or notice her chip-chip-chipping away at his self-confidence; someone whose self-confidence was protected by a hard shell of complacency. And someone who made lots of money.

This made him question the kind of woman he needed. He got a bit stuck on that because he kept remembering kissing Katie at the wedding.

None of this meant he didn't love Geraldine or that they didn't have a lot of wonderful memories to look back on. It didn't mean that breaking up would be easy. Breaking up never was. He'd tried it before, so he should know.

And that's where he always came back to the same point: on the one hand, her reaction had been the straw that broke the camel's back; but on the other, bigger, hand, he was a nervous camel and Geraldine was a piece of straw with a rod of steel going through it. Did he really have it in him to leave her?

They hadn't spoken since he'd told her the news and they'd rowed so apocalyptically. At first he hadn't phoned her because he was angry. Then because he was confused by his thoughts on their relationship. Then it had started to veer from confusion, to awareness that the relationship was over for good, to fatalistic realism that this was probably just another row. Only in the last hour or so had it started to be fear. Because if they were fated to stay together he was in for a right rollocking when they finally spoke.

So he was trying not to think about it.

He stretched over to the phone again. There were only two more names on his list, and he'd already humiliated himself more than he could bear, but anything was better than the ultimate humiliation. He sat through the dialling tone with his eyes shut, hoping against hope that desperation wasn't audible.

As the tone continued, his mind wandered again. It was beginning to do that recently. He was finding it harder and harder to focus since . . . since when? He frowned hard. When had Paul told him he was backing out? Was it really only last night? It felt like weeks. He tuned into the dialling tone again.

Ah well, at least this pointless exercise had reminded him of one thing. He knew exactly why he'd left the city. He could picture the dealing room now, the men's vivid jackets making up for their sallow skins. He might be finding it tough trying to make sense of his new female colleagues' emotional outbursts, but it was better than a testosterone-fuelled office. He was just about to throw the phone away when it clicked into action.

'Charles Gordon?'

'Charley!' cried Dan.

There was a fraction of a pause during which Dan could hear the buzz of a frantic office in the background.

'Dan. My man.'

Dan's heart sank. Charley had been warned.

'Hi, how you doing?' he forced bonhomie into his voice.

'Can't complain, can't complain.'

'Good.'

'What can I be doing for you?'

'Well, it's more what we could be doing for each other,' said Dan, hating himself.

A pause. He could visualise Charley semaphoring to his mates over his computer that the sucker had got round to him.

'I take it you've heard?' Dan couldn't keep up the pretence.

'I had heard something, yeah.'

'We're doing bloody well.'

'Great.'

'Profits are up.'

Charley had the decency to give a wolf whistle.

'But Paulie's got other commitments.'

'Yeah. I heard. Sad bastard.'

'I'm not going to waste your time, Charley boy, I know you're busy. Do you want in?'

Charles gave a big sigh and Dan could see him leaning back on his chair. 'I would mate, but as of last month, I'm investing all my spondulix in property. Just put a deposit on a flat by Tower Bridge.'

'Oh great.'

'Penthouse with views over the river. Hoping it will be my pension.'

'Good for you.'

'Of course if I get the sort of lucky break that that sneaky sod Paulie got, I'll sell up like a shot. Don't care if it means putting tenants out of a home.'

Dan managed the requisite laugh.

'Listen,' said Charley kindly, 'why don't you come down to the pub tonight? All the lads'll be there, and the totty's corking – there's a massive new office next door and it's crumpet city.'

'Yeah, Mike said.'

Charley let out a guffaw. 'Ah yeah, Mikey the Man. He's with a different one every night. It's like live soap opera. Come on. Do you good.'

'Nah, you're all right.'

'OK,' said Charley, relieved.

'Right then.'

'Listen, Dan.'

'Yeah?'

'Keep in touch.'

'Yeah.'

Dan heard the phone click off and sat with it in his hand for quite a while. He looked down at his pad. One more name. Then he watched his hand cross it out and start doodling over the pad.

Maybe he should just go back to the bank. Better to beg a bank manager than his old mates, and with a healthy business forecast they might be only too happy to re-think the loan restriction. On the other hand, did he really want to be that much in debt at this stage of his life? He stopped himself from thinking about a looming wedding and wife. Should he remortgage his flat? Should he sell it?

He looked round his beloved bachelor pad. How the hell had this happened? There he was only a few months ago, living the life of a carefree, solvent, single man, the world his oyster, dreams coming true left, right and centre – and suddenly wham! Business, marriage and financial worries.

He threw the phone back on to the sofa, almost hitting the coffee table, then put it in its cradle. He didn't have the energy to speak to anyone any more. When the phone rang again, he put his hand over his eyes and listened to the answerphone click into action.

Beep, click.

'Hi Dan, it's me. Katie. Um. I just found out you aren't going to be in today and . . . um, well. I think we need to talk. Hope you're OK. Bye then. Um.'

Pause.

Click.

He stared at the silent answerphone, tension pulling his forehead so tight it felt as if his skull was too big for his skin.

What the hell had that message meant? Her voice had been sort of urgent yet soft at the same time. He'd call her. He leapt over to the phone but as he did so it rang again. He froze.

Beep, click.

'Hi. I'm going into a meeting in half an hour. Call me.'

Click.

At the sound of Gerry's voice he almost hopped backwards. He needed to talk to Gerry like he needed a hole in the head. Actually a small hole might be just what his head needed. What did *that* message mean? Was she about to finish with him? Or bollock him again? Make him feel guilty yet again? Or change the habit of a lifetime and actually apologise? Wow. Now that would be worth picking up for.

He supposed he really should speak to her. He was being an utter coward and she deserved more. Or did she? he asked himself as he played back the worst of their row. His hand wavered over the phone. When it rang again, he gave a little jump. He almost started looking for cameras. Could Gerry actually *see* him? He listened again. Maybe she'd give more clues this time.

Beep, click.

'Oh hi, it's me again.'

No, it wasn't Gerry. It was her. The same urgency, the same softness. He listened.

'Um. I think I forgot to say that it was Katie.'

Pause.

'Bye.'

Click.

He picked up but too late. She'd gone. He landed

heavily on the sofa and looked at the phone in his hand willing it to ring again. When it did he started to feel spooky.

Beep, click.

'Where the hell are you?'

Pause.

'Daniel?'

He shrank.

'Are you screening?'

He held his breath.

'I think we both know we have to talk. I have the perfect solution. Call me before my meeting.'

Click.

The perfect solution to what, he thought. Nuclear disarmament? The Israel/Palestine situation? Eczema? Or was she going to suggest they postpone the wedding until both of them had dated everyone else in the world and proved there was no one else out there for them?

When the phone went again, he prayed it would be Katie. This time he would pick up, he told himself. Yes this time he would talk to her. The answerphone cut in. He waited for her voice, flexing his phone hand in preparation.

Beep, click.

'Oh hello love, it's Mum. I don't want to trouble you but I just wanted to let you know that everyone keeps asking me if I have any idea about the date and where your list will be. I keep telling them I don't know and that you'll decide in your own good time, but I just thought you might like to know that they want to know. Because quite frankly they're driving me mad. Dad sends love. Bye.'

Click.

He curled himself into a ball on the sofa. When the phone rang he waited patiently for the answerphone to cut in. This was turning into a modern art exhibit. Maybe he should send the tape to the Tate.

Beep, click.

'Right. I've got to go into my meeting. I really didn't want to have to leave this message, but it looks like that's what you want. So we'll do it your way.'

Pause.

I've had a word with Paul.

Dan sat up.

'I was going to ask him for contact numbers of some of your old pals – thought maybe they'd be able to help you out – but he had a much better idea. He said he'd put in a word with your old boss and he was fairly sure he'd take you back. Obviously not on the same salary, but, well, what do you expect? Daniel, I really don't think you have a choice here.'

Dan lost control of his lower jaw.

'Anyway. Paul wants to meet me for lunch. Can't see why, but no point pissing him off. So, I'm meeting him at one. Thought you might want to speak to me before I see him, but . . . clearly not.'

Pause.

'Right. I'm going into my meeting now, and then I'm going straight to meet Paul. If you want me I'll be on my mobile. If I remember to leave it on.'

Pause.

Click.

Dan fell back on the sofa. Was this her idea of helping him? Humiliating him with all his ex-colleagues? Why didn't she just put an ad in the paper? She probably had. He must remember not to buy the *Financial Times* ever

449

again. What the hell would she do next? Phone his parents? Tell his dad that he'd actually sobbed during their row? He sat bolt upright. Oh my God. This wasn't help. This was revenge. Yes! She was punishing him for shouting at her. Or was it one further – was she finally finishing with him? He gasped. No! It was far worse than that. He realised once and for all that he was dealing with an evil genius. She was making it impossible for him to stay with her, but not actually finishing with him, so that when he was backed into a corner and so utterly humiliated that he was unable to do anything but finish with her – a shell of the man he once was – she could play the victim part again and tell everyone that she'd done everything in her power to help him – she'd even phoned Paul and begged on his behalf – and *this* was how he repaid her! Left her at the altar! She'd even bought the dress! Oh dear God, he could hear her telling this sob-story to all her friends. He hid his face in the cushion. Machiavelli could take lessons.

Beep, click.

'Hi again. Look I'm really sorry to be driving you mad at home, but there's no answer from your mobile and I'd really like to . . . well, make contact with you sooner rather than later. So I just thought I'd give you my home phone number. Look, it is sort of urgent. I mean, not bad urgent. Just urgent. You'll understand when we speak. So hopefully I'll speak to you soon. OK. Well, I . . .'

Pause. Sigh.

'OK, sorry.'

Click.

He turned over and stared at the ceiling for a while, repeating that one in his head.

Beep, click.

'Hello love, Mum again. Your dad's told me off for bothering you. I'm sorry sweetheart. He told me to phone you and leave another message telling you to ignore the last one. We both agreed that there's no point rushing these things, especially when you've found someone as special as Geraldine. You two must take things at your own pace.'

Pause.

'Haven't you got a lot of messages? It took ages to connect me. Anyway, hope all's well and we both send you all our love. It's your cousin Jonathon's fortieth at the weekend. Bye love.'

Click.

He thought he might be sick.

Beep, click.

'All right mate? Just spoken to the lovely Geraldine. Don't want you thinking I'm doing the dirty on you, so just letting you know we're having lunch – all above board obviously. Hey-hey. No but listen mate, she's really worried about you. Says you're off sick this morning. Says she's worried you might have a breakdown. And, well, I know you've been calling all the lads begging them for help with a sob-story. C'mon Dan for fuck's sake call me. There's no need for any of this. I'm sure we can sort something out. C'mon mate.'

Pause.

'Have a good wank and forget all about it. Hey-hey.'

Click.

Yes. It was definitely revenge.

Beep click.

'I forgot to give you my home number! I can't believe it! What a complete twat! You could probably sell these messages to some radio programme. Ooh, that's an idea. A sort of You've Been Framed for radio. Ooh I like it. Somebody must have thought of it already though, eh?'

Pause.

'*Right. Anyway. My home phone number is 0208 555 7693 and I'm in all evening because the TV's good.*'

Pause.

'*Well, um . . . . I think I've been pithy enough.*'

Pause. Laughter.

'*Oh dear, you'll miss me when I'm gone. Bye till next time.*'

Click.

He closed his eyes. 'You'll miss me when I'm gone.' Was Katie going to leave him then? He'd just have to make sure she never got a chance to speak to him again. That way she could never hand in her notice, could she? Katie felt like a different world away. Like she was someone he'd once dreamed about.

Beep click. Sigh.

'*It's Katie. I mean, it was Katie. That last message. The one giving you my home phone number and waffling. By the way, we've been coming up with some great party ideas. Nik's especially worked up about his, and Patsy got so excited she almost swallowed her chewing gum. But it was OK, because Nik very gallantly offered to find it with his tongue. Aaaahh. So you see you're missing loads here. Just thought you'd like to know you have a happy team who are looking forward to seeing you soon. Right. Well. Anyway. Um. Sorry to have kept pestering you. Hopefully speak to you tonight. Bye then. Bye.*'

Click.

And then he felt a cold tear run down over his ear and on to the sofa cushion.

Dan drove to the bank via the back roads so as to avoid passing the café. Geraldine and Paul would be having

452

lunch together now, pretending not to delight in his downfall. After his phone had finally stopped ringing, he'd hauled himself up off the sofa, shaved, showered, dressed and eaten a slice of toast. It felt like a massive achievement.

He didn't get to see his bank manager. He wondered if they actually existed any more. What he did see was his small business advisor, a man safe in the knowledge that he had no financial worries because he still lived with his mum and bought his suits from Suits You. His aftershave was an affectation. They had a full and frank convesation, during which the man-boy told him fairly and squarely that they would need more security. Dan considered offering his kidney but didn't have the heart to make a joke. Then he went home again, via the back roads. When he got home, he'd call the café and tell them he wasn't going to be in again today. It was the least they deserved.

Unbeknown to Dan, on his way home he passed Matt's house and in fact drove past Matt standing outside it. Matt didn't see him because Matt could barely breathe with fear. In fact he had never known terror like this. Everything up till now had been easy. Allowing his mates to spend time with his mother? Piece of cake. Permitting her to come to parents' evening? Walk in the park. 'A' Level exams? Child's play.

This, however, was the stuff of nightmares. This was probably the first time he had ever been truly scared.

'Do I look OK?' asked Eva.

'God yes,' whispered Matt. She looked amazing. She was wearing a sophisticated two-piece summer suit with strappy kitten mules, her hair pulled back, her lips enhanced by deep red lipstick. He was standing next to a schoolboy fantasy. He squeezed Eva's hand as they heard his mum come to the front door. He didn't know who he was squeezing it for, her, him or his mother. He decided it was all of them and squeezed again.

The door opened and he stared in disbelief at his mother. He blinked. She grinned at them both. He blinked again. What the hell was her problem? Would Eva make a run for it or chuck him during lunch?

'Hi!' she greeted them. She put her hand out to Eva and gave her a big smile. 'You must be Eva. Welcome.'

Eva handed her the flowers. 'These are for you.'

'Freesias! My favourite.' She took a big sniff and allowed them in. Matt gave her a look. What was it with her? Did she want to ruin his life? As they followed her down the corridor into the kitchen, he mouthed the word 'Sorry' to Eva. She frowned and then gave him a big grin. She was pretending not to even notice. What a star. He watched his mother flick on the kettle and get the mugs out.

Her hair was in its usual ponytail, her jeans were the latest look and her bright pink T-shirt had glitter on it and little stars. It said 'Motherfucker'.

'Right,' grinned Motherfucker. 'Who'd like a cup of tea?'

Eva started giggling. She'd spotted the joke. 'I *love* your T-shirt!'

'Oh do you?' grinned Matt's mum, joining in. 'I'm so relieved. I thought it might break the ice a bit. Got it at the market. £2.50. Rude not to really.'

Eva laughed loudly. 'It's brilliant!'

'Excellent!' Matt's mum held up the flowers. 'Do you know how to "do" flowers?' she asked. 'You could do them while I make the tea.'

'Oh yes,' Eva rushed forwards.

Sandra watched her trim the flowers and display them in the vase. Eva looked at her and stopped.

'Is this right?' she asked.

Matt's mum nodded. 'Are you sure you're not over-qualified to be going out with my son?' she asked seriously.

Matt grinned as Eva burst into laughter. He decided now was the perfect time to leave and went to sit in the front room. Once on his own, he allowed himself a hearty chuckle. His mum was meeting his girlfriend. That's right. His mum was meeting his *girlfriend*. His girlfriend was *twenty-one years old*. His *girlfriend* was twenty-one years old. He was not a virgin. He looked out through the faded net-curtains of the little bay window and listened to the hooting of laughter coming from the kitchen. He was a man. He could hardly wait to go to school tomorrow and tell his mates.

Meanwhile, a few roads away, Hugh sat in the front room of his knocked through lounge-diner staring through the newly updated sash window with its Heal's gauze curtains. He was surrounded by silence. He'd called in sick today and he really didn't think he was lying. He knew he just wouldn't have been able to go in another day and pretend everything was all right; joking with the lads, smiling at the bosses and concentrating in meetings. He just couldn't do it any more. He felt like he was having a slow-motion panic attack. His body was in fright or flight mode all the

455

time. It had started yesterday, after he'd got into work, and it had been there all day. There was some secret silent madness going on in his head too that no one else could hear. He thought it would be all right when he got home, but it got even worse when he was on his own. It stayed there all night. He couldn't relax, he couldn't think, he couldn't even watch TV. He couldn't do anything.

He hadn't slept a wink. He'd put on the World Service till Radio Four had kicked back in, but he hadn't heard a single word. Perhaps he should pop into the café today and see Katie; it would be good to see someone he knew, someone he could really talk to. Someone he'd once loved. Do him good. He covered his mouth, alarmed by the sound escaping from it.

28

By the time she got to work on Thursday morning, Katie was beginning to feel a tad tetchy. Partly with Dan for not returning any of her calls, but mostly with herself for making such an enormous wazzock of herself. How many times had she called him in the end? For goodness sake, she was supposed to be his manager! How could he possibly respect her when she couldn't even leave a basic answerphone message? Truth was she knew she could hardly blame him for not calling her back – he'd probably pulled a ligament laughing so hard at her messages – but blame him she did. She'd stayed in all evening, tense with anticipation at the thought of sharing a phone call with him. She hadn't been able to go to bed until midnight, assuring herself that he might have been at some important late-night meeting and might yet phone. Then she hadn't been able to sleep till three. Needless to say she was exhausted this morning. And with tomorrow being the big party she really didn't need this. Then when she got in, she discovered that he wasn't in work again, but this time no phone call to explain. What was going on? Was he going to leave them all?

Meanwhile, things were not going quite as smoothly with her own plans of leaving. The purchase of Ye Olde Tea Shoppe wasn't quite going according to plan. It turned out that although Mr Blatchett was very keen to sell the café to someone his mother knew, who knew the area and who had management experience, and although he was a lovely man who was not interested in making a fast buck out of a business his mother had nurtured like a child, he was also very, very keen to get that £10,000. Katie had managed to go up £1,500, thanks to a promised loan from her parents, but he was not budging. He hadn't even come down £500 to pretend to meet somewhere near the middle. It looked like he was not playing. This was the price, take it or leave it.

Katie realised that she had to consider the real possibility of losing the tea shop, and she felt utterly despondent at the thought. How could she not get what she wanted, if she wanted it this much? She realised in an instant why she had put off this moment for so long. Pure self-preservation. Now that she'd finally realised what she wanted to do, she didn't want to wait any more, not even a day. Life was too short. Today was the first day of the rest of her life and she wanted to buy Mrs Blatchett's café.

And typically, for the first time in her life, everything else was on hold too. Dan wasn't in again so she couldn't tell him her monumental news. She couldn't even talk about it to Sukie and make it real that way. She so wanted to tell her about the change in her, and how it had all started with Sukie's bluntness; confess that Sukie had probably changed her life. If not that, just connect with her again; share a joke, a moan, a sarky comment. She'd settle for just some eye contact, but Sukie was refusing to look at her and she was feeling more and more alone as the morning progressed. She'd tried talking to Patsy, but that had made her feel even more alone.

Patsy was nowhere to be found when the commuter queue started, so Katie and Sukie had to work it together.

'One cappuccino with two sugars to go, one almond croissant and a Mars Bar, please,' said the first extremely early commuter.

'Diet going well then?' Katie asked, putting the croissant in a bag as Sukie made the coffee. Surely Sukie would respond to that, she thought.

'Oh *no*,' laughed the commuter. 'I gave up on that years ago.'

'Really?' gasped Katie.

'*Yes*!' The commuter held up her Mars Bar. 'Look!'

Sukie handed the commuter her coffee, unsmiling. 'That's £3.50 and she's taking the piss.'

The commuter handed the money over, smiled uncertainly and thanked them both.

Katie stared in disbelief at Sukie. That was beyond the pale. Some things were sacred, and the Them and Us attitude was one of them. She'd had enough. She did not deserve this. As far as she was concerned the woolly mittens were off.

'Oh I'm *so* sorry,' she said. 'Was I stealing your role of arsy bitch?'

'No,' Sukie replied evenly, giving her a deadened look. 'I just think that not everyone is blessed with your metabolism.' She started wiping the counter.

'Not everyone's blessed with your hair,' Katie replied just as evenly, 'so does that mean you'll stop calling that eleven o'clock Americano Worzel?'

'That's different.'

'Yeah right,' muttered Katie. 'Because that's you and not me.'

'No,' said Sukie, 'because I don't do it to his face. Your woman can't help the fact that a Mars Bar helps her through her boring day at the office. At least she got off her arse and got a job. You've got to respect that.'

'What the hell am *I* doing? Finger painting?'

'Morning ladies!' cried out the first of the 7.14. 'And isn't it a beautiful one?'

'No!' they shouted.

She looked at them. 'OK,' she said slowly. 'My mistake. I'll have a double espresso and two slices of toast please.' As Sukie went to the toaster, she called after her, 'Please could my espresso be blacker than my toast this morning, there's a dear.'

Sukie ignored this and Katie smiled at the commuter. 'Sorry,' she told her loudly, starting to make the coffee, 'but you see, Sukie's the unluckiest person in the world. Count *your*self lucky you only got burnt toast.'

'Oh,' murmured the commuter.

'Do you know,' continued Katie, 'some people believe they're unlucky because they've got a terminal illness or have been debilitated in an accident.' She laughed. 'Did you know some people in this world are blind! Or deaf! But,' she leaned forward, 'not one of them is as unlucky as our Sukie.'

'Why?' Three commuters were now agog.

460

'Because,' she concluded, 'Sukie Woodrow is not famous yet.' She heard Sukie suck in air behind her. 'Of course,' she continued, 'she did go and pick the hardest career in the world because she wanted lots of people to watch her and think she was wonderful. And then for ages she refused to listen to her agent's advice, because she thought she knew better than her agent who had years of experience *and* would actually benefit from her doing well, so had her best interest at heart. But that's what happens when you're unlucky and everyone else is lucky.' The commuters all stared over at Sukie, whose face had gone a funny colour.

'You bitch,' whispered Sukie.

'Shame really,' continued Katie, turning back to the commuters. 'She had such good friends that they came to see every play she was ever in – not just once in the run, but every night of every single run – and they spent hours of their lives listening to the unluckiest person in the world moan on and on and on about how crap it was when someone else got the part instead of her, just because they were better looking than her or taller than her or shorter than her or more blonde than her or less blonde than her or a better actress than her. But I suppose some people are just cursed with bad luck.'

'Have you two had a row?' asked a commuter.

'That's £2.75 please.'

As the commuters left, Sukie ran into the kitchen, probably to get a knife. Katie let out a deep breath and leaned against the counter. She had to face facts. There would be no best-friend making-up scene. Sukie really did hate her. And where on earth had she had found all that vitriol from? She'd always thought she loved Sukie. In wondering, she remembered sitting through the worst open-air *Midsummer Night's Dream* in the world, during which 200 teenage boys had sniggered and hooted every time someone said 'Titania' and after the interval it had hailed. She'd been wearing a summer dress and had caught a cold which then turned into flu. Now she came to think about it, that evening alone had earned her absolute loyalty from Sukie and Sukie had more than reneged on the deal.

She jumped as the kitchen door slammed shut again and Sukie was standing behind her, panda-eyed.

'Oh my God!'

'I know! I'm sorry,' rushed Katie. 'I don't know what –'

'Nik and Patsy are at it on the cooker!' screamed Sukie.

Katie felt her eyes and mouth open wider than they'd ever opened before. It hurt. Then, to Katie's amazement, Sukie started laughing. She tried to say four times that Nik's Homer Simpson underpants were round his ankles, but in the end she just had to push the kitchen door open and pull Katie by the hand. If Katie thought her eyes and mouth couldn't open any wider, she was proved wrong. She did an Edvard Munch silent scream and then, before risking making any noise, ran back into the café and almost burst. Sukie clamped her hands over Katie's mouth and pulled her to the café door and then on to the street where they finally allowed themselves to laugh out loud. Pedestrians stared as Sukie laughed so much she almost started to retch. Katie feared she might need stitches afterwards.

Ten full minutes later, sitting on the café floor behind

the counter, exhausted, they both looked at each other at the same time.

'Ooh that felt good,' said Sukie.

'Not as good as for Patsy and Nik obviously,' said Katie.

'Obviously.'

They smiled at the image again.

'By the way,' said Sukie quietly. 'Thanks for coming to all those plays.'

Katie smiled. ''Salright,' she said.

When Sukie put the café phone down, she called out to the others. 'Dan's not coming in again today.'

Patsy and Katie gathered round. Even Nik came out of the kitchen for this.

'Why?' asked Nik.

'Who?' asked Patsy.

'How did he sound?' asked Katie.

'Not good,' said Sukie. 'Like he had a really bad cold. Or he'd been crying.'

They all looked at each other.

'What the hell has happened?' asked Katie.

'Maybe he's having woman problems,' said Nik. 'Poor bastard.'

Sukie shook her head. 'Surely you wouldn't miss work just because of that.'

'Well,' said Patsy. 'Maybe she's broken off the engagement. Maybe he's broken hearted.'

Katie gasped and turned to Sukie. 'Sukie! That was a secret!'

Sukie was staring at Patsy, who was covering her mouth with her hands. 'Sorry!' she squeaked. 'Nik told me.'

Katie stared at Sukie. 'You told *Nik* as well!'

Nik decided now was the time to return to the kitchen. Patsy stayed put, chewing her gum aggressively.

Sukie sighed. 'Katie, I'm afraid it's not a secret any more.'

'What do you mean?' asked Katie.

'I should have told you,' started Sukie. 'Geraldine came in here when you were away, showing off her ring like it was the first engagement ring in the world. It's massive by the way. I made all the right noises, which was easy because I knew already, even though he hadn't told us, but Geraldine assumed he had. Then he came in while Geraldine and I were chatting, and he wasn't remotely surprised that I knew already. In fact, he seemed to be really relieved about it.'

Katie frowned. 'He knew you knew?' Sukie nodded. 'But he definitely hadn't told you?'

'No,' said Sukie, shaking her head. 'He hadn't said a word about it.'

'And he definitely knew you knew?'

Sukie nodded sadly. 'Yeah. Well, he didn't make any noises about having forgotten to tell me or anything.'

'And he definitely seemed relieved that you knew?'

Sukie nodded sadly again. They all stood in silent concentration.

'You know what this means, don't you?' whispered Katie finally.

Sukie nodded. Patsy shook her head.

'It means I was the only person who could have told you.'

Sukie nodded. Patsy frowned.

'And you know what that means, don't you?' whispered Katie.

Sukie nodded. Patsy shook her head.

'It means he knows I know.'

'I know,' whispered Sukie.

'Know what?' whispered Patsy.

'Which means,' whispered Katie, 'that he knew I knew at the wedding.'

'I know,' whispered Sukie.

'What wedding?' whispered Patsy.

'Which means,' whispered Katie, 'that he's officially a bastard.'

'I know,' whispered Sukie.

They wandered off to the kitchen, leaving Patsy standing on her own. She followed them in.

'Who just phoned?' she asked.

During a quiet break after lunch, Katie phoned her mother. She knew once and for all that she needed to get out of this café, and now wanted to sort out a deal with Dennis Blatchett before Dan came back to work. Not only did she want to be her own boss, but she didn't think she could face him. The thought that he must have known all the way back to London in Hugh's car that she was aware he was engaged, and had done nothing to explain his behaviour or try to placate her, was too painful to bear. Her mother knew something was up – Katie was unable to keep the hurt out of her voice – but Katie told her that she couldn't talk about it now. They would talk properly later. For now she just had to concentrate on finding the money Dennis Blatchett wanted as soon as possible. When her mother explained that she simply didn't have any more money to lend, Katie accepted that she would have to phone Great-Aunt Edna and beg. Once the decision was made, it was easy to make the call and Great-Aunt Edna had surprised her yet again. She too could hear the pain in Katie's voice and guessed all too soon that it was caused by a man.

'My dear,' she said. 'Economic independence is much better than chocolate at a time like this – although chocolate helps.'

'I'll pay you back,' Katie sniffed. 'I promise.'

'Oh nonsense, my dear,' said Great-Aunt Edna with a smile in her voice. 'No chocolate can be that expensive.'

To her surprise Katie heard herself telling her great-aunt that she loved her and the silence from the other end of the phone told her the point had been made and made well. When she rang off, Great-Aunt Edna's voice had a catch in it.

With one elegant sniff, Katie phoned Dennis Blatchett's solicitor and explained that she had the money. She waited while he woke Mr Blatchett in New Zealand. When her phone rang again, she answered immediately.

'Hello?'

'Hello,' said Dennis Blatchett's solicitor. 'Is that Ms Simmonds, new owner of Ye Olde Tea Shoppe, I'm talking to?'

29

The biggest day of Crichton Brown's calendar had finally
arrived. Friday was a textbook summer day: the endless
sky, weightless air and warm breeze made people's limbs
lighter, hearts happier and smiles wider.

Katie arrived extra early, sure that Dan would have to
make it in today and would probably do so at the crack of
dawn. She was wrong, so she had a long morning ahead of
her in which to get riled. She had intended to tell him before
anyone else got in that she was leaving. She didn't want the
rest of them to know until after the party, or possibly after
she'd signed the paperwork with Dennis Blatchett, but Dan
she'd wanted to tell immediately. As she turned the coffee
machine on, her plans changed. If he didn't come in today
she wouldn't tell him at all. She'd just leave, no explanation,
and the sooner the better. She'd given him more than
enough chances to contact her – made an absolute fool of
herself trying to, in fact. So sod him. Time to leave.

By the time today's commuters started arriving, she had
gone one further and decided there was no time like the
present and she'd leave straight after the party. She'd tell
Sukie and Jon on the way home, pack and then drive back

to Glossop during the night. She must remember to scrawl through her contact details on the café list before she left, so that Dan wouldn't be able to call her. Not that it seemed remotely likely that he'd try, but just in case; then it really would be an effective way of getting on with her life. In fact, the thought of getting that wretched roundabout correct this time filled her with nervous determination. Yes, this was it. Tomorrow would be the first day of the rest of her life. She'd pop in on Great-Aunt Edna for breakfast again and then together they'd go to the lawyers and on to the café to celebrate with Mrs Blatchett. Why shouldn't Great-Aunt Edna be in on all this? It was her money after all. She felt a surge of fondness for her and smiled at the thought of pleasing her. Would she cry? Would they both cry?

When only a rather sour Sukie turned up, followed by a nauseatingly happy Nik and Patsy, Katie began to suspect that Dan actually might only come for the party. Paul was rumoured to be coming with his new fiancée and surely that would bring Dan out of the woodwork? Unless he was unable to face them without Geraldine? She grimaced.

At the end of the 7.14 queue she forced herself to dwell on Dan's feelings for Geraldine. Could the reason for his absence really be her? Could he truly be this broken hearted by her? That one hurt. It dawned on her that all this time she'd clung to the belief that Dan had been biding his time with Geraldine. Just like she'd clung to the belief that Hugh hadn't really cared for Maxine. Well, she had to face it. Hugh had been bereft by Maxine's betrayal and Dan was bereft by Geraldine. Yet again, she was a footnote, not the heroine.

As she made the lunch-time sandwiches, she dwelt on the fact that she couldn't have got Dan more wrong. The hardest thing in all of this, she mused, would be reminding herself that the Dan she'd met at Sandy's engagement party and the Dan she'd thought he was at the wedding were figments of her imagination. They did not exist.

'You know,' said Sukie to the room in general, 'when the sun's out, it really does help you forget that your life is a great big pile of steaming poo.'

Everyone agreed with her.

'But my life isn't a great big pile of steaming poo,' said Patsy happily.

Katie and Sukie gave her a look. 'You continue to remind us of that, sunshine,' warned Sukie, 'and we'll do our best to rectify it.'

'To what it?' asked Patsy.

'Correct it,' said Katie.

'Ah thanks,' smiled Patsy.

Sukie, Katie and the commuters rolled their eyes, and then Sukie's and Katie's widened in stunned silence as Dan walked in. He looked at them all and stopped.

'What?' he demanded.

'What?' demanded everyone back and then pretended to get on with what they were doing before.

'What?' demanded Patsy generally.

'You look like you've seen a ghost,' Dan told Sukie and Katie.

'Well, you look as if you *are* a ghost,' Sukie told him back.

'Cheers,' said Dan. ' "Welcome back" would have done.'

A few of the commuters started welcoming him back

but the moment had passed. 'Katie,' he sighed, 'can I have a word?' And he walked past them all into the kitchen.

Katie was reluctant to follow him, firstly because he looked so terrible. Secondly because she was going to miss the group dissection, led by Sukie, out front in the café. Thirdly, because she was now furious that he knew that she knew he was engaged when they'd kissed and had felt no need to defend himself. As soon as she followed him, she heard him tell Nik to leave them alone for a minute. She and Nik stared at each other as they crossed paths and Dan asked Nik to close the door behind him.

Then he stood looking at the floor for a while. She crossed her arms. He looked up and her breath caught. He was crying.

'Oh God!' she gasped. She wanted to go to him but was too confused by all her conflicting emotions.

He bit his trembling lip, coughed and impatiently wiped his eyes.

'I've got some bad news,' he said hoarsely.

Katie swallowed.

'Paul has withdrawn as a partner of Crichton Brown's.' He gave a big sigh and wiped his face with his sleeve. She stared.

'Financially, you mean?' she asked.

He nodded.

'So . . .' she began, 'what does that mean? Exactly?'

He gave a short, hard laugh. 'It means I'm going to have to sell up.' He gave a very long, hearty sniff.

She stared at him for a while.

'Is this why you're crying?' she asked quietly.

He nodded, blinked and wiped his eyes with his sleeve.

'And why you've been off for the past couple of days?'

He nodded.

'And why you didn't return my calls?'

He hid his eyes in his arm. 'Sorry.'

She was unable to speak for a moment; too many thoughts were going through her mind; let alone emotions, which were looping round the spaghetti junction in her stomach. She opened her mouth, then shut it. Then she opened it again.

'How much money do you need?' she asked quietly.

He told her. At this, she was unable to speak again; thoughts, emotions and various bodily functions experiencing momentary gridlock.

To both their surprise, she let out a laugh. He looked up at her and she said affectionately, 'You are a great twerp.'

He frowned. 'Well, thank you for being so honest –' he started, before being unable to continue.

'No,' she cut in. 'I mean – you should have told me earlier.'

'Really? Why?' He gave her an earnest look.

'Because it just so happens that I have that much money.'

Dan gasped. 'Wha-wha-how?'

'None of your business!' she laughed. 'Now . . . let me see.' She pretended to think hard. 'What do I want to do with my money? Hmm.'

'Can I ask what you *had* planned to do with it?' Dan whispered.

She started laughing and then tried to work out where to start.

*

Hugh lay on his rug on the patch of grass that was called a London garden. If he wasn't able to go into work he might as well get a tan. Anyway, he was absolutely exhausted. He was going to the party tonight at Katie's café, and maybe she'd like the new, tanned him.

When the doorbell rang, he woke with a start. He tried to ignore it, but the ringing was persistent. Eventually he got up, wiped his face and chest with a towel, put on his flip-flops and stepped into the house. As he flip-flopped through the hall it took his eyes a while to adjust to the dark, and then, when he opened the front door, it took them a while to adjust to the dazzling light again. Then it took them a while to adjust to who was standing in front of him.

'Hello, Hugh,' said Maxine. 'Are you going to invite me in?'

While Sukie, Patsy and Nik waited impatiently outside the café's kitchen, Sukie's mobile rang. She gave it a quick look before walking over to the furthest table and taking the call.

'Hi Greta,' she rushed. 'Listen, before you say anything, I have to apologise.'

'I beg your pardon?'

'I have to apologise to you.'

'Whatever for?'

'For not taking your advice seriously. For being precious about my stupid art. For moaning about my bad luck when I've got my health and my looks and my youth. For not appreciating all the work you do for me. For being a pain in the backside. I'm really really sorry. I know I don't deserve you. I've never even made you much money. From now on –'

'Well all that's about to change, oh sweetest of hearts,' laughed Greta.

'What? More money?'

'Oh yes.'

'Another advert?'

'No, just the part of Lucie Manette in the BBC's adaptation of *A Tale of Two Cities*.'

Sukie couldn't believe her ears. She made Greta repeat herself and then swear on her mother's grave that she wasn't lying. Greta pretended to be hugely insulted that she should assume her mother was dead – she was a lively octogenarian on a golfing holiday in Malta – but no she was not lying. It turned out that Miranda Armstrong had just won a part in a Hollywood film. It was only a walk-on part, but you don't turn something like that down. Not if you want to be asked twice. Lucie was hers.

'Just remember always to keep some mints on you, my dear,' concluded Greta.

When Sukie finished the call she sat back, gave a squeal and then waited for the elation to hit home. She was rather surprised when she just felt extraordinarily tired and emotional. She wanted to tell Katie and Jon, but forced herself to wait and tell them tonight at the party, when they were all together and when she could toast them a thank you for seeing every single play she'd been in.

Dan stared in disbelief at Katie.

'A café?' he blustered. 'You were going to buy a café?'

'Yes!' breathed Katie, 'I –'

473

'You were going to leave me – I mean *us* – leave the café?'

'Well yes, but –'

'When were you going to tell me?' he cried.

'I tried –'

'After all we've been through together? What the hell was I supposed to do without you –'

'Now hold on a minute!' cried Katie. 'Give me a chance to explain.'

Dan gave her a curt nod. The skin round his eyes seemed to have suddenly shrunk.

Katie took a deep breath. 'I realised when I went home that I wanted to run my own café, not run someone else's. Ideally,' she paused, 'ideally it would have been this one. But you and Paul were the owners so I'd never really be technically in control. So I talked it over with my great-aunt – whose money it is – and we both worked out that it was probably better for me to invest in a café that was more . . .' she struggled to find the right word, 'safe.'

He frowned at her and she spoke quietly. 'I think we both know that our kiss at Sandy's wedding was very wrong. You were – and are – engaged.'

Dan stared at her in shock. So Sukie had told her he was engaged. What else had he expected? His chest tightened. 'I –'

She held up her hand. 'Please. I know I wouldn't have been one of the first you'd tell, but it was not a very nice way to find out.' He grimaced at the thought of Sukie breaking the news to her. 'It's a lot of money to invest in a business,' she said, 'and I need to feel . . . in control,' she

474

raised her voice to stop him interrupting, '*emotionally* as well as technically.' It worked. Dan was speechless. 'I can't be in control,' she clarified, 'when my boss is someone who would kiss one woman when he's engaged to another. It's as simple as that.'

Dan stared at her. 'But-but –' he started, 'you didn't exactly –'

'I didn't exactly *what*?' shrieked Katie, instantly furious.

'You didn't exactly take the kiss seriously.'

'You were *engaged*!' she shouted. 'So does it make it all right if the other girl doesn't –'

'No, of course not.' He tried to say something else, stopped and then shook his head, eyes on the floor. 'I can't say anything,' he finished, almost inaudibly.

Katie realised how much she'd hoped for a contradiction. But no. He really was going to marry Geraldine. The hurt was almost as much as the sudden dip in her respect for him.

She needed to talk to Great-Aunt Edna again. This café would be a wonderful investment and now that she had confronted the painful truth about Dan and accepted him for what he really was, maybe she would fall out of love with him and finally be safe.

Or would she be kidding herself and subconsciously hoping that he would leave Geraldine? If so, would he be able to see through her, and abuse that knowledge? Would it all end in tears? Should she just leave now?

'On my part,' she said finally, 'that kiss was a momentary lapse. I am not someone who wants to do that to another woman – or to myself.'

'I know –'

She held up her hand. 'As for you,' her voice was low, 'it makes you . . . very unattractive.'

'Please, Katie –' his voice was agonised.

'I may not be able to see through a first date,' she said sadly, 'but I've never two-timed anyone. Particularly if one of them was someone I was engaged to.' He hung his head down as if it was suddenly too heavy. 'Anyway,' she took a deep breath. 'My great-aunt and I discussed it at length and eventually we decided that it would be a very sensible idea for me to buy the café in my home village. I could do a lot to it and it could be mine for life. That way I'd be back with my family, I'd see my nephew grow up, and my great-aunt would know that her money was keeping a village institution alive.' Dan gave a feeble nod. 'It was a tough decision to make,' insisted Katie. 'I mean, although I was excited at the idea of taking it over, I knew it was going to be really hard to leave . . . everything here.'

Dan seemed unable to speak. They stood in silence for a while, the only sound his occasional sniff.

'But,' murmured Katie slowly, 'the fact that Paul is no longer involved and that you are actually looking for a business partner –'

'– like you,' cut in Dan throatily, 'a business partner like you, it would be perfect, just think of it –'

She put her hand up and he stopped. 'It does change things,' she conceded. He stared at her. 'I have to talk to my great-aunt,' she said. 'It's all very confusing. I mean for a start, I love this place, but it's yours and Paul's –'

'We'd change it!' he cried. 'You and I would be partners – we'd call it Crichton Simmonds –' She blinked and Dan interrupted himself, 'Simmonds Crichton –

Katie and Dan's!' he rushed. 'Whatever you want! If you were joint owner . . . if we owned it together, every decision – every single decision – would be made together.'

They stared at each other.

'Katie, you know it makes sense,' he whispered. 'We work so well together. We're a team. I can't do it without you. I don't want to do it without you. Please, Katie. I'm begging.'

She looked at him. 'And how the hell would Geraldine feel?'

'Bugger Geraldine!' he cried.

'Dan!' she cried, dismayed. 'That's a terrible thing to say. And it's terrible if you think I'd want you to say that.'

He rushed to her. 'Katie. This is our life.'

She shook her head, annoyed. 'You need my money, Dan. I'm not a fool. And I won't let you hurt Geraldine. Or me.'

'God,' said Dan, ashen-faced, 'what do you think I'm like?'

'I think you're desperate at the moment,' she said softly, 'and you think you've suddenly found the answer. But I deserve more than that. And so does Geraldine. It's her life too,' she insisted. 'You're going to marry her. She matters, Dan. Don't make me despise you.'

His head jerked back like he'd been slapped in the face. 'I have to talk to her,' he murmured, as if to himself.

'Yes. Talk to her. About everything, Dan. About what happened at Sandy's wedding as well as the possibility of me becoming your business partner. Or I'll tell her. And only if she is absolutely fine with that, will I consider putting my money into Crichton Brown's. I won't take anything less.'

He paused and then gave a firm nod. 'I'll tell her everything.'

'All right,' said Katie. 'And I have to talk to my great-aunt. It may be a very wise investment for me, but a very foolish direction. I'm more than money, Dan.'

He held her by the arms. 'Katie, I'd leave this place in an instant and come with you to your café if you'd let me.' She stared at him. 'Sod the money,' he continued. 'I want *you*.' She gasped and he stopped her by talking over it. 'Look, let me talk to Geraldine.' She couldn't move. He suddenly took her hands in his and held them firmly against his chest. 'Katie. Please. Trust me.' She let out a spikey laugh. 'I know you don't believe me because of . . . but I'll tell you everything – I'll explain everything – after I've spoken to her. Believe me. Please, Katie. I need to talk to Geraldine. And then I need to talk to you. Meet me back here before the party. Promise me.' She held her breath. 'Please Katie.'

She gave a small nod.

They stood in the kitchen, hands held, staring at each other for what felt like hours but was probably only moments. Dan seemed to be struggling to say more, but instead he gave her hands one final squeeze and then let go, turned and left.

She watched him go, his words, 'I want you,' ringing in her ears. Did he just mean as a business partner? Or more? Could she ever really be safe with him if she felt like this? Could she ever really trust a man who had treated his fiancée the way he had? She stared at the door after him as if it could explain everything. When it opened again, she almost jumped.

She blinked at him. He stopped. She held her breath. Were the next few words going to answer all her questions? Was her future about to be mapped out? He gave her an apologetic smile.

'Forgot my keys,' he said, picked them up off the counter, turned and left again.

She had to phone Great-Aunt Edna. She needed advice.

30

The café was closing at six so that the party could start at eight, so Katie had two hours to make contact with Great-Aunt Edna before Dan got back from seeing Geraldine. Plenty of time, she told herself, but after forty minutes of no reply, she was beginning to get concerned. She'd give her another ten minutes and then phone home to ask them to pop round and check that she was all right. Meanwhile, it was officially party preparation time. The others got excited and when Matt turned up after one of his exams to join in the fun, he was greeted like a long-lost friend. They all sat at one of the tables with their preferred choice of caffeine for a quick break.

'Is Dan coming back?' asked Sukie.

'Of course,' replied Katie. 'He's just got some business to attend to.' It suddenly dawned on her just how horrible the next two hours could be for Geraldine – and Dan. She stared at her coffee. Was she making a big mistake? Was she getting carried away with the moment? Was she playing people off against each other to get her own way? Oh dear, she really did need to talk all this through with

Great-Aunt Edna. She took out her mobile and went back into the kitchen to try again.

In her flat, Geraldine placed the veil delicately on her bed, just below the tiara. She smiled at it in awe. How could such a fragile thing be so magical? She looked at her engagement ring again and moved it in the light, marvelling at the exquisite twinkle a diamond gave. She placed a box at the bottom of the bed and gently took out the shoes. She lifted them to her nose and drank in the aroma of leather and satin. She pulled the tiny carrier bag out of the wardrobe and eased the stockings out of it as if they were leaves of gold. Then she unrolled them over her knees and up her thighs, where she clipped them on to her suspenders. She slid her feet into the shoes and, with trembling hands, picked up the tiara and veil and secured them firmly on her head.

She turned and looked at herself in the mirror and smiled at her reflection. The basque was simply divine, giving her the waist and cleavage she'd always dreamed of. She couldn't wait for the dress to be ready.

She put her hands round her waist and one leg slightly in front of the other. She had tried on this charming ensemble every day since she'd bought them – until the row. The row had totally immobilised her. It was only the second time in their whole relationship that Dan had ever not apologised afterwards, and the first time had been followed by an unceremonious dumping in Pizza Express. She'd been absolutely terrified he was going to do it again and had waited, petrified, for his call and those four ugliest words in a relationship: We Have To Talk.

But this time had been different. She'd learnt from her mistakes. This time she'd proved that they were beyond rows, they were a partnership. As soon as she'd worked out what to do to help him, she'd acted impulsively. She called Paul immediately and when he said he'd have a word with Dan's old boss she almost burst with pride because Dan would now know how much he needed her. She'd proved they were a team and that she'd grown. She'd been glad that now she'd had an excuse to phone Dan. She had to phone him before actually seeing Paul, didn't she? Otherwise, it would have been a bit too much like plotting. And so she'd called him. She'd wanted to tell him to his face, but in the end, she'd had to tell his bloody answerphone. Hardly ideal, but there you go. She turned her back to the mirror and turned her neck round as far as she could, to see the back view. She smiled. The answerphone messages had done the trick. Dan had just texted her to say he was on his way round and he'd signed off *D x*. She had done it.

She turned to face the mirror again and bit by bit, lowered the veil over her face. She realised now that you earned a wedding, you didn't just get it. You had to prove you were worthy of being a partner. It wasn't just a big party in a gorgeous dress, it was a life-long commitment to someone, and she had proved to Dan – and to herself – that she was ready. She lowered her head demurely behind her veil. She was so glad she'd got the shorter one, it showed off her cleavage at the same time as being virginal. Very sexy. It was at moments like these that she wished her mother lived in this country. But then, she reasoned, she was about to get a mother-in-law whom she found far easier to deal with than her own.

Sitting on the bed now, she slowly rolled her right stocking down the length of her thigh. Maybe Dan had actually been waiting for her to prove to him that she could be the partner he needed. Maybe Dan would even mention it in his wedding speech; say that he'd always known he'd loved her, but it wasn't until she'd helped him win back his job that he knew he couldn't live without her. Dewy-eyed, she looked at her ring again. Maybe for the first time, she could relax.

When she heard the key in her lock, she started. Dan never used his key. She jumped up and walked out of the bedroom into the lounge.

'Dan?' He was standing in the middle of the room and something about his expression brought her up short. 'What's wrong?'

'Gerry,' he whispered. 'We have to talk.'

Back at the café, Katie had still not made contact with Great-Aunt Edna and was now worried. She'd phoned home and there had been no answer there either. She'd left an answerphone message with strict instructions to phone her as soon as they could. Meanwhile, she had one hour to oversee the transformation of the café into a party venue, and without Dan's extra pair of hands, every minute counted. So when Hugh popped in to have a quick word with her and she was only blowing up the third of several dozen balloons, she was not best pleased.

'Can we talk?' he asked. 'Maxine's coming to the party.'

She took a balloon out of her mouth. 'Can you blow up balloons?'

'Er, yes.'

'Right,' she said, handing him one. 'Go on then.'

'Well,' he said, 'I just wanted to say –'

'I don't see you blowing, Hugh.'

'Right.' Hugh started blowing. 'I just wanted to say –'

'That's not big enough.'

He sighed, blew very hard and started tying a knot in the neck. 'I just wanted to say that I don't know what came over me at the wedding.'

'Here's a blue one.'

'Thank you.'

They blew two more balloons.

'I just wanted you to know that I'm sorry.'

'It's OK, Hugh. You were very drunk.'

'Yes. And very lonely. Amazing how much I missed Maxine.'

'Of course. You were missing Maxine.'

'Oh yes, terribly.'

'Here's a yellow one.'

'Thank you.'

They blew up another balloon each.

'Anyway,' said Hugh, 'we're both coming tonight and I do hope everything's going to be all right.'

Katie temporarily stopped blowing. 'You mean you hope I'm not going to say anything?'

'Well, yes, I suppose so.' He took another balloon. 'This is quite fun actually,' he said before starting to blow. Katie watched him for a while. Men were all the same. 'What's it worth?' she asked. Hugh's jaw dropped and his balloon flew all over the ceiling. 'I –'

She started laughing. 'I'm joking,' she said. 'Do you

think I want to incur the wrath of Maxine?'

'Oh thank God,' said Hugh. 'But you won't ever . . . I mean, it's not just because it's your boss's party, is it?'

'What isn't?'

'The fact that you've chosen not to say anything?'

Katie put down her balloon. 'Hugh,' she said seriously. 'That night had nothing to do with me. It was about you and Maxine. I'm delighted you have found your soul-mate. Delighted. I do not want to get in the way of that.'

'Good,' mumbled Hugh. 'Yes, soul-mate.'

'I know now that all the mickey-taking you used to do when we were together in college was because you were in denial about your feelings for Maxine.'

Hugh's eyes lit up. 'Oh yes!' he said.

'It was blindingly obvious to me the minute you started going out with her.'

'Really?'

'God yes. Did you know we spent most of our relation-ship talking about her? You were already head over heels in love with her, you just didn't know it.'

'God, you're right! That's amazing. Have you ever thought of becoming a therapist?'

She smiled. 'Probably.'

'Thanks Katie.'

'It's a pleasure. Here's a gold one.'

'Thank you.'

When her mobile went, she let a half-blown balloon jet off in her rush to answer. It was her mother. She ran into the kitchen to take the call.

Gerry and Dan stood staring at each other in the middle

of her lounge. Eventually Dan spoke. 'Do you want to sit down?'

'Do I look like I want to sit down?' snapped Geraldine. He looked at her. She was wearing a cream basque, matching knickers, stockings – one half-rolled down – suspenders, high-heels, tiara and veil.

'Not really,' he said.

'You do realise it's unlucky to see me in all this,' she said, but she knew it sounded hollow.

He gave her an apologetic smile.

She tried to take off her veil but it got stuck under the tiara. She lost patience and struggled with it, causing her tiara to tip and the veil to knot. She started to whimper and tears of frustration welled up in her eyes. Dan wavered. 'Gerry, don't.'

She stopped and looked at him, tiara wonky and veil a mess, cheeks flushed.

'Just say it, will you,' she said. 'Just get it over with.'

'What . . .'

'Have you any idea,' she breathed, 'how awful it is *waiting* to be chucked?'

He frowned.

'It's like . . .' She closed her eyes as if in thought. 'It's like waiting to be sick. You feel ill but you just have to wait until your body vomits it all out.' She spoke in a dull voice. 'And you know it's going to get a lot worse before it gets any better.' She took a deep breath. 'So stop the nausea, Daniel, and vomit me out.'

He grimaced.

'Say it!' she cried.

'All right!' he shouted back. 'I can't go through with the

486

wedding. I'm sorry I've messed you around but I just can't do it.'

The words stagnated in the air between them.

She suddenly yanked off her tiara, letting out a furious expletive as some hair came out in a clump with the veil. She stood up straight and spoke calmly. 'I have to get out of these ridiculous clothes.' She walked out of the room, her wedding shoes marking the wooden floor as she went.

'I'll wait here,' said Dan.

She turned back to him, silhouetted against her bedroom door. 'Of course you'll wait here, you fuck. You think I'm going to give you one last look while you chuck me? I could just put the footie on and you'd be in lads-mag heaven.'

She turned and slammed the bedroom door behind her.

Dan collapsed on the couch and looked at his watch. The party would be starting soon. Katie would be overseeing all the last-minute details. Oh God, why hadn't he told her earlier exactly what she meant to him? He'd felt he owed it to both women to do this properly, and not go any further with Katie until he was officially a single man, but now he felt he needed Katie's strength to help him do this. He had only really known how much he loved Katie when he'd heard her talk about his engagement as if it were fact. He'd felt pain in his gut at her words – and not because he was marrying Geraldine, but because he was leaving Katie for good. He winced. What a joke. It felt as if he'd been living a lie ever since Geraldine had worn the ring. No. It felt as if he'd been living a lie ever since he'd got back together with her again. No. It felt as if he'd been living a lie ever since he first went out with her. He was now shaking his head in wonder. That was a hell of a long time to be living a lie. Jesus, what on earth had he been doing with her all this time? Had he been waiting for something? And if so what? To fall in love with Geraldine? Or to find Katie?

He pictured Katie bustling round the café and kitchen, issuing orders, insulting the clients and generally burrowing a Katie-shaped tunnel under his skin. He pictured them owning the café together, their countless daughters (all with honey skin and autumn eyes) popping in throughout the day to have a good chinwag with their mum and dad. The thought that he had to wait until he'd got through this excruciating exchange with Gerry and then a car journey before he could hold Katie again – or even see her – was almost too much to bear. And in fairness it did Geraldine no justice. She deserved better than him racing out of here, he told himself. He'd stay as long as she needed him. He'd wasted enough of her life, he could give her one evening. He'd even stay over if he had to, sleep on the couch. Katie would understand. He'd phone her and explain.

When Geraldine came back she was in her business suit, complete with shoes and stockings. She'd even redone her make-up. She stood over him, arms crossed.

'Now,' she began. 'Let's discuss this like two adults. Drink?'

She poured them both a whisky and sat opposite him in the armchair. He felt as if he was being interviewed. As indeed he was.

'Tell me everything Daniel.'

Katie sat staring at the oven, her mother's voice still talking softly in her ear.

'Sweetheart,' said Deanna. 'She died peacefully in her sleep. The best way to go. And she had a wonderful, long and happy life. '

'I-I'd only just got to know her properly,' whispered Katie.

'I know,' said Deanna, 'but at least you did. You'll have that for ever.'

Katie heard her mother talk and then told her very simply and clearly that she had been trying to phone Great-Aunt Edna because she'd decided to back out of Ye Olde Tea Shoppe purchase. To her surprise her mother had sounded relieved. Katie had expected her to be distraught because it would mean she would now be staying in London. Encouraged by her mother's response, she went on to explain, that instead, she was going to put the money towards the café where she already worked. 'It would be exactly what Great-Aunt Edna would have wanted,' she finished. 'I know it.'

There was a long pause.

'Oh my dearest girl, I don't think you understand,' said Deanna gently.

'What?'

'She had an appointment booked with her solicitor for next week. To change her will.'

Katie felt her blood run cold. She didn't really hear the rest of her mother's response. She just sat there, realising that because she'd taken too long to work out what she wanted to do with her life, Crichton Brown's would close and they would all lose their jobs. She and Dan would never be partners. She would probably never be her own boss, let alone own a restaurant. She'd done it again. The orchestra had taken its bow and she'd missed the cue to play her bloody triangle.

Geraldine looked squarely at Dan. 'Well?' she repeated. 'I'm waiting.'

'I'm in love with someone else.'

And to Dan's amazement, Geraldine lost it big time. As great clumps of black guck trickled down her cheeks, he marvelled that she, of all people, didn't wear waterproof mascara.

'Who?' she breathed. 'Who?'

'God, I'm so sorry Gerry –'

'*Just tell me,*' she roared, terrifying him into an admission.

'Katie.'

Geraldine stopped crying. There was a long silence. Then, slowly, she sat back in the armchair.

'You all right?' asked Dan nervously.

She half-smiled. 'You know,' she said quietly. 'It's almost a relief.'

He frowned. 'What do you mean?'

She took a gulp of her whisky and then gave him a long hard look. 'God you must think I'm a bloody idiot.'

'Nothing of the sort.'

'Don't patronise me, Daniel.'

'I'm not. If there's one thing you're not, it's an idiot.'

'Huh.' She took another sip. 'Except where you're

490

concerned.' He didn't answer. 'I know you went out with her while we were on our break.'

'Yeah, well, that all ended rather abruptly.'

'Well, she's been in the wings ever since. Waiting oh so patiently.'

'Come off it Gerry. I wouldn't have seen her ever again if I hadn't taken over the café.'

She gave a sick smile. 'All a bit of an accident, eh?'

'Yes,' said Dan. 'A bit like us getting married, really.'

There was a moment's pause, while Geraldine restocked on anger. 'What?' she asked in a voice that used to turn his insides to ice.

'Well,' he stated, more sad than angry, 'I hardly proposed, did I?'

'What the hell is that supposed to mean?'

'Well, one minute we're all discussing moules, the next you're telling my parents we're engaged.'

'We *were* engaged! I'd been looking for rings! What were they for, my nose?'

'Well, you hardly waited for me to ask, did you?'

'What century do you live in?'

'I'm not saying I had to get down on one knee –'

'Well, that obviously wasn't going to happen, was it?'

'But it would have been nice if it had been a joint decision at least.'

'How could it be when you were too . . . too . . .'

He raised his eyebrows and waited.

She thought carefully. 'Too complacent to get your finger out?'

He let out a laugh. 'I have never dared to feel complacent with you. Do you have any idea what it's like, being with someone you're terrified might suddenly treat you like shit?'

'I didn't treat you like shit; I had mood swings, like anyone normal. Are you trying to blame me for all this?'

He shook his head. 'No. I'm just saying I never felt complacent.'

'Well *good*.'

They both took a sip of their whisky and looked at each other across the coffee table. Then she asked him to promise not to lie if she asked him a question. He gave a small nod.

'Did you ever kiss Katie when you were back with me?'

He paused and she started crying again.

'Only once,' he rushed, but she just cried more. 'And we both felt terrible. We didn't speak after that.'

'When?'

He gave a long sigh. 'At Sandy's wedding.'

There was silence and when he looked up, he saw that Geraldine was sobbing, her glass of whisky spilling on to the floor. He rushed over to her side and she leant into him and then pushed him away. He stayed on the arm of her chair until her sobs subsided. Eventually she spoke.

'That was the day I went wedding dress shopping with your mother,' she managed.

Dan knew there was no way he could leave her here like this. He would just have to miss the beginning of the party. He poured another glass of whisky and held her hand while she drank it down.

Sukie found Katie sitting on the kitchen floor just as the party was about to get going. She practically dived on to the floor next to her and hugged her till she was ready to speak.

Katie told her that she had decided to leave the café and invest her money in one at home. Then Paul had dropped out of Crichton Brown's and that Dan was going to have to sell. Then she'd considered putting her money into the business and saving Crichton Brown's. Then she'd told Dan she'd known he was engaged when they'd kissed and he hadn't apologised or denied it. Then Dan had begged her to go into business with him because they made such a good team and had almost cried. Then she'd insisted he go and tell Geraldine they'd kissed. Then Dan had gone to tell Geraldine and see if she approved of him and Katie going into partnership together. Then she had tried to phone Great-Aunt Edna to ask her what the hell to do, but couldn't get through. Then her mother had just phoned to tell her that Great-Aunt Edna had died, which meant she didn't have enough to save the café, go into business with Dan or buy her own café.

'But I can buy a nice watch,' whispered Katie.

Sukie stared at her and Katie started crying again. 'My life is a very bad farce,' she sobbed.

'Sweetheart,' soothed Sukie. 'Farces always have happy endings. Even the bad ones.'

'How can this one have a happy ending?' asked Katie miserably.

'I don't know,' murmured Sukie. 'But,' she brightened, 'you're not meant to know until the last scene. Until then, you just have faith.'

*

Geraldine sat back in the armchair, exhausted, and Dan stared at the floor.

'You aren't the only one with someone in the wings,' she said. He raised his eyebrows in surprise. 'Bryan, my boss,' she said. 'All those trips.'

'You . . .'

She shook her head. 'Nothing serious. Just flirting. The odd gift. He told me you weren't good enough for me.'

'He's never even met me!'

'I told him all about you.'

'Oh thanks.'

They sat in silence for a while. Then another wave of sorrow swept over Geraldine. She slumped forward over her knees, watched by an increasingly miserable Dan. When it finished, she blew her nose and sat back again.

'You know what I don't understand?' she whispered. 'How women are supposed to want to get married but at the same time not be aware of it, so we have to pretend we're idiots and just wait and wait and wait until it just miraculously "happens".' She started shaking her head. 'It's not meant to be this hard,' she whispered, starting to cry again.

'I know,' soothed Dan.

When Jon came into the café kitchen holding a bottle of wine and three glasses 'just in case', Katie and Sukie knew the party had really started. He joined them on the floor and told them he had some news, and Sukie said that actually, so had she. Katie said that she had enough for a 24-hour rolling news channel, and Sukie made her tell Jon all of it before they got started on theirs. By the end of her recital the three of them were fairly speechless.

'There's absolutely no way I can top that,' said Jon. 'My news is pants now.'

'Yeah,' said Sukie. 'So's mine.' She topped up her own wine and Jon's but when she got to Katie, Katie put her hand over her glass. Sukie gave her a look, but Katie shook her head firmly. She wanted to be clear-headed. Drink made her mind fuggy. And she didn't want to feel fuggy any more.

Geraldine waited until her eyes had dried, took a final gulp of whisky and then, with Dan watching, phoned her boss, Bryan. Dan only left when he knew Bryan was on his way over.

'So what's he like this Bryan bloke?' he asked at the door.

'Rich, hopelessly in love with me and desperate to have babies,' Geraldine said with a smile.

He gave her a questioning look. 'Are you going to marry him?'

She gave a little laugh. 'Well I've got all the underwear, haven't I? And it's terribly romantic isn't it? He's been waiting for me for years.'

He blew her a kiss and she air-punched it back at him. He said goodbye and wished her luck, then shut the door and got the hell out of there. Two minutes later, he climbed into the car, his body trembling. He couldn't remember feeling like this since adolescence. He would be with Katie in a matter of minutes.

*

Back in the kitchen, Sukie and Katie screamed in delight. A publisher had liked Jon's first book and his idea of lager sagas. They were talking to Richard Miller about a possible deal.

Then, as the laughter died down, Katie found her eyes focusing just behind Sukie's and Jon's heads, on the photos of Sandy's engagement party now pinned to the fridge door. There were four pictures in all – one of her and Dan staring intently at each other, one of Dan's mate wearing a lurid green shirt and snogging his girlfriend's best friend, one of her and Hugh talking and one of a very drunk Jon hugging Katie, being watched by Sukie. And it was then that a lot of things slotted into place, like the last piece fitting into a vast jigsaw puzzle. All the other pieces had been assembled years ago; all the times Sukie had popped round to the flat unexpectedly, her asking Jon to help her with her letter-writing, the eagerness with which she had helped prepare Jon for his interviews, the hilarity instead of jealousy at Nik getting off with Patsy. And here was the final image, suddenly clear and complete in front of her. Sukie was in love with Jon.

In the photo, Sukie's face was more radiant than Sandy had looked on her wedding day, with all her make-up and daisies. It looked like there was a torch, just out of range of the camera, shining on Sukie's face. She looked like the Madonna. And all because she was looking up at Jon.

'What's up?' asked Sukie, arm lazily round Jon's neck.

'Nothing!' Katie said as breezily as she could. 'Nothing!'

'Why are you looking at us like that?' asked Jon, his arm round Sukie's waist.

'No reason! Anyway Sukie,' Katie said, pouring more wine in her glass, 'it's time for your news now.'

Dan put the key in the ignition, started the engine and then realised he couldn't drive. He'd probably drunk about a pint of whisky. He pulled the key out, slammed the car door shut and started running.

As he ran, he mused how long he had been waiting for Geraldine and him to crumble. Why hadn't he had balls enough to get out when he'd had the chance? Pathetic. One disastrous date and he'd gone back into that hell without looking back, mistaking the pain he felt after the date with Katie for pain at being single. But he now recognised it for what it was. After only one evening in Katie's company at Sandy's engagement party, he had felt more of a connection – on every level – than he'd ever felt with Geraldine. And that was why, after their date had gone so wrong, he'd been plunged so swiftly into a state of despair. He hardly knew her, yet already he'd felt the loss of her. He hadn't been distraught because he was without a girlfriend, he'd been distraught because he was without Katie. The reason he hadn't been able to recognise the difference was because he didn't know it could happen that quickly. He'd waited so many years to fall in love with Geraldine that he thought falling in love took a long time.

Now that he knew it could take a matter of moments, it was more than annoying to have to stop on his way to Katie, but stop he did, because he already had a stitch.

Jon and Katie could not let go of Sukie. This was the stuff of fantasy. She had won the lead – after all those auditions.

After all the pain. After all the humiliation. Finally, Katie let go of them both and jumped up to sit on the counter, while Sukie and Jon stayed hugging. Katie pretended to look at something else. Then she glanced back. Sukie closed her eyes and, smiling, leant her head against Jon's shoulder. He kissed the top of her head. Patsy and Nik joined them in the kitchen.

'Oh here you all are!' cried Patsy. 'We've been looking for you everywhere.'

Nik put his arm round Patsy. 'We've got some news.'

'Wait,' grinned Sukie. 'We must get Matt in here too.' She didn't move.

'Ooh,' said Patsy. 'Yes we must.' She didn't move.

'I'll go,' said Nik and went to get Matt. Patsy gave them all a grin. 'Isn't he lovely?' she asked and they all nodded. Nik came back with a rather dishevelled looking Matt and Eva. Eva put her hand on Matt's bottom and he put his arm round her.

'Right then,' said Katie. 'All present and correct. What's your news then, as if we didn't know.'

Patsy and Nik looked lovingly at each other and then Patsy gave them a shy grin. 'We're going out with each other. Hope you don't feel upset that we've kept it a secret.'

Sukie pretended she was laughing in delighted surprise.

'You're right,' Katie grinned. 'We'd never have guessed.'

'We're so pleased for you,' said Sukie. 'Let the celebrations begin!'

Dan made his way down Asherman's Hill, but could only achieve the pace of an extremely fit ninety-year-old.

There'd be no point in turning up drenched in sweat, would there? Not for what he wanted to tell Katie, anyway. He slowed down, leant over his shoes and gasped. Then he stood up, squared his shoulders and started walking at a leisurely pace to the party.

The kitchen was suddenly silent. Paul stood staring at his staff and they stared back. He was wearing dark narrow trousers and his party shirt, a lurid green number. A nervous laugh escaped.

'Well, say something,' he grinned. 'It hasn't been that long since I last saw you!'

The kitchen staff all gave him a warm welcome, except for Sukie, who knew he wasn't going to be their boss for much longer, and Katie who was sure she'd seen that lurid green shirt somewhere else. As Paul started greeting all of his staff like some long-lost hero, she turned to the photos of Sandy's engagement she'd been gazing at. Yes, Dan's mate snogging his girlfriend's best friend was definitely wearing a lurid green party shirt. She looked back at Paul. Of course, that didn't necessarily mean it was him. It was probably just a popular Gap shirt or something.

Meanwhile Patsy ran to Paul and gave him a hug, congratulated him on his engagement and ran out into the café, where his fiancée was busy partying. Nik followed her and Matt and Eva decided to get back to the party too.

Katie screwed up her eyes and scrutinised Paul's features before turning back to the photo. Yes, although the image was not quite as clear as it could be, Sandy having been drunk when she took it, and most of Paul's face being hidden by the face of someone else, there was a distinct mule-like quality about what could be seen of his features. In short, it was him.

Paul was now left with Sukie, Jon and Katie. He stepped forward and extended his hand to Jon. They shook hands and introduced themselves to each other. Katie stared back at the photo and then at Paul, just to check. Oh yes, it was him all right. She tuned into the conversation and heard Paul saying that he was finally making an honest woman of his girlfriend.

'After how long?' she asked.

He affected a sheepish grin. 'Far too long I'm afraid,' he said. 'We've been together for five years.'

Katie felt a rush of adrenaline course into her blood stream. And then when Dan suddenly appeared in the doorway she felt quite a bit more adrenaline flood into her blood stream while some more started an orderly queue behind it.

Dan looked at Katie, breathing hard.

'I've done it,' he said. 'I'm not with Geraldine any more.'

'What?' cried Paul. 'You've finished with Geraldine?'

Dan ignored him and suddenly turned to Sukie. 'By the way on that subject,' he said. 'I meant to say well done, that time when you pretended to know that Geraldine was engaged.'

Sukie frowned. 'When?'

'You know,' insisted Dan. 'That time when she was showing you her ring and you pretended to know even though I hadn't told anyone.'

500

'I wasn't pretending,' said Sukie acidly. 'I knew you were engaged.'

'What? How?'

'Katie told me,' Sukie almost gloated. 'Didn't you know? She found out at Sandy's wedding.'

He turned to Katie in shock. 'How? When?'

Katie gave him a measured look. 'I thought we discussed this. Geraldine texted you to say she'd found the perfect wedding dress and I accidentally picked up the message.'

'Wh-when?'

'Just after I'd bared my soul and you'd kissed me.'

There was a gasp and a murmur, but Dan didn't hear.

'Waswaswas that why you suddenly went cold on me?'

'Of course,' said Katie. 'Not a great aphrodisiac.'

'And ran off?' he rushed. 'And pretended it was nothing the next morning?'

Katie bristled. 'Yes.'

'But I thought Sukie told you after Geraldine had shown her her ring,' insisted Dan.

'No,' replied Katie curtly. 'I told Sukie the evening I got back.'

'Oh no!' cried Sukie suddenly, letting go of Jon for the first time. 'She did it to you again!'

'Did what?' asked Dan. 'Who?'

Sukie started jigging, gabbling at Dan. 'Geraldine! When you were on your date with Katie, Geraldine phoned the flat – I was there – and Jon told her Katie was out on a date. He told her Katie was with you 'cos

501

he's a bloke and doesn't get the rules, and so she called Katie on her mobile, and freaked her out about you. Said stuff about you being damaging in a relationship, how you'd patronise her and take her for granted and how you had a foul temper, how she'd have to go to see football every week, blah blah blah. Geraldine knew exactly what buttons to press with Katie and she bloody hammered them with a mallet. Katie had a panic attack. It's a miracle she made it home. When she came into work the next morning she was a wreck.'

He turned to Katie, a grim expression on his face. 'Is this true?'

'Well, yes,' she said quietly, 'but I still acted like a child.'

Dan walked up to Katie. 'Can we just start again?'

'Are you saying you finished with Geraldine?' repeated Paul.

Oh God, how was Katie going to tell Dan she didn't have the money any more?

'I haven't got the money any more,' she blurted out. There. That was how she'd tell him.

'Wha-wha-how?' he asked.

'What money?' asked Paul.

'My aunt just died,' she said, and to her great surprise suddenly started to cry. 'So most of it will get eaten up in inheritance tax and stuff.' She sniffed. 'So you finished with Geraldine for nothing.'

'Wha –' rushed Dan.

'Hold on!' shouted Paul. 'Everyone hold on.' Everyone held on. He turned to Dan. 'First of all: are you telling me you've finished with Geraldine, even after she went to all that trouble to try and get your job back?'

Dan visibly balked. 'Just stay out of this Paul.' He turned back to Katie. 'Me finishing with Geraldine had nothing to do with the money. I'm in love with –'

'That is the most shitty thing I have ever heard –' Paul told him. 'Geraldine put herself on the line for you. She *begged* for you.'

Dan looked at Katie. 'Can we go somewhere private?'

But Katie wasn't looking at Dan. She was looking at Paul. And it wasn't a happy look. She crossed her arms. 'Talking of doing shitty things,' she started slowly, 'you've been doing your fair share recently, haven't you, Paul?'

'Katie,' interrupted Dan. 'There's no need.'

'Oh I think there is,' she said calmly. 'I have a rather important question to ask Paul.'

Paul glanced at Dan. 'I see Geraldine isn't the only woman you need to beg on your behalf.'

'Piss off Paul,' said Dan.

'Oh I'm not going to beg,' said Katie lightly. 'I don't need to. The question I was going to ask was: how would your fiancée feel about seeing this photo?' She went to the fridge door and pulled off the photo of Paul snogging his fiancée's best friend. She held it out in front of her, for him to get a good look at it. Indeed, everyone looked at it. Sukie and Jon gasped. Dan started grinning. Paul went white.

'Will she recognise her best friend,' asked Katie, 'do you think?'

'Give me that –' Paul snatched at it, but Katie was too quick for him. She held it behind her back. Sukie took it from her hand, safely out of Paul's reach. 'You seem to

503

find it really hard to do the right thing by people, don't you Paul?' asked Katie sweetly.

'Give me that photo now,' Paul told Sukie.

'You leave her out of it,' said Jon, putting his arm round Sukie.

'Give it to me now,' repeated Paul. 'Or –'

'Or what will you do?' asked Katie, reaching behind Jon's back and taking the photo from Sukie. She held it over the gas hob. 'Burn it? It won't matter. This is only one copy. It's on Sandy's computer and on Jon's computer. Oh, by the way, Jon's my flatmate.'

Paul swallowed.

'So,' said Katie. 'You're going to go straight out there and tell your lovely fiancée that seeing us all has made you realise how fond you are of the business, and how you just can't let down so many people.'

'I can't,' moaned Paul.

Katie showed him the picture again and gave him a big smile. 'Oh I think you can,' she said.

He stared at them all and they stared back at him. He was about to speak when the door opened and in walked his fiancée, eyes bright with happiness.

'Hello everyone!' she said. 'I'm so glad we've finally met. I do hope you weren't too upset about Paul having to pull out.'

'Actually, honey,' said Paul. She turned to him with a trusting face. 'I've got something to tell you.'

Katie, Dan, Sukie and Jon were touched by Paul's fiancée's response. She had smiled at them all graciously, a bit like the Duchess of Kent meeting a courageous child, and said it was wonderful news and they really hadn't needed the house with the pool; she loved the pool at her gym anyway. If Katie had had a flat cap, she'd have doffed it to her. The couple then did them the honour of staying in the kitchen while Dan opened a bottle of bubbly and Katie genuinely believed that, by the end of his glass, Paul was almost as delighted to have so many people beholden to him as his delightful fiancée was. Dan kept giving Katie lingering looks, and seemed to be trying to move round Paul to her side, but it was a small kitchen and he couldn't manage it without physically moving Paul out of the way. So she made do with the lingering looks. Then, after they had all clinked their glasses to Crichton Brown's and downed their drinks in one, Paul took Dan's arm to lead him outside to the party. The fiancée followed, after giving them all one last sweep of a smile. Dan stretched round to Katie, missed and got Sukie, who had no choice but to join them. She stretched back for Jon, but was out of the door before she got a chance to say anything.

Jon looked at the door for a while. Then he looked at Katie, and did a valiant attempt at pretending he really wanted to be in the kitchen with her, rather than in the party with Sukie. 'So, Dan's the man, eh?' he asked.

She smiled at him. 'So, an interested publisher, eh?'

Jon gave a small smile, hands in pocket. 'Yeah.' He looked at the door where Sukie had just been. Katie handed him the photos. 'Have you ever looked at these properly?' she asked. He shook his head. 'I just printed them out and gave them to you,' he said.

'Well,' said Katie, pointing at Sukie's face. 'Have a

good look, and see if you can *read* what you see as well as you *write* what you see.'

When Katie came out into the party, it was a bit of a surprise. She knew everyone there and felt fond of them all, commuters, journalists, even Maxine. Maxine and Hugh had been busy getting attached at the hip and Katie joined Sukie in watching them with a mixture of disgust and fascination.

'Get a room,' Sukie muttered to Katie.

'Or at least a five-bed terrace,' agreed Katie.

Then their attention was seized by Paul, who stood on one of the tables. He tapped his glass with a fork. The room went quiet.

'Cheek,' whispered Sukie to Katie.

'Do you think he's going to tell his fiancée he cheated on her?' whispered Katie back.

Paul coughed politely until there was complete silence.

'I would just like to say welcome to everyone.'

Katie scanned the room for Dan, but couldn't find him. She saw Jon though, and if she wasn't very much mistaken, he looked like a man possessed. As Paul started telling everyone just how much the café meant to him, and how he and his fiancée were delighted to be a part of something so special, Jon brushed past her to Sukie. Sukie was transfixed. As Paul began the tale of how he and Dan's dream had taken shape, Katie watched as Jon edged his way into Sukie's private space, bent slowly down so that their breaths mingled and, when he was convinced that he had not misread the signals and that she wasn't going to run away screaming, kissed her. Katie felt tears well up in her eyes, then she suddenly realised everyone was looking at her. She blinked.

'*What?*' she asked the room, huffily. '*What?*'

Everyone laughed. Or rather, everyone had hysterics.

'You see?' laughed Paul. 'The rudest waitress I'd ever seen.'

Katie gasped. And then suddenly Dan stood up on the counter, which was higher than the table Paul was standing on. Everyone turned to him.

'But it wasn't until we properly got to know Katie,' he said, 'that we began to learn exactly how much this café depended on her.'

'Yes,' said Paul. 'Absolutely. I was –'

'And not just the café,' cut in Dan. He looked down at her. There was silence. 'But me too.'

The room sighed as one.

'Katie,' he said. 'I absolutely adore you.' He got down on one knee on the counter. The room hushed. 'Paul may be my silent partner, but you are, without doubt, my outspoken one.' The audience gasped. 'Without you, the café would be nothing.' The audience cheered. 'Without you, *I* would be nothing. I know, without a doubt, that Paul will agree with me when I ask you, Katie Simmonds, please will you do me the honour of becoming my official business partner.'

The audience erupted. Katie couldn't remember how she got up on to the counter with him, she just remembered being lifted up and then being held tight, while the sound of cheering drowned out her crying.

And finally, their third kiss. Which was a bit of a dark horse, because it overtook the other two and became the instant Best Kiss Ever. Ooh yes, she thought, tears running down her smiling face, as Dan picked her up and squeezed her to him. They just got better and better. She should definitely ask for the best seven.

Epilogue

Katie sat in the corner of the café, an espresso on the table in front of her, while Patsy showed the new boy how to work the coffee machine. Dan was due back from the jeweller's later this afternoon – he'd insisted that even though they had chosen the ring together, he was the one to pick it up.

She'd waited a long time to open the letter. Great-Aunt Edna's funeral had been surprisingly serene. It was hard to mourn for someone who had so clearly loved her life. There were no great surprises in the reading of the will and Katie's share hadn't amounted to much, just as her mother had predicted. And Katie had been glad. It meant she had no emotion to deal with other than bidding farewell to someone she had grown to love. When the solicitor had handed her the private letter, he had told her, most clearly, that this was not to be opened until she was somewhere that made her happy. That was her Great-Aunt's wish. And so, here she was.

She tore open the envelope and pulled out the sheet of paper.

Katherine Jane,

There are many sayings in this world: Life is not a rehearsal; What doesn't kill us makes us strong; You can take a horse to water but you can't make it drink. All I know is that in a world where speed has overtaken sense, where money is all and where feeding one's soul has become the last priority, you were strong enough to wait until you understood yourself. I did not want you to know the money was safe. I wanted to see if, as I thought, you would make 'finding yourself' a priority over money. I wanted you to learn the value of independence, so that you could then appreciate the value of money. But I had no idea that I would learn from you. The more time you took to make your decision, the more I realised you didn't need anyone to teach you what you knew instinctively. And the more I grew to love you. So I will add another saying that I'm sure you know well: 'Good things come to those who wait.' If one is waiting for the right thing, this one is the truest of them all. And I should know, my love, because I waited until you were ready to know me for me, and not just for what I could offer you.

You have a trust fund in your name, my dear.

Be happy. God Bless,

Edna.

Which was how, when Paul's fiancée decided, upon reflection, that she really did need a house with a pool, Katie was only too happy to buy Paul out and become Dan's partner. In every sense of the word.

If you enjoyed The Waitress, *why not try . . .*

THE NANNY

Melissa Nathan

It'll take more than a spoonful of sugar to sort this lot out . . .

When Jo Green takes a nannying job in London to escape her small-town routine, complicated family and perfect-on-paper boyfriend Shaun, culture shock doesn't even begin to describe it . . .

Dick and Vanessa Fitzgerald are the most incompatible pair since Tom and Jerry, and their children – glittery warrior pixie Cassandra, bloodthirsty Zak and shy little Tallulah – are downright mystifying. Suddenly village life seems terribly appealing.

Then, just as Jo's getting the hang of their designer lifestyle, the Fitzgeralds acquire a new lodger and suddenly she's sharing her nanny flat with the distractingly good-looking but inexplicably moody Josh. So when Shaun turns up, things get even trickier . . .

'One to gobble up in one sitting' *Company*

'Hugely enjoyable' *heat*

'A witty novel about love' *B*

THE TEMP

Serena Mackesy

Invisible. Indispensable. In at the deep end.

This is how it works: school, university – and then Real Life. Real Life is about a boss who trusts you, a wardrobe that suits you, friends who support you and a fabulous relationship.

Unfortunately, Real Life isn't working out that way for The Temp. School and university were fine. But now? A series of jobs ranging from the numbingly mindless to the downright silly to the simply weird! Something isn't right. Who cares about a boss who trusts you? The Temp would settle for a boss who knows her name.

This can't be Real Life can it?

'Brilliantly observed . . . a gripping read' *The Times*

'Mackesy's 400-odd pages whip by in a sitting . . . Say no more, except – more!' *Independent*

'A very funny novel about love, friendship, revenge and finding yourself' *Daily Express*

'A lively romance' *Guardian*

BEHAVING LIKE ADULTS

Anna Maxted

'Modern women don't believe in love. Believing in love carries roughly the same stigma as wearing court shoes. It's as old-fashioned as going on a diet (as opposed to a detox).'

Holly Appleton knows all that, and yet she believes in love so much that she sets up a dating agency, Girl Meets Boy, to help others fulfil their romantic destiny.

Holly's agency is a going success, yet her own love life is beginning to unravel. She has just become un-engaged to Nick (his job – Mr Elephant, children's party entertainer). But Nick won't move on. Holly decides he needs to be shocked into shifting and agrees to go on a date with one of the men who write to her agency. And that's when the problems really start. Not only is Stuart Marshall not her type, he's deeply unpleasant and unaccustomed to taking no for an answer.

Will Nick see sense? Will Holly discover what she really wants and needs? Will Girl Meets Boy survive? Maybe they will, when they stop acting like children and start behaving like adults.

'You'll laugh, you'll cry and you'll feel, and isn't that what a good story is all about?' *heat*

'Powerful without being didactic, moving with being sentimental, riotously comic without being superficial' *Daily Express*

'Maxted is a gifted comic writer and she manages to extract humour from even the most unpromising situations . . . had this reviewer laughing out loud' *The Times*

THE BOY NEXT DOOR

Josie Lloyd & Emlyn Rees

A story of long hot summers, second chances – and learning you're never too old to be a kid . . .

As the 1980s dawn in the sleepy English village of Rushton, Mickey and Fred are next door neighbours and best friends. In and out of scrapes, they share everything, from their first cigarette to their first kiss. They think nothing will ever keep them apart. But they're wrong.

Fifteen years on, Fred is set to marry his girlfriend in just a few short weeks. Mickey is starting her new life with a small flower shop and a tiny flat above it. Then they bump into each other for the first time since that fateful summer.

As they try to rekindle their friendship, can they ever forget the year their worlds fell apart? And is it true what they say about first loves . . .?

'A moving story of childhood friendship and grown-up love . . . you won't want to put it down' *She*

'This husband and wife writing partnership which helped define the twentysomething novel and gave us the best-sellers *Come Together* and *Come Again*, has scored another hit' *Hello!*

'The power couple of popular romance' *The Times*

DIVAS LAS VEGAS

Belinda Jones

A tale of love, friendship and sequinned underpants . . .

Jamie and Izzy, friends for ever, have a dream: a spangly double wedding in Las Vegas. And at twenty-seven, they decide they've had enough crap boyfriends and they're ready for crap husbands – all they have to do is find them. And where better than Las Vegas itself, where the air is 70% oxygen and 30% confetti?

But as they abandon their increasingly complicated lives in sleepy Devon for the eye-popping brilliance of Las Vegas, their groom-grabbing plan starts to look less than foolproof. And those niggling problems they thought they'd left behind – like Izzy's fiancé and the alarming reappearance of Jamie's first love – just won't go away . . .

'A wise and witty read about the secret desires deep with us' *Marie Claire*

'A hilarious riot' *Company*

'Great characters . . . hilariously written . . . buy it!' *New Woman*

FAIR GAME

Liz Young

Up to her eyes with her friends' dramas, Harriet Grey has no time for her own. Let alone getting entangled with John Mackenzie. He might be the most gorgeous man she's met for ages. But he's entangled with someone else. Nina.

Glamorous Nina wasn't exactly Harriet's best friend at school, but Harriet has principles. Still, surely one innocent little drink to repay a favour wouldn't hurt? Her friends aren't so sure.

Harriet tries to be strict, but John Mackenzie won't stay out of her life. When she finds herself alone at Christmas, she'd have to be a saint to walk away. And halos never did suit Harriet . . .

'Feel-good romance' *Marie Claire*

'A warm, sunny read that is as astute as it is humorous'
Good Housekeeping

ANNIE'S NEW LIFE

Maureen Martella

Annie's discovered a case of mistaken identity . . . her own

After thirty years of being Annie McHugh, Annie discovers that she is, in fact, someone else. Her beloved and hugely respectable parents forged her birth certificate.

She hires Gerry, a private detective with a strong look of George Clooney, to track down her real mother. But how is it that when Annie goes to confront her mother in her large mansion in the smart end of Dublin, she ends up working for her instead?

Will Annie reveal the truth to her frosty new employer? Is this the beginning of Annie's new life? And has Annie completely finished with Gerry's services?

Annie has decisions to make . . .

'Quirkily and humorously told' *The Times*

'A hilarious romantic comedy' *Best*

SOMETHING BORROWED

Emily Giffin

'I absolutely loved it . . . I could not put it down' Marian Keyes

Rachel and Darcy are best friends who've always shared everything – from their childhood in Indiana to their twenties in Manhattan. But while Darcy breezes through life getting what she wants when she wants it, Rachel has always played by the rules.

The one advantage Rachel's always had is the four-month age gap which meant she was first to become a teenager, first to drive, first to everything . . . but now she's about to be first to thirty. And so, on the eve of her thirtieth birthday, Rachel finds herself questioning the status quo. How come Darcy still has a charmed life – a glamorous PR job and the perfect fiancé – while Rachel . . . doesn't. Is it just luck? Or are things a bit more complicated?

Then an accidental fling changes everything, and Rachel is suddenly forced to learn that sometimes true love comes at a very high price . . .

'Here's a heroine you'll root for and a book you won't want to put down. I love it'
Lauren Weisberger, author of *The Devil Wears Prada*

'A deftly written and convincing tale of a friendship gone comically – and at times poignantly – awry'
Meg Cabot, author of *The Princess Diaries*

Buy *Arrow*

Order further *Arrow* titles from your
local bookshop, or have them delivered direct
to your door by Bookpost

☐	The Nanny	Melissa Nathan	0 09 942797 4	£5.99
☐	Growing Up Twice	Rowan Coleman	0 09 942768 0	£6.99
☐	The Temp	Serena Mackesy	0 09 940987 9	£5.99
☐	Behaving Like Adults	Anna Maxted	0 09 943988 3	£6.99
☐	The Boy Next Door	Josie Lloyd & Emlyn Rees	0 09 941482 1	£6.99
☐	Divas Las Vegas	Belinda Jones	0 09 941492 9	£5.99
☐	Fair Game	Liz Young	0 09 946335 0	£6.99
☐	Annie's New Life	Maureen Martella	0 09 928058 2	£6.99
☐	Something Borrowed	Emily Giffin	0 09 946146 3	£6.99

FREE POST AND PACKING

Overseas customers allow £2 per paperback

PHONE: 01624 677237

POST: Random House Books
c/o Bookpost, PO Box 29, Douglas
Isle of Man IM99 1BQ

FAX: 01624 670923

EMAIL: bookshops@enterprise.net

Cheques (payable to Bookpost) and credit cards accepted

Prices and availability subject to change without notice
Allow 28 days for delivery
When placing your order, please state if you do not wish to
receive any additional information

www.randomhouse.co.uk